MAKING
Waves

TAWNA FENSKE

sourcebooks
casablanca

Published by Sourcebooks Casablanca, an imprint of Sourcebooks, Inc.
P.O. Box 4410, Naperville, Illinois 60567-4410
(630) 961-3900
FAX: (630) 961-2168
www.sourcebooks.com

Printed and bound in Canada
WC 10 9 8 7 6 5 4 3 2 1

For my parents, Dixie and David Fenske—
for looking the other way when I read under the
covers with a flashlight past my bedtime.

Chapter 1

"I'm sorry, he wants me to do *what*?"

Juli Flynn didn't think to hide the incredulity in her voice. She did, however, think of hiding beneath her mother's kitchen table. If it weren't for the memory of her brother wiping boogers there thirty years ago, she probably would have crawled right under.

Juli stared at her mother. Tina Flynn was chopping carrots for a Jell-O salad that would, in all likelihood, hold as much culinary appeal for the funeral guests as the actual corpse.

"You know you were always Uncle Frank's favorite," Tina said in the same voice she'd used to suggest her children not stick lima beans up their noses. "I think you should be flattered."

"Mom. I'd be flattered if he asked me to read a poem at the funeral or look after his cat or take his clothes to Goodwill. But this—this is just weird."

"Don't be so dramatic, Juli."

"Dramatic? Dramatic is making a deathbed request that your niece travel to the freakin' Virgin Islands to dump your ashes over the edge of a boat near St. John—that's dramatic. Why not spread them off the Oregon coast or on Mount Hood or something?"

Tina finished with the carrots and began chopping beets, her knife making neat little slivers of purple that scattered over the green countertop. Juli sighed and began hunting in the cupboard for sesame seeds to add to the Jell-O.

"Frank had fond memories of his years sailing over there," Juli's mother said.

"He had fond memories of the Polish hooker he traveled with while he was fleeing that federal indictment."

Tina smiled and set her knife down. "That's right—what was her name? Olga or Helga or something like that?"

"Oksana," said Juli, thinking this was *so* not the point.

Juli closed her eyes, hating the fact that at age thirty-seven, she felt like a petulant toddler. She had a sudden urge to stomp her feet and bang her fists on the counter in a full-blown tantrum.

It's not like she and Uncle Frank had been *that* close. She'd been living in Seattle for the past six years, coming home to Portland for the occasional holiday. Until last week, she hadn't even seen Uncle Frank since her birthday party a year ago when he'd gotten drunk on a quart of vanilla extract from Tina's baking cupboard and spent the evening pretending to be a stegosaurus. The rest of the family had been embarrassed. Juli had been delighted that, for once, she wasn't the oddest member of the family. That common bond was the reason she and Uncle Frank had always enjoyed a special relationship.

Well, that, and the fact that advanced dementia had led him to believe his niece was Celine Dion.

"You didn't happen to tell Uncle Frank that I'm—"

"Terrified of the ocean? No, I didn't have the heart to mention that."

Juli nodded and watched her mother consult her hand-written recipe before reaching for the Worcestershire sauce.

"Did Uncle Frank say when I need to complete this mission?" Juli asked, grabbing three packets of orange Jell-O and her mother's fish-shaped Jell-O mold. "Do cremated remains have—um—a shelf life or anything?"

"He didn't really say. He was choking on his tongue a lot there at the end, so it was hard to understand him. Could you hand me that feta cheese?"

Juli gave her the container and scooted a knife out of the way, aware of her mother's tendency to drop sharp objects on her bare feet.

"So maybe you didn't understand him right?" Juli asked hopefully. "Maybe instead of 'throw my ashes off a fishing boat,' he said, 'roll my ass over, you stupid whore'?"

"Those bedsores were sure something! Hand me those Junior Mints?"

Juli sighed, sensing the conversation was going nowhere. Maybe she was arguing the wrong point.

"I can't just pack up and go to St. John. I have a *life*."

Tina beamed at her daughter. "Are you dating someone new, sweetie?"

Juli scowled. "That's not what I meant. I haven't dated anyone since—well, for a long time."

"Oh. Well, you know it can be a little bit intimidating for some men to date a woman with your particular—"

"Mom, can we not talk about this now?"

"Sweetie, I don't know why you're always so embarrassed about your special—"

"Please, Mom," Juli said weakly, feeling her ears flame the way they always did when someone drew attention to the fact that she was—well, *different*. She touched her fingers to her lobes, trying to cool them.

"Could we just stick with the subject of Uncle Frank?" she pleaded.

"Of course, dear. Can you hand me the dill?"

Juli spun the spice rack and located the appropriate jar. "I have a job, Mom. I have a bank account that can't exactly handle the strain of a Caribbean vacation."

"Well, Uncle Frank left a little bit of money in his will to cover some of the cost of your travels."

"Okay. That's half the equation. What about my job?"

"Didn't you say they asked for people in your department to volunteer to take a little time off? That sounds so nice."

That sounds like a layoff, Juli thought, biting into a carrot as she watched her mother mix the Jell-O.

Not that the idea didn't hold some appeal. She'd worked in the marketing department of a software company for less than a year and already she was so bored her skin itched. She'd hardly bothered to hide her delight the week before when the vice president had stood at the center of their cube-farm, running his fingers through his comb-over, asking if anyone was interested in a severance package of three weeks' salary and a scone-of-the-month club membership in exchange for "taking a little time off. *Indefinitely*."

Later that day, Juli had flung herself onto the sofa in her therapist's office and sighed. "I feel like my career is going nowhere," she told Dr. Gordon.

"What makes you say that?" he'd asked, looking wise and vaguely constipated on the edge of his orange armchair.

"The fact that my boss told me yesterday, 'Juli, your career is going nowhere.'"

"Right," Dr. Gordon said, nodding. "And how does that make you feel?"

Juli shot him a look. "Terrific."

Dr. Gordon was not amused. Dr. Gordon was seldom amused. Juli had fantasies about pinning him down on the carpet and tickling him until he peed.

"Juli, we've spoken before about the social oddities you've developed as a coping mechanism to deal with your self-consciousness and your lack of a sense of belonging, which is the direct result of the attention you've generated in the scientific community and the media for your—" He stopped and stared at her, then shook his head. "Are you covering your ears so you don't have to listen, or are you cooling them like you always do when you're embarrassed?"

"A little of both," she admitted, lowering her hands.

"I see," Dr. Gordon said, looking morose. "You're uncomfortable with this subject. Let's talk about your career. What did you want to be when you were a child?"

"The Bionic Woman."

Dr. Gordon didn't smile. "What was your first job after college?"

"I was a newspaper reporter for three months before an on-the-job injury forced me to change careers."

"Injury?"

"I fell asleep in a City Council meeting and stabbed myself between the ribs with a pencil." She lifted the hem of her shirt. "Check it out, five stitches right here—"

Dr. Gordon sighed and began to flip through his notes. "Let's go back over some of the other jobs you've held. After you were a reporter, you spent some time as a data analyst?"

Juli lowered her shirttail and sat up straighter. "Oh. Sure, there was that. And marketing, of course. And I got my helicopter pilot license about seven years ago, and there was that stint as a pet store manager, and four months as a scout for forest fires, six months working in that hat shop, and—"

"Juli, your employment history leaves something to be desired."

She nodded, pleased to be understood. "You're right. I've never been a brain surgeon."

"It's very typical for someone with your IQ level to—"

"Are those new drapes? I like the little tassels."

Dr. Gordon sighed again. "Juli, if you're ever going to have close, intimate relationships with people, you're going to need to work on grounding yourself a bit more."

"My mother never believed in grounding—always thought time-out was a much more effective method of punishment."

"Juli—"

"I know. *I know.* I was making a joke."

He didn't smile. "Why don't you start by taking a step back and reevaluating your career and life choices? Gain some new perspective."

Perspective. That's what she needed.

She'd raced home to Portland from Seattle the day she'd heard about Uncle Frank. Now here she was, chopping steak for her mother's Jell-O salad on the afternoon of her uncle's funeral, wondering if a spur-of-the-moment jaunt to St. John might not be the best thing for her. Or maybe the worst.

"Honey, could you hand me those garbanzos?"

No. Not the worst. Not quite the worst.

The post-funeral reception was still going strong back in the house, but Juli was hiding out in the backseat of the limo, listening to the thrum of raindrops on the roof as she lay back against the plush seat. Her eyes were closed, and she was trying not to notice the smell of Old Spice on the upholstery or the shrill memory of her cousins' voices demanding to know why she was still single.

The limo door creaked open, and someone jumped into the front seat, slamming the door behind him. Juli didn't have to open her eyes to know who it was. She wrinkled her nose as the smell hit her.

"Sorry my Aunt Gretchen dumped the apple cider vinegar over your head," Juli said. "It's a family tradition."

"Family," Brian repeated with obvious intrigue. "Family like kinfolk, or family like *Godfather*?"

Juli sat up and straightened her black wrap dress. She looked at the back of Brian's head, wondering if he knew he was developing a bald patch the exact shape of Zimbabwe.

"Thank you for volunteering your limo service for Uncle Frank's funeral," Juli said, giving Brian's shoulder a squeeze. "And thank you for letting me hide out in here while my family holds the leg-wrestling tournament in the dining room."

Brian loosened his tie and leaned back against the driver's seat. "No problem. Anything for my favorite ex-girlfriend."

Juli gritted her teeth. "You know, we split up seven years ago. I think your wife would appreciate it if you stopped calling me that."

"Nah."

"And if you stopped patting me on the butt when we run into each other."

"Mandy says she doesn't mind that," Brian mused, tugging his tie all the way off and setting it on the dashboard. "She says she's never considered you a threat."

Juli pressed her lips together and tried not to be annoyed by that. "Anyway, thanks for staying late," she said finally, shoving her feet into her black patent leather Via Spigas and smoothing her hair. "I'll get out of here so you can be on your way."

"No rush, actually. The limo's stuck in park, and I can't get a mechanic out to look at it until after *Wheel of Fortune*. You can sit here all evening if you want."

Juli sighed and held out her hand. "Give me the manual."

Brian reached over to the glove box to dig out a leather-bound book the size of a dictionary. He dropped it into her lap and grinned. "You're the best," he said, sliding around on the front seat to look at her. "Why did we break up, anyway?"

Juli flipped the book open to the first page and tried to ignore him. She began to read, starting with the history of the car and progressing quickly to the recommended octane ratings. She felt his eyes on her, knew he was still awaiting a response. She planted her index finger on page 242 and looked up at him.

"You threw my Scrabble board out the bedroom window and yelled that board games weren't considered foreplay even if I spelled dirty words."

"Right," Brian said. "I forgot."

"The neighbor didn't. He's still mad about the vowels in his pond."

"Sorry about that."

Juli returned her attention to the manual, reading faster now that she had reached the section on oil viscosity. "Anyway, it's fine. We weren't right for each other."

Brian laughed. "You're too much woman for most men to handle," he said. "But there's someone out there for you, Jules; I know it."

Juli gritted her teeth, focusing hard on being pissed off instead of wounded. She did that a lot these days. Sometimes she even believed it.

She got to the end of the book and slammed it shut. She leaned over the seat and handed it back to him.

"The electronic release for the transmission is controlled by the same fuse as your backup lights," she said as she picked up the little black clutch she'd carried to the funeral. "It's a safety feature that disables the transmission if those lights aren't working. Check the fuse."

Brian grinned and set the manual on the seat beside him, his expression amused. *Amused, but not aroused*, Juli thought, knowing she didn't care about his arousal anymore, but feeling stung just the same. It wasn't like she'd had a future with him. It wasn't like she'd had a future with *anyone* she'd dated.

The story of my life, she thought.

She watched him reach beneath the dash and pry the panel off the fuse box, poking around inside as the rain sputtered against the windshield outside.

"I'll be damned," he said as he pulled out the dead fuse and held it up for her to see.

Juli popped the door open and stepped out into the rain. "Thanks again, Brian," she said, wrapping her arms around herself as she turned away. "Give my love to Mandy."

—⁓—

Three thousand four hundred miles away, Alex Bradshaw stared at the yellow piece of paper in his hand. Beyond the stuffy, peanut-scented air of the barroom, the Key West sun bathed an army of sailboats bobbing merrily in the bay.

For once, Alex didn't care about the boats.

"It's not pink," Jake Grinshaw muttered beside him, holding an identical piece of yellow paper as the bar lights glinted off his bald spot. "That asshole in Human Resources pointed out the color at least three times. He said yellow is more soothing."

Alex crumpled his own ~~yellow~~ pink slip and took another sip of beer. "I feel soothed."

Over the top of his mug, he watched as Jake wadded his own ~~yellow~~ pink slip and stuffed it in his pocket. Alex tried not to notice the way his friend's hand shook as he hoisted his beer. Jake had been doughy and awkward even twenty years ago when the two of them had started work the same day at Kranston Shipping Enterprises. Over the years, Jake had risen to the top of the accounting department, while Alex had become one of the chief executives for what was now the largest shipping firm in the world.

For all the good it had done them.

On the other side of Jake, Phyllis Prescott sat looking like a startled albino rabbit with great biceps. Catching Alex's eye, she held up an envelope. "Did everyone else get the gift certificate to Sir Loins Steakhouse?"

Alex nodded and took another sip of beer. "I think twenty-five dollars in bad steak is fair compensation for nineteen years with the company."

Phyllis frowned down at her amber ale, her silver-blonde hair falling over one eye. A former Olympic record holder in the steeplechase, Phyllis's fifty-something physique had never surrendered to the squishy curves and motherly bosom of most women her age. Hard-edged and steely, Phyllis looked like she could tear off a grown man's leg with her bare hands if the need arose.

Her perpetual scowl suggested the thought had crossed her mind more than once.

"Sir Loins makes their own croutons," offered Cody Wilkins from the other side of Alex. "They're really good."

Cody's expression was so earnest, Alex's spleen hurt. He patted Cody's massive shoulder. It felt like slapping a ham.

"You're right, Cody, they are," Alex said as he watched Cody dip a cherry in and out of his Roy Rogers.

Looking pleased, Cody lifted his drink. At six foot five and 275 pounds, he looked exactly like an NFL tight end. Not surprising, since he'd been one for three years before a shoulder injury forced him to leave the Seahawks for a safe desk job managing accounts for Kranston Shipping. The irony of it wasn't lost on Alex.

Cody would have been safer getting his head stepped on by linebackers.

"So what are we going to do, Alex?" Jake asked, his voice wilted with desperation. "Did you talk to your lawyer about our pensions?"

Alex nodded and tried to wash down the lump in his throat with a swallow of beer.

"We all signed the same clause saying we'd take the stock options for the bulk of our retirement funds," Alex said. "And we aren't fully vested in the remainder of our pensions until we've worked at Kranston for twenty years."

"Convenient," Jake muttered. "Since we're two months from the twenty-year mark, and those stock options went belly-up last week."

"But Alex, that can't be right," Phyllis protested. "I mean, surely it's obvious to anyone that we signed those forms when we were too young to know better. It was almost twenty years ago! And they were supposed to be rewritten during that reorganization in '03, but then—"

"We still signed the forms, Phyllis," Alex said. "That's binding. And besides, they cut a wide swath so it wasn't obvious they were gunning for people closing in on retirement. They took out younger employees too, like Jim in Sales, Sarah in Marketing, and Cody here."

"But there has to be something we can do," Phyllis said, sounding as close to tears as she had since she'd dropped a Buick on her foot during a power-lifting competition. "Without our retirement savings, what are we supposed to do?"

No one said anything for a minute. Alex returned his attention to his beer, wondering if it had been a wise idea to invite the others to join him. Maybe he'd be better off alone drinking whiskey in his underwear in the kitchen of his air-conditioned condo. Certainly he'd feel better staring out the window at the ocean instead of at a broken neon bar sign advertising cold, refreshing *Bu Ligh*.

He wished like hell he could do something to fix this. Not the sign, his life. *His colleagues' lives*. These guys had been more than just his co-workers. They'd been friends. Good ones.

"I just can't believe it," Jake said, shaking his head as he sipped his beer and wobbled a little on his barstool. Alex put a hand out, ready to catch his chubby pal if he had to. Phyllis patted Jake on the arm, the first time in nineteen years Alex had seen her display any sort of maternal gesture besides slapping a Hershey bar out of Jake's hand and yelling that it would give him zits.

"I'm real sorry about this, guys," Cody said at last, dropping his cherry into his soda.

Alex turned and looked at the hulking figure on his left. "Why are you sorry?"

"I dunno. I feel like it's my fault. I was walking in from the parking lot this morning, and I saw a penny on the asphalt. I just left it there."

Alex stared at him, waiting for the rest of the story. When none was forthcoming, he tried gentle prompting.

"What does that have to do with the layoff, Cody?"

"You know the saying. *See a penny, pick it up, all the day you'll have good luck. See a penny, leave it lay, bad luck you'll have all day.* Only I was in a hurry this morning, so I didn't pick up the penny. It's all my fault."

Alex felt the lump welling in his throat again. "It's not your fault, Cody," he told him. "It's not anyone's fault except fucking Tom Portelli."

"You think the owner of the company ordered the layoffs?" Phyllis asked.

"Of course he did," Alex said. "Portelli's always bitching about the bottom line. This time, we were it."

They all sat in silence for another minute, listening to Jimmy Buffett on the jukebox. Someone had picked "A

Pirate Looks at 40," and Alex listened to Jimmy croon about being drunk for over two weeks. Alex could see the appeal. He was forty-two years old, unemployed, unmarried, and without the pension he'd counted on to keep him in sailboats and cheap beer in his old age.

Between the money he'd just sunk into his boat and the recent market crash, he was pretty much wiped out.

Alone and broke.

Isn't that what his ex-fiancée had said twenty years ago? *You're going to die alone and broke if you don't learn some goddamn provider instinct!* That's exactly what Jenny had yelled as she'd walked out the door and into the arms of her dentist. Apparently *that guy* had provider instinct. As Alex had learned later, the dentist had been providing a lot more than root canals long before Jenny had actually walked out.

Not that he was still bitter. And not that he had trust issues, despite what his last three girlfriends had suggested.

The sound of Jake clearing his throat brought Alex back to the present. "Can you guys keep a secret?" Jake asked.

"No," Alex said and took another sip of beer.

"Don't listen to him, Jake," Phyllis said, turning toward Jake. "You say whatever you need to get off your chest."

Jake eyed Alex dubiously. Alex stared back.

"What?" Alex asked finally. "You going to tell us you knew this was coming all along?"

"No, no," Jake said, shaking his head so furiously Alex thought his double-chin might catch fire rubbing the starched collar of his shirt. "It's just—I know something about a little side project Tom Portelli has going on. A personal one."

Alex raised an eyebrow and took another swig of beer. "You're privy to a lot of the company owner's private business?"

"This one's not exactly on the books," Jake said, grabbing a fistful of peanuts from a dish on the bar. "This one's not even entirely legal."

Phyllis leaned closer, her interest piqued by the prospect of hearing gossip about the man who'd just bitch-slapped the whole lot of them.

"We're listening," she said. "Go on."

"Well, besides all the legitimate shipping operations at Kranston, Tom Portelli has a few side jobs he likes to keep on the down-low."

"Down-low?" Alex snorted. "You make him sound like a gangster instead of an aging executive with bad taste in ties."

"He is!" Jake insisted, almost knocking his beer over as he flung his hands up. Alex made a grab for the beer, setting it safely in front of Cody, who would sooner drink turpentine than Budweiser.

Jake kept going with his story. "Once a year, Tom Portelli sends a cargo ship out of Monaco loaded down with Krugerrand. They head across the Atlantic, through the Panama Canal, and over to the Galapagos Islands where they rendezvous with some guys who illegally export exotic animals. They swap the Krugerrand for the animals—"

"What's Krugerrand?" asked Cody, looking confused.

"Gold coins," Alex answered. "South African, but they're valuable worldwide since they're made of actual gold."

"Anyway," Jake continued, "they swap the Krugerrand for the animals and then head over to

Japan, where they trade the animals for a whole lot more Krugerrand than they started out with. Then they proceed to South Africa and swap the Krugerrand for diamonds—tons of them, about forty-eight million dollars in all."

Alex stared at him. "That's the most fucked up money laundering scheme I've ever heard. No one bothers to say, 'Hey, fellas, where'd you get the crates of gold coins?'"

"Or the Komodo dragons?" Phyllis added.

Jake shrugged. "You can pay off a lot of people with a boatload of gold coins. People are willing not to notice things. Besides, they fill the ship with legitimate cargo and they have the paperwork for that. It's a pretty smooth operation, really."

They all sat digesting the information. Phyllis looked distressed. Jake looked drunk. Cody looked blank. Alex ordered another beer.

"Do you think we should call the police?" Phyllis asked.

"And say what?" Jake asked. "Hi, I'm a disgruntled employee who got laid off this afternoon. Just wanted to let you know that the owner of our company is running gold coins and diamonds and illegal tortoises all over the globe."

"What's wrong with that?" Phyllis argued.

"Who the hell is going to believe it?" Jake shot back.

Jake and Phyllis continued bickering, but Alex had stopped listening. An idea had begun to form in the back of his mind. A crazy, juvenile, dangerous idea.

The idea of a desperate man.

Alex leaned back on his barstool and surveyed his former co-workers. One by one, they looked up at him, their eyes unfocused and a little shell-shocked. Alex took a sip of beer.

"You guys know anything about boating?"

Phyllis rolled her eyes. "Until two hours ago, we were all employees of the world's largest shipping company. I think we know about boats."

Alex shook his head. "Maybe not like this."

Chapter 2

JULI STOOD AT THE COUNTER IN THE ST. JOHN CHARTER boat office. Gulls squawked outside, but Juli could barely hear them over the rattle of an ancient air conditioner. The noise drowned out everything but the Bob Marley tune blasting through the sound system.

Drowned, Juli thought as she glanced out the window.

Over the clerk's shoulder she could see the ocean glittering in the sunlight. Like a pile of smashed glass. Like ambulance lights at a car wreck on Interstate 5. Juli looked away and wondered if the mango salad she'd had at lunch would look as festive and fruity the second time she saw it.

She stared at the colorful brochure in her hand and considered for the hundredth time that day what the hell she was doing. Most women would kill to be standing on a Caribbean island gazing out at the turquoise sea. Most women would love to go swishing out into the ocean, their flowered sarongs fluttering as the salty wind tousled their perfect sun-streaked hair.

Juli was not most women.

Her bikini was an unfortunate pink plaid that had been the only thing on the rack when she'd made a dash through Macy's the night before. The rest of the clothing in her pack was tossed in with such haste, she wasn't certain she'd brought any underwear. After deliberating for several weeks about how best to fulfill Uncle Frank's last wish, she had picked up the phone one afternoon and booked a flight out the following morning. She'd packed with the frenzied energy of a bank robber.

Or a woman who knew that if she gave herself any time to think about it, she'd never get on the plane.

So here she was in the U.S. Virgin Islands, standing in a seaside shop in St. John, trying to summon the courage to book herself on a charter boat trip the following morning.

"So which boat moves the least?" she asked hopefully.

Frank had been specific about wanting his ashes spread near a remote coral cay pretty far offshore. From the research she'd done in advance, Juli had discovered there was only one tour company that got near the spot. A tour company specializing in overnight trips. That meant twenty-four hours in a lurching, tipping, watery death machine.

Juli gripped the edge of the counter.

The clerk gave her a wary look. "Our two-day, one-night adventure on an Ocean 57 leaves tomorrow at 10:00 a.m. and gets pretty close to the spot you're talking about. All meals and drinks are included, and this price on the brochure here includes fuel costs and all the other fees. Bring sunscreen, extra clothes, camera—"

"Will I get a life jacket?" she asked, glancing out at the ocean again.

"Of course. We can even find you those little inflatable water-wings if you want."

"Really?"

The clerk stared at her. "We only have three spots left on tomorrow's trip, so if you want to do this, you'd better act fast. I assume it's you and a boyfriend or husband or something?"

Juli gritted her teeth. "No. Just me. All alone. All by myself on a Caribbean island."

"Okay," the man said. He stepped back a little from the counter. "So just the one spot."

Juli nodded, feeling her stomach flip over again. "Do you have anything for seasickness?"

He reached beneath the counter and handed her a little white box. "That's $12.95. Take it an hour before you get on the boat, and you should be just fine."

Okay. No reason left to stall, was there?

"You take Visa?"

Fifteen minutes later, Juli was out on the pier again, looking for the boat that would, in all likelihood, be dragging her to her death the next morning.

"*Spank Me*," she muttered, glaring at the receipt in her hand. "That's a stupid name for a boat."

It was a big, white boat with a blue stripe. It looked harmless enough. And the clerk had kindly offered a private berth at the front of the boat where he assured her the bedding would be clean and she'd have a bathroom close by.

So that was done. She glanced at her watch, wondering if it was time for dinner yet. Six p.m. was a little early, but maybe a pre-dinner drink at that cute place she'd seen earlier with big flowery umbrellas and barstools planted in the sand. Juli set off down the boardwalk, Uncle Frank's urn tucked snugly in her knapsack for safekeeping. She patted the side of her bag, relieved to discover it was still upright with the top latched tight.

Juli heard the pulse of calypso music before she even reached the quaint seaside bar. Moony-eyed couples, cotton-haired retirees, and scantily clad singles had already packed the place, and a small stage near the bar suggested a rowdy evening to come. She picked the only unoccupied table. It happened to be close to the water, but that was okay. If she was going to go plunging out into the ocean like a maniac, she may as well get used to the sight of it. She set her knapsack on one chair and lowered herself into the other, scanning the turquoise waves for any ships that might be going down.

"Can I get you something to drink, miss?"

Juli looked up at the waiter, then down at the little drink menu tucked inside a coconut shell. "I'll have a mai tai, please," she said. "Make it a double, actually."

The waiter nodded and ambled off, his flip-flops throwing sand up behind him. Juli looked back out over the water. Maybe this wouldn't be so bad. Maybe this was exactly what she needed.

Dr. Gordon had sighed loudly when she'd told him. "So you just quit another job?"

"I didn't *quit*, exactly. I just voluntarily accepted the severance package they were offering."

"Three weeks' salary and a scone-of-the-month club membership?"

"They're excellent scones."

"Juli, we talked last week about your career choices. About the fact that someone of your particular IQ, with an attention span that has prompted"—he consulted the notepad in his hands—"forty-two job changes in the last ten years, could perhaps benefit from something more stable. Something representative of a more mature career decision that isn't such a waste of your intellect and your—"

"I kind of liked that job I had where I washed dogs for that pet groomer."

"Juli—"

"Or the month I sold fireworks at that roadside stand."

"Juli—"

Her ears had begun to burn, so she'd given him a meek nod. "Okay, I've got it. I'll think about it."

"You can belong somewhere, you know. You really can fit in if you try hard enough."

"I know," Juli had murmured, not knowing any such thing.

Yes, this trip to St. John would give her the time and space she needed to think things through. To decide what her next career move should be. Maybe stick with one job for more than a year. Maybe she could be a mechanic. Or a librarian. Or a shepherd.

And maybe if she was really lucky, she could find a way to feel *normal* for a change. To meet *normal* people, to do *normal* things, to maybe feel like she *belonged*. Was that so much to want?

The waiter came back with her drink and she thanked him, twirling the little umbrella between her thumb and forefinger before tucking it behind her ear. She took a sip of her drink, enjoying the way the rum and coconut did a happy little dance on the back of her tongue. She felt tropical and warm, sipping her drink, wiggling her toes in the sand, tapping her fingers to a calypso tune. Then she hit the bottom of the glass, bringing her party to a halt.

Juli signaled the waiter for another, trying not to think about the cost. So what if she was unemployed? She was on vacation. A vacation that involved a dead relative traveling in her knapsack, but still. Juli looked out at the ocean. Not so bad, really. It was kind of pretty in a menacing sort of way.

The waiter brought her second drink and Juli plunged the straw to the bottom, giving it an enthusiastic slurp. She closed her eyes, feeling the rum sliding down the back of her throat as she listened to the sound of the waves. Maybe she wouldn't die. Maybe she could even get used to the ocean. And Uncle Frank deserved to have his dying wish fulfilled.

"Is someone sitting here?"

Juli opened her eyes and looked up to see a broad-shouldered man who had apparently stepped right off the pages of the sailing brochure in her knapsack. Dark, wind-tousled hair with a little gray sprinkled at the temples. A web of tiny lines at the corner of eyes that seemed almost incandescent green in contrast to his tan. Biceps that a girl could really sink her teeth into if a girl had a mind to do such a thing.

Juli blinked up at him, forgetting whatever it was he'd just asked her.

He smiled, seemingly unperturbed by her complete lack of social grace. "I was just wondering if I could join you. Is someone sitting here?"

"Just my Uncle Frank," Juli said, grabbing her knapsack. "I'll move him out of the way."

She set the knapsack in the sand and looked back to see sailor boy with his hands on the back of the chair, clearly hesitating.

"It's okay, I'm not crazy," Juli offered. "I just have my uncle's cremated remains in my backpack."

"Of course. Why wouldn't you?" He sat down. "I'm Alex."

She extended her hand and felt a surge of pleasant heat as he grasped and shook it. *Warm hands*. When was the last time she'd had warm hands—or any hands, for that matter—on her body?

She shook off the thought and smiled at him. "Juli," she said. "Pleasure to meet you."

He looked around the bar and Juli tried not to fixate on how very green his eyes were. "This place is totally packed," he said. "Figured it was smarter to sit down next to someone with reasonably good hygiene than to take a chance on sharing a table with a greasy sailor who hasn't showered for a week."

"Are you always such a flatterer?"

"I try," Alex said with a slow smile.

Juli felt her stomach flip, and she looked down at her drink, trying to get her bearings. "So what brings you to St. John?"

Alex took a swig from a beer he'd brought to the table with him. Something dark that looked more like maple syrup than beer. "Just here with some business associates to take care of a little, uh—"

"Business?"

"Right."

"I'm scattering my dead uncle's ashes at sea."

"I hear that's what all the travel brochures suggest this year."

She smiled and started to ask him another question when a man with greased-back hair and a red silk shirt trotted out on stage. His microphone squealed in protest, then popped loudly as the man waved his hands to the crowd.

"Hey, hey, hey! Welcome to the CoCo Bar, boys and

girls. How many happily married couples do we have with us tonight?"

There were a few whoops and shrieks from the crowd, along with some steely looks from people clearly not pleased with the interruption. Undeterred, the emcee plunged onward.

"You know the drill, kids! It's time for the CoCo Bar's weekly Newlywed Game. A thousand dollars to our top couple tonight, so someone's walking out of here with some nice pocket change. If you want to play, throw your hands in the air and our screener will come over and ask you just a few little questions."

The crowd's enthusiasm was underwhelming. One drunk guy sitting alone in the front row put his hand in the air. Someone in the corner belched. Most of the other guests went back to eating coconut shrimp and sipping drinks with umbrellas.

Juli looked at Alex. *A thousand dollars?* Even split two ways, that was a lot of cash. After the Feds had seized Uncle Frank's assets, what he'd left her had barely covered her airfare down here.

"Want to play?" she asked, taking a sip of her drink.

He stared at her. "Hi, I'm Alex. We just met. I believe you're confusing me with someone you've exchanged rings with."

"Don't be a spoilsport, it's easy," Juli said, raising her hand. "You've seen how these things are played. We just need a system beforehand so we have a shot at picking the right answers."

"Are you nuts?"

"No, are you married or here with a girlfriend or something?"

Alex flinched. "No."

Interesting, Juli thought, and wondered if there was a story there.

"Then there's no problem here if you aren't already attached," she pointed out. "The first question is number one. That means if it's a multiple-choice question, you go with the first one. If the answer has to be a random word, make it start with the first letter of the alphabet. If the answer has to be a number—"

"Right, I get it," Alex said, reaching across the table to pull her hand down. "I just don't think we should—"

"For the second question, we go with two. The answer is two or starts with a *B* or—"

"Hey there, you two," chirped a perky blonde in a pink halter top with a clipboard in her hands. Juli admired the product of several thousand dollars' worth of plastic surgery, blinking against the blinding whiteness of the woman's teeth. She rested her manicured hand on Juli's shoulder and kept right on chirping. "We're having a tough time getting volunteers tonight, so if you're reasonably sane, you're up. How long have you been married?"

"We're on our honeymoon," Juli chirped right back, taking a sip of her drink. She stole a look at Alex, whose expression suggested he was dubious about the sanity requirement.

"You know how this game works?" the blonde asked.

Juli beamed. "Absolutely."

The woman turned her attention to Alex. "How about you, gorgeous? You ready to do this?"

For a brief moment, Juli wasn't sure what he'd say. Hell, she couldn't believe she was roping him into it, but now that the ball was rolling, she didn't want to stop.

She gulped the rest of her drink and signaled the waiter for another, wondering if she'd be doing this without all the liquid courage.

She looked at Alex and felt her stomach do a somersault of lust. Probably.

He met her eyes, his expression unreadable. *A thousand dollars*, Juli mouthed, giving him her best smile. He shook his head and took a swallow of beer. Then he tipped the bottle at her.

"Come on, *honey*. Let's kick some ass."

Three weeks ago, Alex had been sitting in a stuffy office reviewing a fifty-six-page report on shipping export trends in East Asia. Now here he was, penniless and jobless, sitting on a lopsided stage on a Caribbean island, preparing to hijack a cargo ship as he faked marriage to a gorgeous—if slightly disturbed—woman whose last name he didn't know.

Funny the way life works.

"Okay, boys and girls, let's get started!" the emcee yelled.

Alex turned around to look at Juli, who had been seated about ten feet behind him along with the other wives. She gave him a wifely little wave and blew him a kiss.

Jesus. Why had he agreed to this?

Because she made him laugh. Because she had those big blue eyes that reminded him of the color of water near the Whitsunday Islands off the Australian coast. Because he wanted to twist his fingers up in those crazy, sandy curls that looked like someone had chased her around a fun house with a blow-dryer. He felt his libido lunge, and he turned away from her so he wouldn't embarrass himself onstage.

"Okay, audience, we've already met the contestants, now let's get started. Gentlemen, here's your first question: What is your wife's favorite movie?"

Shit, Alex thought. Something that starts with the letter *A. Anaconda, An Officer and a Gentleman, Alien, Ass Pirates III*—

This would be a helluva lot easier if they'd exchanged more than twelve words of conversation before pledging eternal devotion. Behind him, Alex could hear the squeak of markers on paper as the wives wrote out their answers.

"Time's up, ladies. Gentlemen, let's hear your answers. We'll start with Bob from Texas."

Bob from Texas mistakenly believed his wife's favorite move was *Sweet Home Alabama*, when in fact she preferred *Sleepless in Seattle*. Harry from London was certain his wife fancied *The English Patient*, but Sarah actually liked *Citizen Kane*. Then it was Alex's turn.

"*American Graffiti*," Alex guessed, then turned to look at Juli. She held up her little notepad and flashed him a smile that made him forget his name.

"No, I'm sorry Alex, looks like Juli enjoys *Animal House*."

Alex raised an eyebrow, but she just shrugged and blew him another kiss. Alex tried to ignore the surge of warmth that went buzzing through his body.

"Okay, switch seats now, ladies with your backs to the men. Ready? This question is for the wives. What is your husband's most prized possession?"

Alex stifled a groan. A relatively simple question for a couple with more than fifteen minutes of history together. For two strangers restricted to the letter *B*, not so simple.

Boat, thought Alex, and wrote it on his notepad.

"Okay, ladies, let's hear your answers, and we'll see how well you know your husbands."

Apparently Susan from Texas didn't know Bob from Texas as well as expected. She thought he valued his four-wheeler more than anything, but Bob was more fond of his wife's boobs. *Not a bad answer*, thought Alex, resisting the urge to crane his neck and admire Juli's cleavage. What was she wearing under that little pink dress? He thought he'd caught a glimpse of something white and lacy when she'd leaned forward earlier, but maybe if he looked again—

Shit. Alex felt the blood leaving his brain again and forced himself to concentrate on the other couples' responses about favorite possessions.

Sarah thought Harry favored his Porsche, when in reality he preferred his Mercedes. *Rough life*, thought Alex, trying not to think about his lost pension, all the money he'd sunk into his boat, and those damn stocks that had gone belly-up.

Focus, he told himself, and got ready for his turn.

"Juli, can you tell us Alex's most prized possession?"

"Well, he really loves his sailboat," Juli said. "Out there sailing all the time. I can hardly get him to come home for dinner when the weather's nice. I'm going to go with that."

She turned around to grin at him, and Alex almost fell off his chair. He held up his notepad, trying not to look so stunned. The audience went nuts.

Lucky guess, she mouthed.

No kidding.

Alex just shook his head, marveling at their dumb luck.

"Great job, you guys! Switch places again, and here we go. Gentlemen, where is your wife's favorite place to be kissed?"

Shit, Alex thought, his mind churning through half-a-dozen words that started with *C*—most of them wildly inappropriate to suggest to an audience of strangers and his wife of fifteen minutes. Behind him, Alex could hear the markers squeaking.

Cranium, clavicle...um—

"Time's up, pens down, ladies."

Alex felt the back of his neck growing hot. Bob and Susan struck out again, but Harry and Susan both went with lips. *Very vanilla*, Alex thought, still struggling to formulate a response of his own. Then he heard his name. He pictured the sexy neckline of Juli's dress and blurted out the first word that came to mind.

"Collarbone," he said.

He turned and looked at Juli. She held up her little notepad and gave him a coy smile. "Such a sexy place to be kissed," she said.

"Collarbone it is!" the emcee shouted. "Nice work, you two! Okay, Alex and Juli are in the lead with two, Harry and Sarah have one, and Bob and Susan—well, you have a little trouble in paradise, it seems! Okay, folks, switch seats again. If Juli and Alex get this, it's game over for the rest of you. If they miss it and Harry and Sarah don't, we'll go to a bonus round. Ready? On a scale of one through ten, rank your husband's performance in the sack."

Alex grinned, resisting the urge to dance with joy. An easy response, thanks to Juli's system. Had to hand it to her, she'd been smart to think of it. They had it in the bag! He grabbed the pen and started to write.

Then he frowned.

Not a very flattering number. Not flattering at all. He hesitated.

A thousand dollars, he thought. *Shit.*

He scribbled a number on the page.

The emcee came down the row again, this time revealing that Bob and Susan both thought he was a perfect ten. *Great*, thought Alex, listening to Harry and Sarah argue about whether Harry was a nine or a ten. Then it was Juli's turn.

"It's been a rough year for us, what with Alex working late all the time and the doctor making some changes to his cholesterol medication," Juli said with a sigh. "I'm going to have to say four."

Alex turned and shot her a look, but Juli just winked at him. *Sorry*, she mouthed, not looking sorry at all.

Alex grimaced and held up his notepad. Four it was. The audience went crazy.

"Congratulations, you two, you're the winners of our thousand-dollar prize!" the MC hooted. "Maybe you can use the money for a little, uh, marital therapy!"

But Alex wasn't listening to him. He was out of his seat, grabbing Juli up into a giant bear hug. He picked her up off the ground and swooped her around, feeling very husbandly all of a sudden.

"For the record," she whispered, "I don't really think you'd be a four."

Alex set her down and looked at her, feeling warm and

a little light-headed. "For the record," he said, "I could think of better places to kiss you than your collarbone."

———∿∿∿———

Alex wasn't sure how many mai tais his lovely bride had consumed, but he figured liquid courage had something to do with getting her up on that stage.

The gentlemanly side of him wanted to be sure she made it safely back to wherever she was staying. The not-so-gentlemanly side of him just wanted a five-minute walk to watch her breasts move under that dress. Figuring his two sides canceled each other out, he escorted her to her hotel to divvy up the cash.

Juli pushed the door open and led the way into the room. "This is the best honeymoon I've ever had."

Alex hesitated, then followed her in, trying not to stare at the bed. Or to think of tossing her backward onto it. "You've had several honeymoons?"

"None, actually," she said. "I was just being polite."

"You've never been married?"

His tone sounded more incredulous than he meant it to, and he could tell by her expression he'd said the wrong thing. He opened his mouth to tell her how pretty she was, how surprising it was she'd never married. Then he stopped himself, knowing that was a stupid thing to say.

Not like you've ever tied the knot yourself, asshole.

And the mere fact that he was giddy over a measly five hundred dollars was a good reminder of why he'd never made it to the altar way back when.

Broke and alone, he reminded himself. *Jenny was right about that.*

He watched as Juli set her knapsack on the table and counted out half the cash. She handed him his portion and unzipped an outer pocket on her knapsack. She stuffed the bills inside and closed it, then fumbled with the zipper on the main compartment. Alex studied her hands, her fingers long and narrow with lovely, rounded nails. He pictured her raking them down his back and turned away, focusing his attention on an ugly oil painting of a mermaid.

Nice rack on the mermaid. Not as perky as Juli's, but—

He shook his head and turned away from the mermaid. Dammit, he had a mission to focus on. He was a pirate. He was stealing his life back.

"Nice job with the game, *honey*," she said, nudging him with her elbow.

"Thank you *dear*," he replied, nudging her right back. "How on earth did you get boat and *collarbone*?"

"You look like a sailor, and we're on an island, so that one was easy. And you seem like a gentleman, so that ruled out most answers I could come up with that started with *C*. Dumb luck though, really."

"Sounds like more than just luck. You deduced a lot in the first fifteen minutes of our marriage. You're very perceptive."

"That's what my shrink says."

He couldn't tell if she was joking or not, so he said nothing.

Juli smiled at him. "Really, thanks for being a great sport. I needed the cash. I'm sort of between jobs right now."

"Yeah? What is it you do?"

Juli looked away, suddenly very interested in adjusting the zipper on her knapsack. "Oh, this and that."

"You said you just left a job?"

"Right. Marketing."

"Okay," Alex said, getting the sense there was more to Juli's job situation than she was letting on. Not that it was any of his business. He decided to change the subject. "Anyway, I was glad you suggested the contest. It was fun, and I could use the five hundred dollars right now too."

"Glad it worked out."

Alex watched as she chewed her bottom lip, clearly disengaged from the conversation. "Something wrong?" he asked.

She looked up at him, panic evident in those big blue eyes. She shrugged. "I booked this charter boat trip tomorrow, and I'm really nervous."

"You don't like the ocean?"

"The ocean's okay. It's drowning I'm not particularly fond of."

"Try not to do that then."

"Thanks. You're a lot of help."

Juli finally got her pack open and pulled out the most hideous urn Alex had ever seen in his life. Gaudy, orangey brass was adorned with mutant-looking dolphins and little pieces of something that looked like seashell. The lid was fashioned in the shape of an anchor.

"What the hell is that?" he asked.

"Uncle Frank."

"That's Uncle Frank's final resting place?"

"Of course not," Juli said, polishing the top of the urn with the hem of her dress. "The bottom of the ocean is his final resting place. This is just the taxi that's getting him there. He picked it out himself before he died. Look, it's even got this cool switch on the bottom to open it."

"Right," Alex said, edging toward the door. "So listen, Juli—I've got a big day tomorrow. It's been fun being married to you though."

She grinned and set the urn down.

"For a temporary husband, you're not too bad. It was great meeting you." Then she stood on tiptoes and gave him a kiss on the cheek.

Alex knew it was supposed to be sweet and platonic. Nothing his libido should respond to at all.

His libido had other ideas.

Alex slid his hands down her bare arms and felt her shiver under his palms. He held her there for a moment, drinking in the scent of her, waiting to see if she'd pull back. She stilled under his hands, her breath warm against his cheek.

He moved his hands around her back, pulling her closer. She gave a soft little gasp and raised her arms to lace her fingers behind his neck. Her face was scant inches from his, her breath coming faster now.

Then she tipped her head back, bringing her lips close to his as she smiled up at him. "So you want a chance to upgrade your score?"

Alex brushed his lips over hers. "It's only fair, considering we never got a honeymoon."

He kissed her hard on the lips; forget the peck on the cheek. His mouth devoured hers as his hands slid down to fit into the small of her back. Her dress was so thin he could feel every curve and dip of her body. Her breasts pressed against his chest and Alex felt all the blood leave his brain as he thought about how little separated their flesh.

He deepened the kiss, circling his palm low on her back

to feel her move against him. He slid his other hand into her hair, groaning a little at the feel of those crazy curls twisting around his fingers. Her breath was coming hard now, pushing her breasts against him with every inhalation. Her hair smelled like coconuts and lemons, and Alex felt dizzy at the thought of tasting her. He abandoned her lips and began to kiss his way down her throat, lingering on a spot that made her squirm and whimper.

Julie gasped and lifted one bare foot off the floor, sliding it up the back of his calf until she reached the hollow behind his knee. She drew him closer, pressing herself against the fly of his slacks. Alex felt the ground tilt under him and wondered if he was about to topple them both to the floor.

At this point, he didn't care.

His hand left the small of her back and slid down, palming the perfect curve of her ass through her dress. He lingered there, feeling her move warm and soft in his arms. Then he slid lower, not stopping until he reached a bare expanse of thigh. He drew his fingers over that smooth, naked flesh, wondering if the air conditioner was broken or if it was just that hot in the room.

Juli ground harder against him, and Alex slid his hand up again, lifting the hem of her dress higher, higher, then higher still, finding nothing but bare skin—

Juli pulled back and grinned up at him. "Commando," she murmured. "It was hot today, you know?"

"God, yes."

"You should probably lose a layer yourself." She reached for the top button on his shirt and flicked it through the hole. She moved lower, freeing another button, kissing her way down the center of his chest.

. Alex twisted his fingers in her hair as she slid down his body. He made a strangled sound in the back of his throat, wanting to suggest they move toward the bed but not able to form any words besides, "*Oh, God.*"

Her mouth was hot and clever and everywhere at once as she took her time undoing the buttons, kissing each inch of exposed flesh as she moved lower.

His shirt was unbuttoned now, and Julie stood up slowly, sliding her palms over his abdomen, then up and across his chest. She held them there for a moment, then took a step back and smiled at him. She reached for the hem of her dress. She hesitated. Alex held his breath, ready to tear it off her body with his teeth if she didn't do it herself.

"Alex?"

"Mmm?"

"Um, do you have any—um, well—"

Alex closed his eyes, knowing what she was going to say. Knowing damn well that condoms had not been on the pirate packing list.

He shook his head, still too dizzy to form words. He opened his eyes and caught sight of her hands frozen on the hem of her dress. His head started to spin again.

Juli smiled and let go of her dress, placing her palm over his heart instead. "Give me five minutes," she said, pulling back and reaching for the pocket where he'd seen her stash the money in her knapsack. "I saw a drugstore just down the block."

He saw her wobble a little, then catch herself on the back of the chair. She let go of the chair and unzipped her knapsack, fumbling with the bills. Two of them fluttered to the carpet and Juli bent to retrieve them. She teetered, grabbing the back of the chair again with a shaky hand. Alex licked his lips and tasted rum.

Shit. Was he out of his fucking mind?

"Wait," he said, hating the words he was about to say, but knowing he'd hate himself more if he didn't ask. "How much have you had to drink?"

"What?"

"At the bar. You were drinking mai tais. Are you—"

"Drunk? I wouldn't say that, exactly. Tipsy, but not plastered."

"I can't—" He took a breath, shoved his hands in his pockets. "I don't feel right taking advantage of a woman who's had too much to drink."

She looked at him like he'd just sprouted an extra ear, then threw her head back and laughed. "You're joking, right?"

He shook his head, trying to look anywhere but that smooth expanse of cleavage quivering with laughter. "Just a rule I have, okay?"

"You're okay with the one-night stand, but not with someone who's a tiny bit tipsy?"

"It's just something I feel strongly about. I'm trying to be a gentleman."

She laughed again, clutching the back of the chair so hard it tipped over and landed with a thud on the carpet. She didn't seem to notice. "A gentleman who had his hand on my bare ass not thirty seconds ago. Alex, really—"

"I'm sorry—believe me, I want to. But we don't have any protection, and I don't feel right about taking advantage, and I just—I think we should stop here."

She stopped laughing and looked at him for a few

beats. Her eyes were glassy and a little disappointed, but she nodded and straightened her dress. "I suppose I can respect that."

He grimaced, thinking he'd rather be naked than respected. Still, he was doing the right thing. He might be the kind of guy who robbed a cargo ship on the high seas, but he wasn't the kind of guy to take advantage of an intoxicated woman.

Besides, he had a big day tomorrow. He had to get his head in the game; this was no time for a fling with a woman he'd just met in a bar.

"Okay," he said, stuffing his hands in his pockets to hide his arousal. "So I guess this is it."

"You planning to button your shirt before you walk outside?"

"I think I need to cool off."

"They've got the sprinklers running. Maybe you should detour through the lawn."

"Good idea."

He took a step toward the door, wanting to touch her again but knowing damn well where that would lead. He hesitated.

She smiled and smoothed down the front of her dress. "Good-bye, Alex. Happy sailing."

He nodded and reached for the doorknob. "Have a nice life, Juli."

Chapter 3

JULI WOKE THE NEXT MORNING FEELING BLISSFULLY warm and happy. She'd been dreaming of being ravaged on a beach by a handsome pirate who looked an awful lot like Alex.

Alex. Dammit to hell.

Fine, she could admit now she'd been tipsier than she'd realized. Her tongue felt like someone had glued it to the roof of her mouth, and she knew she couldn't blame her nausea entirely on her dread of her impending high-seas voyage. Alex had been right to leave. Still, she'd wanted him so desperately. If only she'd thought to pack condoms. If only she hadn't ordered that last mai tai. If only—

With a sigh, Juli sat up and looked out the window at the ocean.

She lay back down again, feeling queasy.

Once her stomach had stopped rolling, she chanced a look at her watch. 7:02. *Great*. Three hours to fully enjoy the dread of her sea voyage coupled with a slight hangover.

She sat up again and rolled out of bed, padding across the tile floor in her bare feet. She caught sight of Frank's urn on the table and gave it an affectionate pat. "Sorry you had to see that last night," she said as she headed into the bathroom and cranked on the shower.

Despite the derailed tryst, last night had been fun. Really fun. She couldn't believe she'd had the guts to drag Alex up onstage for the contest. Even more amazing, he'd gone for it. Willingly. Eagerly even, totally on board with the game. Guys like that weren't easy to find. It was too bad she hadn't even gotten his last name. He might have been fun to meet up with again sometime, maybe when her life got back to normal.

She frowned at that. *When is your life ever normal?*

Juli showered and shampooed her hair, feeling a little more human by the time she switched off the water. She climbed out of the shower, toweled off, and dressed carefully in a pair of turquoise capris and a white T-shirt with flip-flops that had little seashells on the straps.

Tucking her extra clothes and toiletries into her knapsack, Juli ambled downstairs in search of the most grease she could ingest without an IV. Two cheeseburgers and thirty-six Tater Tots later, she wobbled back up to her room and studied the instructions on the seasickness medication she'd purchased the day before.

"Take each dose with a full glass of water," she read. "Take every four to six hours as needed. Do not take more than four hundred milligrams in one day."

Juli measured out the dose carefully, wondering if a little extra might be wise since she had a full stomach.

Forty-five minutes later, she was standing in front of the hotel admiring the garden hose.

"Shiny," she said to no one in particular.

"Miss? Can I help you with something?"

She looked up to see that the hotel receptionist had four extra ears. That would make answering phones much easier.

Juli smiled at her. "Can I take this dog on the boat with me?"

"That's a lawn mower."

"Okay."

"Are you on—um—some sort of substance?"

"Substance?"

"Drugs. Are you on drugs?"

"Seasick," she said and fished into her knapsack for the little white box. She handed it to the receptionist, marveling that the woman had six hands.

The receptionist took the box and studied it for a moment. Then she looked back at Juli. "Are you by any chance allergic to morphine or codeine?"

Juli stared at her, admiring how fluffy her necklace was.

"Because if you're allergic to those drugs, you're probably allergic to almost any drug with an -ine at the end. Are you hallucinating?"

Juli nodded and took her box of medicine back. "Tell Santa I said hello."

Then she wandered off toward the marina, enjoying the way the sidewalk nibbled on her toes as she walked. When she got to the marina, she looked at her watch. The man had said the boat left at ten o'clock, but it was good to be early. Two hours early was very good.

She tried to find the receipt that told her which boat to get on, but her knapsack had grown at least sixty new zippers. Juli looked out over the marina.

White boat, Juli recalled. *Blue stripe*.

Spotting the boat at the end of the pier, she made her way down there, wondering why the sky was yellow. Stumbling her way on board the boat, Juli tried the door to the cabin. Locked. Looking around, she saw an open window.

"Crunchy," she said and climbed through.

Once inside, she surveyed her new digs. Not bad. The tree growing from the middle of the boat was a nice touch, and she was pretty sure she saw a gnome peeking out of the cupboard.

Juli unzipped her knapsack and pulled out Uncle Frank's urn.

"Here you go," she said, setting it on the bench near a window. "Now you can see the ocean."

Then she stumbled into her stateroom and pulled the door closed behind her, landing with a thud on the bed.

"Everything all set?" Alex called to his fearless pirate crew.

"Ready," said Phyllis as she gave him a thumbs-up. The yellow bandana she'd tied over her hair made her look more like a disgruntled housewife than a pirate, but at least she was smiling.

"Ten-four," chimed Jake, his bald head gleaming in the sunlight.

"Can you tell me again which end is the stern and which end is the bow?" Cody asked.

Jake began to explain it to him for the hundredth time. Alex smiled, thinking how much progress they'd all made since they'd first hammered out this crazy plan in his kitchen just three weeks before.

It was a simple enough idea. The four of them had sailed his forty-five-foot Cabo Rico from Key West to St. John, taking their time over the two-week journey to make sure Jake and Cody and Phyllis got their sea legs and learned the basics of boating. Alex had sailed throughout the Caribbean for years and recognized the intrinsic value of not having to buy plane tickets or check luggage with questionable contents.

An accomplished sailor himself, Alex learned to be patient with his less-than-salty crew. By the time they reached St. John, Phyllis, Jake, and Cody were sailing like pros.

Well, maybe not like pros. But at least not like drunk third graders.

The next part of the journey would be a little trickier. Relying on Alex's boating expertise, their combined years of experience in the shipping industry, and some creative computer hacking by Phyllis, the four of them had identified a tiny island approximately six hundred miles into the Atlantic. The island wasn't on any map, but it was apparently owned by Tom Portelli and used as a refueling station during these off-the-books missions.

The distance and timing involved meant they needed a powerboat. More importantly, they needed an anonymous powerboat. A bareboat charter rental that couldn't be traced to any of them.

Jake had helped with the fake paperwork for their foursome. Phyllis had nailed down the particulars of the cargo boat's voyage by hacking into Kranston's computer system and finding a way to monitor Tom Portelli's ship's GPS throughout the journey. Cody— the only one who knew how to operate a kitchen appliance more complicated than a toaster—had taken over grocery shopping and cooking. He'd also gathered essentials like rain gear and a first-aid kit and extra water.

And ski masks and paintball guns, naturally.

All in all, they were well prepared. Well, as prepared as four terminated corporate rejects could be for their first pirate mission.

"Let me know when the bow clears the slip," Alex called out.

Jake peered over the edge, then turned and gave a thumbs-up. "You're good."

Alex worked the bow-thruster, feathering the throttle of the powerful twin diesels. He steered the Tollycraft 53 out of the marina and through the bay. Someone waved from the shore, then vanished as the boat powered its way out to sea. Alex watched the miles slip past, cruising at five knots until they reached open water. Then he opened it up to ten knots.

He held that speed for a while, navigating north–northwest. The air tasted salty and warm, and Alex lost himself in a daydream that involved Juli and a whole lot of suntan oil. Part of him kicked himself for leaving last night. What would the harm have been? She'd been willing and eager—*God, she'd been eager*—so maybe he should have gone for it.

But no. He had rules of conduct. Taking advantage of drunk women wasn't his style and never had been.

Still, he could think about the way she'd looked last night with her back arched and her face tilted toward him, her lips full and warm and her breasts pressed against him—

Alex distracted himself with that fantasy for a good long while. By the time he looked down at his watch, an hour and a half had passed and the island had vanished behind them.

"Four days," Cody said, jarring him out of his

thoughts. Alex turned to see Cody shoving his lucky rabbit's foot in the pocket of his sailing shorts and kissing his St. Christopher's medal before tucking it back inside the white T-shirt that strained against his muscular frame. "Four days 'til contact."

Alex nodded. "That's the plan. Four days out at eight knots, one day back at twenty knots. You guys want to run through the details again?"

"No, I think we've got it," Jake answered, scanning the horizon. "Not like we haven't had three weeks to obsess about this."

They cruised in silence for a while, each of them seemingly lost in their own thoughts. Alex considered how effortless it had been for all of them to drop everything and go. None of them had kids or spouses or anything that required more care than an asparagus fern. He tried not to dwell on how pathetic that was. They'd all been so focused on their careers, they'd forgotten to have lives.

Ironic, really. Jenny had dumped him because he wasn't making enough money, so he busted ass at Kranston all those years to prove her wrong.

And here he was twenty years later, still alone, still broke, and wrong after all.

He frowned at how pitiful that sounded and looked around at his crewmates. All of them looked a little less haggard out here on the ocean, a little more alive. The layoff had taken the wind out of their sails, and they were all damn determined to get it back. Crazy as this plan might be, he trusted these guys with his life. Trust wasn't exactly his strong suit, so that said something right there.

Alex glanced at his watch. They'd been on the water for just over five hours now. "Anyone hungry?" he called.

"Not hungry, but maybe we could use some coffee," Phyllis said.

Cody jumped up and scrambled toward the galley. "I'll get it, let me."

"Thanks, Cody," Alex said. "Maybe some of those cookies you made earlier?"

"No sweat," Cody said. "Hey, guys?"

"What's that, Cody?"

"I was thinking now that we're at sea, you could start calling me Cookie."

"Cookie?" Jake studied him with a mix of suspicion and alarm.

"Yeah. You know, since I'm the official cook on the pirate ship."

Alex looked at Cody to see if he was joking. He wasn't. "Sure, Cookie," he agreed, watching his shipmate's 275-pound frame disappear down the stairs. "Whatever you say."

Alex turned back to the ocean, his attention focused on the equatorial currents. They wanted to pull the boat westward, which was to be expected here. He checked the GPS and fiddled with the Autohelm, steering them north–northwest and further out to sea.

Fifteen minutes went by with no sign of Cody. Alex looked at his watch again. They were making good time, and the weather forecast had predicted sunny skies all week. If they were going to lose their jobs and resort to illegal pirate activity, they couldn't have picked a better time to do it.

"Here you go," Cody called as he emerged from below deck.

Alex turned to see him carrying a silver tray topped with little blue teacups, a French press coffee maker, and a plate of chocolate biscuits that looked homemade. Cody set the tray down and Alex studied him.

"Nice apron," Alex said.

Cody beamed. "Thanks. I did the embroidery myself."

"You don't say."

Phyllis and Jake trotted over and began helping themselves to the treats. There were cloth napkins on the tray and little saucers painted with blue flowers.

"Hold on a minute. Let me go get the nutmeg grater," Cody said as he scrambled into the cabin again. "I've got fresh whipped cream too."

Alex took a biscuit and watched Cody disappear.

Phyllis chewed thoughtfully for a moment, then turned to Jake. "Has Cody always had this—um—affinity for cooking?"

"I'm not sure," Jake said, shoving a biscuit into his mouth as the sweat beaded along his bald forehead. "But I could get used to it."

"Here you go guys," Cody called as he emerged back out onto the deck. "Nutmeg, whipped cream, and sugar for the coffee. I can't seem to get the top off the sugar bowl though."

Alex turned and saw his life flash before his eyes. There, in Cody's oversized palms, was the ugliest urn he'd ever seen in his life.

Again.

Alex closed his eyes and counted to ten. When he opened them, the urn was still there. Dread pooled in his gut.

Phyllis reached for it, ready to help Cody pry it open.

Jake stared, slack-jawed. "I don't remember packing that. Where the hell did it come from?"

Alex gritted his teeth, tasting salt in the air.

"My wife," he said and headed below deck.

Chapter 4

JULI STOOD BLINKING IN THE SUNLIGHT, TRYING TO make sense of things. A gull was squawking nearby. The ground was lurching beneath her feet. The ocean was hissing and slurping all around her.

And the phenomenally hot guy she'd faked marriage to and then almost slept with a mere sixteen hours ago had just marched her out of bed and now stood glaring at her in a very unhusbandly fashion.

Alex folded his arms over his chest and nodded at her. "Care to explain what you're doing here?"

Juli squinted, trying to bring his features into focus. Her head throbbed, and she wanted to go lie down in her private stateroom again. She cleared her throat, feeling something like sandpaper scraping her windpipe.

"I told you last night," she said. "I signed up for this boat tour so I could spread my uncle's ashes at sea."

Alex stared at her. He didn't speak or even blink, and Juli was tempted to poke him in the chest to see if he was still breathing. Her mind veered a little at the thought of touching his chest again, running her fingers over that hard expanse of muscle, and any additional words of explanation fled her brain.

Alex's icy tone brought her crashing back to reality. "A boat tour?"

"Right. Only I didn't know you were the captain when I paid for it. You could have told me last night."

Alex seemed to be considering his next words carefully. Juli saw a little nerve twitching on the side of his left eyebrow and watched his jaw working.

"You shouldn't grind your teeth like that," she told him. "I had a cousin with bruxism—that's the medical term for teeth grinding—and he wore the enamel right off his—"

"So you think this is your charter boat," Alex interrupted.

"Well duh. *Spank Me*, right?"

Alex looked alarmed. Juli flushed and put a hand to her left butt cheek, where she felt the crinkle of paper in her pocket. *The receipt!* Triumphant, she pulled it out and handed it to him.

"Look, I paid in full," she said, jabbing a finger at the words. "Boarding at 10:00 a.m., it says right here. Okay, I mean I got on a little early because of the drugs and I'm not really sure how long I've been asleep, but I paid for a private room at the front of the boat, so I don't see why that's a problem."

"Drugs?"

"Seasick medication. I think maybe I had a bad reaction to it."

Alex gave her a blank look. He cleared his throat, glancing at the other passengers behind her. It was the first time Juli had actually noticed them, and she was surprised to see two men and a woman regarding her with thinly veiled hostility.

So much for making new friends.

"So let me get this straight," Alex said slowly. "You staggered down to the dock in a drug-induced haze, broke into a strange boat, and fell asleep in my bed?"

"*My* bed, actually," piped the steely-looking blonde regarding Juli like a dog who'd just made doody on the floor. "You found her sleeping in the smaller stateroom up front, right? When we drew straws earlier, I said that was the room that I wanted—"

"But I paid for a private room," Juli insisted, holding up her receipt. "It says so right here. The guy even told me it was at the front of the boat."

She shook the receipt so all of them could see it. No one snatched it from her hand. In fact, no one moved at all. The blonde glowered. The big meaty-looking guy in the apron looked confused. The sweaty bald guy who was manning the controls kept trying to catch Alex's eye. Alex just stared at Juli, unblinking.

Juli put the receipt back in her pocket. "Okay, admittedly my reasoning skills are a little fuzzy right now, but I'm getting the sense that I'm not on the right boat."

The other passengers exchanged looks Juli couldn't read. Well, everyone except Alex. He just kept watching her, as though he hoped at any moment she might disappear in a poof of smoke, to be replaced with something slightly more desirable. Like a leper.

It was the big guy who spoke first.

"Who does your highlights? Those are fabulous."

Juli drew a hand to her hair. "Um, thanks. They're actually natural."

"Really? Wow, that's amazing. Even this little section right here?"

"Well, sometimes in the summer I put a little lemon in my hair and sit out in the sun for an hour or so and then—"

"We should throw her overboard."

This from the heavyset bald guy. Juli shut her mouth, suddenly less interested in the merits of citrus for hair care.

"You think?" mused the blonde prison warden. "I mean, we're one hundred miles offshore, but still, a body could wash up somewhere."

"Well we'd give her a life vest, Phyllis. Geez, we're not murderers."

"Um, what *are* you, exactly?" Juli interrupted.

All four of them gave her a blank look.

"Cartographers," Alex answered quickly.

"Cartographers?" Juli asked. "You mean you make maps?"

"Right."

"I see," Juli said, glancing at each of them in turn. "I wasn't aware that cartographers generally killed people at sea."

"It's been a rough week."

"You don't say."

Juli thought she saw a faint smile tug at the corner of Alex's mouth.

"We shouldn't throw her overboard," argued the big guy who liked her hair. "Can't we just turn around and take her back?"

"We're six hours out to sea, Cody," Alex told him.

"Cookie."

Alex looked pained. "Cookie," he repeated. "That's twelve hours of travel round-trip, not to mention fuel. You know how precise we had to be when we plotted our course."

"Well, okay," Cody said. "But we shouldn't throw her overboard. She's pretty. Maybe we should keep her."

"Jesus, Cody—*Cookie*—" the blonde sputtered. "Like a pet?"

"No, not like a pet. Like a prisoner."

Alex quirked an eyebrow at him. "You want to tie her up?"

Again, Juli caught a hint of a smile. She folded her arms over her chest and leveled a look at Alex.

"Well if you'd suggested bondage a little earlier in the marriage, I might not have rated you a four in the bedroom."

The others looked confused, but Alex was definitely fighting a grin now. He nodded at her. "Can you excuse us for a moment, Juli? Maybe go back to your stateroom for a minute and—"

"*My* stateroom," the blonde insisted. "It's not negotiable. Cody and Jake both said they snore, and you drew the straw for the master stateroom, Alex. I just want to make sure—"

"We'll figure it out, Phyllis."

Juli turned, ready to make her exit. Spotting the urn in the big guy's hands, she reached for it. "May I have my Uncle Frank back?"

"Your what?"

"That's my Uncle Frank. We're traveling together."

He handed the urn over, looking perplexed, and Juli hugged it tightly to her chest. "Okay, so I'll just go back to my room."

"It was nice to meet you, Juli," the big guy— Cookie?—called after her.

Juli smiled over her shoulder. "Um, thanks. Aside from the threats on my life, it's been a pleasure."

———

As soon as Juli was out of earshot, the shouting began. Alex resisted the urge to cover his ears and hide under a deck chair.

"How is this possible?" Jake yelled. "We've got a stowaway on our top-secret pirate mission?"

"I don't understand," Cody said. "Why didn't you see her in your room, Phyllis?"

"Because I didn't get a chance to go *in* my room yet, Cookie! I dropped all my stuff in the salon after you nimrods yelled at me to come help put the groceries away."

"Did you say you knew her, Alex?" Jake asked.

Alex didn't hear the question at first. He was thinking about the way Juli's hair ruffled in the breeze, the sleepy warmth in those big blue eyes, the way her fingers had felt stroking his stomach last night, the taste of her skin as he'd—

"Alex?"

His attention snapped back to Phyllis. "What?"

"Why did you say that our prisoner is your wife?"

"Oh. I met her at a bar last night. There was this stupid game, and we pretended we were married for a few minutes."

Jake grinned and punched Alex in the shoulder. "Only a few minutes, huh? Well, as a man gets older, sometimes it gets a little tougher to—"

"No, really," Alex protested, not sure how the conversation had gone so quickly from the demise of their mission to the downfall of his sexual stamina. "Nothing happened. I mean, not exactly. It was just a game in a bar. I don't even know her last name."

Cody looked confused. "Bradshaw, right? If she took your last name when you got married, I mean."

Alex sighed.

"Seriously, find out her last name," Jake said. "We can do a search online, figure out who the hell she really is. Probably a spy with the CIA or something."

Alex raised an eyebrow. "And you're going to find this in the online public database of CIA spies?"

"I think she looks familiar," Phyllis said. "Like maybe I've seen her on TV before."

"You think she's a celebrity?" Cody asked hopefully.

"Not a celebrity," Jake muttered. "But Phyllis is right—there's something familiar about her."

"Do you think she's a cop?" Phyllis asked.

Jake's eyebrows shot up. "What if Portelli sent her? Like maybe she's a spy for him?"

"What if we put her in the life raft with some food and water and *then* pushed her overboard?" Phyllis argued. "It wouldn't be murder, and she wouldn't screw up the pirate heist."

"Don't be stupid," Jake argued. "We might need the life raft for ourselves later."

Cody scratched his chin. "If she's our prisoner, could we make her do the dishes and scrub the poop deck and stuff?"

"Do we have a poop deck?" Phyllis asked.

Alex closed his eyes, feeling his head begin to throb. He raised his hands to get their attention, feeling like a middle school gym teacher.

"No, we do not have a poop deck," he said slowly. "No, we are not throwing this woman overboard, nor are we setting her adrift in the life raft. And we're not turning around, either. We'll miss our opportunity to meet up with Portelli's ship if we deviate from our game plan."

Phyllis threw her hands up in exasperation. "Well what are we going to do then?"

Alex stared out at the ocean, then looked back at the crew. "There's that little island about 230 miles from here. The one we thought we could use if we had to make an emergency stop? We'll just off-load her there, put out a distress call, and make sure someone comes to get her."

Phyllis looked skeptical. "When will we reach the island?"

"Tomorrow afternoon, maybe early evening."

"So we keep her," Jake said, eyeing Alex with suspicion.

"Just until tomorrow evening."

"What do we tell her we're out here doing?"

"She already thinks we're cartographers," Alex said. "Let's just stick with that."

Phyllis frowned. "Cartographers? An hour ago, Cody was trying to figure out what NESW spelled on the compass."

"Cookie," he insisted.

"And just last week, Jake was reading the map upside down."

"I was drunk, okay, Phyllis?" Jake retorted. "Pirates enjoy their rum from time to time."

"Right, so we're in agreement?" Alex said, hoping for some sign of group unity.

"We're keeping the wench," Jake said grudgingly.

Phyllis folded her arms over her chest. "If she thinks she's getting my room, she can—"

"She can have my room," Alex said. "Cody and Jake, you guys keep the bunks in the middle room. I'll sleep on the flybridge. I like it better in the open air, anyway."

"Okay then," Phyllis said. "So we have our first prisoner."

"A prisoner who's staying in the luxury master suite on a seven-hundred-thousand-dollar powerboat," Jake grumbled.

Phyllis shook her head. "I'm not sure we have this pirate thing down yet."

Alex stepped back, turning toward the stairs. "I'm going to go talk to her. Let her know the plan to off-load her tomorrow. You good at the controls a little longer, Jake?"

Jake grunted in response, and Alex turned away. Behind him, Phyllis muttered something about skipping the honeymoon for now. Alex grimaced, glad they didn't know just how close he'd come to consummating his mock marriage.

When Alex reached the guest stateroom, he hesitated a moment before knocking. What was the proper protocol for entering the bedroom of a phony wife turned botched one-night stand turned maritime prisoner?

"Come in," Juli called from inside.

Alex stepped into the suite to see Juli bent over her knapsack, tossing out wisps of lacy underthings, several cosmetic products, and something that looked suspiciously like a magic eight ball. Alex ducked, narrowly missing the trajectory of a pink tank top.

"I can't find my damn toothbrush—"

"Look, Juli," he began, trying to keep his tone all-business. "I know you hadn't planned to be at sea very long, but we won't reach our first stopping point until tomorrow evening. We're on a pretty tight timeline, and we can't afford the extra half day it would take to turn around and take you back to St. John. Are you going to be okay traveling with us for another twenty-four hours or so until we get to a spot we can drop you off?"

"I know it's in here somewhere," she said, giving no indication of having heard him.

"Juli, we're in a bit of a hurry here, so—"

She looked up at him, her expression quizzical. "Someone has an urgent need for maps?"

"What?"

"You're cartographers, right?"

"Right," Alex said, wishing like hell he'd said they were sightseers or venture capitalists or porn stars.

She stopped pawing through her knapsack for a moment and studied him. She gave him a funny half smile and held up a lacy black thong.

"For the record, I do wear panties on occasion."

Alex swallowed hard and tried to think of something intelligent to say.

"Um—" was the best he could manage.

Juli grinned wider and stuffed the thong back in her knapsack. "Relax, Alex. I'm not going to say anything to your crew about last night, if that's what you're worried about."

"Believe me, that's the least of my worries."

"Oh?"

Her tone was casual, almost teasing. She had to know how desperately he wanted to toss her back onto the bed and make up for last night. Maybe they could just—

"No," he said.

She raised an eyebrow at him. "No what?"

"Nothing. I was talking to myself. Look, Juli, about last night—"

"Don't worry about it. Really. You were right, okay? I probably was too tipsy to take things any further. I appreciate you being a gentleman."

Alex nodded, feeling no satisfaction at all in being right. "Gentleman. That's me."

Juli went back to pawing through her knapsack and Alex lost his train of thought again as another bra went flying across the room. He was just about to say *the hell with being a gentleman* when Juli reached into the depths of her knapsack and produced a purple toothbrush with silver stars on the handle. Not even bothering to dust off the lint, she shoved it in her mouth and began scrubbing vigorously. While she brushed, her eyes explored the spacious expanse of the cabin.

"Pretty nice boat you've got here," she observed, her words coming out garbled around the toothbrush.

"It's a rental."

She raised an eyebrow. "So I guessed wrong when I said your boat was your prized possession?"

"I've got a sailboat. This is a powerboat."

"Mwuffa ifnus?"

"What?"

Juli extracted the toothbrush. "What's the difference?"

He stared at her. "Are you joking?"

Juli shoved the toothbrush back in her mouth and kept scrubbing. Her eyes didn't leave his.

Alex sighed. "A sailboat has sails. It's powered by the wind. A powerboat has a great big engine that makes it move. Better for going longer distances at higher speeds."

Juli nodded, considering this as she gnawed the head of the toothbrush.

"Do you want some water or a sink or some toothpaste or something?" Alex asked.

Juli extracted the toothbrush again. "No. This is how I brush my teeth."

Alex stared at her, feeling fairly certain this was the strangest woman he'd met in a long time. Strange, but maybe that wasn't such a bad thing. She made him laugh, and it had been a helluva long time since he'd done much of that. And God she was gorgeous, even with the toothbrush making her cheek balloon like a hamster's pouch. Her eyes were that perfect, aqua blue of Caribbean water. Her hair made him want to tangle his fingers through those loopy curls again. And that body...

As though reading his thoughts, Juli grinned at him around the toothbrush.

"So where am I sleeping?" she asked.

"The master stateroom."

"Wow. Sounds fancy. How'd I score that?"

"There are three sleeping quarters on the boat. This room—which Phyllis has dibs on—and the guest room with two bunks—which is where Cody and Jake are sleeping, since they both snore. And then the master stateroom."

Juli grinned. "So you're sleeping with me?"

"No." Alex shook his head and tried to ignore the surge of lust that hit him in the gut at the thought. "Out here—no. Bad idea for a lot of reasons. I'm sleeping on the flybridge, if the weather holds. If it doesn't, I'll be in the salon."

"Flybridge? Salon? Do any rooms on this boat have normal names?"

"The flybridge is the open area on the upper deck. You can drive the boat from there or from the pilothouse on the main level where Jake is right now. The salon is sort of like the living room. It's the one right off the pilothouse."

"Where the cockpit is?"

"Right. And bonus points for knowing your boat terminology."

Juli grinned. "I saw that in the pamphlet for my boat tour. Only whoever designed it couldn't fit the word on one line, so it looked like two words. Cock. Pit. Funny, don't you think?"

Alex stared at her. Juli shrugged and stuffed the toothbrush back in her knapsack. Then she looked at him again. "So you have your own sailboat."

"Yes," he said cautiously.

"Expensive. Must be a real chick magnet."

"Right. That's pretty much why I bought it. I don't even know how to sail."

She grinned again, and Alex felt some of the tension leave his shoulders. Then he wondered what the hell he was tense about in the first place. It wasn't just the pirate mission or the job loss. There was something about discussions of women and money that always made him want to bite the head off large rodents.

"You're a funny guy," Juli said.

"I'm here to amuse you."

"Great! So now what?"

He raised an eyebrow. "What do you mean?"

"Well, are there any onboard activities or anything?"

Alex stared at her again. "I appreciate your enthusiasm, but did you miss the part where we said this isn't really your charter boat?"

She rolled her eyes. "I get that, wise guy. But don't you guys have anything fun to do? A drinking game or a crossword puzzle or an entertaining interlude where you name all the marine life or something?"

Alex wanted to give her a stern look, but he could feel her exuberance making him smile in spite of himself. He fought it hard. "I think Cody brought Battleship—"

"Battleship! Wanna play?"

"Um—"

"The bald guy is driving the boat now, right?"

"Well yes, but—"

"So just a quick game."

This was definitely not how he'd envisioned this pirate mission. Not at all. But Juli stood grinning at him, looking like a deranged mermaid, and Alex felt something warm inside him. Those eyes. And were those freckles on her nose? There was something so undeniably sweet about this woman. So fresh and warm and—

"I think I'm going to puke," she gasped, her face turning an interesting shade of green faster than Alex could register the change.

Alex jumped back, frantically scanning the room for a suitable receptacle. Snatching a high-heeled leather boot from a corner of the floor, he handed it to her.

Just in time. Juli grabbed the boot and hurled into it.

Alex froze, not sure whether to give her some privacy or pat her back and murmur comforting words.

"Hold my hair?" she choked.

"Um—"

Alex grabbed a fistful of blonde curls and then studied the grain of the woodwork, trying to imagine himself anywhere but here. When Juli was finished, she set the boot on the floor and fished a water bottle out of the side pocket of her knapsack.

Alex watched her rinse her mouth, the color returning slowly to her face.

"Sorry about that," she said, looking sheepish. "The ocean doesn't really agree with me."

"You still feel seasick?"

"Well, the drugs have probably worn off by now."

"What did you take?"

Juli reached into her knapsack again and handed him a half-crushed cardboard box. He read the back and then studied her again. "You allergic to morphine?"

"Dunno."

"If you are, it's no wonder this stuff made you loopy. Come on. Let's get you moved into your new cabin, and then out into the open air. I'll give you something that'll work a little better."

He expected a joke about him luring her to the master suite on their wedding night, but Juli just stuffed her belongings in her pack, avoiding his eyes.

"Really, I'm sorry," she said, shoving a shoe into the pack with more force than necessary. "I didn't mean to ruin your trip."

"You didn't ruin our trip," Alex said, feeling an odd pang in his chest. "Not yet, anyway. The day's still early."

"I'm such an idiot," she said. "I always do stuff like this."

"Stow away on strangers' boats?"

"No. I mean I do the wrong thing and then everyone knows I don't fit in."

"You weren't on our passenger list," Alex pointed

out. "I'm pretty sure we would have noticed you didn't belong."

She gave him a weak smile. "You know what I mean."

He smiled back and touched her elbow. "Come on. You got everything?"

Juli glanced around the cabin. "Um, the boot?"

"Right," Alex said. "We can dump that overboard in a sec. Sorry, I hope it wasn't expensive."

"The boot? Wasn't mine."

Alex grimaced. "Shit. Phyllis?"

"I doubt it. It's a size 15 wide. Nice leather. Excellent detailing. Prada, actually. I wouldn't have puked in it if I'd looked at it a little more closely. Cody maybe?"

Alex winced, wondering if this trip could possibly get any weirder. With a sigh, he hoisted his wife's knapsack onto his shoulder.

"Bring the boot, and let's go."

Chapter 5

"I THOUGHT I WAS SUPPOSED TO LOOK OUT AT SOMETHING not moving," Juli said, taking a sip of the tea Alex had given her as she stared out over the ocean from her lounge chair on the flybridge. "The horizon or something."

Alex leaned down and took the tea from her before placing something sticky and amber-colored in her palm. "We're in the middle of the ocean. Everything's moving. Have some crystallized ginger."

Juli accepted the amber lumps without much of a glance, preferring to stare straight into Alex's eyes. They were the most interesting shade of green. Even with her aversion to the water, she couldn't help but conjure up a plethora of ocean metaphors. Deep-sea green. Green as a glass float. Seaweed green.

Seasick green.

God, why did she have to puke in front of him? Was there anything more embarrassing? So much for her efforts to be *normal* for a change. So much for trying to fit in.

Alex frowned. "You okay? Your ears just turned really red all of a sudden."

Juli touched her chilly fingers to one earlobe, holding the ginger lumps in her other palm. "I'm fine, really."

"Are you going to eat that ginger or just fondle it?"

"Will fondling it be enough to get rid of the seasickness?"

"No. And neither will eating it. If you're already seasick, there's not much we can do about this round. We're trying to prevent the next round. Are those bands tight enough?"

Juli fiddled with the odd little wristbands he'd slipped over her hands just a few minutes earlier. Small plastic beads pressed between her tendons, performing some sort of acupressure miracle Alex swore by.

"Tight enough for what?" she asked.

"Your wrists seem awfully small. Can you feel pressure?"

"Sure. Am I supposed to have circulation?"

"Preferably. I'd rather not have to amputate your hands at sea."

Juli turned her wrist up to look at it. "Do they come in other colors? Seems like they could market pink ones for women, maybe yellow ones for kids—"

"Why don't you phone me the next time you decide to stow away on my boat and I'll be sure to have a full palette of colors for you to choose from."

Juli grinned and grabbed the tea back from him, taking another sip as the wind ruffled her hair. The warm air above deck certainly felt better in her lungs than the stale stuff down in her cabin. Of course, that may have been because the air below deck smelled like regurgitated breakfast.

"Did Cody handle it okay when you told him about the boot?" she asked as she took another sip of tea.

"Cookie."

"What?"

"He wants us to call him Cookie out here. And yes, he was fine with the boot. He offered to let you use the other if you need it."

"That's sweet."

"That's Cody."

"He seems like a nice guy."

"The best," Alex agreed, easing himself onto the deck chair beside her.

"You seem very protective of your crew. Kind of paternal, really. You have kids?"

"No."

"And you never got married?"

Alex stared at her. "Drink your tea and eat your ginger so you won't have to take Cookie up on the boot offer."

"Thanks for having him bring Uncle Frank up here." Juli patted the top of the urn. "I promised he'd get to see the ocean as much as possible on this trip."

"Don't mention it. That thing's latched, right?"

"Yes."

"I'm not a fan of cremated remains flying around my boat."

"I'll keep that in mind." Juli took another swig of the brew, then opened her palm and eyed the sticky lumps. "Candied ginger root?"

"Plenty of sailors swear by it."

"My mother puts it in tuna casserole."

"You don't say."

Juli tossed the lumps into her mouth and chewed, watching Alex as she washed the gummy, spicy mess down with another mouthful of tea. Reclining in a deck chair beside her, Alex might have appeared relaxed to the casual observer.

But Juli wasn't a casual observer. She saw the odd glance he'd exchanged with Cody when he brought the tea. She heard him murmuring something to Phyllis earlier when the two of them went rooting for the acupressure bands. Heard the sharp notes of worry in the older woman's voice. Something was up with these guys. Nervous cartographers? Was this really a high-stress occupation? It didn't seem likely.

Or rather, it didn't seem likely that was truly what they were doing out here. But why would they make up a lame story like that?

"You done?" Alex asked, taking the mug from her hand.

"Done. Thank you. For taking care of me, I mean."

"You're welcome."

"Really, I mean, I'm a stowaway on your ship and all. You don't have to be this nice."

"I do have to. I don't want you to puke again. It's a rental. There's a cleaning fee."

"I'm touched by your concern."

Alex grinned, his eyes crinkling pleasantly at the corners. "I'm a touching kind of guy."

Juli felt the heat creep into her cheeks and took a sip of tea, hoping he wouldn't notice. "So your friends— the other cartographers—they don't like me much," Juli said, wincing a little at the neediness in her own voice. "Did you tell them I'm sorry about all this?"

"It's okay. You were just a surprise to them. And anyway, they don't dislike you. Didn't Cody ask you like a dozen times if he could braid your hair?"

"I thought that was part of the plot to throw me overboard."

"No, that's Phyllis who wants to throw you overboard. And Jake. And they wouldn't really do it. Probably. It's just that you weren't in the plans."

"I see," Juli said. "And what are the plans, exactly?"

Alex stared at her for a few beats. "Like I told you. We're mapping deserted islands. Do you know how many uncharted islands exist in the region where the Caribbean meets the Atlantic?"

"Isn't that a trick question? If they're uncharted—"

"There are a lot of them," Alex said, ignoring her question. "This is a popular area for cartographers to work."

"Why do I have the feeling there's something you guys aren't telling me?"

He grabbed her cup and swung his legs off the edge of the deck chair. "More tea?"

"Please."

"You'll feel better once you've got something in your stomach. Cody—*Cookie*—is down in the galley right now getting dinner ready, so that should help. You feeling okay?"

"Sure. So am I still going to get to spread my uncle's ashes in the place I told you about?"

Alex looked out at the ocean for a minute, his expression thoughtful. When he returned his gaze to her, Juli felt her stomach give a pleasant little flip.

"Tell you what," Alex said. "No matter what happens, I'll make sure you get to do that. One way or another."

"Promise?"

"Promise."

"That's very nice of you," she said. "Uncle Frank also asked me to throw two vodka tonics in the water and play Loverboy's 'Turn Me Loose' when I toss the ashes. Will I get to do that?"

"Don't press your luck."

A soft, tinny tinkling sounded beneath them. Juli cocked her head to the side, listening. "Is that a triangle?"

"I'm not sure."

Beneath them, Cody's voice boomed. "Hey, guys! I'll be serving hors d'oeuvres in the galley in six minutes. It's black tie optional, of course."

"Good thing," Alex muttered. "I'm not sure where I packed my black tie."

"You know, I actually do have a little black cocktail dress," Juli said. "I brought it in case I ended up on one of those fancier cruise ships."

"Save it," Alex said. "Maybe you'll get lucky and end up on one of those boats soon."

Alex stood and extended a hand to her, hoisting her up with almost no effort. *Nice arms*, Juli thought, watching him turn and start toward the stairs. *Nice ass, too,* she amended, then chastised herself for ogling the captain. He'd made it clear they weren't going to be picking up where they left off last night. He was all-business out here, though she had to admit she was curious about the nature of the business. Alex was definitely hiding something, though she had no idea what.

"So how do you guys decide who drives the boat?" Juli asked.

"We drew up a shift schedule, so we take turns. It's mostly Jake and me, since Cookie is handling all the galley duties and Phyllis is dealing with all the computers and navigation."

"Can I have a turn?"

Alex glanced over his shoulder at her. "You can operate a powerboat?"

"I don't know. I've never tried. And maybe it'd be like motion sickness in a car—you know how you don't get sick when you're driving?"

"Right. It's just like that. Without the fur dice on the rearview mirror."

"Are you mocking me?"

"Yes."

"Fair enough. Anyway, maybe once I get past the seasickness, I could even learn to like boating."

Alex raised an eyebrow at her. "Thirty minutes ago you said you'd rather shave your legs with a carrot peeler than spend another hour on this ship."

"I was puking at the time. The ginger has given me a new perspective."

"Powerful stuff, ginger."

They descended the narrow stairwell together, Alex a few steps ahead of her, reaching back to steady her once when she wobbled a little. They stepped into the pilothouse and moved toward the U-shaped dinette area where Cody—*Cookie*—had set the table with blue linen place mats and perfectly pressed linen napkins folded into the shape of a swan.

"Wow, Cookie, something smells delicious!" Juli said, taking a seat and spreading her napkin over her lap. "I hope you didn't go to all this trouble because you have a guest onboard."

Cody beamed at her. "No, no. This is just something I'd planned to do once we started this leg of the journey. I have a complete gourmet menu drawn up for the duration of our mission."

"Mission?"

"That's what cartographers call it," Alex said, glancing up as Phyllis stepped into the room. "Right, Phyllis?"

Phyllis nodded and settled into the chair beside Juli. "Right. I'm starving."

"I've selected wines that complement each course of the meal, so we're starting with a crisp Pinot Gris from Napa Valley," Cody said, filling their glasses from a bottle plucked from an ice bucket at the center of the table. Juli took a cautious sip as she watched Cody set the bottle back in the bucket and return to the table with a silver tray.

"Here we have bacon-wrapped dates in a port wine demiglace. And these are miniature quesadillas with brie and fresh grapes."

Juli pointed at the pretty green flourish on the quesadillas. "What are the green swirly things shaped like flowers?"

Cody beamed. "That's green pea guacamole. I used a pastry tool to achieve the exact shape of a gardenia."

Juli clapped her hands together. "It's lovely! Thank you."

Phyllis looked like she was trying hard not to smile as she used some small silver tongs to help herself to the appetizers. Juli watched as the older woman darted a glance toward the cockpit where Jake was steering the ship. The look of hunger was palpable, though it wasn't clear whether the food or the man had prompted it.

Juli shot a look at Alex, who seemed oblivious to everything but the navigational chart he'd brought with him to the table. His eyes didn't leave the chart as he reached out and plucked a bacon-wrapped date from the tray.

He began to chew, then looked up in obvious surprise. "Wow, nice job, Cookie. These are excellent. I usually just eat Chef Boyardee when I'm at sea."

"Chef who?"

"Chef—oh, never mind," Alex said, helping himself to another. "This is really good."

Remembering the fate of her breakfast, Juli suddenly realized how starving she was. She used the little tongs to grab a couple quesadillas, then carefully dotted each with some extra green pea guacamole from a dish on the side.

"Ohmygod, Cookie, this is amazing!" she gasped between bites. "Have you worked as a professional chef?"

Cody beamed as he piled more dates on the platter. "Never professionally, but I've always cooked. When I got laid off, I decided to spend more time getting serious about it, maybe trying to find myself, you know?"

Juli cocked her head at him. "Laid off?"

"From my job at—"

"At a rival cartography firm," Alex interrupted as he grabbed another date. "We snapped him up very quickly, of course."

"Of course," Juli said, eyeing Alex. She helped herself to another quesadilla and two dates, careful not to drip sauce on the beautifully starched tablecloth. "Which appetizer is your favorite, Phyllis?"

"Hmmm?" Phyllis asked as she tore her eyes away from Jake. For all intents and purposes, Jake seemed unaware of the smorgasbord behind him, or of the woman who was shooting daggers of lust at his backside.

Alex, too, seemed oblivious, or maybe it was just that he was focused on the complicated-looking navigational chart. Juli looked back at Phyllis, who was staring wistfully at Jake again.

"That sure smells good," Jake called from the helm.

Juli glanced at Jake, then back at Phyllis. Phyllis met her gaze, her expression uneasy.

Juli gave her an encouraging smile. "Maybe you should take some of this over to Jake. Since he's busy driving the boat and all."

Phyllis looked as though Juli had just suggested stripping naked and painting her breasts with the port wine demiglace.

Of course, she didn't appear to think the idea was entirely unappealing.

Juli picked up an empty plate and handed it to Phyllis. "Just grab a couple of each and feed them to him," she encouraged. "You don't want him to have to take his hands off the controls, right?"

"Right," Phyllis said, biting her lip. "Jake, you want to try this stuff?"

"Yeah, that'd be great," he called. "Better get it now before you guys eat it all."

"Oh. Okay." Phyllis eyed the spread of food. "Well then."

She gripped the plate and piled a couple dates and some mini quesadillas on it. Juli reached over and spooned some guac on the side, then gave Phyllis a conspiratorial wink. Phyllis looked mortified, but she stood and wobbled her way over to Jake.

Juli smiled at them before turning back at Alex, who was shoveling food into his mouth with single-minded determination. He'd missed the whole thing. Probably missed the chemistry between Phyllis and Jake, too.

Alex looked up at her and stopped chewing. "What?"

"Nothing."

"Am I missing something?"

"Probably. That makes two of us in the dark, doesn't it?"

Alex eyed her suspiciously. "You still feeling drugged?"

"Nope."

"Maybe you should take some more."

"I thought you preferred your bride sober for the honeymoon."

"Honeymoon's over. I'll take you as you are."

Juli swallowed hard, blinking as Alex smiled. She tried to pull her gaze away, but her brain wasn't obeying the command.

"More Pinot Gris, anyone?"

Startled, Juli looked up to see Cody brandishing the bottle beside her. She held up her glass, grateful for the distraction. From the corner of her eye, she could see Phyllis feeding Jake a mini quesadilla with a shaky hand. She wore an expression of grim determination, not unlike a woman tasked with feeding a school of piranhas.

"Which one do you like best, Jake?" Juli called, picking up her glass and sipping her wine.

"This one with the green stuff is good," he said, shooting her a wary glance before turning back to let Phyllis shove another one in his mouth.

Okay, so Jake didn't like her yet. At least the others were warming up a little. She wasn't doing too badly so far. She might even make some friends before this was all over.

Cody sidled up to the table with another tray in his hand and placed a small crystal dish in front of Juli. "So next we'll be cleansing our palates with a key lime and basil sorbet," he announced, placing a dish in front of Alex.

Juli looked down at the tablespoon of ice cream melting in her dish. She swirled her spoon through it before smiling up at Cody. "Are these flecks of fresh basil?"

"I brought my herb garden with me," Cody said, beaming. "These guys said I wouldn't need it, but obviously…"

"Obviously," Juli agreed, and she dug into her sorbet. She groaned aloud. "Ohmygod, this is incredible!" she said, closing her eyes and licking the back of her spoon. "Cookie, you're a genius!"

She plowed her spoon back into the dish, scraping up the last traces of sorbet. She licked the spoon again, savoring the tangy, crisp flavors.

She looked up to see Alex staring at her mouth, his expression unreadable.

"Enjoying that?" he asked.

Juli licked the spoon once more, watching as Alex kept his eyes fixed on her mouth. She flushed and set the spoon down. Alex took a deep breath and looked down at his own sorbet.

"This is incredible," Juli said. "Seriously, my mother is the world's worst cook, and I'm a pretty close second. I can barely boil water for Top Ramen. If Cookie isn't married, I'd like an annulment right now so I can snatch him up."

"I'm hurt," Alex said as he scraped the sides of his dish with a spoon. "And here I thought we had this deep, meaningful connection in our marriage."

She patted his hand. "Deep meaning is one thing, but a man who can satisfy my appetite is a rare thing indeed."

Alex quirked an eyebrow at her, and Juli realized

at once that she'd sounded a whole lot sluttier than she'd intended.

Great. In addition to being socially backwards, you're also a tramp.

She realized she was still patting Alex's hand and started to pull back, but he caught her wrist and held it. Then he smiled.

"Judging from your appetite, that's a big order to fill."

He released her hand, but Juli's flesh tingled where he'd touched her. She held his gaze and saw his eyes were flashing with something—humor? Lust? She honestly couldn't tell.

She looked back down at her empty dish as her cheeks burned. Feeling silly, she glanced over to where Phyllis was spooning sorbet into Jake's mouth. The two of them looked a little more relaxed now, which was good. Phyllis glanced up and Juli gave her an encouraging wave. Phyllis bit her lip and returned a weak smile.

"Okay, gang!" Cody announced as Phyllis returned to the table with the empty plate and wiped her hands on a napkin. "Up next we have ankimo monkfish foie gras with dijon miso sauce and tobiko."

Juli watched as Cody set the next dish in front of them. She had to concentrate hard on not drooling as she reached for the platter.

"Let me get it for you," Cody said. "I've got this new serving spatula I've been dying to use."

Juli drew her hand back. "It's a very lovely spatula."

Cody beamed. "It's a genuine stainless steel blade with a red porcelain handle," he said. "I've wanted one since I was eight."

"I'm glad you finally got one," Juli said, admiring the food more than the spatula. "This looks amazing! If there's enough to go around, I'd love an extra helping."

Cody smiled down at her as he heaped the food on her plate. Juli gave a small groan of pleasure as she forked the first bite into her mouth.

"Are you always this passionate about food?" Alex asked.

"Yes," Juli said around a mouthful of fish. "Always. I love food. Especially decadent food like this."

"It's a shame we never had a wedding cake."

"Oh, I've already picked out my future wedding cake. I got to help make it once at this bakery where I worked as a cake decorator—"

"Didn't you say you worked in marketing?" Alex asked.

"Anyway," Juli said, spearing a bite into her mouth and chewing blissfully. "The bottom layer is a white champagne cake layered with fresh strawberries, and the middle layer is a red velvet cake filled with amaretto cream cheese, and the top layer is chocolate fudge with an apricot glaze filling, and the whole thing is covered with ivory fondant and fresh flowers."

"No kidding."

"No kidding," she said. "Best cake in the world."

Alex smiled and shook his head. "What about the ring?"

"Ring?"

"Wedding ring. Some big, expensive, hunkin' rock. Or the wedding dress that costs more than a down payment on a house. Aren't those the things women generally care about?"

"Oh. Probably. I don't know. The ring just needs to be round with a hole in the middle to stick my finger through. The dress should be white, I guess. Lacy, frilly, blah, blah, blah." She speared another piece of monkfish and looked up at Alex.

He was staring at her oddly and Juli tried to remember if she'd said something provocative or offensive this time. She couldn't think of anything, but then she often didn't catch her own faux pas until it was too late.

She turned back toward the kitchen. "Cookie," she called to him. "Who taught you to make food like this?"

"Serge Lightfoot."

"Serge Lightfoot, the famous TV chef?"

"He's my older brother."

"No kidding?"

"Nope. He's always been an inspiration to me."

"I thought Steve Largent was an inspiration to you," Jake called over his shoulder.

At the sound of his voice, Phyllis smiled prettily and began to load up another plate of food for him. She stood and carried it over to him, her hips swaying just a little as she moved. Jake smiled appreciatively—a look that wasn't lost on Juli, even if the rest of the conversation was.

"Who is Steve Largent?" Juli asked.

"Steve Largent?" Jake snorted. "The best wide receiver to ever play the game."

"What game?"

"Football. The great American sport?"

Juli rolled her eyes. "Ugh. Football."

"Ugh? Football? Are you kidding me?" Alex stared at her. "You're from the west coast and you don't have a Seahawks tattoo?"

"What?"

"The Seattle Seahawks. Best football team in the history of the sport. Steve Largent? Jim Zorn? Walter Jones? Lofa Tatupu? Any of these famous Seahawk names ringing a bell?"

"I have no idea what you're talking about."

"That's my team," Cody said, drizzling some sort of sauce on another platter.

"Your team?" Juli said, paying more attention to the food than the conversation. "That's nice."

"No, he means it," Alex said. "Not in a 'those are my boys' armchair-quarterback kind of way. Cody used to play for the Seahawks. I know that's not a big deal to someone who doesn't know a football from a salami, but trust me, it's huge. Cody here—*Cookie*—is one of the best tight ends to ever play the game."

Juli eyed Cody with renewed interest. "You really are a novelty then, Cookie. A football playing, gourmet cooking, cartographer pirate."

"What?"

Alex dropped his fork. Phyllis choked on her wine. Jake's shoulders went rigid. Even Cody looked uncomfortable.

"What? What did I say?" Juli asked, looking from one face to the other for a clue. "What?"

"Nothing," Alex said, staring at her. "Have another piece of ankimo monkfish foie gras with dijon miso sauce and tobiko."

Juli sighed, forking up another generous portion. "You guys are the weirdest cartographers I've ever stowed away with."

In the middle of the night, Juli tiptoed out of her state-room and peered into the pilothouse. Alex was tilted back a little in the chair, looking more natural at the helm of a boat than he did anywhere else she'd seen him. Juli watched him, feeling a shiver of voyeuristic excitement.

His shoulders were beautifully muscled beneath the rumpled linen shirt. The dark hair looked windblown, not in that phony movie star fashion, but genuinely blown by the wind. He glanced at something in his lap, then punched some numbers on a gadget beside him. *Beautiful hands*, Juli thought, then shivered at the memory of those hands all over her body.

Obviously she'd been celibate a little too long. *Be normal*, she told herself, wishing it was that easy.

She forced herself to concentrate, watching Alex from behind. Something odd was going on. There had been more than a few awkward moments during dinner, strange bits of conversation that left little doubt in Juli's mind that these guys were not cartographers. Not even close.

Now that she wasn't puking her guts out, she was almost enjoying herself out on the water. Okay, there was the perpetual fear of sinking to a watery grave, but really, was that much worse than working in a marketing office? Certainly the coffee was better here.

So maybe she could convince them to keep her. Maybe she could really *belong* here. Certainly they were nice people. A little strange, but nice. Maybe there was even a new career for her here somewhere. Maybe she could be an investigative journalist. Or a cabana girl. Or a deckhand. Or maybe, if her suspicions were right—

"Quit spying on me and go back to bed," Alex said without turning around.

Juli jumped, stubbing her toe on a stair. With a yelp, she grabbed her foot and pulled it up to eye level for inspection. *Ouch*. She'd chipped the corner right off her big toenail.

"I'm not sure whether to be more impressed with your flexibility or your balance, but it's good to know you have talents," Alex said. "Since spying clearly isn't one of them."

Juli looked up to see he'd turned in his chair and was studying her with a look of amusement. She felt her face flush, though embarrassment wasn't the only culprit.

"Don't mind me," she said, lowering her foot to the floor. "I'll just stand here and bleed to death on your boat."

"You're not bleeding. But if you are, try not to get any on the woodwork. It's teak."

"Aye-aye, captain," she said, saluting him as she turned. "If I don't survive the night, it's been lovely knowing you."

"Come back here," he called, his tone nowhere near as stern as his words. "Want me to make sure it's not broken?"

She turned and looked at him, ignoring the shiver of lust that snaked down her spine. "Are we playing doctor now, or do you have actual medical training?"

"Neither, but I figure if your toe is hanging off your foot by one tendon, Cody's got some sharp knives in the galley."

Juli shrugged and hobbled back toward him. Her toe didn't hurt anymore, but she liked the idea of Alex's hands on any part of her body. She sat down on the high-backed stool beside him and lifted her foot into his lap, grateful she'd gotten a nice pedicure before the trip. She watched as he prodded and probed, her blood pressure kicking up a few notches as his fingers moved deftly over her toes and skimmed the ball of her foot.

"Looks okay to me," he said.

She sighed with pleasure. "If I sit here long enough will this turn into a foot massage?"

"No, because you know where foot massages lead?"

"Where?"

He grinned and lifted her foot off his lap, setting it neatly on the rung of the stool. "With both of us naked in the pilothouse."

"Oh," she said, momentarily speechless. "That would be bad."

"It would actually be quite good, under normal circumstances."

Juli swallowed. "Normal?"

"Right. But these aren't normal circumstances. I've got work to do, and you've got secrets you aren't sharing."

"Don't be silly. I don't have secrets. I'm an open book."

Alex snorted and shook his head. He said nothing more and turned his attention back to the task of driving the boat.

Juli nudged his shin with her toes. "You're one to talk, Mr. Don't-mind-me-I'm-an-innocent-cartographer." She delivered another light kick for good measure.

He leaned down and caught her foot before she could kick him again, drawing it back up into his lap and squeezing her big toe. She wasn't sure if it was supposed to be punishment or seduction, but it worked for both.

"So you agree we both have secrets?" he asked.

"Maybe one or two. Who doesn't?"

"My point exactly."

She grinned. "Know what we should do?"

"Yes, but I still don't have condoms. Pity, that."

"Not *that*," she said, rolling her eyes as though it had been the furthest thing from her mind instead of an obsession from the moment she'd met him. "We should play Truth or Dare."

"Truth or Dare?"

"Exactly. It's the perfect game for two people trying to get to the bottom of each other's secrets."

He stared at her. "Are you certifiably insane or still awaiting diagnosis?"

"Truth or Dare?" she insisted, ignoring the prick of embarrassment over the insanity comment. He was stroking the ball of her foot with his thumb, which made things considerably easier. She sighed again as the pad of his thumb made a lazy circle over her arch, then stroked upward toward her toes. Juli resisted the urge to close her eyes.

"I thought you were going back to bed," he said.

"This sounds like more fun. Truth or Dare?"

Alex shrugged. "Fine. Dare."

"That's no way to get to the bottom of each other's secrets, but okay. I dare you to give me a foot massage for the next five minutes and *not* use it to seduce me."

Alex grinned and reached for her other foot. Juli leaned back on her stool to let him prop both feet on his lap. He began to stroke her arches in tandem, his thumbs strong and clever over the tense band of muscle. The rest of his fingers curved over the top of her insteps and Juli marveled at how small her feet looked in his oversized hands. His thumbs stroked upward over the outside of her arch and Juli gasped in pleasure.

"The foot massage I can do," he said. "I make no guarantees about the seduction. Not my fault if you melt in a puddle at my feet."

"I'll try to avoid it."

She would have been a lot more convincing if her voice hadn't cracked. Alex slid his thumbs over her arches for a few more pulse beats before moving up to the balls of her feet. He stroked her there, kneading the pad of flesh on each sole until Juli had to bite her lip to keep from moaning.

"Truth or Dare?" he asked.

She jumped, having forgotten already that they were playing. "Truth."

"Who are you and why are you on my boat?"

She laughed. "Don't beat around the bush, sailor boy. Aren't you supposed to work up to that sort of question? Like foreplay or something."

"I think I've got the foreplay covered," he said, caressing her arches again. "I'll repeat the question—who are you and why are you on my boat?"

"Has anyone ever told you that you have serious trust issues?"

"Yes. Who are you and—"

"All right, all right," she said as his thumb slid over her arch and made her gasp. "That's a waste of a good question." Her voice sounded high and strained, so she cleared her throat and tried again. "I've already told you everything. My name is Juli Flynn, and as God is my witness, I got on your boat thinking it was my charter. I just want to dump my uncle's ashes and go home."

His eyes bored into hers, the green of them flashing in the dim light of the cabin as the heel of his right hand pressed firmly into the heel of her left foot. He moved the pads of his index fingers along the narrow hollow at the base of each toe, his touch not soft enough to tickle, not firm enough to hurt. Juli concentrated on breathing so she wouldn't crawl into his lap and force him to put those hands on other parts of her body.

"Why do I think there's more to your story?" he asked.

"There's always more to a story," she replied. "Truth or Dare?"

"Truth."

"How daring of you."

"I try."

Juli cleared her throat and tried to think of something besides the suggestive way his thumb had worked its way into the crease between her big and middle toe. He massaged her there for a moment, increasing the pressure as the pressure in Juli's brain built to a point where she thought her head might explode.

"Where is your favorite place to be kissed?" she asked.

He raised an eyebrow but didn't stop what he was doing to her toes. "I thought your big idea here was to get to the bottom of my deepest, darkest secrets."

"Would you tell me yours?"

"No."

"Exactly. So this is what I want to know. It's not collarbone, is it?"

"No," Alex said, looking thoughtful. "Close though. You really want to know this?"

"Absolutely."

"Fine. Anytime a woman does anything with her mouth anywhere near my neck, I lose it completely."

"Completely?"

"Not completely. I'm just saying—it's my Achilles heel."

As if reminded by his own suggestion, he slid his thumbs downward and began to stroke the tendon along the back of her heel. Juli gasped as he hit a spot that sent an electric jolt all the way up the back of her calves and through her thighs, delivering pulses of pleasure between her legs.

She gave up playing it cool and closed her eyes, only dimly aware of the soft hum in the back of her throat. She let her thoughts roam to dark places where she could back him up against a wall and breathe warm against his neck, trailing her tongue along the tendons there and up toward his ear—

"My turn," he said, his voice soft and dark like melted chocolate. Juli opened her eyes, not sure what he was suggesting. Alex licked his lips. "What do you do for a living?"

She smiled. "I didn't say I wanted truth."

"Dare, then?"

"I'm thinking," she said. "Yes, dare."

"I dare you to tell me what you do for a living."

She rolled her eyes. "Lame, sailor boy. Very lame. I have nothing to hide, though. I am currently unemployed, though my most recent position was in the marketing department for a software company. Would you like to phone my references or take my word for it?"

He shook his head. "You're giving me nothing here."

She shot a pointed look at his lap, then lifted her right foot from his grasp. Slowly, gently, she grazed him with her heel. "I'm pretty sure I'm giving you something."

For the first time all evening, Alex looked startled. He shifted on his stool but didn't break contact. Juli angled her leg the other way and felt him get harder beneath the ball of her foot. She felt a shiver of triumph knowing she was the cause. She flexed her calf and continued to stroke him through his trousers, making slow, gentle circles.

Feeling him grow harder still, she increased the pressure. Alex closed his eyes and gripped her other ankle so hard Juli gasped. She slid her arch over the length of him, satisfied to feel him moving against her.

"You're killing me here," he murmured.

"How unfortunate."

She stroked him again, curling her toes over the hard length of him.

"We have to stop." Alex opened his eyes and swallowed, looking down at her feet as though noticing them for the first time. "Your second toe is much longer than your big toe."

"I know. It means I'm destined to be the one in charge in my family."

"Yeah?"

"That's the old wives' tale," she said, keeping the ball of her foot pressed against him. "I've also heard in men it means they're particularly well-endowed. Are you picking dare next?"

"Maybe."

She grinned. "Good. Take off your shoes."

Alex laughed and slid his palms under her feet. He took a deep breath, then lifted them off his lap and set them on the rungs of her stool. When he sat back up, his expression was an odd mix of desire and regret.

"Your five minutes are up, darlin'," he said in a voice that didn't sound very steady. "You got your foot massage and I didn't seduce you. Much."

Juli nodded and bit her lip. "I thank you for that."

"So are we done playing?"

For a second, she wasn't sure what he meant. Was he going to shove her up against the wall of the pilothouse and have his way with her? She swallowed, met his eyes. "Oh. The game?"

"The game."

"Yes, we're done."

"And sadly, neither of us got anything from your intensive truth-finding mission."

She shrugged and gave him a small smile. "I wouldn't say that."

He grinned back and angled his body away from her, turning his attention back to the controls of the ship. "Neither would I," he said. "But we'd better stop now. Jake is going to be here soon to relieve me at the helm, and it would be best if I weren't sitting here with a raging hard-on."

"Relieve you at the helm? That's a euphemism I haven't heard before."

"Go to sleep, nut-job."

Juli stood up, her body still humming with pleasure and need. She straightened her top, noticing how it clung to her body. She looked up to see Alex noticing too.

He shook his head, looking pained. "Get out of here."

"Good night, sailor boy."

She turned and sashayed back to her cabin. Once inside, she latched the door behind her. Her body was still tingling everywhere Alex had touched her—not to mention a few places he hadn't. Ignoring that for now, Juli moved toward the bed and reached under the pillow. She pulled out the laptop she'd sneaked from the salon when no one was looking. Phyllis had just left it there when she'd gone to bed, and no one else had been paying attention.

Juli fiddled with the wireless Internet connection, disabling it. She ignored the pang of guilt she felt. They'd figure it out sooner or later, or Juli could show them how to fix it eventually.

She just needed some time. A little more time before they found out about her. Just a little more time to fit in.

If only she could figure out how to do that.

Chapter 6

THE NEXT MORNING, ALEX LAY STRETCHED OUT ON A deck chair on the flybridge. He wasn't asleep. Just resting in the early dawn air, the sun drizzling through a light cloud cover to pool on his arms and legs.

Jake had relieved him at three o'clock that morning and he'd come up here intending to sleep. But sleep hadn't come. Usually he slept soundly under the stars with the ocean rocking beneath him, soothing him into a slumber.

But nothing about him was feeling soothed at the moment.

When they'd sailed to St. John, it hadn't really hit him what they were attempting to do. It had seemed like a far-off fantasy, something in an action flick or a pirate novel.

Okay, admittedly they weren't the cast of *Ocean's Eleven*, but still.

Of course, now that they'd boarded the powerboat and were headed toward their rendezvous with the cargo ship, everything had changed. They were really going to do this. Really going to take charge of a ship and pilfer thousands of dollars worth of diamonds.

Illegal diamonds, he reminded himself. *Diamonds acquired in a shady transaction. Diamonds that just barely cover the amount of the pensions Portelli stole from us.*

So it wasn't his conscience keeping him awake. When he closed his eyes to sleep, the face he saw on the inside of his eyelids wasn't Tom Portelli. Not unless his former boss had sprouted a mass of golden curls and flashing blue eyes.

Thirty more seconds last night and he would have had her pressed up against the wall, wrists pinned over her head as he drove himself into her over and over and over. He was lucky she'd gone to bed when she had. Hell, they were both lucky.

He thought of his ex-fiancée and her damn dentist lover and suddenly didn't feel so lucky.

The last thing you need right now is another woman you can't trust, he told himself. *You're penniless and jobless, and you're about to commit an act of high-seas piracy. Hardly the time to start dating.*

They were ditching Juli in a matter of hours. No one had been able to get a straight answer from her about who she was or what she did for a living. The story about the dead uncle seemed fishy. The idea that she'd *accidentally* stowed away on the boat didn't add up.

And Jake and Phyllis were right—there was something oddly familiar about her. He couldn't put his finger on it, but it was there.

No, there was no reason to complicate things. No sense getting to know her, making love to her, getting attached to her. No sense risking their pirate heist for anything. Not even a beautiful pair of—

Alex cleared his throat and forced himself to relax, throwing an arm over his face to block the sun as he lay back on the deck chair. At least the weather was beautiful. And the boat handled like a dream. If they were going to commit a felony on the high seas, at least they'd chosen a good time for it.

When he heard footsteps, he tried not to move. Even though he knew it was her. Even though he wanted to look.

"Ahoy, matey!" she called. "Prepare to be boarded!"

What the—?

Alex opened his eyes and stared at the inside of his elbow. He closed his eyes again, not sure he wanted to move his arm. Maybe she'd think he was asleep. He was sure as hell trying to be.

The feeling of her knee pressing against his chest dispelled that possibility. He tried to focus on being annoyed, but all he could think was how good it felt to have any part of her body pressed against any part of his.

"Fancy a walk on the plank before breakfast?" Juli chirped. "Come on, lad! Scrape the barnacles off your rudder and get up!"

Okay, he couldn't *not* look. She sounded like a deleted scene from a bad pirate movie, and curiosity was getting the best of him. He could sleep another time.

Alex drew his arm away from his face and sat up, blinking in the sunlight.

The first thing he noticed was the eye patch. Though he'd certainly admired the black thong panties when she'd tossed them out of her knapsack the day before, this wasn't quite how he'd imagined her wearing them.

The second thing he noticed was her left hand tucked up in the sleeve of her blouse.

"What are you doing with my boat hook?"

"I'm a pirate," she informed him. "Arrr."

"Arrr," Alex repeated, sure he hadn't heard her right. He was starting to wonder if he'd fallen asleep after all, and this was just a weird dream. Any minute now, a unicorn was going to appear on deck and ask to borrow a bottle of ketchup.

"Shiver me timbers!" she said. "Is that a cutlass in your trousers, or are you just—"

"Oh, Jesus." Alex lay back down and closed his eyes. Juli nudged him with her toe.

"Come on. This is funny. You have to admit, it's funny."

"What's funny?"

"You're pirates. Come on, you didn't really expect me to believe you're cartographers, did you? Cody asked me last night why we couldn't see the stripes in the water like we could on the map."

Alex gritted his teeth, trying to hide his alarm. And trying not to notice how beautiful she looked with the sunlight glinting in her hair.

"You're delusional," he muttered.

"And then there was the way you all freaked out when I made the pirate joke last night."

"Truly, truly delusional."

"And then I overheard Jake talking about booty—"

"Jake always talks about booty."

"And I saw Phyllis reviewing some diagrams of a really big boat that doesn't look anything like this one."

Alex groaned inwardly, praying like hell she'd give up this line of questioning and go away. Okay, so maybe he didn't want her to go away. He *really* didn't want her to go away. He just wanted her to stop talking about pirates. And to stop jiggling around under that top. "You're insane."

"And yet, you deny nothing. I'm right. You know I'm right. You're pirates."

"Have you been taking that seasick medication again?"

She nudged him again with her knee. "Come on, Alex. I want to be a pirate too. I'll be good at it. Really, I will. I promise, I'll be a big help."

"Juli, seriously. You're nuts."

"Arrr."

Alex sighed. She wasn't giving up. And she clearly wasn't going away. Alex sat up again and stared at her.

"Nice pirate pants," he observed.

"You like? They're pajama bottoms. I didn't really have anything that worked as a pirate shirt."

"No, the blouse over the plaid bikini top is a nice touch."

"I was going for a Scottish pirate thing."

"Scottish pirate. Of course. A formidable bunch. Do you have any aspirin?"

"If I give you some, will you let me stay?"

Alex sighed. "Juli. Seriously. Drop it. This isn't what you think."

"Then why don't you explain it to me?"

"It's not that simple."

"Come on. I watch CNN. I know piracy has been increasing globally in the last few years. Estimated worldwide losses of about sixteen billion dollars a year. Mostly near Somalia and places like that, but still. It's a blooming industry. I want to be a part of it. I want to join you."

"Stop jumping around. The stripes on those pants are making me queasy."

"You want some candied ginger?"

Alex folded his arms over his chest. "Juli. Come on. You're getting off this boat in less than twelve hours. You'll have a nice adventure getting back to St. John, and then you're going to go home and forget you ever knew us."

"Alex, please—"

"No."

Juli sighed. She raised her thong eye patch and crossed her arms over her chest, wincing a little as the boat hook caught on her bikini top.

"I don't want to leave," she said. "And do you really want to leave *me*? Think about it. You ditch me on a deserted island and call someone to come get me, how do you know I won't scream? How do you know I won't tell anyone who comes to rescue me exactly who you are and what you're up to? I could tell them which way you're headed and what the boat looks like. I could even tell them about that little anchor tattoo on your left shoulder blade. I'm very observant."

Alex narrowed his eyes, trying to remember when he'd been shirtless with his back turned to her. Perhaps she was a better spy than he'd thought.

"White linen," she said, reading his thoughts. "Very see-through."

Alex sighed. "So maybe we just leave you on the island. What do you think about that? Maybe we don't call anyone to come rescue you. Maybe we just leave you there to fend for yourself. It's not inhabited. Maybe no one will find you. Did you consider that?"

Juli shook her head and smiled. "You may be a pirate, but you're not an evil one. No way you're going to leave me on a deserted island alone. Jake and Phyllis might, but not you. You're one of the good guys, Alex. Or is it Dread Pirate Alex?"

"Juli—"

"Alex, please." Her expression was so earnest that Alex felt something soften inside him. He wasn't sure if the desperation in her eyes was real or not, but obviously her intention was sincere. She truly wanted to stay.

Why was another matter.

Alex closed his eyes and sighed. "Go change. Okay? Ditch the pirate outfit and let's talk. Like sane people. Think you can manage that?"

Juli grinned at him, clearly pleased.

"Aye-aye, captain," she said, saluting him before she turned and scampered toward the stairs. "You won't regret it. Really!"

"And put my boat hook back where you found it," he yelled after her.

"Yes, sir!"

"And don't forget my aspirin."

He tried to lie back down for a minute and gather his thoughts. But all he could see were visions of Juli in that pink plaid bikini top. *Dammit.* He stood up, pressing his fists to his eyes to clear his vision. *Dammit. Dammit to hell.* This was not in the plans. He tried to summon up some genuine anger, maybe to hit something.

But there was a tiny part of him that felt just a little pleased she wanted to stay.

She doesn't know you're broke, his conscious pointed out. *She thinks you're a rich guy who owns a boat, not a jobless executive who couldn't afford a corn dog right now.*

He shook his head, trying to clear his thoughts. This wasn't about him. Not once had Juli said, "I want to stay because I'm hot for you, Alex." Hell, that wasn't even what he wanted to hear. He had a job to do.

A job that had just gotten a lot more complicated.

He stood up and strode toward the stairs, descending to the main level with the enthusiasm of a man heading to the execution chamber.

When Alex stepped into the pilothouse, Cody was whistling to himself as he ladled something fragrant into bowls. "Fresh sautéed Moroccan grains with dried pears and goat milk yogurt?"

"Thanks, Cookie. That sounds—interesting. Is that Juli's urn on the counter?"

"I thought Uncle Frank could use a change of scenery. Juli said it was okay, as long as I didn't flip any switches."

Alex shook his head, trying not to think about the hygienic implications of having cremated remains in a kitchen. He glanced toward the cockpit where Phyllis was manning the controls, Jake standing beside her looking oddly flushed. What was that about?

"Stone ground cardamom?" Cody asked.

"Of course," Alex said, not caring what that meant. He sat down at the table and unfolded his napkin in his lap.

Cody nudged a bowl in front of him and stepped back from the table. "Will Juli be joining us?"

"That's what I wanted to talk to you guys about," Alex said as he spooned up a mouthful of sautéed grains. "Juli wants to stay."

"What do you mean?" Jake sputtered, stepping away from Phyllis. His bald head reflected the light off the ocean, making him look like a pudgy pink beacon. "Stay where? Not with us!"

Phyllis shot a nervous glance over her shoulder as she gripped the wheel. "What happened, Alex?"

"Well, she dressed up like a pirate and suggested

she might rat us out to authorities if we didn't keep her. Things got a little confusing after that."

"Is she serious?" Jake growled.

"Rarely." Alex spooned up a piece of pear.

"I thought she didn't like the water," Cody said, looking confused. "She wouldn't make a very good pirate if she doesn't like water."

"Good point, Cookie," Alex said. "I'm honestly not sure what she's up to. Maybe she thinks it's a game. Maybe she was joking about the pirate thing. Maybe she's insane. Any of those things seem likely."

"Maybe she's Portelli's spy," Jake said. "Did you ask her that?"

"It didn't come up in conversation, no."

"There's something suspicious about her," Jake insisted. "Did you notice how she changed the subject last night every time one of us asked her about her job?"

"She just lost her job."

"So she says."

"We should check her out," Phyllis said. "I can do a complete background check right away as soon as I figure out what's going on with the damn satellite Internet. I'm going to run some diagnostics on it after breakfast. What did you say her last name was?"

"Flynn," Alex said. "Juli Flynn."

Jake's brow furrowed. "Why does that sound familiar?"

Alex shrugged and ladled up another mouthful of grains. "Beats me, but you're right, a background check is a good idea. In the meantime, though, I'm reconsidering our plan to dump her on the island."

Jake threw his hands in the air. "Great. Just great. We invite the spy to stay."

"For now," Alex said as he chewed. "The alternative is that we leave her for authorities to find without knowing who she is, what she knows, or what she might say about us to anyone who asks."

"We don't trust her, so we're going to keep her?" Phyllis asked, her tone even.

"If she already suspects we're pirates, there's no telling what she might say to someone," Alex pointed out. "Even if she thinks it's a joke, she might say something to the authorities that would put our mission in jeopardy."

Cody smiled. "Right. It's like that expression about keeping your enemies close and your friends—no, wait. Keep your friends close and your—"

"Exactly," Alex said. "So we let her play pirate for a while until we figure out what she's up to."

Jake pounded a fist on the table, sloshing orange juice onto Cody's linen place mat. "No! She can't be a pirate! She doesn't even look like a pirate!"

Alex stopped chewing and eyed Jake, chubby and seething in his mint green polo shirt. "A worthy consideration."

"She's not in the plans," Jake argued. "How will we divide the diamonds?"

Alex sighed. "We're getting ahead of ourselves here. Maybe she'll get bored or seasick and want off tomorrow or the next day. Maybe she just wants to dump her uncle's ashes and go home. Maybe we'll find out she's an escaped mental patient."

"Or a cop," Jake muttered.

"In which case we'll have a chance to check her out and discover that *before* we dump her off for the authorities to rescue," Phyllis pointed out. "I'm with Alex on this one. Sorry, Jake."

Jake glowered at her. Phyllis glared back, then turned her attention to steering the boat.

"So what would she do?" Cody asked. "We all have to have jobs on the pirate ship, and I've got the cooking covered. And Phyllis deals with the computers and navigation and stuff, and you and Jake handle the boat most of the time. What does Juli do for a living?"

Alex shrugged, trying to ignore the fact that he was growing increasingly worried about that very thing. "Her occupation is apparently something of a mystery."

"She could scrub the poop deck," Cody suggested as he carried two glasses of orange juice over to Jake and Phyllis.

Alex closed his eyes. "There's no poop deck. But you're right, she could be in charge of cleaning. That's something we'd planned to split among the group. She could do that."

Jake shook his head, his expression grim. "I can't believe you're even considering this."

"What choice do we have, Jake? We can't make her leave if she refuses. Not without doing her bodily harm."

"So?"

Alex leveled him with a look. "Despite your efforts to be an evil pirate, Jake, I'm not buying it. You used to dig the poinsettias out of the trash every year after Christmas and nurse them back to health. You're not going to harm a person."

"Especially not a cute one," Cody piped.

Jake frowned and looked away. "Fine. But I still don't like this. I don't like this one bit. Seriously, Alex. This could ruin everything."

"This is temporary," Alex assured him. "Remember,

we identified islands at several places along our course where we could stop in case of emergency. We can still dump her off if we need to. For now, it just makes sense to keep her close."

Jake grunted but stayed silent, clearly trying to think of a way out of this. Alex glanced at Phyllis, who seemed deep in thought.

"Phyllis, how long do you think it'll take to do that background check?"

"Once the Internet is back up? Not long at all. Hopefully I'll be able to figure out what's wrong with it pretty soon. A couple hours maybe?"

"Okay," Alex said, nodding. "In the meantime, we tell her nothing. No details about who we worked for, where we're going, what we're after—nothing. Just let her play along with the pirate fantasy. Agreed?"

The other heads nodded. Alex looked to the only other female on board. "Phyllis, you haven't said much. Are you okay with Juli staying for now?"

She was quiet for a moment, and Alex wasn't even sure she'd heard him.

"She doesn't seem so bad," Phyllis said finally. "I think she should stay. And Cody's right. She can scrub the poop deck."

Alex gritted his teeth. "For the last time, there's no—"

"Isn't my shift up?" Phyllis interrupted with a quick glance over her shoulder. "I was just supposed to cover breakfast, right?"

"Right," Alex said, not sure he was following the swing in conversation. "Jake's up next."

"Okay," Phyllis said, looking flushed. "So that settles it."

"So we're all good?" Alex asked. "Juli stays?"

"Juli stays," Cody said, delighted as a boy permitted to keep a stray kitten.

"She stays," agreed Phyllis with a brisk nod.

"Fine," Jake muttered, spooning sautéed grains into his mouth with one hand as he grabbed the controls with the other. "It would have taken too long to find that damn island anyway."

"Okay then," Alex said, surveying the crew. "Who wants to tell her?"

"Let me," Phyllis said. "I'll do it."

Alex eyed her, trying to figure how Phyllis had gone from plotting to throw Juli overboard to apparent eagerness to keep her around. "Why the change of heart, Phyllis?"

Phyllis straightened the yellow bandana on her head and shrugged. "It's—um—it's a girl thing."

"A girl thing?"

"Right," she said, pushing past him on her way toward Juli's cabin. "I need to borrow—um—female products."

"Oh," Alex said, still confused. "Okay then. You go do that."

"Thanks. I will. We'll talk about girl stuff and do girl things."

Alex nodded. "Have fun with that."

~~~

Juli was refolding her favorite black thong when she heard a knock at the door.

"Come in, Captain Alex," she called, stuffing the panties into her knapsack. "Door's unlocked."

But it wasn't Alex at the door. It was Phyllis, so tense she looked electrified.

"Phyllis," Juli said, straightening up. "Good morning. It's nice to see you. Did you sleep well?"

"Yes," Phyllis replied, looking everywhere but at Juli. She picked up a shoe, then set it down, her eyes darting around the room. "I slept well. And you?"

"Great, great. No seasickness in the night, so that's good."

"Yes, very good. Very good. Very good indeed."

Juli eyed her uncertainly. Had Alex sent Phyllis to give her bad news? To say she wouldn't be allowed to join them on their pirate mission?

Okay, admittedly it was a dumb stunt she'd pulled. Wasn't Dr. Gordon always saying she needed to work on her social skills? Obviously this was what he meant. Well, he hadn't specifically said anything about not dressing like a pirate and threatening men she wanted to sleep with, but that was probably the general idea.

She'd been mostly joking when she'd accused Alex of being a pirate. It had seemed funny at the time. She just really wanted to stay with them out here, to be a part of whatever they were doing.

And she'd wanted to see him smile. She craved it.

She sure as hell hadn't expected him to react the way he had.

But there was something going on with these guys, and the pirate thing did have a certain plausibility. Whatever was happening here, she wanted to be a part of it.

Juli tried again, hoping to get Phyllis to relax. "So was the stateroom everything you thought it would be?"

"The room is fine."

"Did you have breakfast?"

"Yes."

"Did Cody make something really amazing?"

"Yes."

"You going to watch more *Olympic Steeplechase Highlights* videos today?"

"I already did."

"Okay then."

Juli waited a moment, keeping a wary eye on the steely blonde. She looked like a muscular albino rabbit, minus the pink eyes and cottontail. Phyllis fiddled with a corner of the quilt, her fingers twisting the fabric in a knot. The quilt began to fray, releasing a puff of stuffing.

Juli couldn't take it anymore. The sympathy stress was making her eyeballs hurt.

"Why are you here, Phyllis?"

Phyllis looked up. She bit her lip. "I want to talk to Jake."

Juli frowned. "Jake's not in here."

"No, *talk* to Jake. Not just about boats and work and things like that."

"Right," Juli said, beginning to grasp the situation. "Talk. Like—*talk*."

"Exactly," Phyllis said, looking unsure. "Last night at dinner, you seemed to understand that—"

"You've got the hots for Jake," Juli finished, trying hard not to grin. It was clear this was uncomfortable territory for Phyllis. "Of course."

Phyllis's pale skin went two shades lighter. "Is it that obvious?"

"Not to the men. They're oblivious."

Her relief was palpable. "The thing is, I've worked with Jake for years. But it wasn't until we started this mission a couple weeks ago that I really started to think that maybe—"

"You want to jump his bones," Juli supplied.

Phyllis winced. "Right. Well, so what do I do about that? I mean, besides feeding him dinner. That was good, I mean, but I need to do more than that. And I don't have much experience with this sort of thing."

"With flirting?"

"With men in general. Except my workout partners. And you seem like you probably know a lot about men."

Juli grimaced. Obviously she wasn't doing so hot with Alex these last couple days. Even before that, her love life wasn't anything to write home about. She was thirty-seven years old, never married, no serious man in her life. She knew the reasons for it, but that didn't make it much easier to deal with.

But here was Phyllis, looking at her like she expected Juli to be some sort of love guru. Juli studied her, considering.

"I'm really no expert," Juli said. "I mean, asking me for advice is like the blind leading the blind. Not that I'm suggesting you're blind, but—"

"You're so pretty. And you seem to know things about men. *Know* things. Like that Jake would want some extra guacamole with his quesadillas last night."

"Right. Yes, that is unparalleled insight into the male psyche."

"Please?"

Juli bit her lip. "So in the years you've worked with

Jake, have you ever had any indication how he feels about you?"

Phyllis considered this. "Three years ago he offered to share his bag of microwave popcorn. Only I said no because the fumes in microwave popcorn can give you lung cancer."

"Okay, well, that's good. I think. Maybe you need to start with the basics."

"Basics?"

"Well, unless you want to just show up naked in his cabin and crawl into bed with him."

Phyllis turned a little green. "No. Unless you think that's best? Oh, but he's bunking with Cody."

"I was kidding about that. Sorry, dumb joke."

Phyllis watched her without smiling, and Juli cringed at the thought of offering love advice to anyone— even Phyllis.

"Tell you what," Juli said, folding her pirate pants into her knapsack and zipping it up. "Let me watch you guys for a little while and assess the situation. That's assuming I'm staying. Did Alex happen to bring up the subject?"

"Oh, that," Phyllis said with a dismissive wave of one hand. "Yes. He said you know we're pirates. He said we're not dumping you on the island."

Juli stared at her for a few beats. "Oh. Pirates. Okay, well that's a relief." She paused, regrouping. "So you won't throw me overboard or leave me for dead on a tropical island. And I'll do my best to help you get together with Jake."

"Right. Get together."

Phyllis looked down at the quilt again, her cheeks

crimson beneath her white-blonde hair. Juli watched, struck by the peculiar color contrast, not to mention the strangeness of being asked for advice by a woman she was pretty sure could bench-press her.

Juli cleared her throat. "Is something else bothering you, Phyllis?"

Phyllis shook her head slowly. Then she changed course and nodded. "It's just—like I said, I'm not very experienced with men."

"Uh-huh."

"But see, this thing with Jake—it's giving me these urges. Like *urges*, you know?" Phyllis scratched a spot on one leg. "But I don't know what to do about it. And I don't want to be too forward, but I just really, *really* want Jake. Bad. And it's hard to concentrate on the mission with all these *urges*. But I just don't know what to do."

Juli tried not to grimace, picturing balding, scowling Jake as a man who could ignite such desire in a woman. And honestly, why was Phyllis talking to *her* about it?

Phyllis covered her face with her hands and sat down on the edge of the bed. Juli gave her an awkward pat on the shoulder, considering an appropriate response.

Clearly, Phyllis was distressed. And clearly, Phyllis was a woman in need. Juli bit her fingernail, considering how very desperate Phyllis must be to be counting on *her* as an authority on sex and romance.

"Well," Juli said slowly, "I don't think you should jump Jake right away. I know you have *urges* and all, but I'm not sure a quickie is the right solution just yet."

"So what do I *do*?" The final note came out as a wail,

and Juli scooted back in case she turned violent. "I feel like I'm going to *explode* or something!"

"Um, well," Juli tried. "You do have a private room. Can't you just—um—take matters into your own hands?"

Phyllis frowned. "What do you mean?"

"Right. Uh, maybe there's one of those handheld shower massagers around here or something?"

Phyllis's eyes flew so wide Juli braced herself to catch an eyeball if it went rolling.

"Or not," Juli amended. "I'm sure there are a lot of good books you could read or crossword puzzles to solve or dumbbells to lift? Plenty of things to take your mind off your, um, *urges*."

"A vibrator," Phyllis said thoughtfully, getting to her feet again. "I've never had one of those."

"Oh. Well, the odds aren't good you'll find one out here if you didn't happen to bring it. But you can probably mail-order something when you get back to land. In the meantime, why don't we focus on the essentials?"

"The essentials," Phyllis repeated, looking perplexed.

"You do whatever you need to do to, um, keep yourself from getting too distracted by your *urges*," she said. "And I'll pay attention to your interactions with Jake and will offer whatever advice I can."

Phyllis nodded a little shakily. "Okay."

"And you won't throw me to the sharks," Juli added. "It's almost like we're friends."

"Friends," Phyllis agreed, trying the word on for size. "Yes. That sounds nice. I don't have any girlfriends."

"Oh, it'll be great. We'll paint each other's toenails and talk about boys and have pillow fights in our underwear."

Phyllis looked alarmed. "Pillow fights?"

"Or we could play computer games and spot each other when we lift weights," Juli amended.

Phyllis smiled. "That sounds lovely."

———⁓———

Back in the galley, Alex was helping Cody with the dishes while Jake steered the boat and muttered under his breath about spies and cops.

"I like Juli," Cody said. "I don't care what you guys say. I think she's nice."

Alex toweled off a plate and sighed. "No one's saying she's not nice. We're just saying we don't trust her. Not completely, anyway."

"I still think we should throw her overboard," Jake muttered.

"We're not throwing her overboard." Alex draped the towel over a hook and leaned back against a cupboard. Beside him, Cody began wiping down the counter. He picked up Uncle Frank's urn and set it gently next to Alex.

Alex studied the ugly bronze façade, hoping like hell his final resting place would be someplace slightly less hideous. He turned it around, a little disturbed to realize some of the dolphins were copulating. "Anyone else think it's odd how she lugs the urn around with her everywhere?"

"No," Cody said. "I think it's sweet. She said Uncle Frank liked being on boats, so she wants him to experience the whole trip."

"Right," Alex said, and picked up the urn. It was ridiculously heavy, though he had no idea how much urns and cremated remains normally weighed. "Have you looked inside?"

Cody gaped at him. "Of course not! Why would we do that?"

Alex shrugged. "Maybe she's lying. Maybe there isn't a cremated body in here at all."

Jake turned, his eyes wide and frenzied. "Yeah. Open it! Maybe she's transporting weapons of mass destruction."

"What the hell kind of weapon would fit in an urn?"

"Drugs then," Jake growled. "Heroin or cocaine or something."

Alex pondered that. "I'm not sure I'd be able to tell the difference between heroin and cremated remains."

"Open it!" Jake snapped again. "Hurry, before she comes back."

Cody reached over and snatched the urn from Alex's grasp. "No! That's rude. I'm taking this back to Juli right now and I don't want to hear another word from either of you about disrespecting her poor dead uncle."

Alex watched Cody march away with the urn held reverently between his meaty palms. He sighed and picked up the dish towel again.

Behind him, Jake went back to muttering. "Damn woman's going to ruin us."

"Probably," Alex said, and tried not to look forward to it.

Chapter 7

THE NEXT MORNING, JULI MADE IT HER MISSION TO talk to Jake alone. Regardless of whether she really had the expertise to help Phyllis with her love life woes, she was damn well going to try.

It wasn't hard finding Jake by himself. Alex was napping after a long shift at the helm, Cody was busy preparing a rotisserie lamb shank for dinner, and Phyllis was in the middle of her sixty-fourth set of crunches with at least two-dozen more sets to go.

That left plenty of time for conversation while Jake steered the boat from the flybridge.

"So, Jake," Juli said, trying to look casual as she leaned against the railing. Instead, she looked down at the ocean and felt queasy.

She stepped back and moved toward the deck chair, lowering herself onto the padded seat. She felt a puddle of water sink through her shorts and sighed. Things weren't off to a very good start.

Steeling herself, she looked up at Jake, who was scowling at the ocean. Or maybe scowling at her; it was tough to tell.

"Phyllis tells me you're an excellent bowler," she said. "That's great. I like to bowl sometimes."

"Yeah?" he muttered. "They teach you that in spy school?"

"No, I knew how to bowl before spy school. They

did teach me how to kill someone with a bowling pin, though."

Jake looked at her over his shoulder. She couldn't tell if he was trying not to smile or trying to decide if she was serious.

"Anyway," she said, "it sounds like you guys have all known each other awhile. You and Alex and Phyllis and Cody? That's really great. Long-term friendships are important."

"So?"

"Just wondering if there's ever been any—I don't know. *Romantic tension* in the group? You know how those things sometimes happen?"

Jake looked startled. He stared at her, his frown deepening.

"I don't think we should be talking about this," he said.

Julie widened her eyes and feigned innocence. "Talking about what?"

"A man's personal business is his own and no one else's," Jake snapped.

"Absolutely."

"And it's not your place to judge."

"Well, of course not."

"And if Alex and Cody want to go see *Brokeback Mountain* together, that doesn't mean anything at all."

"Oh," Juli said, confused. This wasn't going the way she had hoped. Regrouping, she tried another tack.

"So Phyllis is sure pretty," Juli tried.

"Phyllis?" Jake eyed her with deep suspicion. "Yeah. She is. Real pretty."

"What a great figure for a woman her age! What is she—forty-seven, forty-eight?"

"She's fifty-four," Jake growled, though the flush in his cheeks gave Juli a little hope she was making progress.

"Wow!" she said. "Fifty-four? She doesn't look it. That's great!"

Jake scowled. "I don't think she swings that way."

"No, Jake—that's not what I was getting at."

Jake frowned, looking her up and down. "Is that what this is about? Are you one of those groupies looking to score with a famous former steeplechase record holder and go tell the tabloids all about it? Because I've got to tell you, that's not okay with me, lady. And I'm pretty sure it's not okay with Phyllis."

"No, Jake, that's not what I meant—"

"And even if she did swing that way—which she doesn't—and even if you were her type—which you aren't—I really don't think she'd let me watch anyway, so—"

"Uh—no," Juli interrupted. "No, Jake. That's not what this is about. And really, I'm not sure the tabloids would be interested in—"

"What, the steeplechase isn't glamorous enough for you? Her record stood for twenty-six years—*twenty-six years!* And it's, like, the hardest track-and-field event there is. Three thousand meters with water pits and jumps and stuff. That's not good enough for you?"

Juli gritted her teeth and wondered if she should just throw herself overboard to get it over with. "Jake, really—I'm not after Phyllis. And I have the utmost respect for the sport of steeplechasing. Really, I do."

Jake stared at her for a minute, assessing. "You promise?"

"I swear."

Jake looked relieved. "So you're just a spy."

Juli sighed. "Good talk, Jake," she said, standing up and heading for the stairs. "Good talk."

They had been out on the ocean now for a little more than twenty-four hours. Alex glanced at his watch, amazed to realize they were a quarter of the way into their carefully plotted timeline to reach Portelli's ship. The details of the boarding were swirling in his brain, fighting for space with the images of Juli in her bikini top.

Dammit all.

Phyllis had spent the last couple hours hunched over her laptop, trying to get an Internet connection. Inexplicably, the system had been down for almost twenty-four hours, and the pirates were growing restless.

"Maybe there's a weather system somewhere that's impacting the signal?" Alex suggested as Phyllis retreated below deck muttering something about urges.

"Maybe the spy we're transporting has figured out a way to crash the Internet," Jake grumbled. "I still say her name sounds really familiar. And I swear I've seen her on TV. *America's Most Wanted* or something."

Only Cody seemed not to care. "Would anyone like a crumpet with some lemon curd and clotted cream?" he asked.

Alex focused on keeping their course, fighting a hefty wave slap that wanted to push them sideways. He was driving from the helm on the flybridge, which gave him a wider view and the fresh air he craved. But the shelf clouds on the horizon were making him edgy. The wind had kicked up to fifteen knots in the last couple minutes. He glanced at the radar, not particularly liking what he saw.

Alex was fiddling with the instrument panel when Juli sidled up to him.

"Cody loaned me Battleship," she announced, parking herself in a deck chair beside him. "I tried to get Jake to play with me, but he's being a sore loser after I beat him earlier this morning. And Phyllis is busy doing bicep curls with the anchor. And Cody is making the maple glaze for his cider-brined pork ribs. Wanna play?"

Alex stared at her. "I'm kind of busy right now," he said. "This big thing we're on? Someone has to keep it moving through the water."

Juli rolled her eyes and glanced at her watch. "I know that, smartass. Doesn't your shift end in fifteen minutes? That's what Jake told me earlier."

Alex nodded toward the horizon. "See those flat-looking clouds out there?"

Juli followed the direction of his finger. He saw her frown as she nodded.

"That means the wind is going to start kicking up in about ten minutes," he said. "I'll feel better if I keep the wheel for a while longer."

From the corner of his eye, Alex saw Juli go pale.

"A storm?" she asked. It was obvious she was making an effort to keep her tone light, but was failing miserably.

"A squall."

"Isn't that a fancy way of saying 'storm'?"

"Squalls are usually over fast. Storms can last awhile."

"Based on that description, I think my last boyfriend was a squall."

Alex looked at her again. She was cracking jokes, trying to keep things light, but her expression was anything but casual. She was scared shitless. He felt her shiver beside him and resisted the urge to put an arm around her.

"You have rain gear?" he asked.

"I grew up in Oregon. We wear rain gear to bed."

"Might want to grab it. Go put that urn someplace safe while you're at it, unless you want it getting tossed around."

Juli frowned down at the ugly hunk of metal in her lap, and Alex wondered again what the hell was inside. Probably just a bunch of powdered bones. He was being paranoid, like always.

"Okay," Juli said, her voice a little strained. "Should I stay down below or come back up here?"

"Come back up," Alex said. "The water's getting choppy and the waves are breaking in a couple different directions. These rolling swells drop the stern like sort of a slow-motion roller coaster. Not good for seasick travelers. If you don't mind getting a bit wet, you'll do better up here."

"Oh."

At a loss for any smartass comments, and looking much greener than she had two minutes earlier, Juli disappeared down the stairs without another word.

"Can you let the others know too?" Alex called over his shoulder.

"Let the others know what?" Jake asked as he dropped into the deck chair Juli had just vacated. "And why is your wife looking green again?"

Alex nodded toward the clouds. "Weather coming."

Jake looked out at the ocean and sat up straight in his chair. "Oh. Shit. Just in time for my shift."

"It's fine, I've got it. We haven't had a chance to see how this tub handles in a squall. I'd like to get a feel for things, if that's all right with you."

"Sure, no problem. Can I help?"

"You could close up the hatches, put away anything that could fly around if things get really rough."

"Got it," Jake said. He stood and picked up one of the deck chairs. He folded it carefully before grabbing another and stacking it atop the first one.

Alex studied him from the corner of his eye. "So what's going on with Phyllis?"

"Phyllis?"

"The angry blonde woman traveling with us? I believe you've met before."

Jake suddenly seemed very interested in scratching a spot of goat cheese on his shirt. "What do you mean?"

"It just seems like maybe something's happening with the two of you."

"Happening?"

"Are you just going to repeat everything I say? Because if you are, I'm going to make you pledge to stop using my utility scissors to trim your ear hair."

Jake stopped scratching the cheese spot and shrugged. "I like Phyllis."

"Like?"

"Now you're doing it."

Alex sighed. "There's a reason men don't have these conversations."

"What conversations?"

"About women. And feelings. About relationships."

"We're having a conversation about feelings?"

Alex sighed. "You seen Porsche's new 918 Spyder?"

"Yeah, a two-hundred-mile-an-hour fucking hybrid that gets seventy-eight miles per gallon. Nice! So who do you like in the Pac-10 this year?"

All around Juli, the crew seemed to be focused on keeping the boat afloat. Not that there was any risk it *wouldn't* float, Alex had assured her. Even so, Juli was fighting hard to squelch the butterflies in her stomach.

Not to mention the curried prawn and fennel salad that still hadn't decided whether or not to stay down for good.

"You doing okay, Juli?" Alex called over his shoulder.

"Fine. Thank you."

"Those wristbands helping?"

"I think so."

"How about the rest of you—Jake, Phyllis, Cody?" Alex said. "You sure you want to stay up here? It's probably going to get pretty windy."

"I want a good view of the squall," Jake said.

"Me too," Phyllis agreed. "We can always head down if it gets really bad."

Juli nibbled another piece of ginger and watched them work. Cody lurched through the doorway as a wave hit them from the side. He regained his balance and tucked his beloved spatula in his apron pocket before moving through the group to pass out personal flotation devices. Satisfied everyone knew how to use the devices, he went to the helm to stand beside Alex. A gust of wind blasted them from the side, plastering Cody's wet apron against Alex's leg.

Jake and Phyllis were putting away the rest of the deck chairs, so careful not to touch each other that Juli wanted to give them a hard shove so they'd end up wrapped around one another on the floor. Not that she had any desire to see that, but cultivating romance between Jake and Phyllis was proving more difficult than trying not to stare at Alex's butt as he steered the ship.

Even so, she was up to the task. Both tasks.

Juli snuggled deeper into her windbreaker and squinted against the misty raindrops that had started to splatter against the deck. The boat was certainly rocking harder than it had, and the waves were definitely bigger, but the crew seemed to have everything under control.

"You sure I can't do anything useful?" she called for the hundredth time.

"We're good," Alex yelled back. "Keep your eyes straight ahead and breathe deeply."

"Okay. But let me know if I can help."

"Just don't puke."

"Got it. I can do that, I think."

Cody turned to look at her, his face etched with concern. Suddenly, a gust of wind snatched the spatula from his apron pocket. Juli watched as it hurtled end over end, flying through the air in slow motion, headed straight for Jake's skull.

"Jake, duck!" Juli screamed.

Too late.

There was a loud *thwack*—the sound of sharp metal connecting with Jake's shiny pink forehead.

Juli was on her feet in an instant.

"Sit! Now, Jake—sit down."

Juli grabbed his shoulder while the others gawked. Before anyone could ask what she was doing, she pushed him down onto the deck and knelt in front of him. Grasping his hand, she yanked it away from his forehead.

"Let me see it!"

Like an obedient dog, Jake pulled his paw back. Juli sucked in a breath as she saw the blood well up through a two-inch gash just above his right eye. The cut was ugly, fringed with ragged bits of skin, and it was bleeding hard.

"Phyllis, give me your bandana," Juli ordered.

Visibly startled, Phyllis pulled the bandana off her head and handed it over. Juli folded it into a square that she pressed hard against the gash.

"Hold this here," she told Jake, moving his fingers into place and demonstrating the pressure she needed him to apply. "Are you dizzy?"

He tried to peer around the yellow bandana. "The ground is moving."

"You're on a boat. The ground is supposed to be moving. Do you feel dizzy or light-headed? Is your vision blurry?"

"No. No, I don't think so."

"How about your neck? Does it hurt anywhere?"

"No."

Juli got to her feet and glanced at Alex. He was alternating between staring at the ocean and staring at her with visible disbelief. His hair was plastered wet against his scalp as the rain pelted down around them. Juli braced herself against a sudden gust of wind and turned to Phyllis.

"Phyllis, help him hold pressure on the wound. Cody, could you please get him some water and give him a drink? I'll be right back."

Juli dashed down the steps, catching herself once as the tide rolled and pitched her against a wall. She breathed deeply, hoping thirty seconds below deck wouldn't make her queasy again. She reached the door of her stateroom and pushed it open, locating her knapsack on the floor where it had fallen.

She dug through it as fast as she could, tossing out clothes and toiletries until she found what she was looking for. Snatching the neon orange case, she clutched it to her chest and dashed through the door, taking the steps two at a time.

She dropped to her knees again in front of Jake, who was almost on his back, pressed up against the side of the boat with his limbs flailing. Phyllis was holding the bandana against his forehead, and Juli made a note to be more specific when directing a woman who bench-pressed the mini-fridge to apply pressure.

Juli snapped open the medical kit and dug out a bottle of antiseptic. Then she yanked on a pair of surgical gloves and grabbed her penlight.

A big wave hit them from the front, and Jake grabbed Juli's shoulder for support. Juli spit out a wet curl and aimed her penlight in his eyes.

"Um, Juli?" Alex called behind her.

"Yes?"

"See, the whole thing about playing pirate was kind of funny, but I'm not sure if playing doctor is really—"

"I'm a nurse."

"What?"

"Haven't worked in a hospital for years, but my license is current and I've dealt with plenty of head wounds like this before. Unless you'd like to give it a go?"

Alex was silent behind her as the wind shrieked and threw up another blast of water. Juli glanced over her shoulder at him. He was staring slack-jawed at her, looking no less surprised than if she'd told him she rebuilt Italian motorcycles as a hobby.

Actually, she should probably mention that at some point.

Juli waved a gloved hand at him. "Shouldn't you be driving the boat instead of gawking at me?"

She turned her attention back to Jake, who for his part didn't look particularly shocked. Then again, he was pretty focused on avoiding Cody's over-exuberant efforts at hydrating him.

"It's okay, Cookie—I think he's had enough to drink. Thank you. Could we maybe get a towel? And Phyllis, I'll take over holding pressure now. Jake, you want to go ahead and sit up for me?"

Jake pulled himself upright with as much dignity as he could muster and peered at Juli from behind the yellow bandana.

"You look like you know what you're doing," he muttered.

"Thanks for the vote of confidence."

Juli moved the bandana aside and shined her penlight in Jake's eyes. The pupils looked fine, no real evidence of head trauma. She didn't think he'd need stitches, which was good. She'd stitched wounds on plenty of less visible body parts, but putting sutures into Jake's shiny bald forehead was like practicing her painting skills on a billboard. And with the boat rocking like crazy, there was no way to do it safely.

"I'm going to slowly pull the bandana off and have a look," she said. "It'll probably bleed a lot—head wounds always do—so no one freak out, okay?"

From the corner of her eye, Juli saw a couple heads bob. Jake nodded against her palm, and Juli pulled the cloth back. The wound was deep, but not as bad as she'd feared. A big wave hit the ship from the side, and Juli clutched the edge of the deck rail to hold herself in place.

"I'm going to irrigate it a little with saline, then clean it with a bit of antiseptic. I think we can do without stitches, which is good, since this isn't exactly a sterile setting and I've never stitched anyone on a moving boat in the middle of a squall. But we'll give it a couple hours and see how you're doing. You all right?"

Jake nodded, then winced.

"Phyllis, maybe give him your hand—something to hold on to. This will probably sting."

As gently as she could manage, Juli began to clean the cut. She could feel the others watching her, but she kept her focus on the task at hand. The rain was easing up, but she was already soaked to the bone.

"Okay, I'm going to move the edges of the wound together and then put a pressure bandage on it. This might hurt a little bit. Can you think of something pleasant for a minute to take your mind off things?"

Jake looked at Phyllis, whose tank top was rain-soaked and plastered to her chest. He stared down the front of it. A look of serene calm came over his face.

Phyllis seemed delightfully oblivious. What was it with these people?

Gently, Juli dried the skin around the wound as a gust of wind ripped at the gauze in her hand.

"Here we go." Juli moved the edges of the wound together and pressed the bandage into place. Then she covered it with a light gauze pad, securing the edges. Satisfied, she sat back on her heels.

"All right, Jake, you're good for now. Try to take it easy for a little bit. Maybe Alex or Phyllis or Cody can cover your shift for now? I really don't want you driving the boat right away."

"I've got it," Phyllis piped, stepping up to take the controls from Alex. "Alex needs to sleep for at least a couple hours, and Cody needs to get dinner ready. Are we through the squall yet?"

"Pretty much," Alex said. "You guys missed the worst of it while you were reenacting scenes from *Grey's Anatomy*."

"And Juli didn't puke," Cody said, beaming at her with obvious pride.

Alex folded his arms over his chest, regarding Juli with a curious look as Phyllis took the wheel. "No," Alex said, his tone flat. "Juli definitely didn't puke."

His eyes were cold as he studied her.

Juli felt herself shiver. She had some explaining to do.

Chapter 8

"So let me get this straight," Alex said, forking a piece of seared yellowtail tuna into his mouth at dinner that evening. He chewed and pointed his fork at Juli. "You're a nurse."

"Yes."

"And you work in marketing."

"Well, not anymore. But yes, I did."

"*And* you said something yesterday about working as a cake decorator?"

"Um, yes. A few years ago."

"Any other jobs I should know about?"

Juli raised an eyebrow at him. "Are we exchanging résumés now? If so, I'm excited to see your cartographer's license."

"Cartographers don't have licenses. And that's not the point."

"What is the point?" Juli snapped as she spooned more pomegranate crème fraîche onto her wilted spinach salad with a shaky hand.

Alex looked down at his braised leeks and tried to regroup. This wasn't going quite like he'd planned. "The point is that you haven't been straight with us about who you are and why you're on our boat. The point is that it would have been useful to know we had a medical professional on board."

"As soon as you needed one, I told you. What's the problem?"

"More saffron risotto?" Cody offered.

"No thank you, Cookie," Alex said.

"Yes, please, Cookie!" Juli piped, holding up her plate. "It's amazing; is this Spanish saffron or Indian?"

"Imported from Azerbaijan, actually."

"Wow, no kidding? I really like the white asparagus in there. You're a genius with flavors!"

Cody blushed, and Juli got to work devouring everything on her plate. Alex watched, impressed in spite of himself. The woman certainly had a passion for food. And a passion for other things.

Dammit, focus!

"So back to the discussion at hand," Alex said, tearing the corner off a loaf of homemade bread and reaching for the truffle infused olive oil. "What are you, exactly?"

Juli leveled him with a look. "So we're defining ourselves by our careers? Because if that's the case, you and the rest of the pirate crew can—"

"Juli, come on," Alex said. "Just tell me what you do for a living."

Jake dropped his fork with a clatter, clearly done beating around the bush. "Are you a cop?" he demanded. *"Are you a goddamn cop, Juli?"*

Alex kicked him under the table, but Jake was on a roll, with little beads of sweat clustered on his forehead like dewdrops. "Well come on, that's what we want to know, isn't it?" Jake snarled. "I mean, we don't care what her job *is*, do we? We care what it *isn't*." He wiped his mouth with his napkin and glared at her.

"Juli, are you a cop or a spy or a representative of the shipping industry?"

Juli seemed to consider the question as she sipped her cocktail of rosemary-infused vodka and fresh lime juice.

"No," she answered finally. "I am definitely not a cop or a spy or a representative of the shipping industry. Those are all jobs I haven't held." She seemed pleased as she took another sip of her drink.

"So who exactly *are* you?" Alex asked.

"Why is this relevant?" she fired back. "I'm not asking *you* for a résumé."

"Dammit, Juli," Alex said, setting his glass down. "You're the one who stowed away on our boat. You're the one asking to stay. How the hell are we supposed to trust you if you keep unveiling these little surprises? What's next, you confess you're a hit man?"

"Hit woman," Juli muttered, sipping her drink without meeting his eyes. "I'm not. A hit woman, I mean."

"Juli—"

"Well I'm not," she insisted, her voice breaking a little.

Alex gritted his teeth. "Juli, what is your deal? What the hell are you?"

Juli sighed, looking defeated. "I got my degree in nursing when I was fifteen. Just for fun, not a long-term career or anything."

"Fun," Alex repeated, not comprehending. "At fifteen?"

Juli closed her eyes and shook her head. "I'm also a licensed gemologist. And a dog trainer. And a massage therapist. And a computer programmer. Oh, and I drove the compactor at the landfill for eight months. And I worked in a handbag boutique for a while until I realized I was spending more than I was making. I was a finish carpenter for about a year, but that got boring. I worked in the entomology department at the zoo off and on for a few months. And I sometimes work as an interpreter for German, Danish, French, Spanish, Yiddish, Cherokee, Japanese—"

Alex set his fork down. "You're being funny, right?"

She pressed her lips together and looked up at him. "Well, my spoken Yiddish is a little rough, but my written skills are perfectly adequate."

Alex stared at her, trying to figure out what to say. Juli looked down at the table and didn't meet his eyes. Her cheeks were flaming, and her ears were even redder. She set her fork down and reached up to press her fingertips against them.

Jake flung his spoon across the galley and slammed a fist on the table. "I told you she was a spy!"

"I'm not a spy," Juli cried, her voice watery with unshed tears. "I swear, I'm not a spy. Come on, guys, just let it go. Let me be normal here."

Phyllis frowned. "Normal?"

"*Normal*," Juli insisted, looking wild-eyed at Phyllis. "That's all I want here, just that. It's not so much to ask, is it?"

"Normal," Alex repeated, trying to understand. "What the hell are you talking about?"

Juli looked miserable sitting there with four pairs of eyes boring into her. Her ears were the color of Roma tomatoes, and she looked like she was ready to bolt from the room. Alex blinked, trying to make sense of what was going on.

She'd clammed up now, feigning intense interest in the kumquat garnish on the side of her plate. She picked up her fork again and poked at her food, though she didn't eat it. She touched one of her ears with her free hand, making it redder than it already was. Alex continued to stare. Even Cody was looking at her, his expression more perplexed than normal.

Finally Juli set her fork down and met Alex's eyes.

"Look, I get bored easily, okay? I change careers a lot. And I like taking classes to learn new skills."

"Someone who gets bored easily generally jumps between waitressing at IHOP and manning the front desk at a hotel," Alex said flatly.

"Oh, I've done both of those things—"

"Juli, cough it up. What the hell are you hiding?"

She sighed. "I have an IQ of 186, okay? And I have a short attention span. I like to try different things, and I'm usually pretty good at most of them, and I really don't like to talk about this. You happy now?"

Alex just stared. Words failed him. Either she was pulling his leg, or—

"Look, if you don't believe me, go Google my name," she said. "You were going to find out anyway, I guess. Every now and then, some reporter gets bored and decides to write an article or do a TV spot about the career-hopping genius. I hate it. I'm sure you can find something about me online."

"I was right!" Jake yelled, jumping out of his chair. "I knew I'd seen you on TV! World's smartest woman, right? *Guinness Book of World Records*?"

Juli frowned and reached for the cocktail shaker.

Phyllis shot Jake an annoyed look from her spot in the captain's chair. "We've been trying to do a search on you, but our Internet has been down all day."

Juli frowned. "I may have had something to do with that. I was trying to keep this to myself. I just wanted to fit in with you guys, and I didn't want you to find out right away."

"You screwed up our computer?" Phyllis asked. She sounded more impressed than annoyed.

"I'll fix it after dinner." Juli said. "It shouldn't be hard. But until then, I can assure you that I've never been a serial killer or an executioner or a lawyer or whatever else you guys are so worried about."

"A cop?" Jake asked.

"Or a cop."

"A spy?" he pressed.

"No. Never a spy."

"What about an aesthetician?" Cody asked hopefully.

"That I've done," Juli said, forking a piece of hoisin pressed duck into her mouth. "I do excellent pedicures."

"So why didn't you tell us this earlier?" Alex asked.

She looked up at him, her eyes still shimmery with tears. "You need a pedicure?"

He sighed. "It might have been helpful to know we had someone with all these specialized skills in our midst. A celebrity of sorts."

"Oh, and you've been straight with me from the start, Pirate Alex?"

Alex tore off another piece of bread. "Fair enough."

Juli looked at him, her eyes pleading. "Look, my whole life, I've been the freak show. The odd duck. The weird, smart girl who doesn't fit in. I just wanted to try something different for a change, you know?"

Alex stared at her. "And this is why you want to stay on our boat?"

Juli shrugged, her shoulders still slumped in defeat. "I like you guys. And I like new careers. This seems like one worth exploring."

"What does?"

"Piracy. Duh."

Alex felt a stabbing pain behind his eyes. This was definitely not turning out the way he'd planned.

"I think it's suspicious," Jake said. "I'm sorry. I know you fixed my head and all. Thanks for that. But seriously, something seems odd about all this. How do we know you're not a spy?"

"How do I know you're not all criminally insane?"

"You don't," Alex said. "For that matter, we're not sure about it ourselves."

"My point is, we're all stuck on this boat together," Juli said. "Maybe we should cut each other some slack?"

"I'll drink to that," Phyllis said from the helm, lifting her glass of mineral water.

Alex stared at her, trying not to grit his teeth. In almost twenty years of working with Phyllis, he'd never known her to have any particular loyalties to girlfriends.

Come to think of it, he'd never known her to have any girlfriends.

Beside him, Jake was muttering something under his breath as he forked salad into his mouth.

Cody just looked intensely pleased as he began uncorking a bottle of red wine. "Sangiovese, anyone?"

Juli nodded and lifted her glass. "I worked as a sommelier once," she said, her voice still shaky. "That's an excellent vintage."

—◦—

Juli wasn't really asleep when the tentative knock sounded at her door. It was 2:00 a.m., and she had spent the last two hours mentally kicking herself as she stared at a spot on the wood paneling that looked like a misshapen eggplant.

"Come in," she called, turning away from the eggplant and sitting up in bed. The door creaked open, and Alex tiptoed in, looking sheepish. He was holding a pillow.

He paused when he saw her in bed. "I'm sorry, were you asleep?"

"Why, were you planning to smother me with that?"

Alex glanced down at the pillow, then back at her. He shrugged. "Not a bad idea, but no. It's raining."

"And you felt the need to tell me this at 2:00 a.m.?"

Alex stepped into the room and pulled the door shut behind him. He turned back around, and Juli saw his eyes drop to her cleavage and stay there for a few beats. She resisted the urge to cover up with the sheet. Let him look if he wanted to, at least he wasn't staring in horror like they all had over the IQ announcement.

Ogling seemed like a plus at this point.

"I was sleeping on the flybridge, but the rain is coming in sideways now," Alex said. "And I tried to sleep in the salon, but Cody is making homemade fettuccine and has the pasta draped over everything so it can dry out."

"Fettuccine?" she asked hopefully. "Whole wheat or semolina?"

"Focus, Juli. I need a place to sleep. And you've got the biggest room with the built-in bench that could be doing more than holding your clothes right now."

"And Uncle Frank. He's kind of comfy there."

"Right. Uncle Frank would be equally comfortable on the nightstand."

Juli looked at Alex for a moment, trying not to think about how well his T-shirt fit, or how nice it would be to have some companionship. She was still reeling with embarrassment from her dinnertime confession. She felt silly and lonely and very, very vulnerable.

Not the best time to have an attractive, half-dressed man in her room. Especially not a half-dressed man she'd come close to sleeping with twice now.

"I didn't hear a 'please' in there anywhere, but you look so pathetic, you can stay," Juli said, swinging herself out of bed to clear her things off the bench. "Isn't Jake at the helm? Why don't you sleep in his bed?"

"Would you sleep in Jake's bed?"

"Good point."

"And Cody snores. Besides, I wanted to talk to you. I wanted to apologize, actually."

"Apologize?"

"For getting so angry about the fact that you didn't tell us about your—um—"

"Freak-of-nature status?"

"Right."

"Apology accepted. Blanket?" She held it out to him, willing her hand not to shake.

"Thank you," he said, and took the blanket. His arm brushed the edge of her breast as he moved past, and Juli shivered.

"Tight quarters."

"No kidding."

Juli picked up Uncle Frank's urn and set it carefully on the nightstand. Alex reached out to touch it.

"That really is the ugliest urn I've ever seen."

She smacked his hand away. "It's what Uncle Frank wanted. Be respectful."

"Can I look at it?"

"No. Make your bed."

Alex shrugged and began settling himself on the bench, making a cozy little nest just a few feet from her bed. He was almost too tall, and his broad shoulders barely fit in the space. Somehow, he managed to wedge himself in there with a pillow propped beneath his head.

Juli bit her lip. It seemed silly that he should sleep there when she had this perfectly spacious queen-sized bed all to herself. The sheets were soft. There was plenty of room.

But he'd already made it clear that high-seas sex wasn't in the cards for them. How wise would it be to lure him into her bed at this point?

Some World's Smartest Woman you are.

She felt annoyed with herself all over again.

He did look excellent in a T-shirt though. Beautiful pecs, and shoulders so broad she thought about clawing—

"Something wrong?" Alex asked. He was watching her as he readjusted his pillow.

Juli shrugged. "I was just hoping maybe you could tell me more about your pirate mission. About who you are and what you're all doing out here."

"No. Anything else?"

She watched him for a moment longer, her guilt mounting as he kicked viciously at the blanket and tried to twist his legs into the small space.

"Are you sure you're comfortable there?" she asked. "Because if you want—"

"I could sleep with you?"

Juli sucked in a breath.

Then choked on her own spit. *Classy.*

When she finally stopped coughing, Alex was grinning at her.

"Believe me, I'd like nothing more than to climb into bed with you, but it's a terrible idea," he said. "Isn't that the romance cliché? Boy meets girl, some mix-up requires them to share a room, they end up in bed together, and—"

"You can stop there," Juli said, feeling her face grow warm. "And I've never read a romance novel where the hero and heroine fake marriage three minutes after meeting, then almost sleep together, then the heroine has an allergic reaction and stows away on the hero's ship, then she finds out he's a pirate, then—"

"You forgot the part about the heroine being a famous genius," Alex said with a smirk. "I like that part."

Juli gritted her teeth, feeling her ears grow warm. "I don't."

He watched her in silence for a moment, his expression going from smug to thoughtful. "You really hate talking about this?"

She crossed one arm over her chest and touched her ear with the fingertips of the other hand. "What tipped you off?"

He smiled, and Juli realized it wasn't just her ears flaming anymore. Every part of her body felt warm all of a sudden. She tried to tell herself it was anger or embarrassment, but she knew it wasn't just that. Alex was standing so close, and her fingertips recalled every detail of what his chest felt like beneath them.

"Sorry," he said, sounding like he meant it. "I'll drop it, okay? I didn't realize the genius thing was such a touchy subject."

"It's fine," she said. She hugged her arms around herself, softening in spite of her annoyance. "It's just—I'm tired of always being different, you know?"

"No," he said. "I really don't. That's your whole charm. You're different as hell—in a good way."

Juli bit her lip and tried to think of a response that didn't make her sound more pathetic.

She couldn't come up with anything.

"Anyway," he continued, "back to the romance cliché. Just so you know, I'm not diving in to save you if you do happen to fall overboard, so don't get any ideas."

"This is *so* not a romance cliché," Juli said, stomping away and flopping back on the bed. She jerked at the covers, tugging them loose from the foot of the bed as she pulled them up to her chin. *Dammit, the lamp.* She sat back up, struggling to find the switch and then flicking the light off and dropping back onto the bed. She gave her pillow a few violent jabs, trying to get comfortable.

Alex was silent for less than ten seconds. "What is that you're wearing?"

Juli turned and looked at him in the darkness. "I thought you were going to sleep."

"I was. But then you started jiggling around under there and I woke up."

"You're rude. Even for a pirate."

"Is it silk?"

"No. It is not silk. It's probably nylon or polyester or something."

"Very slippery. Fits well. Victoria's Secret?"

"Are we going to sleep now?"

"Good night."

Juli sighed and lay back against her pillow. The sound of Alex breathing a few feet away was soothing. The feel of the water sloshing beneath the boat had even become comforting—not terror-inducing like it had been before.

So what was the problem? She sure as hell wasn't feeling very relaxed. Every nerve ending she owned was sizzling under the surface of her skin.

Juli turned over on her side and stared at the eggplant again.

"Can't sleep?" Alex asked.

Juli glanced at the travel clock on her bedside table. "It's been two minutes."

"Because I can't sleep. And I was thinking."

"This should be good."

"What are the odds that we'd *just happen* to meet up in a bar, the night before you *just happen* to end up on my boat, which we don't discover until it *just happens* to be too late to take you back?"

"Are we still on the romance cliché? Because I really don't think this is fate."

"I'm not talking about fate. I'm talking about the fact that the circumstances of our meeting, coupled with your presence on this boat, coupled with the fact that you seem to have a very bizarre existence—all of that makes me a little suspicious."

Juli turned back onto her other side to face him in the dark. His features were stark in the glow of her digital travel alarm clock, and she could see his chest rising and falling beneath the thin cover.

"You've been in my room for five minutes, and so far, you've accused me of stalking you, called me bizarre, ogled my sleepwear, and suggested that I'm attempting to lure you into my bed for illicit purposes," she said. "This is fun. We should have sleepovers more often."

"I'm just saying, I think there's something going on. You were terrified of the water two days ago. Now you want to stay?"

"Yeah, well, you told me you were a cartographer. Then I find out you're a pirate. What is it you're after, anyway?"

Alex was quiet for a minute. "This bench really isn't very comfortable."

"Get over here, you jerk. There's plenty of room."

"Your seduction skills need work," Alex said, but he got up and moved around to the other side of the bed.

The instant he crawled under the covers with her, Juli felt her skin electrify. No part of her body touched any part of his, but she was aware of just how close he was. How solid and warm and touchable. Just a few inches and her fingers could brush the side of his chest—

Juli grimaced and drew her leg away from him, putting a little distance between them. She focused on breathing in and out, keeping her hands safely at her sides —

Alex flopped his leg over the top of hers, pinning her knee beneath the underside of his so he could drag her leg back to his side of the bed. He sighed in the darkness.

"Your skin feels soft."

"Yours feels hairy."

"You're warm too."

"Your feet are cold," she said. "You need socks or something."

"Now that we've established that—"

Alex leveraged himself up on one elbow so his face was inches from hers. "I know you don't trust me and I don't trust you and we said this was a bad idea right now. But on the big list of bad ideas I've had lately, this one seems pretty good."

Before Juli could protest, Alex had found her lips in the dark. And then, protesting was the furthest thing from her mind. Alex slid a hand beneath her head, pulling her closer, twining his fingers in her hair. Juli responded with a whimper she hoped didn't sound too pathetic, sliding her nails down his neck, over his shoulder, gasping against his mouth.

His lips were warm and soft and so good at what they were doing. Juli's head swam, her torso liquefied, and her other leg somehow wrapped itself around his hip to pull him to her. He kissed her harder, making her arch her back so she could press against all that male hardness.

She remembered what he'd said the other night about his favorite spot to be kissed. *Anytime a woman does anything with her mouth anywhere near my neck, I lose it completely.* Did she want him to lose it?

Yes. Yes she did.

She began to kiss her way across his jawline, savoring the scratch of stubble against her lips. She slid down, wriggling against him. Her nightgown bunched up around her hips up as she kissed her way down his chin and then lower until she found the spot along his throat—

"Oh, God."

Juli smiled into his skin and kept kissing him, loving the feel of his pulse throbbing against her lips. His breath was ragged and the way he moved against her told her she was achieving the desired effect. She circled her tongue in the hollow beneath his jaw and heard him gasp.

"I can't believe I told you this," Alex murmured as Juli dragged her teeth lightly over the sensitive flesh of his throat.

"You would have been safer just telling me you're a pirate," she breathed against his neck, trailing her fingers along his hairline. "Now you're at my mercy."

She kissed him again, exploring the tendons, his Adam's apple, all that heated flesh against her lips. He was salty and warm and the best thing she'd ever tasted in her life.

She could feel his arousal pressed hard against her thigh, and Juli felt herself go dizzy with the thought that she was responsible. She slid her legs apart, letting him slip between them so only her nightgown and his shorts separated them. She ran her tongue up to that tender spot behind his ear, then back down along his throat, savoring him.

"You're killing me," he whispered.

He pulled away then, angling himself up on his arms. He hovered there above her, the planes and angles of his chest glowing sharp in the dim light of the clock radio on her nightstand.

"I really don't have anything," he breathed. "Condoms, I mean. It's not like I planned for this. For you to be here on this boat or for—well, this is probably not a good idea."

"Right," Juli agreed, squirming beneath him just to feel his body hard against hers. "So we should stop."

"Probably."

Neither of them moved. The ocean rocked beneath

them and they both breathed in and out and stared into each other's eyes.

"Or not," Alex said and lowered his lips to her throat. He began to kiss his way down her body, his mouth traveling along her sternum. He tugged the spaghetti strap of her nightgown down over her shoulder and kissed the newly bared skin before moving south. His tongue found her nipple and began making warm, lazy circles as his other hand cupped her left breast. The pad of his thumb skimmed her nipple with such aching softness Juli thought she might sob from pleasure.

Then he moved lower, kissing his way down the center of her body. He found the hem of her nightie and slid it up and over her ribs, his tongue dipping into her navel before Juli could register the fact that she was so exposed. His hands gripped her hips, pinning her to the bed.

"I thought we were stopping," she gasped.

He raised his head and grinned in the darkness. "You are. I'm not."

"But—"

"Shut up." He lowered his head again, his mouth moving down over her belly, off to the side where he nipped at her hipbone. Juli gasped and clenched the sheets in her fingers. He kept moving down, leaving no question about his intended destination.

She still cried out when he found it.

"Oh my God."

Her hips started to rise off the bed, but he pinned her in place as he drove her crazy with his lips and tongue and teeth and fingers and what felt like an entire army of other skilled parts converging on that single spot with the sole purpose of bringing her the most intense pleasure she'd ever felt in her life.

She cried out, then bit her knuckle to keep quiet, her brain barely registering pain as wave after wave of sensation washed over her. Alex stroked her hip with one hand, using the other to caress and tease and probe as he drove her mindless with his mouth.

Juli felt the explosion building inside her, felt the scream building in her throat, and she pulled the pillow over her face and bit down hard to keep from waking the rest of the crew. Alex pressed his palm against her abdomen and Juli screamed into the pillow again and again, arching her back and twisting her fingers in his hair.

She wasn't sure how long she lay there like that, just breathing into the pillow as her mind whirled and her body pulsed with pleasure. Her breath was still coming fast when she felt the bed move as Alex slid back into place beside her. He lifted the pillow off her face.

"You okay under there?"

She nodded, still too breathless to speak.

"Good," he said, and he pulled her against him spoon-fashion. "I was hoping not to kill anyone on this mission."

Juli swallowed, finding her voice at last. "If someone's gotta die, that's the way to go."

Alex laughed and snuggled against her, wrapping his whole body around hers in a protective cocoon. Juli took a deep breath and felt herself slipping into oblivion.

"I couldn't agree more," he murmured into her hair.

Chapter 9

DAY THREE, AND I'M STILL ON THIS BOAT, JULI thought, staring out over the ocean from the flybridge the next morning as she sipped her ginger tea. *How the hell did this happen?*

Okay, she knew how it had happened. It didn't make the situation any more believable, but at least she was aware of how she'd ended up here. Her uncle's ashes were still in the urn below deck, and according to the navigational chart she'd seen the night before, she was further away from Uncle Frank's spot than she'd been before she boarded.

And then there was Alex. Last night had been amazing. More than amazing, it was mind-blowingly spectacular.

But what did she know about him besides the fact that he was ridiculously skilled with his hands and mouth and... well, pretty much everything else? Who was Alex, really? What would possess a seemingly sane man to embark on a high-seas pirate mission?

"Hey, Juli, have you seen my spatula?"

She looked up to see Cody, trailed by Jake and Phyllis, emerging at the top of the stairs.

Before she could answer, Jake rolled his eyes. "Just because she's the World's Smartest Woman doesn't mean she knows where your damn spatula is, Cody."

Juli gritted her teeth and took a breath. "See, this is why I didn't tell you guys," she said, hoping she sounded mad and not wounded. "I just wanted you to treat me like a *normal* person."

Jake snorted. "Normal. Right."

Juli swallowed the lump in her throat and got ready to fire off an angry retort. But before she could say a word, Phyllis stooped down to pick up the spatula from under a deck chair. Standing up, she swung it at Jake, smacking him hard on the shoulder.

"Ouch! What was that for?"

"You. Stop picking on Juli. That's not nice."

"Ouch, stop it! I was only kidding. She knows I was kidding. Right, Juli?"

"Right," Juli said, leaning away from them as Phyllis drew her arm back again.

"So tell her you're sorry," Phyllis insisted.

Jake made a grab for the spatula. "I'm sorry. Geez, *I'm sorry*."

"Me too," Cody said, reaching down to pat Juli on the arm. "I mean, I was the one who left my spatula out."

"It's okay," Juli said, not quite understanding the connection but enjoying the bubble of hope she felt at this odd new level of inclusion. "I'm probably just too sensitive about—about—well, anyway." She felt her ears go hot, so she stopped talking.

"You boys go finish breakfast," Phyllis insisted. "We're going to talk about girl stuff."

"Girl stuff," Jake repeated, looking mystified.

"Girl stuff," Cody repeated, looking eager.

"Go!" Phyllis told them as she handed the spatula to Cody.

Both men retreated, bickering all the way down the stairs. When they were out of earshot, Phyllis turned to Juli.

"Can I join you for a minute?"

Juli gestured to the deck chair beside her and smiled up at Phyllis. "Be my guest. And thanks for that."

"Oh, no problem," Phyllis said, hesitating a little. "That's what girlfriends do, right?"

"Right," Juli said, trying to remember if she'd ever had a girlfriend who assaulted bullies with kitchen utensils on her behalf. "So I take it the guys aren't quite done with breakfast?"

"Cody said the Grand Marnier sauce didn't come out right on his first batch of blintzes, so he insisted Alex stay at the helm in the pilothouse for a while longer until the next batch was ready."

"I hope I didn't use up all the fresh whipped cream earlier."

"No, he made more." Phyllis eyed the chair next to Juli for a moment, then eased herself into it, her posture rigid and her hands clasped in her lap.

"So have you had time to, um, observe?" Phyllis asked in a voice that was surprisingly timid for a woman with biceps the size of a small automobile.

"You and Jake?" Juli nodded, trying not to feel ridiculous in her new role as love advisor. "Yes. I have."

Phyllis swallowed. "And?"

"Well, despite the fact that you beat him with a kitchen gadget, I think he likes you. And I know you like him. But I think we could all die of old age before either of you makes a move to do anything about that."

Phyllis stared down into her lap, her knuckles whitening. "I'm just not very good with men. I mean, a man like Jake—well, I'm sure he has so much experience with beautiful women, and, well, I'm not really the caliber of woman he's probably used to."

Juli raised an eyebrow at Phyllis, not sure which part of her assertion called for correction first. Seeing the obvious discomfort on the older woman's face, she took her best stab at it.

"Phyllis, you're a very attractive woman."

"You're just saying that because you think I still want to throw you overboard."

"Um, no. I thought we were past that. But thank you for reminding me. Seriously, Phyllis, you just have to gain a little confidence in your attractiveness. In your appeal to the opposite sex. In your womanly wiles."

Phyllis looked dubious. "Womanly wiles?"

"Yes. You have them. You just have to learn to use them."

"I don't understand."

Juli set her tea down and folded her legs beneath her, feeling nervous all of a sudden as Phyllis regarded her with rapt attention.

"Let's say you catch Jake staring at you. What do you do?"

Phyllis frowned. "Do I have spinach stuck between my teeth?"

"No. No spinach. And you don't want to ask him that. What you want to do is smile at him."

"Smile?"

"Yes, smile. It's when you curl up the corners of your mouth and show some teeth."

"I know what smiling is," Phyllis said as she pulled a tiny notebook out of the pocket on her shirt. *Smile*, she wrote. *Teeth*.

Juli continued. "If you smile at Jake, you're giving
him just a little bit of encouragement. It's not as direct
as, say, putting him in a headlock and sticking your
tongue in his ear, but it lets him know you're interested."

Phyllis was scribbling furiously in her notebook. *No
headlock.*

She stopped writing and looked up at Juli. "Okay, so
how do I, um—"

"Move things to the next level?"

"Right."

"Well, you can start by asking him questions. Men
like to talk about themselves, and it lets him know you
want to know more about him. That you're interested in
really getting to know him."

"Questions," Phyllis said aloud, writing the word in
her notebook. She frowned and looked up at Juli. "Like
how to unclog the toilet?"

"Well, that wasn't quite what I had in mind. Do you
know anything about his family? Where he's from?
What he likes to do for fun?"

Phyllis chewed on the end of her pen. "I think he
plays Frisbee golf."

"Frisbee golf. That's excellent. See, you have exer-
cise in common. So you can talk with him about Frisbee
golf and workouts and outdoor recreation."

Phyllis looked dubious. "But I don't want to be his
workout partner. I want to rip off his clothes with my
teeth and—"

"Er, right," Juli said, hoping to avoid hearing the
end of that sentence. "But you have to work your way
to that point. Show him you're more than just a work
buddy. Let him see that you're pleasant to be around,

that you're enjoying his company. That you're a fun, sexy woman."

Fun, sexy woman Phyllis wrote, pressing so hard with the pen that she put a hole in the paper.

"So to accomplish the fun, sexy aspect of that—"

Phyllis balled her fist around the pen. "Is this the part where you pull out your big cosmetic kit and give me a makeover and dress me up in girly clothes like in the movies?"

"Um, no. Not unless you want to."

"I'm allergic to cosmetic products. Everything except ChapStick."

"Okay, so no makeup. And obviously we're not in a position to make any real wardrobe changes out here, but maybe just a few alterations."

"Like what?"

"Well, you've got great arms. And excellent legs. You're in fabulous shape all around."

Phyllis beamed, so Juli kept going.

"And you've got a great smile. And nice hair. And your boobs are good too."

Phyllis gaped at her. "Boobs?"

"Hooters, blouse bunnies, sweater potatoes, lady balls, dumplings, chesticles—"

"I know what boobs are," Phyllis said, her complexion two shades paler than normal. "I just, well, I mean—"

"Look, I'm not an expert here," Juli said, chewing her lip. "But watching the way Jake responds to you, I've determined that he is a boob man. And since you happen to be in possession of a perfectly lovely pair, it makes sense that you show them off just a little."

"Oh."

"You have to be subtle about it. Nothing overt. But you want to make him notice you as a woman instead of a just a workmate."

Subtle, Phyllis wrote in her notebook, then underlined it twice.

"So try to work on that, and see if you notice a difference."

"Smile, ask questions, find common interests, show boobs," Phyllis said, reading from her notes.

"Exactly. Let's regroup later today and see how things go."

Phyllis nodded, then closed her notebook. She gave Juli a faint smile and stood up, looking relieved. "Thank you, Juli. I'm glad you stowed away on this boat."

"My pleasure, Phyllis. Actually, I was hoping maybe we could trade information."

"Oh?"

"Like maybe you could tell me a little more about this pirate mission. Alex has been pretty closemouthed about the whole thing."

Phyllis remained standing, her expression unreadable. "Well, yes. Piracy isn't legal. It's important to be discreet."

"Right. So are you just planning to attack a ship at random, or what?"

Phyllis nibbled the end of her pen, considering. "No, we know the boat we're after. There's a plan."

"Can you tell me more about the plan?"

Phyllis looked down. "I really don't think so."

"What about telling me where the boat is?" Juli tried. "Do you know that?"

Phyllis looked uncertain, clearly under orders not to reveal too much. "We're tracking it," she said finally. "With GPS. And proprietary navigational software. We know where it is now and when we'll make contact."

"Oh. So when will the rendezvous take place?"

"At our current rate of speed, we'll connect with the ship in 22 hours and 17 minutes."

Juli sat up, surprised by this revelation. "Really? Wow. So do I need to do anything to be ready?"

Phyllis frowned. "Alex hasn't talked to you about this yet?"

"Talked to me about what?"

"Oh. Well, maybe he was going to do that later this morning. I'm pretty sure he was planning to talk to you after his shift ended."

"Phyllis, come on. You're a part of this mission too. You have a right to tell me things if you want to. Alex isn't in charge of *everything*."

Phyllis looked so conflicted that Juli almost felt bad for her. Still, Juli had a right to know, didn't she?

Phyllis sighed. "I guess Alex was going to tell you anyway," she said. "Look, you're not going to take part in this heist, okay? We're hoping you'll just cooperate, but if it's necessary, Alex suggested we may have to restrain you—"

"*What?*" The word came out as a shriek, but Juli didn't care. She was livid. "Restrain me? He's going to tie me up?"

Phyllis took a step back and bit her lip. "Well, there are handcuffs, actually. And maybe a blindfold. And I think Alex was going to have you stay in your stateroom until we get everything sorted out."

Juli stood up, her face flaming. "I can't believe it. I can't fucking believe it! Tied up? Like a prisoner?"

Phyllis turned a few shades paler and glanced at the stairs. "It would just be best if you don't get too involved—"

"Involved? I'm already involved! Who the hell does he think he is?"

"Um, well. The captain of the ship."

Juli scowled. "Captain Alex. That's right. Dread Pirate Alex. Well, if he thinks he's going to handcuff me and leave me out of everything, he's got another think coming."

"Oh, Juli. Don't. Just—well, *don't*."

Juli shook her head, trying to ignore the sting of hurt pricking the back of her throat. It was just like always. She had started to think she belonged, that she was a part of something.

But that wasn't true, was it? It would never be true, not for her.

She swallowed hard. "Why the hell shouldn't I go talk to Alex right now?"

"Why don't you wait until you calm down? I'm sure Alex is planning to talk to you about it. Just give him a chance. He's a very reasonable man."

"Reasonable," Juli said, thinking that was not one of the first adjectives that came to mind when she pictured Alex.

She tried to ignore the adjectives that *did* come to mind.

Sexy. Gorgeous. Fabulous kisser.

Phyllis sighed. "It's just—there are reasons for leaving you out. Reasons we can't talk about right now."

Juli frowned, still seething, trying to decide whether to feel mad or hurt. Maybe she had no right to feel either one, but dammit, she thought she was finally becoming a part of the team.

Phyllis eyed her warily. "Okay, so I'm going to get ready for my shift at the helm. And Juli?"

"Yes?"

"Really, thanks for the help with Jake."

"No problem," Juli said, feeling herself smile in spite of her frustration. "And thank *you* for assaulting the man of your dreams on my behalf."

Phyllis nodded. "My pleasure."

When Alex strolled up to the flybridge with a boating magazine in hand, he was just looking for an hour of quiet relaxation.

Instead, he found himself looking at the most perfect legs he'd seen in—well, probably ever.

"Um—" he said, trying not to stare at Juli lounging there in her teeny little bikini. Was it his imagination, or had the top shrunk considerably since he'd seen it on her the day before?

"What are you looking at, sailor boy?"

"You know, I'm really better off not answering that question."

Juli lowered her sunglasses and peered over the top at him with narrowed eyes. "Really? Because I've got some more questions for you to answer."

"Can I ask mine first? Because I was just wondering why Phyllis is down in the cockpit in her bra looking really happy about driving the boat."

"What?"

Alex put on his sunglasses and stretched. "Jake looks pretty happy about it too, for that matter."

"Oh, hell," Juli said, and jumped out of the lounge chair, heading for the steps.

Alex watched her go, enjoying the view.

"If it's any comfort, her bra covers more than that bikini top you're wearing," he yelled after her before settling into her abandoned deck chair. He leaned back, noticing the smell of coconuts and lemon on the cushion. The same smell he'd enjoyed the night before in bed with Juli, nuzzling against her hair, devouring her body.

Okay, maybe he'd been dumb to kiss her last night. And he'd been *really* dumb to take it further than that, especially with so many questions about who she was and what she was doing out here. He really didn't know what he'd been thinking. She'd just looked so beautiful lying there in the half-lit room, those crazy curls spread across the pillow and her mouth looking warm and soft and inviting.

And yeah, he had to admit it—the genius thing was kind of a turn-on. He knew it made her uncomfortable, but seriously—was there anything hotter than a smart woman who was also funny as hell?

But getting in bed with her had been a stupid idea, and he wouldn't do it again. He was here on a mission. A mission to rescue his pension, to regain his identity, to help his friends do the same. There was no sense getting involved with a woman he didn't trust. Not when he was broke with no career future. He'd learned that lesson once before.

He needed a romantic entanglement like he needed a French manicure.

Alex sighed and closed his eyes, trying to ignore thoughts of Juli as he enjoyed the feel of the sun on his eyelids. He must have drifted off to sleep, because the next thing he knew, he felt a shadow fall across his chest. He opened one eye and peered up at Juli.

She wasn't smiling.

"Did Phyllis put her top back on?" Alex asked.

"Yes, as a matter of fact she did."

Alex yawned, stretching his arms overhead. "Too bad for Jake."

"I'm not concerned about Jake right now. What I'm concerned about is the fact that you intend to handcuff me in my room during the pirate heist."

Alex groaned and closed his eyes again. "Phyllis told you?"

"Never mind who told me. Were *you* ever planning to clue me in?"

He opened his eyes and sighed. "Come on, Juli—"

"Don't *come on Juli* me," she said, her eyes flashing with indignation and something that looked a lot like hurt. "I thought we agreed I wasn't a prisoner. I thought I was going to be a part of the team out here. I thought—"

"Juli, there's a lot you don't know about this mission. A lot you're better off not knowing about us, about me, about what we're all doing here."

"Like what?"

Alex threw up his hands in exasperation. "Did you just miss the part where I said you're better off not knowing?"

Juli rolled her eyes. "Give me an *example* then. What's so top secret?"

"Has it really not occurred to you that we don't

exactly fit the profile of real pirates? That there's probably more to this mission than you realize?"

"Gee, Alex, no it didn't. I thought pirate heists were really what you did for a living."

"Juli, let it go. Seriously. Just let it go."

She folded her arms over her chest and stared hard at him. "And you'll do what?"

"Huh?"

"What will you do for me if I let it go?"

He raised an eyebrow at her. "I don't know that you're in a position to be negotiating."

Juli sighed. "How about a challenge then?"

"A challenge?"

"Right. Give me a chance to win the right to help you guys with the heist."

"Juli, I really don't think—"

"Just one chance."

He sighed. "What sort of challenge do you have in mind?"

"A game."

Alex snorted. "I've played games with you twice now. The first time I had my sexual prowess mocked onstage in front of several hundred strangers, and the second time I got roped into giving you a foot massage."

"You got a foot job out of the deal, if I recall."

"Foot job?"

"Like a hand job, except—"

"Right."

"And we both ended up five hundred dollars richer in the first game, sailor boy. It wasn't all bad, was it?"

No, he thought as he watched her moving fluid and warm under that bikini top. Watched her eyes flash with fury and passion and that quirky brand of humor he was pretty sure had been keeping them all from throwing themselves overboard in the midst of all this high-seas drama.

Definitely not all bad.

"Fine." Alex sighed, sensing there was no way he could possibly win an argument with Juli. *Ever.* "What are you thinking?"

"One game of Battleship. My rules. If I win, no handcuffs. And I get to be a part of this mission."

"And if I win—"

"You can handcuff me without argument. I'll sit in my cabin like a good little wench while you four go off to pillage and plunder."

"You make it sound so tawdry."

"Isn't it?" she asked.

"Probably."

"Do we have a deal?"

Alex considered for a moment. "One game of Battleship?"

"One game."

"Winner takes all?"

"You could say that."

"Sounds easy enough."

Juli smiled. "You've never played with me before."

Alex tried to ignore the dread pooling in his gut. At least he thought it must be dread, but lust was another contender. It was tough to tell these days. "Why do I have a feeling there's more to this game than you're letting on?"

"There's always more to the game," Juli said, looking him up and down once before turning away. "Now if you'll excuse me, I've got a date with Cody to catch our dinner."

———

"So what are we fishing for?" Juli asked, adjusting her pole as she glanced over at Cody's hulking frame.

Cody leaned out over the railing and fiddled with his line. "A sailfish or a marlin would be great, but I have a really good recipe for zebra-striped wahoo that I've been wanting to try."

"You too?" Juli mused as she cleaned the lenses of her sunglasses on the hem of her shirt.

Cody grinned, either appreciating her humor or genuinely anticipating a recipe exchange. Juli wasn't sure. She still couldn't figure out how to read Cody.

At any rate, it was nice to be out here with him in the sunshine, enjoying at least a brief, uncomplicated interlude in a journey that hadn't had many uncomplicated moments thus far.

"I can't believe how big these poles are," she said, adjusting hers to let a little more line run out. She glanced at Cody, whose impressive bulk made the pole look like a chopstick in his hands.

"Deep sea fishing is pretty different than fishing in lakes or rivers back home," Cody agreed. "I'm just glad I brought the ingredients to prepare a variety of marine life. I mean some of the basic staples are the same, but obviously you wouldn't use alder to wood-fire a Pompano filet the way you might with salmon or something."

"Obviously."

"Anyway, I'm really glad we have the chance to catch fresh fish out here."

"Me too," Juli agreed. "Your cooking is fabulous."

Cody's cheeks flushed pink, and he adjusted his line as Juli leaned forward, admiring the sparkle of the ocean beneath them. She listened to the wet smack of waves hitting the side of the boat and considered how terrifying that sound might have been just a week ago. Now that she had her sea legs, she was actually beginning to enjoy the water.

Just to be safe, though, she gave an extra tug on the straps of her personal flotation device and checked for the hundredth time to make sure she was properly tethered to the side of the boat. No sense taking any chances. Satisfied she wasn't about to topple into the water, she grasped her fishing pole again and turned her attention back to Cody.

"So how did you get to be a pirate, Cookie?" Juli asked, trying to keep her tone innocent.

Cody's smile evaporated, and he looked down at his feet, suddenly very interested in the toe of his sandal.

"Alex said we're not supposed to talk with you about our mission," Cody said apologetically. "And Jake still thinks you might be a spy."

"I promise you, I'm not a spy. I tried to join the CIA once, but they required this polygraph test, and I kind of screwed that up."

"That doesn't seem fair."

"Well, there was this whole complicated family business with the mob and—well anyway, it didn't work out."

Cody sighed. "I'd better not say much. Alex doesn't want us to give details, and I don't want to make Alex mad."

"Is he—violent?"

Cody looked startled. "Alex? No. Not violent."

"What about Jake?"

Cody shrugged. "They're nice guys."

"Nice guys can do bad things."

"Not these ones."

The vehemence in his voice was enough to make Juli drop the subject. She studied the side of his face, waiting for more information.

"So how long have you known Alex?"

Cody thought about it. "Three years or so. He was a lot higher up the food chain at—well, at work. But he was always really nice to me. Invited me to be in the football pool and took me out for a drink when I got picked as employee of the month, even though he was a big shot at the company and I was just a—"

He stopped, then frowned down at his feet. He'd obviously been coached not to reveal his job title or company name.

Juli smiled. "That sounds like Alex. I mean, I don't know him well, but he doesn't seem like a guy who's very hung up on job titles or who makes how much money or the lines between one level of employee and another."

Cody looked at her oddly for a moment, then turned back to the ocean. "I guess not," he agreed.

"What?"

Cody shrugged. "Jake's known Alex a lot longer than I have. He says Alex almost got married once."

"Married?"

"To someone besides you, I mean."

"Right," Juli said, annoyed at the sudden pang of jealousy that socked her in the gut. "So what happened?"

"Alex hadn't gotten his job at—well, he wasn't in a job that made much money yet. And the lady he was planning to marry wasn't happy about that. She wanted to start having kids right away and stay home with them, and she couldn't do all that if they both had to work, right?"

"I see. So she—"

"She left. Married someone else. A dentist, I think."

Juli swallowed. "And Alex?"

Cody shrugged again. "I don't know. I think he had a lot of girlfriends, but they weren't really around very long. He worked a lot but—" Cody stopped himself and looked at Juli. "I probably shouldn't be telling you this stuff."

Juli blinked. As intent as she'd been on fishing information out of the crew, there was something about this that felt a little too personal. Cody was right. She should let the subject drop. "It's okay. I won't tell Alex. It does give me a little more insight into who he is, though."

Cody nodded. "And now we all know who you are. World's Smartest Woman. That's kind of cool."

Juli gritted her teeth. "Sometimes it is."

"Being smart seems like a good thing."

"It is, but—" she stopped herself, not wanting to feel more pathetic than she already did. "It is."

Cody looked at her. "But?" He gave his fishing line a tug, but he didn't take his eyes off her. "But you're too smart for most men."

She stared at Cody, taken aback by his observation. "Well, I—I guess that's part of it. Too smart, I mean. But the smart thing maybe makes me a little—well, different."

Cody grinned. "That's why you fit in with us then."

He turned back to the ocean then and became absorbed in adjusting something on his pole. Juli just stared at him, struck by this new side of Cody. She'd pegged him as just another dumb jock in an apron—not that she'd met many dumb jocks in aprons, but she knew the type.

It was obvious now there was more to Cody than she'd guessed.

Suddenly, Cody jerked forward. Juli stepped back and watched as something gave a vicious yank on the end of his line.

"Fish!" Juli shrieked. "Cody, you have a fish!"

"Cookie."

"*Cookie!* Get the fish!"

She watched Cody's enormous shoulders strain as he worked the reel, pulling his catch toward the boat. He leaned back, sweat springing up on his forehead as his pole bent nearly in half. He kept cranking on the reel, working it expertly as he brought the fish in closer.

"Holy cow, it must be huge!" Juli panted.

"It's heavy!"

"Don't fall in!"

"Get the net!"

Juli squealed and grabbed the net they'd set on the deck behind them. Cody grunted, and Juli held the net out, braced to capture the monster fish. Cody gave another heave, his apron fluttering in the breeze, and he jerked the line.

"Ohmygod!"

Juli closed her eyes and lifted the net, bending her knees a little to brace herself. There was a loud grunt from Cody and then something heavy dropped into the net. Juli's shoulders sagged, and the net hit the deck with a thud.

She opened her eyes. They both stared at their catch.

"You think we should poach it in a court bouillon?"

Juli looked at the waterlogged shipping crate, empty and covered with grimy barnacles. "Maybe with an aspic glaze?"

Cody grinned. "That sounds delicious."

Chapter 10

"YOU'VE GOT TO BE KIDDING ME."

Alex stared at Juli in disbelief. It was 8:00 p.m., and he was back in her stateroom—against his better judgment—and sitting on her bed—*really* against his better judgment.

But it wasn't his judgment giving him heart palpitations at the moment.

Juli smiled. "You've never played Battleship this way?"

Somehow, her voice was both innocent and taunting all at once. Alex grimaced and ignored the fact that he desperately wanted to shove the game boards aside and toss her back against the pillows.

He sighed. "I don't actually recall reading about this in the instruction booklet."

"Are you chicken?"

"Chicken? No. Sane? Yes. This wasn't part of the deal we made."

"One game, my rules. You agreed."

"You failed to tell me the rules."

"You're just afraid you'll lose."

Alex shook his head, wishing like hell all the blood didn't leave his brain whenever Juli came around. "I am *not* afraid I'll lose," he insisted.

"Then what is your problem?"

"My problem is that I'm not in the habit of playing Strip Battleship with insane women who've stowed away on my boat."

"That is a problem." She opened the box top and began unpacking the game parts.

Alex watched her and tried to ignore the little voice in his head that insisted any game that offered the possibility of seeing Juli naked was definitely worth playing. And fine, if he had to admit it, the game did sound fun.

"What's wrong with regular Battleship?" he asked.

"I've been playing regular Battleship with Jake and Phyllis and Cody for three days," she said. "I'm bored with it."

"I see. So if I'd only agreed to play sooner, I'd be off the hook and Cody would be down here ready to lose his boxers."

Juli grinned as her gaze traveled down his shoulders and chest and lingered awhile in the middle before journeying back up. She shrugged. "Probably not," she said. "I know how to pick my battles wisely."

He sighed and grabbed one of the game boards from her. "Fine. One game."

She laughed. "That's the spirit. You're going down!"

"If my memory serves correctly, I already did."

Juli's cheeks turned pink. "Thanks for that."

"My pleasure," Alex said, grinning. "Truly, *my pleasure*."

Her color went from pink to bright crimson, and Alex couldn't believe how beautiful she was. He considered offering to skip the game and satisfy her again.

"Let's play." Juli popped open her game board, angling it carefully away from him as she began sorting the white pegs from the red ones.

"Give me some of those," Alex muttered. "Do I have all my ships?"

"There should be five. An aircraft carrier, a destroyer, a submarine, a patrol boat, and of course, your battleship."

"Quit looking at my board."

"Relax, sailor boy. I'm not that desperate to see you naked."

Alex snorted and began placing his boats on the game board in strategic locations.

"G4," Juli said, eyeing him.

"Will you wait a minute?"

"Hurry up."

"Fine, I'm ready. What did you say again—G4?"

"Well not now. Now you've had a chance to move your pieces around. B9."

"Miss," Alex said, pleased she'd failed to hit him on the first try. He angled his board a little, shielding it from her view.

"Your turn," she said as she smirked at him.

Alex glanced at her over the top of his game board, considering his move. Juli leaned forward, dashing his hopes of catching a glimpse at her board but giving him a nice glimpse down the front of her shirt.

"C6," he said, tearing his eyes away from the view.

"Miss," Juli said, clearly delighted. "E2."

Alex frowned. "Hit."

"Excellent! And I'll take your shirt, please."

Alex raised an eyebrow. "You got to pick the game. You don't get to pick the clothing. Have a shoe."

He reached down and pulled off his deck shoe, handing it to her without ceremony. Juli shrugged and took the shoe from him, tucking it behind her on the bed.

"Makes no difference to me," she said. "I'll have it all before too long."

"A6," Alex said, ignoring her.

"Miss! E3."

"Ha! Miss. J7."

"Hit!" Juli shrieked, and Alex felt himself grinning at her enthusiasm. She leaned down and pulled off her flip-flop and Alex grew light-headed as he tried not to look down the front of her blouse again.

"Here you go," Juli said, slapping the shoe into his palm with more force than needed. "And I'll take F2, please. And how about your wristwatch, if it's a hit. Which I know it is."

"It's a hit," Alex said, unsnapping his watch. "What, you don't want the other shoe?"

She accepted the watch with a smile, brushing her fingernails over his wrist in a way he was sure was deliberate. "Just trying to keep things interesting," she said.

"Right. Because we were running the risk of boredom."

Juli grinned, and Alex had to admit he was beginning to enjoy losing. Not as much as he'd probably enjoy winning, but still.

"I7."

"Good guess. Hit," Juli said and handed him her other flip-flop. "And since it hasn't sunk yet, I've obviously got either your aircraft carrier or your battleship, so let's go with D2."

"Miss! Ha!"

"I'm still sinking your boat, sailor boy. You won't be laughing when I get your other shoe."

Alex studied his board. "Actually, I might. The shoes smell pretty bad."

"All this charm, how did I get so lucky marrying you?"

"Can it and play, blondie. H7."

"Hit. You sank my submarine."

"Excellent. And hand over your top."

"Patience, Pirate Alex, patience," Juli said, grinning at him as she moved her fingers to the buttons on her blouse. She hesitated for a moment, her eyes challenging him.

"You sure about this?"

Alex tried not to stare, then gave up. The game was her idea, after all. Wasn't staring the whole point? "Positive," he said, ignoring the voice in his head that told him he wasn't being a gentleman. "Take it off."

Juli grinned, apparently unconcerned with gentlemanly conduct. With obvious deliberateness, she began to unfasten the buttons on her blouse. She started at the bottom, her fingers graceful and nimble as she slid the metal bits through the fabric, angling her torso away from him slightly to impede his view. She held the edges of the shirt together, not showing any skin at all, taking her time.

Alex swallowed hard, trying to remain unaffected but failing miserably. He couldn't see a thing, not even a sliver of skin as she worked the buttons, deftly holding the shirt closed. Even so, he found himself struggling just to breathe evenly. Juli clutched the edges of the blouse together with one hand, her modesty somehow more arousing to him than if she'd just torn the shirt right off. Her other hand reached the last button and hesitated. She looked at him and smiled, her fingers poised at the final buttonhole.

Alex didn't breathe.

Juli unfastened the last button.

Alex blinked. "You're wearing a tank top underneath? That's not fair."

Juli laughed, visibly pleased with herself. "Life's not fair, sailor boy. Technically, it's a camisole and not a tank top. G2."

Alex frowned and glanced down at his board. He'd forgotten for a moment they were even playing a game. And dammit, there was his boat, on the verge of sinking.

"Hit," he muttered.

"The other shoe, please."

Alex sighed and handed it over.

"Bet you're sorry you didn't wear socks, huh?" Juli chirped. "You could last a whole lot longer if you had."

"Your concern for my staying power is touching. Unnecessary, but touching. Let's try F5."

"Miss. H2."

Alex sighed. "Hit. You sank my funny-looking whatever boat."

"That's your battleship. Have you never played this before?"

"Not since high school. And I don't recall anyone taking my clothes from me at the time."

"Pity. Hand over the shirt."

Alex pulled the T-shirt over his head, conscious of Juli's eyes on him. Conscious of the fact that she wasn't even pretending not to stare.

She kept watching him, her eyes wide, her voice silent for the first time all evening.

"What?" he asked, settling back on the bed as he handed her the shirt. Juli reached out and took it, a smile crossing her face as her fingers closed around the cotton. The color had risen in her cheeks, and her eyes were still fixed on his chest. She glanced up, meeting his eyes.

"My my, Pirate Alex," she said, her voice teasing. "We've been doing our ab workouts, haven't we?"

"Phyllis would beat me up if I didn't. She's been the office drill sergeant for the last twenty years."

"Office?"

"Stop chatting and play. H10."

"Miss. I5."

"Miss," he said. "C3."

"Miss. D7."

"Miss," he said. "How long are we going to do this?"

"Until I win and you're naked. Did you miss that part of the plan?"

Alex shook his head and grinned. "You're nuts, you know that? H2."

"Miss. You suck at this."

"I don't see you getting any hits."

"A1."

"Damn," he said. "Hit."

"Yes! Shorts, please."

Alex raised an eyebrow at her. "This is your idea of fair?"

"Fair?"

"You've got a tank top, a bra, your shorts, and under-wear. You started with a lot more clothing than I did."

"You sure about the underwear?" Juli asked, crossing her legs with a saucy smile. "Maybe I'm going commando again."

Alex ignored the sudden rush of blood to his head as he stood up and stripped off his cargo shorts. He kept his eyes on Juli, almost hoping to see her blush or turn away. Anything to see he was beating her at her own game. Instead, she stared openly, her gaze approving as she sat there in her thin little tank top—a garment that, honestly, left little to the imagination. Did she even have a bra under there? He couldn't tell.

Alex kicked his shorts aside and Juli grinned. Alex sat back down on the bed and pulled his game board close.

"Boxer briefs," Juli said, smirking at him over the top of her board. "You have excellent taste in underwear."

"Quit ogling and play. C9."

"Hit. It's about time, sailor boy."

"And yet, you're still wearing a top."

He sat back and watched her, no longer caring that it was a piggish thing to do. She'd suggested this game after all, and it wasn't like she hadn't expected to lose an article of clothing or two.

You knew full well you'd both end up naked.

He should probably feel bad about that, but he was too busy watching Juli to care at the moment.

She stood and, with an unself-conscious grin, stripped off her top. Alex watched her arms crossing and uncrossing beneath the flimsy fabric, her ribs appearing one by one like a row of piano keys. Her belly was flat and firm, her navel the perfect dimple in the middle of it all.

And just like that, she was standing in front of him in her bra. A bra that left nothing to the imagination.

"Jesus," Alex muttered, wishing he were a better man who could force himself to look away politely. "If Phyllis had worn that bra this morning, Jake would have had an aneurism and fallen overboard."

"You think?" she said, grinning through her mock

simper. She pivoted a little, clearly enjoying the effect she was having on him.

"I think that bra might be illegal in several states."

"It's sheer."

"No kidding."

"The lace is French."

"God bless the French."

"So where were we?" Juli asked, sitting back down. "My turn, right?"

"What?"

"B1," she said. "And stop staring."

"Miss. D9. And if you didn't want me to stare, you wouldn't have suggested the game."

"Good point," she said, grinning. "Also, that was a hit. Now you've got a choice to make."

Alex was feeling light-headed, not sure he was up for any decision more important than what sort of preserves to have on his toast in the morning.

He looked at her. "What choice?"

"A choice. Shorts or bra?"

Alex swallowed. "I get to choose?"

"It's the least I can do, since you're going to be naked on the next round anyway. You may have several ships left, but you're out of clothes. Your game is up, Pirate Alex."

Juli's eyes flashed in challenge. Alex watched the slow rise and fall of her chest, her breasts moving with the weight of her breath. A gold curl drifted lightly over her shoulder, coming to rest against the sheer lace of her bra. Her nipple tightened.

Alex made a noise in his throat. Juli smiled, her breath coming faster now. She pushed the curl back and met his gaze.

"What's it going to be, sailor boy?"

"Neither."

Her eyes registered surprise. "Neither?"

"Neither. I want something else."

Her face flushed, and he watched the column of her throat ripple as she swallowed. She rested a hand on her game board, her fingers brushing the forgotten ships along the clear surface.

"What do you want?" she asked, her voice almost a whisper.

"What do you think?"

She bit her lip. "I thought we weren't going to do this."

"You're the one who suggested getting naked. You started it. Did you really think it wouldn't end up like this?"

She smiled. "My intent was to get your defenses down. Anything else was just a bonus. The stripping seemed like an easy way to win."

"Yeah? That mirror over my shoulder probably helped too."

Juli's eyes widened in surprise. "You knew about that?"

"It was pretty obvious. You could see my board the whole time."

She laughed "But you didn't say anything."

"We're both mostly naked now. At this point, is there really a winner or a loser?"

Juli stared, words obviously failing her. Alex stared right back, cooler than he actually felt.

"So now what?" Juli asked, her voice almost a whisper.

"Well, the way I see it, we've got a couple choices."

"Only two?"

"Option one—"

There was a sudden knock at the door. Before either

of them could grab for their clothes, Phyllis burst through the entrance. Alex threw himself in front of Juli in a vain attempt to cover her up. He grabbed for his T-shirt and started to protest the intrusion.

But one look at Phyllis's face stopped him short. He froze, shirt in hand, and stared at her.

"What is it?" he asked, feeling a chill that had nothing to do with his lack of clothing. "What's wrong?"

"We have a problem," Phyllis said, her knuckles white as she clutched the doorknob. "A big, big problem."

Chapter 11

"OKAY, PHYLLIS, EXPLAIN IT AGAIN SLOWLY," ALEX SAID.

They were all fully dressed now, and everyone was clustered around the table in the pilothouse looking faintly green. Jake was steering the boat, but his eyes were on the group, and his expression was grim.

Juli folded her hands in her lap, uncertain what was happening but certain she didn't want to miss a word of it.

"I started getting some funny readings on the GPS tracker," Phyllis said, taking a swallow of the water Cody handed her. "I thought it was a glitch at first, but then the alert went off for the ShipSafe system."

"Jesus," Jake hissed.

"Is something wrong with our boat?" Juli asked, trying to keep the panic out of her voice. "Are we sinking?"

Alex shook his head. "Our boat is just fine."

Juli stared, trying to understand. "The boat you're hijacking?" she guessed, still lost in the conversation.

Cody set a tray of cookies down beside a milk pitcher on the table. "Isn't ShipSafe designed to alert the authorities?"

"Normally, yes," Alex said, glancing warily at Juli. "That's what the system is supposed to do. But obviously they would have disarmed that part of the software for an off-the-books operation like this."

"I don't understand," Juli said. "What's ShipSafe? What are you talking about?"

Jake sighed and broke a cookie in half, then ignored the two pieces. "It's an alert system used in the shipping industry," he said. "It uses a hidden computer to monitor the ship's position. If anyone breaches a fiber-optic network around the perimeter of the vessel, it sends a signal to the ship's crew and to the authorities on shore."

Juli stared at the faces around the table, each more grim than the other. She frowned, trying to put the pieces together. "So something's wrong on the ship you're planning to rob. How do you know about it?"

Alex took a piece of cookie from Jake and began breaking it into smaller bits. "Let's just say we've got a connection to the company operating the ship. We know the systems, the technology."

"So you're monitoring the ship," Juli said. "And now something happened."

"Which way is it headed, Phyllis?" Alex said, moving around her to check the controls.

"Southwest, last I checked," she said.

"It'll go right past us at that rate," Jake said.

"It's heading back the way we've just come?" Cody asked, clearly confused.

"Someone else must be controlling the ship," Alex said. "Not our guys anymore. That has to be it."

"Maybe that's not it," Jake argued. "Maybe the system malfunctioned or something."

Phyllis folded her arms over her chest and glared at Jake. "I designed that system. It didn't malfunction. No way."

Cody frowned. "Maybe they're rerouting for some reason? Bad weather? Just a change of plans?"

"We've been monitoring all their communication," Alex pointed out. "We'd know about any foul weather or changes in plans."

"Well, they're sure as hell not going to be at the re-fueling station tomorrow afternoon," Phyllis said. "That much we know."

Alex stared at the controls, a frown etched on his face.

"So let me get this straight," Juli said, grabbing a small stack of cookies and biting into one. "You're out here on your pirate mission to rob this ship. Only now, it looks like, for some reason, the boat isn't going to be where you thought it was."

Jake scowled. "Fuck."

"Who else knew what was on that boat?" Phyllis asked. "Really, could it just be a random hijacking, or is something else going on?"

Juli frowned. "So if the boat is headed our way, can't you just attack when it comes by?"

She couldn't believe she was sitting here calmly suggesting a pirate attack the same way she might suggest a trip to the mall, but no one blinked.

Alex rubbed his eyes, all traces of playful lust gone for now. "You can't board a moving cargo ship at sea from a fifty-three-foot powerboat. Even if it were physically possible, we're not equipped to do that."

"What was the plan originally?"

Everyone frowned, clearly uncertain how much to reveal.

Phyllis glanced at the men, then sighed. "We knew the ship was stopping to refuel at a private island that belongs to the owner. We planned to sneak aboard and take what we needed while the ship was docked for the night."

"No violence," Cody said.

"A good plan," Jake growled. "An easy plan."

Juli shoved a cookie in her mouth and chewed. "So you need a new plan."

"It's not that simple," Alex muttered.

"You know which direction the boat is headed, right?"

"We don't know who's on it," Alex said. "We don't know where they're going, how heavily armed they are, whether they've killed anyone on board, or whether they even know the particulars of the cargo onboard. We didn't come out here prepared for a heist like this. It was supposed to be peaceful."

"Mostly," Jake added.

"It could be a random thing," Phyllis said. "Maybe they're ransoming the crew or something."

"It could even be a mutiny," Jake said. "Maybe a few members of the crew overthrew the others and now they're headed to some pre-planned rendezvous or something."

"But why wouldn't they still stop for fuel like they planned?" Cody asked. "That doesn't make sense."

Alex was fiddling with the radio, a scowl etched on his handsome features. Juli watched him, wondering what she could do to help.

"You've had the VHF on channel 16?" he asked Phyllis.

"I started listening for distress calls right away," she said, looking pale. "Nothing."

"More milk, anyone?" Cody asked, obviously feeling the same desperation to be useful.

No one answered, so Juli smiled at him and raised her glass. "The cookies are really good."

"Amaretto and chocolate pecan," Cody said. "My mother's recipe."

Alex continued fiddling with the radio. A hiss of static came over the airwaves, followed by a string of voices. Someone was chattering about weather conditions. Another voice with a German accent rattled on about his difficulty obtaining a Marine Identification Number. A third voice came crackling through, reporting something about floating debris.

"Try channel 68," Phyllis said. "They were using that frequency earlier."

Alex glanced at the radio. "Yeah, but if the ship really is being controlled by someone else now, they probably wouldn't use the same channel."

"It's worth a try, isn't it?" Phyllis shot back, not bothering to hide the agitation in her voice. "Maybe they forgot and just left it switched on or something."

Alex shrugged and began fiddling with the controls. Another clatter of static sounded in the small cabin and Cody winced at the burst of noise. More voices, these ones raised in anger.

Everyone was silent, listening. Juli reached for another cookie and began to nibble.

"What the hell is that?" Alex muttered. "Spanish?"

"Sounds like it," Jake said, standing up to listen.

"They sound angry," Cody said.

"Try another channel," Phyllis said. "Maybe 72."

"It's not Spanish," Juli said, taking another bite of cookie. "It's Bajan."

Four pairs of eyes swung toward her. Alex's hand froze on the radio dial, his stare boring into her.

Juli picked up her milk glass and took a swallow before biting into another cookie. She chewed quietly, listening to the voices over the radio as all four of her shipmates stared at her. Alex was the first to speak, in a voice that was anything but pleasant.

"What did you say?"

Juli finished chewing and swallowed. "That language. It's Bajan. It's an English-based Creole that uses a combination of British dialect with African syntax."

They all gaped at her, no one speaking. No one except the voices on the radio, raised in angry urgency. Juli scrunched up her forehead and listened.

Alex glanced at the radio, his brows knitted together in concentration. He looked back at Juli.

"What is Bajan, Juli?" he said slowly. "Where do they speak it?"

"Barbados."

Alex stared at her. "Would it be unreasonable to ask if this is one of the four million languages you just happen to speak?"

"No."

Alex frowned.

"No, it wouldn't be unreasonable," she said, grabbing another cookie. "And yes, I speak Bajan."

Alex gripped the edge of the counter. The voices began chattering again, this time more urgent. Alex gritted his teeth. "Any chance you can translate what they're saying?"

Juli stood up and grabbed her milk glass, along with another stack of cookies. She walked over to stand beside Alex, setting her glass on the counter and leaning in close to the radio so she could hear better. She listened, cocking her head to one side as the others watched her with rapt expressions.

Another crackle of static, more voices. Juli turned toward Alex.

"I might be able to translate," she said, taking a drink of milk. "You still planning to leave me out of your pirate mission?"

Jake threw his arms up in the air, exasperated. "Jesus, Juli, tell us what they're saying," he barked.

Phyllis waved a hand at him and scowled. "We don't even know this has anything to do with the cargo boat," Phyllis pointed out. "It could be anyone on the radio."

Juli ignored them both and looked at Alex. She said nothing, waiting for his response. He closed his eyes and muttered a curse.

"Whatever you want," he growled. "Just tell us what they're saying. If it's even relevant."

"Well, earlier, that first guy—the one with the raspy voice? He was saying they got it. Whatever that means. And then the other guy asked how big, and the first guy just laughed. Then they made a bunch of penis jokes."

More voices, more static. Juli listened, picking out words.

"The raspy-voiced guy is on a boat at sea, but the second guy is talking as though he's on land somewhere. At a harbor, maybe? Is that possible?"

"Boat to shore," Alex answered. "Sure, very common."

Juli nodded and went back to listening to the voices. "The second guy says the space at the Arawak Cement plant is too small—that they should try coming in somewhere else. Something about Oistins Bay?"

"It could be anyone," Jake pointed out.

Juli held up a hand to silence him, listening hard. "He's giving a bunch of numbers. Eight-seven-four-eight-one-two-five-nine-seven-nine."

Jake scribbled the digits on a piece of paper as she said them. He looked up, his face white. "Oh, shit. It's their MIN number. That's the boat."

"It *is* them," Phyllis groaned, dropping into a chair.

"Phyllis, quick—look up ports in Barbados," Alex said. "Look for Oistins, Arawak, any of those things Juli just said. Anything that sounds close."

Jake grabbed a chart off the table, frantically scanning the configuration of islands and water.

"The first guy—the one on the boat—his accent isn't native," Juli said, cocking her head again. "He speaks Bajan well, but I don't think he's from Barbados."

"What does that mean?" Jake asked.

Juli shrugged. "Just an observation. The guy on the boat may be headed to Barbados, but I don't think it's where he's from. The guy he's talking to—the one on land? He sounds native."

Jake was frowning, trailing a finger over the map. "Son of a bitch."

"If they're headed to Barbados, they're going to pass right by us," Cody said, staring over his shoulder.

"Not if we beat them there," Alex said.

Jake and Cody stared at him. Phyllis kept clicking keys on her laptop.

"Oistins and Arawak Cement plant are both places to dock large boats in Barbados," she said, nodding at the screen.

"Phyllis, can you find out all the specs on docking there—visas, entrance requirements, permits, that sort of thing?" Alex asked.

She pulled the laptop closer and punched a few more keys. "Sure, no problem. What are you thinking, Alex?"

"We'd planned to ambush the ship on land. Maybe we can still pull it off."

Jake stared dubiously at the controls. "Do we have enough fuel to make it there?"

"We'd planned to haul ass coming back anyway," Alex said. "Twenty knots, remember? We planned on burning some fuel. Let's crunch the numbers."

"You want to take the helm for a minute?" Jake asked. "I've got the charts right here; Phyllis and I can plot it out."

Alex took the controls, and Jake grabbed a fistful of charts out of a cupboard. Striding over to the table, he dropped into the chair beside Phyllis with a notebook in his hand and a determined expression on his face.

"Cookie, would you mind checking into the weather and the currents along that course?" Alex asked. "And Juli?"

"Hmmm?" she said, biting into another cookie as she watched them all work.

"Keep an ear on that radio," Alex said. "You're now the official translator of this pirate mission."

Juli grinned, wiping at her milk moustache as she surveyed the rest of the crew. "Cool. I'm the medic *and* the translator."

Jake shook his head as he stared down at a chart. "Unfuckingbelievable."

Juli just smiled and dragged a stool over to the controls. Perching on the seat, she took a bite of cookie and got to work.

She was officially part of the team. It felt damn good.

～～～

Jake scowled at the numbers in front of him, pencil poised in one hand as he anchored the chart with the other.

"So we can do this," Phyllis said, sounding like she was trying to convince herself.

"Maybe," Jake said. "There are a lot of *ifs* here. And no offense, Juli—I mean, we all like you and everything, but it's pretty fishy that this is all happening while you're stowed away on our boat."

Juli grinned at him. "No offense taken. I'm flattered you think I could figure out how to hijack a ship that's several hundred miles away."

"Let's stay focused on the *ifs* here, guys," Alex interjected from his spot at the helm. "*If* we're right about where they're headed. *If* whoever's driving the ship isn't armed to the teeth. *If* we're not completely wrong about what just happened out there. *If* we can even figure out where to dock once we hit Barbados."

"*If* this guy doesn't stop telling stupid jokes on the radio, I'm going to throw myself overboard," Juli said, scowling at the controls. "Seriously, blonde jokes in Bajan aren't any funnier than blonde jokes in English."

"Just keep listening," Alex told her. "Tell us what they're saying."

"He says the trade winds have been really bad the last two days, so they'll have to be careful. Now the other guy is saying something about taking care of the details with customs at Bridgetown Harbour so they can make it through without a problem."

Jake glanced over her shoulder at the notepad where she was jotting all the information.

"Hell," he said, turning back to Phyllis. "Can we use the same doctored-up paperwork we used before?"

"I think so," Phyllis said, frowning. "It looks like we can come in either through Bridgetown Harbour or

Port St. Charles, but we'll be required to leave customs through the same port we entered."

"Something to keep in mind," Alex murmured.

"So how long until we make it there?" Juli asked, keeping one ear tuned to the radio. The voices had fallen silent, and she wasn't sure what that meant.

Alex frowned down at the calculations Jake and Phyllis had jotted on a notepad beside their stack of charts. "We've got about three hundred miles to cover. Factoring in the windstream and the currents we're likely to hit along the way, we can make it in about twelve hours if we average twenty knots."

Juli studied him, noticing dark circles under his eyes. She couldn't remember the last time Alex had gotten a solid night of sleep, but it hadn't been in her bed. They'd been much too busy for that. "Maybe you should go sleep for a little while," she suggested. "You didn't get a lot of rest last night."

Alex frowned, his hands still on the controls. "I'm fine."

Juli rolled her eyes. "Look, I'm no expert, but you're obviously the most experienced member of the crew. I don't know much about boating, but it seems like it would be a dumb idea for our captain to be falling asleep at the wheel by the time we arrive."

Alex seemed to be on the verge of protesting, but Phyllis interrupted. "She's right, Alex. We're going to need you when we dock. None of us can get the ship into port without you."

"I can take the next six hours," Jake offered. "And Cody and Phyllis can split up the rest. We want you to be sharp for the next part of this mission."

Alex sighed. "We don't even know what we're going

to do when we get there. We need to have a plan. We can't just pull up alongside the cargo ship and ask if they have any Grey Poupon."

"We have Grey Poupon," Cody offered helpfully.

"We've got twelve hours," Jake said. "We'll chew on it while you sleep, and we'll wake you up with plenty of time to spare so you can help us hammer out the details."

Alex glanced at his watch. "It's 10:00 p.m. now. Wake me up at 4:00 a.m., okay? No later. I'll just rest my eyes."

"Go," Juli said. "We've got it covered."

Alex looked at her and shook his head. "Why does that not reassure me?"

"Go!" Juli said again, this time more forcefully. "Are you waiting for someone to tuck you in?"

Alex gave her a tired half smile. "Actually, that's not a bad idea. There's a Battleship game we need to finish."

Juli rolled her eyes. "The moment's gone, sailor boy."

"I'm good at creating new moments."

His tone was playful, but something in his eyes made her go warm all over. Her mind flashed an image of him wearing nothing but his boxer briefs, his body hard and lean and ready to—

She dropped her cookie.

"Got it," Alex said, stooping to pick it up.

He handed it to her, and Juli was so dizzy at his touch, she shoved the cookie in her mouth without thinking.

"Five second rule." She flushed and looked down at the radio. "Can I just detach this handheld thingy on the radio here if I need to move around the ship for a second?"

"Sure," Alex said. "You coming with me?"

"I need my sweater from my room, and I want to get

Uncle Frank. I'll follow you down there, but I'm coming right back. I don't want to miss anything."

Alex shrugged. "Mi casa es su casa."

"It's *my* room," Juli pointed out.

"Yeah, but it's my boat."

"Technically, isn't it a rental?"

"Are you going to gab all night, or are you going to get your sweater?"

Juli grinned and pushed past him, making her way toward the master stateroom. Alex followed. In the doorway, they both paused for a moment, surveying the Battleship carnage.

"Quite a game," Alex said.

"That it was."

"Tell me again what it was you were hoping to accomplish there?"

Juli moved past him and set the portable radio on the bed. Grabbing her knapsack, she felt the tingling sensation she'd come to recognize as Alex's eyes on her body. She bent over the bag, pawing through the contents in search of her sweater.

"I was hoping to distract you," she said, tossing out shorts and shoes and other random articles of clothing. No sweater. "Put you off your game so you wouldn't notice you were losing the challenge."

"It's tough to make a man forget he's sitting there in his underwear."

"I didn't care about the underwear," she said. "I just wanted to get your defenses down so you'd forget about your plan to cut me out of the heist."

"You're right then. I forgot about that part."

Juli found her sweater and pulled it out of the pack,

tugging it over her arms as she avoided his eyes. She felt very naked all of a sudden, even more than she had in her bra.

Naked wasn't a bad thing, but not what they needed right now.

"Anyway, it's a moot point now," she told him. "You're not going to handcuff me, and I'm going to be a part of the mission one way or another."

"That you are."

Juli was quiet a moment, hesitating there at the foot of the bed. Alex moved first, stooping to collect the Battleship pieces. Juli joined him, pulling the little red and white pegs out of the boards and collecting them in little bags. When she finally spoke, her voice sounded small to her.

"Should I be scared?" she asked. "About what's happening with the mission, I mean."

"No."

"Are *you*?"

Alex was quiet for a moment, his expression unreadable. "I'd be an idiot if I pretended this wasn't risky."

Juli frowned and rubbed her hands over her arms.

"This mission is personal, Juli," Alex said, handing her a bag of red pegs. "It's not about money or power or pirate booty or anything like that."

"Really?"

"Okay, it's a little bit about money."

"Money can be important," she agreed. "Seems to matter a lot to some people."

He flinched—just a little, but Juli noticed. She opened her mouth to ask about it, but he cut her off.

"Anyway," he said, "there's a lot at stake here. That's all."

Juli nodded, not sure they were still talking about money or pirate missions. She waited, wondering if he'd continue. When Alex said nothing, Juli reached for the Battleship box. Her fingers brushed his arm as she leaned across the bed, and she shivered a little at the contact.

Drawing back, she put the box in front of her and began setting the game boards and little bags inside. Alex handed her the bag of gray plastic boats, and Juli dropped them in the box and set the lid in place.

"So one of us will come wake you in six hours," she told him.

"Feel free to join me if you need a nap."

Juli rolled her eyes. "If you and I continue sharing a bed, I think the odds are pretty slim we'll get much sleep."

"Probably true. Kind of a shame. I'll miss sleep."

She giggled. "I thought we agreed we weren't doing this."

"That's right." He took a step closer, and Juli felt his breath ruffle her hair. "Why was that again?"

"I might be a spy, you might be a criminal, and we're on a ship with no condoms," she said, feeling dizzy at his closeness. "Or something like that."

"Right. Other than that, though—"

Juli lifted the box and smacked him softly over the head with it. "Good night, sailor boy."

He grinned and grabbed her around the waist, pulling her against him before she had a moment to lower her arms or protest. Then he was kissing her again, his fingers twining in her hair as Juli held the Battleship box awkwardly above them. She whimpered and leaned into his chest, enjoying the kiss, craving his body, wishing she weren't standing there like a moron with a Milton Bradley box raised over her head.

She wasn't sure who pulled away first, but they were both breathless. Alex looked down at her, his gaze unfocused at first.

"I didn't mean to do that," he said.

"Okay."

"I'm not sure what came over me."

"Well—"

He smiled. "Next time, try putting the box down first."

Juli rolled her eyes and lowered her arms. "Next time, give me a little warning."

Alex's smile widened. Juli could feel his breath ruffling the curls around her face. "Funny how we both assume there'll be a next time."

Chapter 12

By the time Juli returned to the cockpit, the others seemed to have settled into a routine. Jake was steering the boat, his brow furrowed as he checked the compass every few minutes, guiding the ship back toward the Caribbean again. Juli watched him for a moment, noticing the way he stole glances at Phyllis every couple of minutes, the tension in his forehead relaxing each time he did it.

Phyllis was hunched over the laptop, studying something on-screen as she tapped a pencil against the map. She was frowning slightly, but it was obvious she was in her element as she scrolled a page with one hand on the mouse button.

"The weather's clear, but those guys on the radio were right about the trade winds," Cody announced, moving past her and setting a coffee urn on the table beside a pile of charts.

Phyllis glanced up just long enough to accept a mug from him, then went back to focusing on her computer. "Direction?" she asked, taking a sip of coffee.

"Prevailing easterly. Sugar?"

"Thanks, Cookie."

Keeping an ear tuned to the radio, Juli accepted a mug of coffee as well, allowing Cody to add a splash of homemade vanilla-infused creamer. She took a sip, wondering what it meant that there had been no chatter on the radio for several minutes.

"So we promised Alex we'd brainstorm a plan," Jake said. "Anyone have any ideas?"

Phyllis set down her pencil and looked up. Lifting her mug, she took a long sip of coffee and sighed. "Has anyone ever even *been* to Barbados?"

Jake and Cody shook their heads.

"Nope, sorry," Juli said. "Want any help researching it?"

Phyllis took another sip of coffee. "I think I've got it covered for now. We're aiming for 13 degrees N Latitude, 59 degrees W Longitude, and that we'll reach Barbados sometime around 10:00 a.m. local time if the wind and the weather cooperate with us."

"Have you figured out where we should berth once we get there?" Jake asked.

"Two options," Phyllis answered. "Either Bridgetown Harbour or Port St. Charles, which is about ten miles north of Bridgetown on the west coast."

"Which is better?"

Phyllis shrugged. "Clearance is easier up in Port St. Charles, since it's not a commercial port. That might be our best choice."

"What about the other boat?" Cody asked. "Will they come in the same way?"

Phyllis shook her head. "They'll need a lot more room with a cargo ship. There's Esso Jetty, just outside the breakwater. That can accommodate tankers up to 244 meters long and 11.6 meters draught. That's the most likely place. There's also the Arawak Cement Plant—which they mentioned on the radio earlier—or Needham's Point, which is used for crude oil imports."

"Can they take a cargo ship like that?"

"Arawak can handle ships 121 meters long, 9.0 draught. And Needham can take them 193 meters long and 11.6 meters draught."

Jake nodded thoughtfully. "It doesn't sound like a huge place. No matter where they put the ship, I don't think we'll have much trouble keeping them in our sights."

"True enough."

"When we get closer, we'll want to switch over to VHF 12/6."

"What's the port call sign?"

"Eight, Papa, Brava."

Juli listened to the comfortable rhythm of their banter, understanding more of their boat-speak than she would have just a few days ago. She knew the situation was dire, but it was nice to feel like a part of the action. Cody was wiping down the counter with a rag, glancing at his watch every now and then.

"So who will get there first?" Juli asked, taking a sip of her coffee. "Us or them?"

"Hard to say," Jake answered. "They're bigger and faster, but we've got a head start."

"We can adjust our speed a little bit, so it's pretty likely we'll arrive close to the same time they do," Phyllis added. "Maybe even an hour or so before them."

"So are we just better off waiting to form a plan?" Juli asked. "I mean, without knowing who they are or what they're doing, we can't narrow things down much."

Jake shrugged. "Maybe so. We can come up with some elaborate plot to sneak onto their boat and run recognizance, but who knows what'll happen when they get there? They might have someone waiting to unload the cargo the instant they berth."

"In which case, we'll be chasing them across land?"

"Or not," Phyllis said. "Who knows, maybe they're just planning a handoff to another ship."

Jake shrugged. "It's also possible they don't have a clue what sort of cargo they're dealing with. This could be a random thing, right? You hear about pirates stealing boats sometimes just to get their hands on the boat itself."

"True," Phyllis agreed. "And there's still the possibility it's a mutiny—that it's the same guys who've had the boat all along.

Juli took another sip of coffee, jumping a little as she heard a quick bark of static on the radio. She waited, but no one spoke. For a few more moments, everyone sat in silence, waiting for voices.

"So we wait for another clue on the radio," Juli said finally. "And if we don't get one, we stay the course to Barbados."

"We've still got the GPS tracker," Phyllis added. "Even if these guys don't say anything else on the radio, we'll be able to see where they're headed."

"Okay," Juli said, trying to stifle a yawn. Even with the coffee, she was fighting to stay awake. She looked up to see Cody staring at her.

"You should take a nap," he said.

"Gotta listen to the radio," Juli said, giving in to the urge to yawn.

Jake glanced up at her and shrugged. "So sit right there. Put your head down on the counter so you hear the radio if anything happens. It'll wake you up."

"Oh," Juli said. "Maybe. I don't think I could fall asleep, but maybe if I just rest my eyes."

It was the last thing she said before she trundled off into dreamland.

———

When Alex woke at 4:00 a.m. to the sight of Jake's bald head, he was admittedly disappointed.

"Where's Juli?" he asked, blinking against the over-head light Jake had just switched on.

"Napping," Jake said. "What, I'm not cute enough to wake you up?"

"No, you're plenty cute. You just don't fill out your shirt the same way."

"Few people do," Jake agreed.

Alex yawned and sat up, swinging his legs out of bed. "Everything go okay?"

"No problems. We should be hitting Bridgetown Port in about six hours."

"Anything else over the radio?" Alex asked, scrounging on the floor for his T-shirt.

"No word since just before you went to sleep. We're keeping an eye on them, but they seem to be making a pretty straight line for Barbados."

"So we guessed right."

Jake snorted. "Not completely a guess. What the hell would we have done if Juli hadn't known what they were saying?"

"We would've followed the boat anyway."

"Probably. But we wouldn't have had a clue how far they were headed or whether we had the fuel to follow them. At least this way we got a chance to plot the route and figure out whether we could make it there."

Alex tugged his shirt on over his head and smoothed

down his hair with his fingers. "So she saved our asses, more or less."

Jake gave a grudging shrug. "Hate to admit it, but she's proving to be useful. That's why I'm not sure what to make of what Phyllis found online just a minute ago."

Alex looked up at Jake, startled by the sudden grimness in his voice. "What do you mean?"

"Juli wasn't lying about all the IQ crap," Jake said, dropping onto the bench beside the bed. "We found a bunch of information about her. She's pretty damn famous. There have been a lot of scientific studies and articles written about her."

"So what's the problem?"

Jake was quiet a minute, toeing a spot on the floor. When he looked up at Alex, his expression was somber. "You know the dead uncle she's been toting around in that urn? Uncle Frank?"

"Yeah," Alex said, trying to read Jake's solemn expression. "What about him?"

"We did some digging online," Jake said, rubbing his palms against his knees. "Uncle Frank was also known by another name. Frankie-Two-Toes."

Alex felt a chill run up his arms. "Frankie-Two-Toes the mobster?"

"You know of another Frankie-Two-Toes?"

"Shit," Alex said as he sat back down on the edge of the bed.

"Yeah."

Alex was quiet for a long time. He looked up at Jake. "So we're transporting a notorious mobster's famous genius niece."

"Pretty much."

"Not exactly part of the plan."

"Nope."

"It could be a coincidence."

Jake shrugged. "This trip has been one long string of them, hasn't it?"

Alex looked around the room. "You notice she took the urn with her?"

Jake nodded. "She even fell asleep with her hand on it. No chance to pry the damn thing away from her and see what's in it."

Alex shoved his feet into his shoes and stood up, shaking his head. "I don't like this."

Jake grunted. "Me neither."

Alex pulled the covers up and straightened the pillow, trying not to meet Jake's eyes. "So we keep holding our cards close to our vest. *No details*. And we watch her. Constantly."

"Agreed," Jake said, nodding. "And Alex?"

"Yeah?"

"Don't get too close."

With that, Jake turned, patted Alex on the shoulder, and headed toward the door. Alex sighed.

"Too late," he muttered and followed Jake out the door.

―⁂―

Juli was the first to spot land. Of course, it may have been because she'd swiped Alex's binoculars.

"What do you see?" he asked, trying to wrestle the binoculars away from her.

"Sand," she said. "Buildings. Trees. Give me a minute. I haven't seen any of these things for three days. I want to savor it."

"Savor it later," Alex said, grabbing the binoculars at last. "I need to see where I'm going."

All hands were on deck, and Juli watched as the rest of the crew bustled about, preparing for their arrival. For the last twelve hours, they'd been hauling ass—at least three times faster than they'd been going just a day earlier. She had asked Jake about it, but he'd been decidedly vague. She knew the original plan had called for a slower trip out and a fast trip back, but she wasn't sure if it was a matter of fuel conservation or making a quick getaway.

Now as she watched, she was fascinated by the complexity of the process of bringing a large boat into a small space.

"How big was the entrance channel again?" Alex asked.

"13.5 meters," Phyllis called.

"Breakwater is 522 meters long," Jake added.

Juli looked on as Alex performed a series of complicated-looking maneuvers to bring the ship into port. They'd all been oddly hush-hush about the arrangements they were making, so Juli wasn't sure whether to expect a lei greeting or a hail of gunfire upon their arrival.

One important thing she *had* managed to pick up— they'd beaten the other boat by nearly two hours. Alex seemed pleased about that.

Things seemed to happen fast once they brought the ship in. There was a lot of hasty dialogue among the crew about port-of-clearance and berthing orders, and Juli tried hard to stay out of the way. She held her breath as they cleared customs, more than a little worried about some of the phony paperwork Jake had thrust into her hands just before they docked.

"Don't ask," Phyllis had said. So Juli didn't.

Instead, she beamed at the customs agent, complimented his tie, held her breath as he studied Uncle Frank's urn, and finally marched right through as though she wasn't a member of a fearsome pirate crew.

"Ditch the apron, Cody," she heard Alex whisper behind her.

"*Cookie!*"

"Shit."

Finally, they were all through customs and standing there on dry land with the Caribbean sun beating down on them and waves of jaunty calypso music bouncing through the air from a nearby ice cream shop. Phyllis fiddled with the handheld GPS, while Jake kept a firm grip on the portable radio.

"Now what?" Jake asked, fastening the radio to his belt and looking at the assembled group.

Alex glanced at his watch. "We should catch a cab over to the port where we think they're coming in. Find a good spot to watch the harbor, maybe find a cheap room so we can shower and set up our land-based headquarters?"

"A shower?" Juli asked hopefully. "You mean one where I don't have to prop my foot on the toilet to shave?"

"Says she with the master stateroom," Jake muttered, though he didn't sound particularly put out.

"You can have the first shower, Jake," Juli told him, waving frantically as a cab appeared, then zipped passed them. "I want to take my time anyway."

Alex cleared his throat. "How do the rest of you guys want to work this when we get to a hotel? It'll be suspicious if all five of us go marching into some place and ask for a room."

"Shouldn't we send in the least memorable person?" Phyllis asked, glancing at the assembled group. "Cody's too big—people will remember him. And Juli's too pretty, so they'll remember her too."

"Phyllis, why don't you and Jake go in as a couple?" Juli piped, giving Phyllis a gentle nudge toward Jake.

At least the nudge was supposed to be gentle. Instead, Phyllis went toppling into Jake's chest, an impact that resulted in an unpleasant "oomph" from their colliding bodies.

To Jake's credit, he caught Phyllis without wincing. And he immediately fastened his arm around her and returned her to an upright position.

"Um, sorry," Juli said, watching conflict play over Jake's features as he decided whether to keep his arm there or not.

"A couple?" Phyllis asked, looking nervous.

"Sure," Juli said. "You're illicit lovers here on a secret romantic rendezvous or something."

At that, Jake grinned. He stole a glimpse down the front of Phyllis's blouse. She looked up and raised an eyebrow.

"What?" he said. "Just getting into character. I'm a wealthy oil tycoon with a frigid wife who only stays with me for my money and power, while my adoring mistress fulfills all my wildest fantasies and desires."

"Wait," Phyllis said. "Am I the mistress or the wife?"

"Definitely the mistress," Jake said.

"Um, how about if you just ask for a room," Alex said, waving as another cab zipped past. "A cheap one."

"And it's important to stay inconspicuous," Juli said, stooping to study the sign on the little roadside stand behind them. "Oh, look—they have fresh pelau."

Cody looked delighted, ducking his head to look inside the booth at the menu scrawled on a blackboard. "Breadfruit cou-cou? Ohmygod, you have *got* to give me the recipe!"

"Inconspicuous," Alex muttered. "Right."

———

By the time they'd all trooped into the room—a free upgrade to a luxury, multi-room suite for the moony-eyed lovers—Alex was getting edgy. Edgy and irritable.

He was sitting in the room next to the window in a chair with one leg shorter than the others, peering past the curtains at the ocean. Jake and Cody and Phyllis were out on the balcony, but Alex felt safer being inside. Every few seconds, he'd stop scowling at the ocean and start scowling at the portable FHS radio.

When he wasn't scowling at the radio, he was stealing looks at Juli, alternately enjoying her cleavage and wondering what the hell it meant that the niece of Frankie-Two-Toes had stowed away on his boat. Something was going on, but he didn't have a clue what it was.

"Why aren't they saying anything else?" he muttered, fiddling with the radio. "It's been almost ten minutes since the last transmission. They should be coming in soon."

He glanced up at Juli, who was rubbing her wet hair with a fluffy white towel, looking unconcerned. He tried not to notice the way her robe gaped open a little in front, revealing a lovely triangle of flesh beneath her collarbones.

Juli noticed him not noticing and rolled her eyes, pulling the robe closed with one hand. Strolling over to him, she grabbed the radio out of his hand and set it on the windowsill.

"Gee, maybe because they've stolen a boat and don't feel much like chatting about childhood memories over the radio?"

Alex frowned. "You're sure you heard that last transmission right?"

"Well, they either greased the palm of the customs guy and arranged to pull the boat into that berth you guys were talking about earlier, or they were sharing a recipe for banana bread. Of course I'm sure, Alex."

She draped her wet towel over his knee and put one hand on his shoulder, using him as leverage to peer around him out the window. This time, Alex could see right down the front of her robe. He felt his mood improving as all the blood left his brain.

"So that's where they'll be coming in, huh?" Juli said, nodding out the window toward the water. "Pretty nice that Jake talked the receptionist into giving them a room with such a great view of the harbor."

"I'm not sure it was luck," Alex replied, fixated on an entirely different view. "I think they were just eager to do whatever it took to make sure Jake and Phyllis didn't start necking in the lobby."

Juli angled her body away from the window and looked at him. She was so close she was practically in his lap.

"So they played the illicit lover thing well?"

"I'm not so sure it was acting. I think they might actually have the hots for each other."

She shook her head. "You're just now figuring this out, sailor boy?"

There was a distinct buzzing in Alex's brain, and the smell of her shampoo was giving him a craving for lemon and coconut and something else he didn't want to admit. The sight of all that flesh moving beneath the robe was making him dizzy.

You can't trust her, a voice reminded him. *Just get the damn diamonds and get out of here.*

God, he hated that voice.

Alex stood up, glancing at his watch before moving past her and out onto the balcony where the others were gathered.

"Hey, guys? I know it's nice out here and everything, but don't you think you look a little conspicuous?"

Three pairs of eyes looked up at him with expressions of identical puzzlement. At least he assumed that was puzzlement behind their gaudy plastic sunglasses. Cody picked up his virgin daiquiri from the arm of his Adirondack chair and nudged the pink umbrella out of the way, taking a big gulp. Phyllis and Jake shrugged and went back to smearing suntan oil on each other's legs. Alex sighed.

The floral shirts they'd purchased in the hotel gift shop were so bright he couldn't stare directly at them. And Cody's garish orange sun visor was covered with pictures of copulating flamingoes.

"We're incognito," Cody insisted, slurping on his drink. "We're just tourists looking at the ocean."

"Yeah," Jake agreed, smiling down at Phyllis's calves. "Regular old tourists."

"With high-powered binoculars?" Alex asked. "And a GPS tracking device?"

Jake shrugged. "We're well-equipped tourists."

"Come back inside," Alex muttered. "We can see just as well from here."

There was much sighing and grumbling, but all three filed back through the sliding glass door. All at once, the radio squawked to life. Alex snatched the radio off the ledge.

"What are they saying?" he snapped, thrusting the radio at Juli. "What was that all about?"

"They're approaching the harbor," Juli said, glancing out the window. "Hey, look! Is that them?"

Alex stared out on the horizon. An enormous gray cargo ship was barely visible, sliding through the crevice between blue, blue sky and even bluer ocean.

Portelli's ship.

The radio squawked again and Juli listened as the voices chattered.

"They're thanking the customs guy who, um, greased the skids," Juli translated. "They're laughing about it. They're being subtle, not really saying anything outright, but it seems like they're implying something's going on."

More words over the radio, more laughter. The boat was drawing closer. Alex looked at Juli. She was scowling now.

"What?" he asked. "What are they saying?"

Juli's frown deepened. "Well that's not very nice."

"What?"

She waved at him to shut up, a gesture that might have annoyed him if he weren't relying so completely on her translation skills.

"Juli?"

She made a squeak of indignation and glared at the radio. "I don't believe it!"

"What?" Alex asked. "What's going on?"

"Honestly, is that all you guys think about?" She turned her scowl on Alex, then at Jake. Jake, at least, had the good sense to look ashamed.

"Juli—"

"*Alex*," she snapped as the radio grew silent again.

"What did they say? Please?"

Juli folded her arms over her chest.

"I'm not repeating most of the words he just said," she said, meeting Alex's gaze with fire in her eyes. "But I can tell you where our boys are headed the second they hit land. And I've got an idea what we can do about it."

Chapter 13

"TELL ME AGAIN WHY YOU PACKED A BUSTIER FOR THIS trip," Alex said, staring at Juli as she tugged her curls into a complicated twist on top of her head.

"Tell me again why I'm wearing it," Phyllis said, frowning down at her cleavage.

Jake was the only one not frowning. In fact, he seemed downright joyful with this unexpected turn of events.

Juli blinked at Alex through six coats of mascara, her blue eyes fringed with terrifying black spikes of lashes. "We're giving them what they want. That's it."

"No kidding," Jake murmured appreciatively, his gaze fixed on Phyllis.

Phyllis tugged at her leather miniskirt and scowled some more. Juli ignored Jake and directed her ire at Alex.

"They're looking for hookers," she said, grabbing hold of Alex's shoulder to steady herself as she stabbed her feet into impossibly high heels. "At least that's what the guy said on the radio. And from what the guy in the harbor said, there aren't a lot of hookers in Barbados."

"Pity, that," Jake muttered.

Alex smacked his palms on the counter in exasperation. "So you think it's your civic duty to fill the gap?"

"You have a better plan, sailor boy?"

Alex tried not to stare as Juli made a series of adjustments to the pushup bra that raised her cleavage to dizzying heights beneath her flimsy black cocktail dress.

The straps on the dress were so thin she could floss with them after a meal.

"I just think this is a dangerous way to—" Alex sneezed, cutting himself off midsentence as he tried to dodge the cloud of perfume Juli was spritzing into the air.

"They're coming ashore in search of hookers," Juli said, setting the perfume bottle down. "If they don't find them, they're going to return to the boat. If they *do* find them, they'll stick around awhile, maybe leave the boat unattended while they try to figure out the best way to conduct their illicit transaction."

"It's too risky," Alex protested. "For both of you."

"I can't feel my left boob," Phyllis muttered, tugging at the lacing on the side of her bustier.

Jake stood up, grinning like mad. "Here, let me help you feel your left—"

"Stop!" Juli said, throwing her hand up. "Nobody should feel Phyllis's boob right now except Phyllis. We're on a mission here, and Phyllis is a smart, sexy, confident woman who shouldn't be groped while she's getting ready."

Jake looked forlorn. Phyllis looked conflicted. Juli sighed and looked back at Alex.

"You guys want to get onto that boat," she said. "The crew is obviously coming ashore, but they're not going to want to leave things unattended for long. If they don't find what they're after, they're going back to the boat, right?"

Alex closed his eyes. "I don't like this."

"You don't have to like it," she said. "You just have to work with us here. I'm pretty sure we can keep these guys distracted for at least an hour. That gives you time to sneak onto the ship, disarm any guards they've left behind, figure out what happened to the original crew, check out the cargo, and get the hell off the boat without being caught."

"Look, just put some clothes on and we'll find another way to—"

"You want to wear the dress?"

Alex gritted his teeth as Juli stood back, surveying her handiwork with Phyllis. Alex had to admit he'd never seen her look quite so sultry. Come to think of it, he'd never seen her look like she wasn't preparing to crush someone's skull between her thighs.

Still, this was a crazy, risky plan. There was no way he could let them do this.

He turned his attention back to Juli, who was now slathering some sort of sparkly lotion on her bare legs. He stared, following the path of her fingers as they slid further up her thigh.

"I can't believe Cody just happened to have a red leather miniskirt in his bag," Juli was saying to Phyllis. "What are the odds?"

"I'd say pretty good," Alex muttered, grateful Cody was in the shower and not here to witness this fiasco. He stared at the thigh-high, patent leather stilettos on Phyllis's feet and raised an eyebrow at Juli.

"That's not the boot you puked in, is it?"

Juli rolled her eyes. "No. The other boot was Prada. This is a Manolo Blahnik."

"Duh," said Phyllis.

Alex looked at her. "Two days ago, you asked if Manolo Blahnik was an appetizer or an entrée."

Phyllis beamed. "I'm a new woman."

"Just what we needed," Alex muttered.

Phyllis tugged at the ruffled edge of her bustier. "Is it supposed to itch this much? Because it really itches."

"It's the price we pay for being desirable, sexy women," Juli told her. "Discomfort, misery, and itchy boobs."

"Speaking of the price you pay—" Alex began.

Juli turned on him. "We're not actually going to accept money in exchange for sex, Alex. We'll just titillate a little until we suddenly have an 'emergency phone call' we have to take care of. Then we'll sneak out the back door and never see these guys again."

"Titillate," Jake repeated.

"Anyway, you'll only be a couple minutes away on the boat, and we can radio you if anything happens," Juli pointed out. "And it's a public place. There will be tons of people there in the bar."

"So one of us will go with you," Alex said. "Just for safety's sake."

"As a pimp? No. Besides, you need all three of you to deal with any guys they may have left behind to guard the boat. You guys are walking into a much riskier situation than we are. You deal with that, and let us handle ours."

Juli grabbed a hairbrush off the counter and made a few quick passes through Phyllis's white-blonde hair, fluffing and teasing as Phyllis sat there looking amazed. "We'll get out fast if things don't feel right, okay?" she said, smiling at Alex.

"Things don't feel right now," Phyllis muttered, tugging at the bustier again. "Things are very itchy."

Juli beamed at her. "You look amazing, Phyllis. Beautiful. Isn't she stunning, Alex?"

Alex sighed. "You both look gorgeous. Really, *too* gorgeous. You're going to give these guys a heart attack."

Juli nodded. "So they said on the radio they were going to start off at that little tavern just down the alley," she said, tucking her brush into a tiny silver clutch. "We'll go work our magic. You guys work yours. And we'll see you back here in an hour."

"We don't have to do it this way," Alex argued, still not ready to surrender. "We have our paintball guns. We've got ski masks. We can do this by force."

Juli shook her head. "I've got mace in my purse, and so does Phyllis. But anyway, you can kill more flies with honey than with vinegar."

Cody stepped out of the bathroom and smiled, rubbing his head with a towel. "You can kill them with orange oil too."

Juli grabbed her clutch and walked over to the bathroom door, where she stood on tiptoe to kiss Cody on the cheek. "We'll keep that in mind."

Alex stared after her as she flounced toward the door, key in hand. Phyllis flounced after her, looking fairly new to the whole business of flouncing. Alex resisted the urge to catch her when she tripped over her own boots.

At the door, Juli pivoted and looked at him. She smiled, making him want to run up and grab her and tie her to the bed so she wouldn't take this crazy risk.

"Good luck getting the booty," she said cheerfully, smiling at him.

"Good luck peddling yours," Jake called back.

Alex shook his head and sat down on the edge of the bed, watching them strut out the door.

------ᴧᴧᴧ------

The throb of club music made Juli's feet rattle inside her stilettos as she stepped into the darkened bar and looked around.

"See anyone?" Phyllis whispered, tugging at the bustier again.

"I'm not sure what we're looking for," Juli whispered back. "I think if we go sit down at the bar, they'll probably just approach us."

"Do we need to make up a 'hookers for sale' sign or anything?"

Juli swatted Phyllis's hand away from the ruffled edge of her cleavage and shook her head. "Dressed like this, we don't need to advertise. We just need to wait."

Phyllis nodded, not looking convinced. Juli gave her an encouraging smile.

"You look totally hot, Phyllis."

"Yeah?"

"Yeah. I'd buy you. If you were really a hooker, I mean."

"Thanks, Juli. That's really sweet of you."

The two of them strolled over to the bar, Phyllis wobbling a little in her high-heeled boots. Juli pulled out a barstool and slid into place, setting her clutch on the wooden surface. Phyllis followed suit, looking like a nervous pre-teen girl on a first date—if a nervous, pre-teen girl were allowed to dress like a prostitute.

"What do hookers drink?" Phyllis whispered as Juli tried to catch the bartender's attention.

"I forgot to consult my *Guide to Hooker Etiquette*," Juli whispered, directing a flirty little wave at the startled-looking man wiping a wet rag across the other end of the bar. "How about if we just wing it?"

"Wing it. Right. Maybe champagne? Or a lime vodka collins? Or how about a cosmopolitan?"

"We'll have two gin and tonics," Juli called, smiling up at the bartender as he approached them with a cautious expression.

"With a twist," Phyllis added, beaming at him. "It's a special night."

"Really?" he said, his vaguely British accent offering an odd contrast to boyish features.

Phyllis beamed. "Yes. We've got some coochie for sale."

The bartender dropped a glass. Juli closed her eyes.

"That's the name of our boat," she interjected, kicking Phyllis under the bar. "The *S.S. Coochie*. If you know anyone in the market."

"A boat," he said, staring at her in disbelief as he filled their glasses and anchored a lime twist on the rim of each one, pushing them across the bar.

Juli took a sip of her drink, choking only slightly as she tried to remember details from the sale flyers she'd seen posted outside the marina. "Right. A boat. It's a beautiful sixty-nine-foot Steem AmShip Custom Built workship."

"You're selling a tugboat?"

"Um, yes. A tugboat. That's right."

"Named *Coochie*?"

Juli took another sip of her drink and shot a pleading look at Phyllis. "Great weather we're having here, don't you think?"

"Sure is nice," Phyllis agreed, yanking at the edge of her bustier and turning to survey the crowd.

The bartender wandered away, shaking his head as Juli tried to decide whether to beat Phyllis over the head with her right shoe or the left one.

"For future reference," Juli hissed when the bartender was gone, "I think we'll be a lot more convincing as hookers if we don't announce it to people."

Phyllis shrugged and began nibbling the edge of her lime. "I don't know," she said, pointing across the bar. "Those guys seem to be buying it."

Juli followed the direction of Phyllis's finger and nearly choked on her drink again.

Seven of the biggest, meanest-looking guys she'd ever seen were staring across the room at the two of them, looking like they'd just spotted an all-you-can-eat lobster buffet with a blowjob station beneath the butter tray.

"Don't they look like pirates?" Phyllis asked.

"They look like inmates," Juli hissed, thinking perhaps Alex had been right about the absurdity of this plan. At the thought of Alex, Juli felt a pang of longing.

"Inmates, pirates—same thing, right?" Phyllis said. "And it looks like they're coming over here. Is my lipstick straight?"

"You're not wearing lipstick."

"Oh. Right. Here they come. Look pretty."

Juli felt every ounce of bravado evaporate from her pores as the men ambled toward them like an approaching team of defensive linemen. "I think I just wet myself," she whispered. She thought about Alex and tried not to consider how disappointing it would be to end up dead in an alley without knowing for sure if the sex would be as amazing as she imagined.

The men lined up in front of them, their eyes hungry and

mean. "Well, well, well," said one of the men in a voice Juli recognized instantly as the one from the radio. "What are you sexy bitches doing here this evening? Looking for a little play? I think we can help you out with that."

He reached out to grab her with a hand that looked like it hadn't seen soap since the '80s. Juli winced.

Suddenly, the man beside him whirled and punched him in the nose. The other men jumped back, dodging the body of their fallen comrade as he hit the ground in front of them. One man grabbed a napkin to staunch the bleeding, while the man who'd thrown the punch crossed his arms over his chest and stared at the rest of the men with a look of reproach.

"That is an entirely disrespectful way to communicate with a lady, Phillip," he intoned in a voice more suited to a Rhodes scholar than a thug. "I insist that you apologize immediately for your barbaric behavior."

The other man was on his feet in an instant, looking like a beaten cocker spaniel. He stared at the floor with remorse practically dripping from his forehead. "I'm sorry."

The other man sighed and smacked him across the back of the head. "What are you sorry *for*, Phillip?"

"For my barbaric behavior."

"And for your disrespect of the fairer sex."

"And for my disrespect of the fairer sex," he agreed, looking like he wished to be anywhere else.

So did Juli, frankly.

"Very good," the man said, turning around and bowing slightly before Juli and Phyllis. "My name is Malcolm. And these are my brothers Blythe, Percy, Winchester, Prescott, and Pierson, and, of course, Phillip."

"Um, pleased to meet you," Juli said, extending her hand. Phyllis did the same, looking dumbfounded as Malcolm lightly grasped her fingers and planted a delicate kiss on the back of each of their hands.

"Please, allow me to apologize for my brother's boorish words by purchasing the libation of your choosing," he said, gesturing to the bartender. "Steven, we'll have seven glasses of your finest sherry, and whatever these lovely and sophisticated ladies would like to drink."

"Right away," the bartender said, eyeing the lot of them as though he wished they'd all fall through the floor. Then Malcolm pulled out a wad of cash the size of his arm, and Steven suddenly looked a whole lot happier to be serving them.

Malcolm eased himself onto the barstool beside Juli and pulled a linen handkerchief from his breast pocket. He used it to mop his brow before turning to Juli with a smile. "So, my enchanting ladies, what brings you to such an uncivilized establishment on this fine evening?"

The other six brothers dragged barstools over and arranged themselves in a circle around them, keeping a wary eye on Malcolm.

Phyllis lifted her drink and took a swallow, then beamed at Malcolm. "We're here trying to—"

"We're just here enjoying a drink," Juli said, kicking Phyllis again.

"Hey!" barked one of the men, rubbing his shin and glaring at Juli. "She just kicked me!"

Malcolm picked up his sherry with one hand and slapped his brother with the other. He took a sip of his drink.

"Apologize for your disrespect, Winchester," Malcolm said, taking a sip.

"But *she* kicked *me*."

Malcolm kicked the legs of his brother's barstool and sent the whole thing toppling backwards into a table. The table shattered, the barstool snapped in two, and Winchester's skull hit the floor with a thud.

Malcolm took another sip of his drink.

"Um…" Juli said, edging away from Malcolm as she glanced down at Winchester. "Is he going to be okay?"

Malcolm seemed not to hear her at first, absorbed as he was in his sherry.

"He's fine," declared one of the other brothers. Percy? Pierson? "He's got a steel plate in his head."

"Oh. Okay." Juli made a mental note not to say or do anything else to provoke Malcolm.

"So do you ladies enjoy literature?" Malcolm asked, taking another sip of his sherry. "Because I do so enjoy postmodern American poetry, particularly the Projectivists. So very avant-garde! You are American, right?"

"Um…" Juli said.

"Of course you are. As I was saying, I'm particularly fond of William Carlos Williams. *Paterson*—his modernist, epic collage of place—truly captures the essence of its locale while examining the role of the poet in American Society in the 1950s. Don't you agree?"

"Um…" Juli said.

"But of course, we mustn't forget the impact his tutelage had on other poets associated with the San Francisco Renaissance—obviously Williams's affiliation with Kenneth Rexroth impacted Rexroth's exploration of Japanese poetic forms and his deep fascination with transcendent love, wouldn't you agree?"

"Um…" Juli said.

"Want to see my boobs?" Phyllis asked.

Malcolm smiled and took another sip of his sherry. "Absolutely, my dear. But first, I'd love to hear your thoughts on ancient Greek lyric poetry."

———

A mile away and on another planet, Alex, Jake, and Cody were standing on the starboard deck of their former boss's cargo ship, trying to assess the situation.

"Are they unconscious?" Jake asked, staring at the two large men Cody was holding by the shirt collars with their feet dangling limply beneath them.

"Either that or faking it," Alex said. "I didn't think he'd hit them that hard."

"I didn't realize he was carrying a spatula," Jake muttered.

Alex sighed. "Cookie, you can go ahead and put them down now. Maybe you can tie them up while Jake and I check things out down below?"

Cody dropped the men in a heap on the deck. "Okay," he agreed. "You sure you guys don't need any help?"

Jake hefted his paintball gun and smiled. "We've got it covered. And we've got our map of the ship's layout. You stand guard and yell if you see anything odd."

Alex reached over to straighten Jake's ski mask for the hundredth time, positioning the eyeholes over his eyes instead of his mouth. "You really think the rainbow-striped ski mask is the best idea?"

Jake's grin widened between the blue and purple stripe. "We're outlaws. This is what outlaws wear."

"Right," Alex said. "You think the girls are okay?"

"Yeah. They're smart. They'll get out if things go bad."

"You notice if Juli took the urn with her?"

Jake shrugged. "Not sure. We can check the room when we get back."

"Okay, let's head below deck and get this over with."

Alex turned and started moving toward the stairs. He knew the layout of the ship like he'd come to know the freckle at the top of Juli's left breast. The boat was one of Kranston Shipping Company's most popular vessels, utilized for hauling lumber and machine parts and steel around the world. Now they just had to find the diamonds.

Alex moved down one set of steps and turned left, jogging down a long corridor before hitting another staircase. He could hear Jake panting behind him, but he kept going, eager to get the hell out of there fast. They'd seen no trace of the original crew, and Alex was trying hard not to think about it. He was having a tough time thinking at all, worried as he was about Phyllis and Juli's safety, wondering if they were okay, wishing like hell he hadn't let them go off alone like that. He thought about how beautiful Juli had looked, how many men would kill just for the chance to touch her. If anything happened…

"Down here, you think?" he called over his shoulder to Jake.

"That'd be my guess."

"Here, we'll try this door."

"You have the lock pick set?" Jake asked, breathless as he caught up to him.

Alex grasped the door handle and pulled. "Don't need it."

The two of them stepped into the cargo hold and blinked into the darkness. Alex fumbled on his tool belt for the flashlight and flicked it on, spreading a thick swath of yellow light across the yawning gulf of blackness. There was a musty smell in the air, something like wet cardboard and old seawater. He slid the beam along the wall and hit the light switch.

Alex was the first to see it. "What the—"

"Holy shit."

They both stood staring, not sure what to make of the cargo surrounding them from all sides of the room. Alex turned and surveyed the rest of the cargo bay, seeing more and more of the same.

They both stood blinking in the dusty air, trying to make sense of things.

Jake shook his head in disbelief. "I don't understand."

"But I thought we checked—"

"We confirmed it, Alex. We did. I just—"

"Are those really what I think they are?"

"Well what the hell else would they be?"

Jake took a step forward and reached out, but Alex pulled him back. "Wait. Don't touch anything. Not yet."

"But—"

Before either of them could argue further, they heard sounds above deck. A distinct hum, the rev of an engine. The thud of footsteps. A gunshot.

"Oh shit," Alex said, dropping Jake's arm. "They're back early."

"They can't be back yet," Jake hissed. "It's only been fifteen minutes. Phyllis looked too hot for them not to stay longer."

"Cody," Alex said, heading for the stairs. "We've got to make sure Cody's okay."

He sprinted out the door and headed down the

narrow hall, taking the stairs two at a time. He could hear Jake plodding behind him as the blood pounded in his ears. Alex rounded a corner and reached for the gun on his belt.

"That's not a paintball gun, is it?" Jake whispered behind him.

Alex stopped short, flattening himself against the wall on the other side of the deck where they'd left Cody. He braced himself to pounce.

"No. Not a paintball gun. Yours?"

Jake shook his head. Alex gripped the gun and peered slowly around the corner.

What he saw made his blood run cold. On the deck of the cargo ship, the two unconscious men were still tied motionless, back-to-back, their wrists pinned together with the strings from Cody's apron.

And in the distance, a cigarette boat was racing full speed toward the horizon, four hulking men silhouetted against the screaming orange sun.

Three men holding automatic weapons.

One very tall man with his arms behind his back.

"Jesus," Jake hissed.

"Cody," Alex said, and he took off running.

Chapter 14

"SO YOU AGREE DECONSTRUCTIONIST AND OTHER poststructuralist strategies toward the interpretation of New-American poetic dissidents are ultimately futile?" Malcolm asked, staring thoughtfully at Juli as he signaled the bartender for another sherry.

Juli leaned forward, fully engaged in the conversation with Malcolm now that she'd determined he was more interested in a theological discussion of literature than in allowing his brothers to gang rape them. Frankly, she was enjoying a little friendly, poetic banter with a rival pirate.

"I agree that literary works don't yield fixed, single meanings, but this effusion of philistine approaches to poetic deconstruction presents a challenge in the basic ideological notion that the social milieu implicit in the literary works are little more than an assessment of their relation to the pedagogy of Marxist interpretations."

"No shit," Phyllis said, taking another slurp of her drink as Blythe and Percy stared adoringly at her cleavage.

Juli glanced over at Phyllis, enjoying the sight of the older woman basking in more male attention than she'd probably seen in all her previous fifty-four years. Juli looked at her watch, surprised to see that more than an hour had passed since they'd entered the bar. Plenty of time for Alex and Jake and Cody to have conducted their spy mission.

She should probably begin wrapping up their discussion and making excuses to cut the evening short, but she was having such a lovely time. Besides, Malcolm's six brothers were so enraptured by the sight of Phyllis's décolletage, it seemed a shame to deprive them.

Suddenly, Alex burst through the door, his face ashen. His shirt was damp, and he was breathing like he'd just run to the bar from the other side of the island. Jake flew in behind him and doubled over, hands on his knees, his expression grim.

Juli jumped off her barstool, spilling her drink in the process. "Alex—Jake—what are you doing here?"

"There's a problem," Alex growled as he moved toward her. "We need to go."

Juli bit her lip and looked from Alex to Jake and back at Alex. Oh God, where was Cody? She gripped the edge of the bar as her knees started to give. Alex reached out and caught her elbow, holding her upright.

She opened her mouth to speak, but Malcolm beat her to it.

"A problem?" he asked, standing up beside Juli. "Perhaps I can be of assistance. Malcolm J. Forthwald III. Always a pleasure to meet an acquaintance of such lovely and charming ladies."

He extended his hand to Alex, who took it with an expression that was equal parts bewilderment and suspicion.

"Alex," he said as he shook Malcolm's hand. "Um, Juli—can I see you alone for a minute?"

"Well, yes," Juli stammered with a quick glance at Malcolm.

Malcolm set his drink on the bar and regarded Alex with a serious expression. "Sir, if I may, I can assure you that I completely understand any needs you may have for the utmost discretion, and perhaps my knowledge of this island and my familiarity with delicate business matters can help you in your—"

"It's Cody," Alex interrupted, looking at Juli. "Three thugs with automatic weapons just kidnapped Cody and took off in a cigarette boat."

"Oh, merciful heavens," Malcolm said and clucked disapprovingly. "Was the boat, by any chance, a thirty-six-foot Racing Gladiator with a rebuilt 750-horsepower Richie Zul engine and a Bravo One XR drive?"

Alex stared at him. Then he looked at Juli. She gave him a small nod. "It's okay," she whispered. "I trust him."

"Trust," Alex said. "Right." He looked at Malcolm. "I couldn't tell for certain, but that sounds right on the boat. Why?"

"Oh, dear." Malcolm turned to his brothers and began chattering rapidly in Bajan. Juli perked up, trying hard to eavesdrop without looking like she was eavesdropping. Alex caught her eye and gave her a questioning look.

"You two are okay?" Alex whispered.

Juli nodded. "We're fine. We don't need rescuing. But Cody—"

Malcolm turned back to them as his brothers lined up in a row behind him.

"Let us help," he said. "We're partly responsible, after all. The cigarette boat is ours—it was tied down right beside a boat we recently *acquired* in a routine business transaction. And if my hunch is correct, the formidable crew you speak of were captives who've apparently escaped our control and are now, obviously, wreaking havoc and committing unsavory acts."

"Captives?" Juli asked, feigning innocence. "You're a literary theologian and a thug, Malcolm?"

Malcolm waved his hand, dismissing the details. "Gentlemen who were crewing a ship we gained control of the other day. Purely business; we required the boat for other cargo. These hostages, they're friendly chaps—the original crew of the ship, you see. But they're certainly not the most intellectual specimens. Truly, I'm sorry for the inconvenience."

Phyllis frowned. "So let me get this straight, Malcolm. You stole a boat and took some hostages, but now the hostages have stolen *your* boat and taken Cody as *their* hostage?"

Malcolm looked thoughtful. "Yes, that does sound correct, my dear."

Jake tucked his ski mask in his pocket and gave Phyllis a warning look. "Alex and I were just out for a stroll down by the harbor when we saw Cody being kidnapped. Isn't that right, Alex?"

Alex didn't reply. His eyes were on Juli, his expression guarded. "There's a note," he said and reached into his back pocket. Juli saw his hand shake as he unfolded it and held it out.

"May I?" Malcolm asked, extending his hand. Alex looked at Juli again, and she nodded.

He handed him the note, and Juli peered over Malcolm's shoulder.

"'Dear Pirates,'" she read. "'We borrowed you're boat—'" She stopped and threw up her hands in exasperation. "God, I hate that, don't you? The contraction for 'you are' is misused so often it just makes me want to scream!"

"Indeed!" Malcolm agreed. "Truly, this abuse of the English language is an atrocity of the highest magnitude."

"Focus, guys," Alex said, tapping the corner of the note.

Juli grabbed the note and kept reading: "'We borrowed you're boat, and we borrowed you're guy. Just let us get away fast and we'll send you're guy back tomorrow with you're boat. If you come after us, we'll—'" Juli scrunched up her face. "What is that word there?"

Alex closed his eyes. "I believe that's supposed to be 'torture.'"

"Spelled with a *ch*?" Malcolm said, aghast. "Honestly, I don't understand this lack of education in—" He stopped and looked at Juli. "You've gone very pale, my dear."

"Cody," she whispered and looked at the note again. "Someone would torture Cody?"

Alex gritted his teeth. Juli saw a tiny muscle twitch at the corner of his eye.

"It appears that way," he said.

"We have to get him back." Her voice sounded very small to her.

Malcolm nodded once, then turned to his brothers and gave two sharp claps.

"Blythe, Percy, Winchester, Prescott, Pierson, Phillip, shall we see what we can do to be of service to our new friends?"

The six brothers were still staring at Phyllis's legs. Malcolm sighed, then sucker punched Percy in the gut.

"Gentlemen?"

"Yes, Malcolm," they murmured and bowed their heads.

Alex just stared, words failing him. Juli gave him a guarded smile and touched his arm.

"Honor among thieves, right?" she said.

Alex closed his eyes and shook his head. "This was really not part of the plan."

Alex was trying hard to understand what was going on. Apparently, Juli's new pirate friend was more interested in literature and chivalrous conduct than in acquiring prostitutes or pondering the technicalities of illegal activity.

"He doesn't know we're pirates," Juli pointed out back at the hotel room as she and Phyllis hastily swapped out their hooker garb for more practical attire. "For all he knows, we're just hapless vacationers whose friend has been kidnapped."

Phyllis was hunched over her laptop, alternately tapping at keys and wriggling out of her bustier. Alex wasn't entirely sure what she was looking for online, but it seemed important that he keep his eyes averted as she undressed.

Jake, on the other hand, offered no such courtesy.

"You need any help with those little hook things, Phyllis?"

Alex sighed. He had bigger things to worry about than Phyllis's privacy. Like where the hell those guys were taking Cody. And how the hell he might go about getting him back. And whether Cody's kidnappers had a clue their new hostage was a former employee of Kranston Shipping—the same company that wrote *their* paychecks.

"Are you sure Malcolm is trustworthy?" he asked Juli, ducking as she flung her bra across the room and began tossing clothing out of her knapsack.

He watched as she pulled out the urn and set it on the nightstand before reaching back into her bag to continue flinging clothing. She yanked a pale blue tank top over her head and wriggled her arms through the holes before turning to give him an incredulous look. "Define trustworthy," she said. "I don't think he'd hurt us, but he is a pirate. He's probably missing a few scruples, but isn't that exactly why we need him?"

Jake looked up from where he was chivalrously assisting Phyllis with the zipper on her thigh-high boot. "We sure as hell need his boat and his firepower. Where else are we going to get a go-fast boat on short notice?"

"Or the ability to clear customs with no questions asked," Phyllis added. "Which is something Malcolm seems to have."

Alex sighed. They had him there. Wherever the hell those guys were taking Cody, they could get there about three times faster in their cigarette boat than Alex and the crew could possibly move in the fifty-three-foot powerboat.

Not that they had any idea where they were going. The thugs in the cigarette boat had been headed north–northwest when he and Jake had lost sight of them, but they could be anywhere by now. Lucky for them, Malcolm was willing to provide a boat and assistance slipping into foreign harbors with minimal hassle. Trustworthy or not, Malcolm and his brothers were good allies to have right then.

Alex couldn't stop checking his watch. Couldn't stop

blaming himself. Twenty minutes. Cody had been gone twenty minutes. They could be anywhere by now.

"Ohmygod! Check this out!" Phyllis shrieked, buttoning up her blouse with one hand as she scrolled through something on her laptop with the other.

Phyllis finished buttoning and turned the laptop screen toward Alex. "I've been monitoring communications since the boat was seized yesterday, and there hasn't been anything at all about the hijacking. Not a word, which seems weird since he would have gotten the ShipSafe alert too. But look what came through just a few minutes ago."

Alex stared. It was a simple e-mail, vague enough to sound like correspondence conducted through the normal course of business. But to Phyllis, Alex, and Jake — who'd spent the last twenty years reading between the lines in Tom Portelli's communications — it was clear the hijacked crew had gotten in touch with him. The same guys who now had Cody were communicating with Portelli, and now they were set to rendezvous.

"St. Lucia," Alex said, snatching a map off the counter. "Makes sense. It's the closest neighboring island."

Jake nodded, already penciling it out on a chart. "It's one hundred miles due west. They've still got a half-hour head start, but we can make it in under two hours if we take Malcolm's cigarette boat."

"Malcolm's not just loaning us the boat, right?" Juli asked. "I mean, he's going with us?"

"They want their stolen boat back," Alex said. "I'm sure they'll want to be there to reclaim it from the guys who took it."

"So how many people can fit in one of those little cigarette boats?" Juli asked.

"There's only room for four or five people, and I'm sure Malcolm will want at least one or two of his brothers along," Alex said.

Phyllis frowned. "Shouldn't someone stay here in case Cody's kidnappers try to contact us for ransom or something?"

They all stared at each other. Jake was the first to speak. "Alex, you and Juli should go. Phyllis and I will stay here in case Cody gets in touch."

Alex scratched his chin, not sure that was the best plan. "Well—"

"He's right," Phyllis said. "Malcolm loves Juli; she needs to go. It'll keep him in line. And at least one of you boys needs to be on that boat, and one needs to stay here."

"And someone needs to be here to make sure the cargo ship doesn't disappear before we figure out what's going on," Jake added. "Maybe we can even get back on board while you're gone, get a closer look at that cargo. Maybe see if you and I missed something the first time through."

Alex looked at Juli. She'd been terrified of the water less than a week ago. Now she was getting dragged out into the open ocean in a cigarette boat. Could she really handle that?

Juli looked up at him and offered a weak smile. Alex cleared his throat. "Juli? You all right with this?"

Juli's eyes were wide and a little fearful, but she nodded. "Got any ginger?"

He tossed her a bag, and Juli caught it with one hand—a hand, Alex noticed, over which she'd already slipped her seasick bands. She was ready.

"Do I have time to pee?" she asked.

Alex nodded and watched as she disappeared around the corner and into the bathroom. The second she locked the door behind her, he picked up the urn.

"Alex, no!" Phyllis hissed. "Not now."

Jake glanced in the direction Juli had vanished, then back at Alex. "Do it quick."

Alex hesitated. Was it wrong to invade her privacy? Not to trust her after how much they'd shared?

"Hurry," Jake urged. "Just a quick peek inside. Then we'll know if she's hiding something."

Alex shook his head. "No." He started to set the urn back on the nightstand. Then he picked it up again, studying it.

"Oh, give it to me," Jake snapped, marching over and snatching it from his hand.

"Jake, wait—"

With a quick flick of his thumb, Jake popped the lever on the bottom. The top of the urn flipped open and Jake squinted inside.

Alex held his breath.

"Son of a bitch," Jake said.

"What?" Phyllis asked. "What is it?"

Alex heard the water running in the bathroom and felt his heart speed up. He looked at the door, then back at Jake. "What is it?"

Jake closed the lid and set the urn back on the nightstand. "Cremated remains."

Alex felt his chest tighten. "You sure?"

Jake nodded and stepped back. "I'm sure. Looks just like what spilled out of my grandma's urn when my brother and I knocked it over playing football in the house last Thanksgiving."

Alex nodded, not sure whether to feel disappointed, relieved, or just plain guilty over snooping. He *wanted* to trust her, he really did. But still—

Juli came rushing out of the bathroom drying her hands on the leg of her capris. "Ready?" she asked, looking at Alex. When he didn't respond right away, she looked at Jake, then Phyllis. "What? Is something going on?"

"Nothing," Alex said. "Just worried about Cody."

"Uncle Frank," Juli said and scooped up the urn.

Alex stole a glance at it to make sure they hadn't left the lid off, but everything looked just like it had before. "You're not bringing that, are you?"

"I have to. I can't just leave him here. It's my job to look after him."

Alex sighed as Juli stuffed the urn into her knapsack. "Let's go then."

———⁓———

Alex seemed edgy on the boat ride to St. Lucia. Juli tried several times to talk to him, but the noise of the boat and the darkness of his mood made it impossible. It was just as well, since she had plenty of her own dark thoughts to contend with. Where was Cody? Had he been hurt?

The second they hit St. Lucia, Malcolm and the two brothers he'd brought along hustled off to deal with customs officials. Alex hopped out of the boat and turned to offer Juli a hand up. She took it, annoyed with herself for feeling light-headed at his touch even now with Cody in trouble and their mission in shambles.

Once she was standing on the pier beside him, she

took a deep breath. "So the owner of the cargo ship is meeting these guys in St. Lucia?" she asked. "That's what Phyllis said, right?"

Alex nodded. "There wasn't a lot of info, but he has access to a private jet. He should be there in a couple hours. They're meeting at the airport."

"And what about the cargo on the boat—the stuff you guys were after in the first place?"

Alex's expression darkened. "Let's just say things weren't quite what we expected," he said stiffly.

"What do you mean?"

Alex looked out at the ocean, not meeting her eyes. "Cody was taken before we really got a chance to assess the situation, but there may have been a misunderstanding."

"Oh. Not a good one?"

"No," Alex said, looking grim. "Not a good one."

"So what did you—"

"Could we maybe not talk about this right now? It's just—I haven't really had a chance to digest things."

Juli took a step back, trying not to feel stung. What did she expect, really? Alex still wasn't willing to lay all his cards on the table. He didn't trust her, probably never would.

She was spared the need to say anything more as Malcolm and his brothers rejoined them at the ocean's edge.

"Your friend, he's a big guy?" Malcolm asked.

"Huge," Alex said. "Former NFL tight end."

"The gentlemen at customs may have seen him, but they didn't notice which way they went."

Alex glanced at his watch. "Should we split up and look for them? We've got two hours before they're scheduled to meet up with their boss. They couldn't have gone too far."

Malcolm nodded. "Juli and I will venture inland, toward the south. You and Phillip and Percy can try the north."

Alex shook his head and took a step closer to Juli. "She'll go with me. We work best as a team."

Juli felt an odd flutter in her belly, and she couldn't be sure if it was joy at Alex's protectiveness, or the sheer pleasure of having him so close.

Or possibly a little terror. Okay, a lot of terror.

Malcolm stared him down for a moment before nodding. "Fine. We meet back here in one hour. You have protection?"

Alex gave an almost imperceptible nod, and Juli felt the hair prickle on her arms. She was pretty sure they weren't talking about safe sex.

"Okay then," Percy said. "Back here at 7:00 p.m."

The three brothers turned around and stalked away, not once looking over their shoulders as they retreated to the far end of the dock.

"Let's go," Alex said and turned away.

Juli hurried to keep up, and they walked in silence for a few moments. She kept an eye out for Cody, noticing every figure, every movement around them. They passed a funky little bar with a terrible sound system blaring reggae music into the street, and Juli peered inside, hoping for a glimpse of Cody.

Nothing.

They kept walking, checking out a bakery, a roadside stand selling T-shirts, and a kiosk hawking timeshares.

Still no sign of Cody.

Juli bit her lip and looked up at Alex. He was scowling. "You think he's okay?" she asked.

"Yes. I have to believe that."

"What if—"

"Don't," Alex said, halting his steps to turn and look at her. "We can't even think that way."

Juli stopped too, taken aback by the intensity in his eyes.

"Sorry. I won't. Cody's fine. He's probably teaching his captors to make a spicy Creole remoulade as we speak."

"That's the spirit," Alex said and started walking again.

Juli wasn't sure how long they'd been searching when they heard raised voices coming through the cracked window of a ground-floor room at a cheap hotel. She and Alex froze in their tracks and looked at each other. The voices continued, louder this time.

"You just ate the last spring roll, asshole!" someone shouted.

"Yeah, we ordered enough for everyone to have three and that was your fourth. I saw it!"

Alex raised an eyebrow at Juli, ready to keep walking, but she shushed him. Then they heard another voice inside the room.

"But you guys, the sauce is really good! It's just the right blend of lemon and ginger, with the little flecks of zest in there."

Juli gasped. Alex made a fist.

"Cody," he mouthed.

"Shit," she mouthed back, stepping closer to the window, trying to keep her head down. Alex joined her, his arm brushing her rib cage as they crouched together.

"What do we do?" she whispered.

"I don't know yet."

They were both silent again, listening to the voices on the other side of the grimy window.

"All the breadfruit custard is gone too!" someone complained. "Dammit, I told you we didn't need a hostage. Especially one who eats like this."

"Of course we needed a hostage, Todd," another voice shot back. "You have to have a hostage if you're stealing a boat. Duh! That's just how it works."

"Give me those noodles!" shouted a third voice, definitely too high to be Cody.

"Seriously, don't you think those pirates are going to be mad we took their guy?"

"We needed him to drive the cigarette boat back to them after we meet up with the boss," reasoned a man with a bullfrog voice. "We were being helpful. Thinking ahead. Don't we get, like, pirate points for that?"

"I get to drive the boat?" Cody asked, clearly delighted. "Awesome! I've never driven one of those fast boats before. Can I have some more sauce?"

Juli moved below the window and slid up the wall, trying to get a peek inside the room. She squinted into the dim interior, spotting three strange men, two machine guns, Cody, and about eighteen takeout containers. She slid back down the wall.

"*Guns?*" Alex whispered.

Juli nodded, holding up two fingers. Alex grimaced. "How many guys?"

"Three, plus Cody, all of them sitting on the floor eating," she whispered back. "Apparently everyone's confused about who's who. I don't think they know who Cody is, and Cody doesn't seem to know who they are. They're all just sitting there glaring at each other."

The voices continued inside, sounding increasingly agitated.

"What, the rest of the pirates never let you drive the boat before, big guy?" shouted the man with the bullfrog voice, responding to Cody's last statement.

"Well sure, but we had a big powerboat," Cody said. "Not one of those little fast things."

"You jerks were in a cigarette boat when you hijacked our ship," Bullfrog argued. "That's not a big boat at all."

"We didn't hijack your boat," Cody said with exaggerated patience.

"Well, stole it then. Whatever you call it."

"We *didn't* steal it," Cody insisted. "We were just going to take some stuff onboard, but not the boat. We were going to leave that with you guys."

"Well then why the hell did you steal the boat?" Bullfrog asked, clearly angry now.

"We *didn't* steal the boat! We didn't even make it to the boat before the pirates got it."

"I thought you said you *were* a pirate. You were on the goddamn boat!"

"I *am* a pirate," Cody said, his voice now equally agitated. "But I'm a good pirate. The ones who stole your boat were the bad pirates."

"What the hell are you talking about?"

Cody sighed loudly. "We're pirates now, but we used to work for Kranston too. Just like you guys. I don't know who the bad pirates are, but they didn't work for Kranston. And we didn't steal your boat."

"This guy is crazy," Bullfrog said. "Pirates who work for Kranston. What a crock of shit!"

There was a loud whacking sound inside the room. Juli looked at Alex, alarmed.

Smack!

"Ouch! Dammit, he did it again."

Smack!

"That's it," Bullfrog said. "I told you the last time—"

"Hey, give me back my spatula," Cody said.

Alex put his head against the wall, looking pained. Juli stretched up again, trying to catch another glimpse through the window. Alex yanked her back down.

"I've got a better idea," he whispered. "Come on."

He tugged her by the arm, leading her to the crooked front door coated with six shades of peeling paint. He paused for a moment, composing himself. Then he knocked.

"What the hell?" someone inside yelled.

"Don't answer it! It might be the pirates!"

Alex shook his head and knocked again. The door flew open and one man peered around the edge of it, looking alarmed.

"Hello, boys," Alex said, shouldering the door open wider and pushing his way inside.

Juli saw his hand go to the middle of his back where she'd watched him tuck the pistol. She sucked in her breath. If she'd been Catholic, she would have crossed herself. Instead, she stepped inside the room behind Alex.

"A word with you, if I may?" Alex asked, and he kicked the door closed behind them.

Chapter 15

"SO HERE'S THE THING, BOYS," ALEX SAID, LEAVING HIS gun tucked in the back of his pants for now and raising his hands in his best impression of a harmless guy. "I know who you are. You're the crew of the Kranston cargo ship that got hijacked yesterday. And I also know you've just stolen a cigarette boat and taken a hostage. That doesn't make you any better than the pirates, now does it?"

Alex watched as two of the men shook their heads in shame and looked at the floor, blanching a little at his words.

Good, he thought. *That's good. A little guilt could be a powerful weapon.*

A third man frowned, looking confused. Fortunately, none of them were looking at their guns. That was a positive sign.

Cody opened his mouth to say something, but Alex shot him a warning look. The last thing he needed was Cody revealing too much.

"But they started it!" one of the men protested. "Those pirates who stole our cargo ship—they started the whole thing, I swear!"

"I know, I know," Alex said, holding up his hands again. "But see, they're real pirates. Bloodthirsty ones. And you stole their cigarette boat. They don't take kindly to that. In fact, they're very angry."

At that, all three men turned pale. Alex continued, edging almost imperceptibly between one of the men and his automatic weapon. For now, they seemed uninterested in violence, but Alex wasn't taking any chances.

"Who are you?" one of the men asked. "Are you one of the bad pirates?"

Alex ignored him, focusing on the basics, on keeping his voice calm. "Here's the thing. The bad pirates are pretty upset about the boat and the hostage. But I know you're due to meet Tom Portelli in less than an hour."

At that, all three men looked startled. From the corner of his eye, he saw Juli's eyes widen.

"Hey, that's how I know you!" one of the guys said. "Aren't you like a VP or something for Kranston Shipping?"

"That's right!" another guy chimed. "His picture's in the company newsletter all the time. He's a real big shot."

Alex tried not to react to the words, but he could feel Juli's eyes boring into him.

"Forget about me," Alex said, folding his arms over his chest. "You guys just need to get out of here alive, hop on that private jet of Portelli's, and get the hell out of here, right? You don't need a hostage. And you sure as hell don't need a bunch of angry pirates slitting your throats when you're almost home free, do you?"

Three heads shook side to side, their expressions grim. From what Alex could tell, he was dealing with stupid here, as opposed to violent. Not that stupid wasn't every bit as dangerous, but if he handled this right—

"The, um, pirates," one man said, swallowing hard. "They're here?"

"They followed you," Alex said. "They came all the

way to St. Lucia to get you. They're very angry, and they're looking for you right now. As a matter of fact, we're helping them look."

One of the men sat down hard on the bed and pulled his knees to his chest, rocking back and forth. Another gave a pitiful whimper and covered his eyes.

Alex glanced at Juli and quirked an eyebrow at her. She took her cue and nodded gravely.

"Should I call the pirates now and let them know we've found the guys who stole their boat?" she asked Alex.

"And stole their man," Alex said. "Don't forget that."

"You're right," Juli agreed. "They were pretty mad about that part."

"But he wasn't even their guy," one of the men protested. "He just told us he wasn't really one of them."

"Who's fault is that, *Todd*?" one of the guys muttered. "I told you we didn't need a hostage. You couldn't even get the right guy, stupid."

"Who are you calling stupid, stupid?"

"You, stupid. You're a big, *stupid*—"

Alex turned to Juli. "Make the call," he said loudly enough for the men to hear.

Juli, who didn't even have a cell phone that Alex knew of, began rummaging through her bag. Alex suppressed a smile as he watched her hair fall forward, framing her face as she focused on playing her role.

"No, wait!" one of the guys interrupted. "See, we took Cody here so he could bring the boat back to the pirates after we escaped. We were helping. Honest!"

Juli looked up and shook her head sadly. "I don't think the pirates will see it that way, do you?"

Alex sighed. "No. I don't."

"Please!" Todd said, falling to his knees in front of Alex. "You've got to help us. Don't call the pirates."

"Here's what I'm thinking," Alex said, and Juli stopped rummaging. "You give us the hostage. No hassles, no guns, no violence. We go back and tell the bloodthirsty pirates we've already killed you—"

"But—"

"We won't *really* kill you," Alex said. "We'll let you continue on your merry way to meet the boss. We'll call the pirates off, and you can jump on that plane, sip champagne, and forget this whole thing ever happened."

The three of them frowned, clearly trying to figure out how they were being trapped.

"Or I could just call the pirates," Juli offered helpfully, digging in her bag again.

"Here, take him," one of the guys said, giving Cody a nudge toward them as he stepped back. "We don't want him anyway. He eats too much."

"Hey—" Cody started to protest, but Alex grabbed his arm and yanked him closer.

The man named Todd frowned at them. "So you'll make sure the pirates don't kill us. You'll tell them, um, you took care of things already?"

"We'll tell them we butchered you in cold blood and left your corpses to rot in an alley," Juli said cheerfully. "They'll be happy to hear it."

Cody looked at Alex. "You have a gun, right?"

"Well—"

"Use it to get my spatula back from these guys before we leave, okay?"

None of them spoke as they walked away from the hotel room, their pace as brisk as they could manage without actually running. Since Cody and Alex both had a good twelve inches on her, Juli was practically running just to keep up.

As soon as they were out of earshot, Cody was the first to speak.

"That was so cool! How did you guys know where I was? That was the coolest thing, really, really cool!"

"Our first rescue mission," Juli agreed. "Nice job, Pirate Alex."

Alex grinned and looked down at her. "You weren't so bad yourself. Now we just have to find Malcolm and the rest of the guys."

Juli glanced at her watch. "You're right—we only have two minutes before we're supposed to meet the pirates."

Cody paled and stopped walking. "You mean the pirates are really here?"

"They're really here, but they were helping us find you," Alex said. "And their boat, of course."

"And they're really not bloodthirsty," Juli added. "Much."

Cody frowned, then started walking again. "So now what?"

"Well, I guess we head back to Barbados," Alex said.

"The cargo ship?" Cody asked hopefully.

Alex frowned. "Things weren't quite what we expected. Jake and I didn't have much time to look before you were kidnapped, but I think there was a misunderstanding about the cargo."

"Misunderstanding?" Cody repeated.

"The cargo we expected wasn't there."

"Oh." Cody frowned and glanced at Juli before looking back at Alex. "That doesn't sound very good."

"No. It's not good at all."

Cody looked like he might be on the verge of tears, and Juli saw Alex give him a sympathetic pat on the back.

"It'll be okay," Alex said. "The five of us can regroup once we're all back in the hotel room. Maybe figure out our next move."

Juli watched the exchange in silence, trying to decide whether to feel disappointed about the unknown cargo or hopeful they were considering her a part of whatever came next. Alex had said *five*. That meant she was included.

As they approached the meeting spot, Juli spotted Malcolm barking orders at his two brothers.

"Right there! On the other side, next to the flat box. No, not that one, the other one. Good!"

"Um, Malcolm?" Juli asked, stepping beside him. "What's going on? Why are the boats full of boxes?"

Malcolm turned and grasped her hand. "My dear. There's been a change in plans. We had the opportunity to procure some rather valuable cargo on short notice. There's a certain urgency involved in transporting it from the area as hastily as possible, you see."

"I see," Juli said, not seeing at all.

"Hey, Malcolm," Phillip called. "If there are a dozen books in each of these four boxes, can't we just consolidate them into these other two and split them up between the boats?"

Malcolm scowled. "No, you can't reorganize them! The first editions are in those boxes, and the ones over there have autographed copies! They're already alphabetized and organized by genre as well."

Alex poked at one of the boxes with his toe, then raised an eyebrow at Malcolm. "You boosted a rare bookstore?"

Malcolm sighed. "Boosted is such a gauche word." He turned his attention back to Juli and to the hand he was still grasping. "So you see, we really must go quickly, my dear," he said. "And there really won't be room for all of us, but we've taken the liberty of securing a luxury hotel room here on the island for your friends, Alex and young Cody."

He pressed a key into Alex's hand and smiled. "You gentlemen can go freshen up and nap for a few hours, and we'll be back bright and early in the morning to pick you up, along with the rest of our cargo."

"Gentlemen?" Juli asked, feeling alarmed. "What do you mean?"

"There's only room for four now, my dear," Malcolm said, smiling at her. "Phillip and Percy will take one boat, and you and I will take the other. We'll come back for your friends in the morning."

Juli opened her mouth to speak, but Alex got there first.

"No way. Sorry, Malcolm, I appreciate your help getting Cody back, but Juli stays with us. Not negotiable."

Malcolm pressed his lips into a thin line, and for a moment, Juli feared he was on the brink of throwing a punch. Alex folded his arms over his chest, nowhere near backing down.

Juli stepped in front of Alex just in case. "It's okay, Malcolm, really. The three of us will stay here and wait together. It's already dark now, anyway. Alex and Cody and I will just go to the room and get some sleep and see you here in the morning."

Cody frowned down at her, then looked at Malcolm. "But I have to get back. My herb garden needs to be watered, and I have a pork loin marinating. It needs to be turned."

Juli looked at Cody. "It's just a few more hours. We can all return to Barbados together in the morning when they come back for us. Your meat and herbs will be fine."

Malcolm shrugged and glanced at his watch. "We have room for a fourth, but you must make your decision quickly," he said. "We simply can't delay any longer. We certainly would appreciate young Cody's strength in off-loading the cargo, of course. And we could use some extra hands with the makeover I mentioned earlier."

Cody's face brightened. "A makeover?"

"A boat makeover," Malcolm clarified. "We've recently acquired a rather sizeable cargo ship that requires a very different look."

Juli looked at Alex, who was watching Malcolm, Phillip, and Percy with guarded interest. Then he turned to Cody, motioning him aside.

"Cody, can I talk to you for just a sec?"

Juli watched as the two men moved to the edge of the dock and bent their heads together, conferring quietly as Malcolm checked his watch again. When Alex and Cody rejoined them, Cody was beaming.

"I'm going with you guys for the makeover," Cody said, bending down and hefting the remaining boxes in one hand. "Maybe later I can have a tour of the galley on your new cargo ship? I heard it has four ovens and a gas stove with eight burners."

Malcolm studied Cody with interest, then nodded to Juli and Alex. Smiling at Cody, he gestured to a seat in the second cigarette boat and stepped around to the other side.

"Why yes, son. That's true. Tell me, how do you feel about Aristotle's *Poetics* with respect to the concepts of mimesis and catharsis and the notion that poetry is imitative and secondary?"

"What the hell was that?" Juli demanded as soon as the boats had pulled away. "I can't believe you just let Cody go with them alone like that! Are you nuts?"

Alex turned and looked at her, beautiful in her fury, and momentarily forgot what she was saying.

"What?" she demanded as she blew an unruly curl out of her eye. "What are you looking at?"

"Nothing," he said, regrouping. "I let Cody go with them so we can keep tabs on the cargo ship. I wasn't worried about it disappearing without Malcolm around, but once he's back in Barbados, anything can happen. Jake and Phyllis should have an extra set of hands to help keep an eye on things until you and I get there."

Juli gave him a dubious look. "So you sent Cody as a spy?"

"Should I have sent you instead?" Alex asked, folding his arms over his chest. "All alone, with two boatloads of actual pirates?"

Juli scowled at him. "I can handle myself."

"I'm sure you can. I'd prefer it if Malcolm and his brothers don't handle you as well, which is why I didn't want you alone with them."

"You really think Cody can be a spy?"

"He's smarter than you'd guess. Come on," he said,

nodding toward town. "I'm starving, so I know you have to be completely famished, considering how much you like food."

Juli shrugged. "How about that burger place up the hill? The one with the 'all-you-can-eat onion rings.'"

"Works for me."

Alex started up the hill, conscious of his need to slow his steps so she could keep up. She was panting a little beside him and he tried not to notice the way her breasts rose and fell beneath her thin tank top.

"That was pretty cool how you rescued Cody," she said. "How did you know you could pull that off?"

Alex shrugged and looked down at her. "I didn't. But I could tell right away they were just a bunch of dumb, scared kids more interested in getting the hell out of here than in hurting anyone."

"Ballsy," Juli muttered appreciatively. "Almost as ballsy as trying to rob a cargo boat owned by the largest shipping company in the world. A company that happens to be your former employer?"

Alex winced. "I was hoping maybe you missed that part."

"I don't miss much," Juli said. "So you were a VP for Kranston?"

"Can we not talk about this?"

She laughed. "You guys did a pretty good job hiding the details from me, but I figured it was something like that. Did you work for Kranston long?"

"Really, let's talk about something else."

"You know the owner well?"

"Here we are at the restaurant," Alex said. He stopped and held the door open for her. "So sorry we won't be able to continue the conversation. Would you like a booth or a table?"

Juli rolled her eyes. "I'd like the bathroom, right now. Order for me, okay?"

"What do you want?" he shouted at her retreating back.

"Everything," she shouted back. "In the biggest quantities I can get it."

Alex watched her disappear down a darkened hallway, admiring the curve of her hips. He'd probably have to talk with her about the Kranston thing, but not yet. Not until they both had some food in them and their heads on straight.

He surveyed the dimly lit room in search of an empty table. He found a nice booth in the back corner and ambled over to it, grabbing a menu from the counter on his way.

"Someone will be right over to get your order, hon," called a waitress with a gravelly voice and a giant snake tattoo on her arm. "Need anything to drink?"

"Two waters for now, thanks," Alex said as he dropped into the booth.

He studied the menu for a second, watching for Juli out of the corner of his eye. Funny how quickly she'd gone from an inconvenient distraction to someone who laid claim to at least one out of every three thoughts he had. And he'd known her only four days.

True, there'd been a marriage in there, and a pirate heist, and some of the hottest near-miss hookups in his entire life—just the things to bond two people together. And now they would spend the better part of a night together alone in a hotel room.

He wasn't sure what to think of that.

Of course, at the moment, he really shouldn't think

about that at all. This mission was far from over. They still had to get back to the cargo ship. They still had to figure out what happened to the diamonds—if they ever existed at all. He was still broke, still unemployed, still a total loser.

Just like Jenny said you'd be.

Not to mention he was falling hard for a woman he wasn't sure he trusted. He wanted to trust her—*God knows he did*—but something was holding him back. What was it about Juli? Okay, so there hadn't been anything nefarious in the urn. She still hadn't told him about her mobster uncle and had only shared the genius thing under duress. What else was she hiding?

A waitress wandered over, order pad in hand, and Alex set his menu down.

"I'd like everything on the appetizer menu, to start with," Alex said. "We'll get back to you on the rest."

The waitress frowned. "Everything? There are ten items. You're expecting a large group?"

"My friend likes food. A lot."

"I see," the woman said, and scribbled something on her notepad.

Alex stood up. "Can you tell me where the restrooms are?"

"Down that hall, out the back door, in the little alley right outside the restaurant. Men's room is the second one on the left. The one without a door."

"Thanks," Alex said. "If you see a cute blonde wandering around, point her to this table and give her some crackers or something. Otherwise, she may start eating furniture."

The waitress nodded, and Alex made his way down the hall and out the back door. He smiled a little to himself as he heard Juli's perky soprano coming from the women's room, humming an off-key version of Jimmy Buffet's "Cheeseburger in Paradise."

Alex stepped into the men's room and froze. The hair on his arms stood on end.

A pistol was pointed straight at his chest.

And holding it was his old boss, Tom Portelli.

"Hello, Alex," Tom said, flashing a familiar smile as he leveled the gun at him. "Good to see you again, son. I hear you tried to rob my fucking boat."

Alex closed his eyes and raised his hands over his head.

Next door, the humming went on undaunted.

Chapter 16

"COME IN REAL SLOWLY AND CLOSE THE DOOR BEHIND you," Tom said, holding the pistol at Alex's chest.

A light Caribbean breeze ruffled Tom Portelli's white hair, giving him the comical look of a man with wings on the side of his head.

It was the only thing comical about the moment.

"There's no door, Tom," Alex replied, keeping his voice even. "Would you like to try the women's room? I'm sure there's plenty of privacy there."

Tom narrowed his eyes. "Don't get smart with me, boy. Move in here where I can see you. Over there, next to the urinals. And don't try anything stupid."

"May I pee?"

Tom frowned, clearly unsure whether that was allowed in a hostage situation. Alex didn't wait for a response, though his mind was racing a million miles an hour. He'd stood shoulder to shoulder with the man at countless board meetings and company urinals for twenty years. Somehow, this wasn't how he'd pictured the future of this business relationship.

Alex unzipped as Tom angled away from the door, ensuring no passersby would have a glimpse of any of the proceedings inside the cramped space.

Alex glanced over at him, hoping like hell Juli had found her way safely to the table and was peacefully devouring her onion rings. He couldn't hear her humming anymore, so the odds were good.

Then he froze. Juli?

She couldn't be behind this. But she had picked the restaurant, and now here he was with a gun pointed at his back—

Tom leaned casually against the wall as though he pointed pistols at pissing men on a daily basis. "So Alex," he began. "I was wondering where you and the rest of the gang had gone after the layoff. Seemed like you just dropped off the face of the earth. Now I know. Sounds like Cody shared a few choice details with my boys from the cargo ship."

Alex swallowed his thoughts of Juli and zipped up his fly. He turned to face Tom with his heart slamming hard against his rib cage. "What is it you think you know, Tom?" he asked, wondering what would happen if he went for the gun tucked under his shirt in the back of his pants.

A shootout in a Caribbean bathroom, he thought grimly. *What a way to go.*

"What I think is that you tried to fuck me over," Tom snarled. "I don't appreciate that."

"No? I didn't particularly appreciate losing the pension I'd spent twenty years building. Call it even."

Tom's eyes narrowed. "Where's my goddamn boat, Alex?"

He laughed. "Not here. In case your boys left out a few details in their telling of the tale, someone else beat us to the punch."

"I know it's in Barbados. ShipSafe alerted me, of course, and my crew told me about the hijacking. I was merely hoping you'd cooperate in helping me get it back. Now that I see you're not in a cooperative mood, I'm frankly more interested in revenge."

Alex took a step back as Tom straightened his arm, leveling the gun. Alex felt everything in his body tense as the breath left his lungs.

There was no choice.

In one quick motion, Alex slid a hand to his back, reaching for the pistol. His heart was hammering loudly in his ears.

Or was that footsteps?

"Hey, there! How's it going?"

Both men whirled around and stared. There in the doorway, with her blonde curls fluttering around her ears and an angelic smile on her face, was Juli.

She stuck her hands in her back pockets and grinned into the men's room, leaning back a little. Her cheeks were rosy in the moonlight, and her expression was one of unfathomable perkiness. Alex felt his heart twist in his chest. He opened his mouth to speak—to tell her to get the hell out of there, to ask her if she had something to do with this—but Juli beat him to the punch.

"Tom! I haven't seen you for ages," she chirped. "How are you? How's Ginny and Fran?"

There was a moment of silence as Alex stood there dumbfounded, his fingers frozen on the handle of his pistol. He didn't speak. He didn't breathe. He stared at Tom's profile, wondering what the hell was going on.

Tom blinked at Juli. Then blinked again. His eyes closed for an extra half second, like he hoped she might be gone when he opened them again.

Then he cleared his throat. "Ju-Ju," Tom said. "My God, what are you doing here?"

"Oh, you know. Working on my tan, doing some sightseeing, relaxing on the beach, tossing Uncle Frank's remains into the ocean."

Tom swallowed, his gun still trained on Alex's chest, his torso turned toward Juli.

Juli, for her part, was doing a damn fine job of pretending not to see the gun.

Shit, Alex realized suddenly. She really *couldn't* see it. She couldn't see *him*. From where she was standing in the alley, she could probably see only the first couple feet of the men's room and the first couple feet of the women's room. She couldn't see him at all. Alex closed his eyes and breathed deeply.

Maybe that was best. Assuming she hadn't set this whole thing up, she might just go quietly without trying to be the hero, without getting hurt.

But how the hell did she know Tom Portelli?

"I was so sorry to hear about Frankie," Tom continued solemnly, taking a step to the left, ensuring he completely blocked Juli's view into the restroom. "You know Frank's been like a brother to me all these years."

"I know," Juli said, her voice perfectly angelic. "We were all really heartbroken, but it was just his time."

"He led a good life, honey."

"You're so right. You know, he spoke fondly of you there at the end."

"Did he? That's so nice to hear. Tell you what, pumpkin. Why don't you head inside and grab a table. I just need to, um, finish up in here, and then I'd love to sit down and visit with you. Hear about the funeral and everything. Are you here vacationing with someone, or all alone?"

"All alone," she said. "I'd love the company."

Alex frowned.

"I'm so glad, sweetie. I'll just be a minute."

"Sure thing, Tom. Don't forget to wash your hands, okay?"

Tom smiled, looking relieved. "Okay, honeybunch. I'll be right there."

"Great," she said. "Oh, and Tom?"

"Yes, lollypop?"

"Uncle Frank really did talk about you on his deathbed. In fact, he talked a lot."

Tom's face went a little pale. "You don't say?"

"In fact, he told me every little detail about the heroin ring you've been running together for the last fifteen years. A perfect partnership—a mobster and the owner of an international shipping company. What a great team! And you guys made a pretty nice profit. At least, that's what Uncle Frank said. He gave me spreadsheets and everything."

"Did he, now?" Tom said, shifting his weight from one foot to the other.

"Yes. As a matter-of-fact, he had quite a lot of documentation that he included in his memoirs. Did I mention that I'm the executor of his estate? A friend of mine at a publishing company in New York City was really excited when I handed it all over to her just last week. Have they not been in touch with you about it yet?"

Tom stared at Juli.

Alex stared at Tom.

Tom turned and looked at Alex.

Suddenly, he whipped the pistol around and pointed it at Juli.

Alex raised his own pistol, taking aim at the side of Tom's head.

Outside in the alley, Juli rolled her eyes and laughed.

"Oh, please, Tom. The book is already at the publisher, so killing me won't do you any good. And if you shoot me, these four FBI agents standing right here in the women's room will not look too kindly upon it. They'd like to have a word with you, actually. They were really interested when I called them right after I heard your plane would be landing here on St. Lucia today."

"You're bluffing," Tom said. "There are no FBI agents in the women's room."

Juli leaned back, craning her neck to the right to yell into the women's restroom. "Hey, guys?"

"Yes, ma'am?" called a gravelly voice from the other side of the wall.

"Can you tell this jerkoff that he probably shouldn't shoot anyone right now?"

"Sir, you probably shouldn't shoot anyone right now," the voice shouted. "We would take that amiss."

"Very amiss," another voice agreed.

"And we would be inclined to shoot you, sir," piped a third voice. "Really hard."

"So you see," Juli said, turning back to Tom, "you may want to put the gun down and step out with your hands up. Because I'm looking at you, and I'm looking at them, and I've gotta say—their guns are a lot bigger than yours."

Alex watched Tom's face in profile—watched him go from anger to indignation to bluster and finally, defeat. The whole time, Alex held his pistol ready, waiting.

"Fine," Tom said, stepping out into the alley and bending slowly forward to set the gun on the ground at

Juli's feet. He looked up at her and lifted his hands into the air. "I want my lawyer," he snarled. "Right now! Bantam and Royal Law Group, same as Frankie always used. Get them right now, dammit."

"Sure thing, Tom," Juli said, stooping down to retrieve the gun, handling it like a pro. Alex started to tell her not to—that the FBI would want it as evidence.

That's when he noticed the four FBI officers were not rushing from the restroom to cuff Tom Portelli. They weren't barking orders over radios or whisking Juli to safety. In fact, they were peculiarly silent on the other side of the wall.

Fuck me, Alex thought, shaking his head as he yanked off his belt before tucking his pistol back in his pants. Stepping up to his former boss, he gave Tom a nudge with his knee and jerked his ex-boss's arms behind his back.

Juli fluttered a wave at Alex, keeping the gun trained on Portelli's head.

"Hi, Alex. How's it going?"

"Just great, Juli," he said, genuinely meaning it. "Just great."

She beamed as Alex cinched Tom's wrists together with the belt. "Excellent. Did you order already?"

"Absolutely," Alex said. "Food should probably be there by now. Hopefully it's not getting cold. That'd be a real shame."

Tom frowned and craned his neck to look into the women's room. "But the FBI. My lawyers."

"I'm sure they'll all be joining the party soon," Alex said. He raised one eyebrow at Juli and watched as her smile broadened.

"Who's in the bathroom?" he asked as he secured the belt around Tom's wrists.

Juli beamed. "Bob, Gretchen, Sal, and Sadie. Our waitress, the busboy, the cook, and a diner unlucky enough to get caught in the shuffle when I was herding everyone to the bathroom after I heard you guys talking over here. Oh, and PS, these bathroom walls are really thin. Peeing during a stickup, Alex?"

Tom's expression was incredulous. "But, but—I don't believe this. You tricked me. This is an abomination! This is unacceptable! Untie me right now!"

Alex clamped his hand on Tom Portelli's shoulder and shook his head. "Let's go, Tom. We can find the police station and tell them how sorely you were mistreated. I'm sure they'll be very sympathetic."

―∿―

It took a couple hours to sort through all the confusion, but eventually, Tom Portelli was ensconced safely in a holding cell at the Royal St. Lucia police station, waiting for his attorneys. The FBI was already en route and very interested to hear that the man they'd had an eye on for several years was safely in custody.

The three crewmen from the cargo ship were rounded up and shuttled to the police station as well. Remarkably, Juli and Alex were allowed to go. Despite their plans to commit several crimes over the course of the last few days, they were relieved to discover they hadn't actually succeeded in committing any that were worth detaining them for. Juli felt it unwise to point that out to the police.

By the time they found the hotel room Malcolm had reserved, it was nearly midnight.

"I'm starving," Juli said as she flopped onto one of the king-sized beds and looked around the room. Alex was still standing by the door, looking wary.

"Do you think they have room service here?" she asked him.

Alex hesitated, then moved into the room and began pawing through the brochures and booklets arranged atop the table near the window. He handed her the room service menu and kept moving past, careful not to even brush her hand.

"Didn't you box up all those appetizers at the restaurant?" he asked. "I thought you already ate."

"Sure, but I ate it all at the police station. Now I'm hungry again."

Alex shook his head and sat stiffly on the edge of the other bed. He folded his hands in his lap while Juli studied the menu and wondered what the hell was going on with him. He had been strangely quiet on their cab ride to the hotel, but she'd chalked it up to exhaustion. Now, seeing his shoulders rigid and his forehead creased in a frown, she could tell there was something on his mind. She saw his eyes slide over her body, then quickly dart away.

"Want anything special?" she asked as she picked up the phone. "Cheese sticks? Club sandwich?"

Alex looked at her again. "I want to know how you got to be such good buddies with Tom Portelli."

Juli turned the menu over and shrugged. "I don't see that on here. How about a chef salad instead?"

"I take it you've known him awhile?"

"Maybe a nice Denver omelet?" she offered hopefully.

"How about Uncle Frank—or Frankie-Two-Toes, as

he's more commonly known," Alex said, not giving up. "I take it you two were close?"

"I know! A piece of cheesecake. Strawberry or passion fruit?"

Alex stared at her for a moment, then shook his head. "Do they have burgers?"

"Cheese or regular?"

"Cheese, please. Make sure you get extra fries."

Juli dialed and placed an order for a Denver omelet with a triple order of sausage links, french fries, two cheeseburgers, a garden salad, two Cokes, and two pieces of cheesecake—one strawberry, one passion fruit. When she hung up, Alex was still staring at her. She couldn't read his expression at all. Was he preoccupied? Hungry? Horny? Honestly, it could be any of those things.

Juli was hoping for the latter.

Alex continued to stare and Juli shivered under the weight of his gaze. "What?" She rubbed her arms to make the fuzziness die down, but it only made her skin feel hot and achy with the need to be touched.

"Is any of that food for me besides the cheeseburger?"

She smiled and set the menu down on the nightstand. "The fries, of course, but I'm not sharing my sausages. I'll fight to the death over sausage links."

"Now that I've seen you in a fight, I'll consider myself warned. Nice job with Portelli, by the way."

"Thanks. You too."

Juli moved toward the end of her bed where she'd dropped her bag. She bent forward and rummaged around for her toothbrush, intent on doing something to cut the tension. She pulled out Uncle Frank's urn and set it on the edge of the dresser, then dug back in her knapsack for the toothbrush. She found it tangled in a sock and pulled it out. Alex was quiet for so long that Juli glanced up to see what he was doing. He was staring openly, right down the front of her shirt.

"Enjoying the view?" she asked, still bent over, bolder than she felt. "Let me know when you'd like to retrieve your eyeballs from my cleavage."

"Actually, I'll just leave them there awhile if it's all the same to you."

She shrugged. "Suit yourself."

Alex watched her for a few more seconds, then shook his head. "This shared luxury suite thing is a bad, bad idea," he said as he flopped back on the bed. "This bed's mine, that one's yours. No more strip Battleship. No more staring down the front of your shirt. We're going to behave like responsible adults. This isn't a good time for—well, for—"

"Whatever you say, boss," she said with a shrug as she began strolling the room. "Nice place." She flicked a lamp on and off and on and off again as she chewed the head of her toothbrush. She switched sides, working the rest of her teeth, still aware of Alex's gaze. Finally, she looked up to see him studying her, an amused smile playing over his features.

"The toiletries are pretty fancy," she said, extracting the toothbrush. "Did you check out the bathroom? Little soaps in their own box, mouthwash, a shower cap, shampoo *and* conditioner—not that all-in-one crap."

She chewed the toothbrush again, watching him.

"No toothpaste?" Alex said. "Because normal people brush their teeth at a sink with toothpaste and water. Ever tried it?"

"You really think the only thing separating me from *normal* is how I brush my teeth?"

"Good point. Let's return to the original line of questioning." Alex sat up on the bed again. "How long have you known Tom Portelli?"

Juli sighed. He wasn't going to let this die. And really, there was no reason not to tell him. He already knew her freak-of-nature genius status. What were a few family mob ties on top of all that?

"Uncle Frank brought Tom to Christmas dinner when I was three," she said finally. "He was pretty much a fixture at family events whenever he was in town. His wife, Ginny, used to braid my hair and even bought me my first training bra."

Alex nodded, looking a little distracted by that detail. "How well did you know Tom?" he asked. "Or your Uncle Frank, for that matter?"

"Well enough, on both counts," Juli said as she dropped onto the edge of her bed and bounced a little.

She saw his eyes fall to her breasts again, watched him swallow hard and look away. He reached behind him and tugged one of the pillows out from under the duvet. Propping it behind him, he leaned back, folded his hands over his chest, and settled his gaze on the ceiling.

Probably figured it was a safer place to look.

Pity, that, Juli thought.

"What else?" Alex prompted, and Juli felt the room tilt as she considered what he might be suggesting.

"Oh—you mean Portelli and Uncle Frank?" She folded her arms over her chest, annoyed. "Why, because you've been so forthcoming with information to this point?"

He looked at her again, those green eyes pinning her with such intensity she was sure he could see right through her clothing.

I'll tell you anything you want, she thought. *Just keep looking at me that way.*

"I knew Uncle Frank and Tom Portelli were business partners," Juli said at last. "As I got older, I figured their business wasn't always legal. I didn't know for sure until Uncle Frank told me everything just before he died, but I guess you could say I wasn't surprised by anything he said."

Alex nodded. "So that was true. The part about the deathbed confession, I mean. After the fake FBI thing, I wasn't really sure which parts of your story were true and which parts you just made up."

Juli shrugged and stuffed her toothbrush back into her bag and scooted back to the edge of her bed. She pressed the balls of her feet against his knees to stretch her calves. "Let's see, the deathbed confession part was true. The part about the memoir, not so much. I don't even know anyone in New York City, much less a publisher. I did actually call the FBI as soon as I heard Tom would be here. I wasn't lying about that. They just hadn't arrived yet, so I had to improvise."

"Nice job with that," Alex said. "Seriously, you probably saved my life."

"Nah, he wouldn't have shot you."

"Sure he would have."

"Okay, he would have." She wiggled her toes against his calf, savoring the feel of the thick hair and muscled flesh. "So how about you? How long have you known Tom?"

Alex sighed. "More than twenty years. Started at Kranston right out of college, when I was broke and trying to figure out what I wanted to do with my life." He laughed. "Kind of ironic, considering where I am now."

"What do you mean?"

He shrugged. "Right back where I started. I was at the bottom of the corporate ladder in the beginning, and I made my way up to becoming a VP at Kranston. Worked closely with Tom the whole time. Had a pretty nice pension, good benefits, the whole nine yards."

"What happened?"

Alex was quiet for a long time, and Juli thought he was going to avoid the question again. She was so used to having him withhold information, she was surprised when he finally spoke.

"Portelli hosed us," he said at last. "Me, Phyllis, Jake, Cody—and a bunch of others. Our pensions, stock options, benefits, everything we'd worked for—gone. Just like that."

"So you were getting even," Juli said, understanding at last. "That's what you meant when you said the pirate mission was personal. But you didn't get your money back since the cargo wasn't there. So now what?"

She saw him wince, and wished like hell she could take back the question. Smiling Alex was gone, replaced by Surly Alex now.

"I don't know what's next," he said. "I sunk most of my savings into my boat last year, and lost more in the stock market a few months back. Figured I had time to make it up with a steady job and a great pension, but now—" He shook his head and looked away. "I am jobless and penniless at forty-two years old. Hot, huh?"

Juli frowned. "What does *hot* have to do with anything?"

He looked away. "I should be at the peak of my earning potential right now, and instead, I'm starting from scratch."

"Don't be silly," she said. "I've only known you a week, but you're one of the most resilient people I've ever met. I'm sure you'll land on your feet."

"Sure."

"Alex—"

He looked at her. "When's the food getting here?"

"Soon." Juli looked at him a moment longer, then shook her head. Clearly, money and job security was a touchy subject.

Maybe mobsters would be better.

"So Uncle Frank is the reason you refused to tell me any details about the mission?" she asked. "Because of the whole mob thing?"

"No, actually," Alex said, shifting his leg a little to trap her feet under his calf. Juli grinned and wiggled her toes beneath the weight, enjoying the sensation of having any part of her body pinned under any part of Alex's on a bed.

"We didn't figure out you were the niece of a famous mobster until just yesterday morning," he continued, still not looking at her as he squashed her toes under his calf. "I'd heard of Frankie before, obviously. Notorious guy. But I didn't know he had any connection to Tom. That part was news to me."

Juli wiggled her toes some more, then pulled them free and sat up. She stared at Alex, willing him to look at her, trying to figure out how to make him smile again. Keep him talking, maybe that would do it.

"So what can you tell me about—"

"Look," he interrupted, "why don't we call it quits

with the Twenty Questions for now. When do you think the food will be here?"

Juli clapped her hands together and grinned. "That's a great idea!"

Alex gave her a puzzled look. "The food? You already ordered it."

She shook her head and dropped onto his bed beside him, crossing her legs. "Twenty Questions. Let's play!"

He shook his head, but he'd started to smile. "You're something else, you know that?"

Juli grinned back. "I'll take that as a compliment. You want to go first?"

"Really, when is the food coming?"

Juli checked her watch. "Ten minutes. We've got time for at least one round of Twenty Questions. Come on, Alex, it'll be fun."

He grabbed Juli's foot and tickled it, making her squeal. "Fine," he said. "One game. Why do I have a feeling I'll regret this?"

"You always have that feeling," she pointed out. "Do you ever regret it?"

"Not yet."

~~~

Alex couldn't believe he'd let her talk him into another game. *Jesus*. The first one had gotten him married. The second had gotten him a foot job. The third had gotten him naked. Now what—conversion to a religious cult?

Sharing a room with her was insane, especially with all these secrets that kept popping up like something out of a deranged jack-in-the-box. The genius thing, the mobster uncle, the ties to Portelli. Sleeping with her would be stupid. What the hell else was she hiding—a sex change operation?

He looked at her, flushed and round in that tank top. No, probably not a sex change.

Still, he had to stay focused. He had to figure out what to do about the cargo. About his vanished pension. About the fact that he was forty-two years old and jobless with no retirement package and no clue what the hell had gone wrong with his plan to get it all back. Now wasn't the time to get distracted.

"Okay," he said finally, willing to do anything to get Juli to stop bouncing around, moving under that thin tank top, making him want her so badly he was five seconds from pushing her backwards onto that bed and really making her toes curl.

"You ask questions first," he said. "I picked an object. Go."

Juli jumped up, and Alex couldn't help but watch as she grabbed all the pillows off her bed and began tossing them onto his.

"What are you doing?"

"Sitting by you," she announced, leaning over him to straighten the pillows, reaching back to grab two more before crawling across his lap to sprawl out beside him. She flounced and jostled for a minute longer before settling beside him and matching his pose. She grinned.

"Your bed is closer to the air conditioner," Juli informed him. "I like it better over here."

Oh, good, Alex thought. *Juli in a flimsy top next to the air conditioner.* He looked at his watch, willing the room service staff to hurry up. Maybe he could get his burger raw?

"Animal, vegetable, or mineral?" she asked.

Hell, he'd forgotten they were playing a game. He looked up at the ceiling, his mind racing, feeling around in dark corners for an object, any object. His brain swam in images, but few lent themselves to an innocent game of Twenty Questions.

He looked away from the ceiling and down at Juli, considering. Well hell, she was the one who came up with Strip Battleship, wasn't she?

"Animal," he told her, already regretting his choice.

"Is it bigger than a zebra?"

Alex raised an eyebrow at her. "A zebra?"

"Just as a point of reference."

"No. It is not bigger than a zebra."

"Is it bigger than a sheep?"

"No."

"Bigger than a tarantula?"

"Yes. Bigger than a tarantula."

Juli nodded, looking thoughtful. "Is it soft?"

Alex winced. "Yes."

"Striped?"

"No."

"Does it live on land?"

"Yes."

"How many questions is that?"

Alex smiled. "Counting this one and the animal-vegetable-mineral one, eight."

She frowned at him. "You don't count that one. That's not fair."

Alex grinned down at her, enjoying his advantage. "Neither was using a mirror to cheat at Strip Battleship."

"Good point."

"You going to ask another one?"

"I'm thinking," she said, shifting again, her curls tickling the side of his chin as she wriggled to adjust one of her pillows. He felt dizzy as he caught a breath of her shampoo and another glimpse down the front of her shirt. He looked away and checked his watch again. Where was room service? And why the hell hadn't he been smart enough to request two separate rooms?

And for that matter, what was happening one hundred miles away with Jake and Phyllis and Cody and the pirates and all that damn cargo? He should be focusing on that. Not on Juli, no matter how soft and beautiful and—

"Is it a mammal?" Juli asked at last.

Alex considered that one. "Yes. I suppose it is."

"Had to think about it though?"

Alex smiled. "Is that your tenth question? You're going to have to start guessing soon."

Juli crossed her arms over her chest. Alex felt light-headed.

"Is it a cat?" she asked finally.

"No."

"Dog?"

"No."

"This is hard."

Alex closed his eyes. "Actually, you already established that it's soft."

She slugged him in the shoulder. "Is it furry?"

"God, no."

"Does it have a tail?"

Alex laughed, looking down at her again. "No. No tail. Are you going to take another swing with the guessing or just burn up the rest of your questions?"

Juli met his eyes, holding them for one beat, two, three. She gave him a devilish grin and leaned against him, making her top gape open again.

Jesus, she was driving him nuts.

"Well, since you keep looking down the front of my shirt when you think I'm not paying attention, I'm going to go ahead and guess that it's my breasts."

Alex felt his jaw drop. He tried to respond, but no sound came out. Juli grinned and performed a triumphant fist pump.

"Score!"

Alex shook his head in disbelief. "You got that from me looking down your shirt? I would think you'd be used to that."

"Was I right?" she asked, bouncing on the bed, looking infinitely pleased with herself. "I got it? It was really my breasts?"

"You're taking this well, considering I just objectified and ogled you. Really, very chauvinistic of me." Alex straightened, swinging his legs out of the bed as he moved away from her. "I should be going now. Maybe there's another room in this place just for the night."

Juli grabbed his sleeve and yanked him back down onto the bed beside her.

"I've been trying to get you to objectify and ogle me for the last hour," she said, so close now her breath tickled his ear. "Winning the game was just an added bonus. Ogle me some more. Pretty please?"

The room felt suddenly hot. The pressure of Juli's hand on his sleeve, her curls brushing his arm, the lemony, coconut scent of her, the delight flickering in her eyes—all of it was making Alex dizzy.

He was either going to kiss her or take a cold shower. He closed his eyes.

Cold shower, he decided. *Much safer.*

"It was actually just your left breast," he admitted between clenched teeth. "Just one, not both."

"Just the left one?"

Alex opened his eyes to see her looking even more delighted. She was still gripping his sleeve, pinning him there beside her. He could break free if he wanted, flee the room and get away. Hell, he could even sleep in the hall.

"The left is my favorite," he conceded.

Juli smiled. "We've known each other less than five days and you have a favorite breast? I'm touched."

Touched. Something about the way she said that last word made Alex's throat go dry. He tried to ignore the buzzing in his head, the itching in his fingertips, the urge to slide his hands up her arms and make her shiver.

He looked back at her. She held fast to his sleeve and smiled.

I didn't need a shower anyway, he thought. He leaned down, capturing her mouth with his, sinking into that soft heat.

He was rougher than he meant to be, but Juli pressed against him, spurring him on, kissing him back with the same urgency. He felt her fingers move into his hair, gripping the base of his skull, pulling him to her.

Alex moved one hand over her hip, sliding into the perfect hollow at the small of her back. Her spine curved with the pressure of his palm as she arched against him, pressing her breasts to his chest. Alex felt his pulse quicken as Juli made a soft whimpering sound in the back of her throat and began to kiss her way down his neck. Alex closed his eyes, near delirious with pleasure as her lips moved soft and warm against his throat. Every nerve in his body came screaming to life and he tightened his hold on her, making her whimper again.

Her hands surprised him, hot and hungry and eager. She moved down, gliding her fingers over his biceps, detouring down the edge of his chest, clutching him there for a moment, then slipping down his ribs, dipping low over his abdomen, lower, then lower still. Alex groaned.

The blood was pounding in his head now, hammering so loudly he thought he might go deaf. His ears were ringing as he eased her body back against the pillows, craving more of her, loving the feel of her fingers fumbling with his zipper, freeing him, grasping him tightly in her hot hand. His heart was beating wildly, loud and crazy and eager.

"Sausage," Juli gasped, angling away from him.

Alex drew back and looked down.

"What?" he said, dizzy with her heat and the softness of her body and the pressure of her hand gripping him.

"Room service is here," she panted. "Sausage."

"Oh," Alex said, trying to focus, dimly aware of the knocking at the door. "Right."

Juli drew back further, her eyes burning into his. She didn't blink. Was she even breathing? Alex swallowed, trying not to lunge for her again.

Juli bit her lip. "This won't be one of those movie moments where the mood is ruined and we eat our dinner and go to bed without clawing each other's clothes off. I want this. I want you. And I don't care if the hotel catches fire and the entire mob shows up to gun us down. I need you to make love to me. Here. Tonight."

"Um," Alex said, getting dizzy all over again.

"But first, sausage," she said, releasing him and jumping up off the bed.

"Sausage," Alex repeated and lay back against the pillows, wondering how his life had gotten so complicated. And why he wasn't more concerned.

Chapter 17

JULI FELT FULL. FULL AND HAPPY.

"I can't believe you just ate all of that," Alex said, taking his eyes off the glittering black swirl of the ocean long enough to watch her.

Juli smiled and set the plate down, licking the last of the french fry grease from her fingers. Alex smiled and turned back toward the water.

They were sitting side-by-side on the second-floor balcony of their hotel suite, basking in the moonlit view of the beach with their legs stretched out straight in front of them, touching at the knee.

"You helped with some of it," she pointed out. "I gave you the croutons off the salad."

"Very generous of you," he agreed. "Want the last bite of cheesecake?"

"Only if you don't," she said, feeling pleased when he forked the piece straight into her mouth. She chewed blissfully, aware of the solidness of his shoulder against hers, the gentle hiss of the ocean splashing up onto the beach, retreating, rushing up onto the sand again.

Juli watched the waves for a moment, intrigued by the motion, the salty smell, the soothing rush of water.

A week ago, I would have rather pierced my own nostril with a toothpick than sat on a balcony over the ocean.

A week ago, I was eating my mother's carob meatloaf instead of passion fruit cheesecake.

A week ago, I didn't even know this guy.
Now I belong to a pirate crew.

Juli looked over at Alex and smiled.

"What are you thinking about?" he asked, setting the plate down beside him and dusting his hands off.

Juli looked at him, considering her next words.

"What were you guys hoping to steal from Tom's boat?" she asked finally, surprising herself with her bluntness. "That's the only part you haven't told me yet. If we're laying all our cards on the table, I want to know what you were going after out there."

Alex frowned, staring out at the ocean again. "Diamonds. Forty-eight million dollars worth of diamonds, to be exact."

"Really?"

"Yup. We had some pretty good intelligence that told us what was on that boat. An illegal transaction, something we could intercept without getting caught. We even had a plan to fence them through a connection in Antwerp. I'm still not sure what went wrong."

"They weren't there?"

"Nope."

She put a hand on his leg, feeling the heat beneath her palm.

"I'm sorry," she said at last.

"Not your fault."

"I know, but this isn't how you planned it."

Alex shrugged. "I'll survive."

Juli turned back to the ocean, trying to think of how to permeate the grim haze that had fallen over them. She felt sad for Alex, no doubt about it. Really, very sad.

But she still wanted to roll around naked with him.

Okay, so that made her an insensitive trollop. There it was. Even as she wanted to cradle his head in her lap and stroke his hair and tell him things would be okay, she also wanted to tear his clothes off with her teeth and lick her way down his abdomen.

Of course, they'd obviously lost their mood mojo in the last hour. Somehow, they'd gone from passionate groping to companionable, somber dinner conversation with the dark ocean crashing beneath them.

Not that there was anything wrong with that.

But really, more groping would be nice.

Juli frowned at the ocean. How to get the mood back? The women's magazines never really addressed the proper method for jumping back on track with a derailed hookup. Maybe running her hand up his leg? Sticking her tongue in his ear?

No, maybe something sensitive. Perhaps she should gaze meaningfully into his eyes, whisper something sweet and sultry, give him her best come-hither look—

"Oh, baby! I want to rub your cheese doodle 'til my hands turn orange."

Juli jumped, sending her fork flying off the edge of the balcony. There was another loud whoop, followed by something that sounded like yodeling. Juli frowned and looked at Alex. His expression was equally perplexed.

"You rub my doodle, baby, and I'll give it to you so good you'll tattoo my name on that sweet little tushy of yours."

Juli winced, disgusted. But also curious. She craned her neck to see where the voices were coming from, baffled by sounds that reminded her of the time the raccoons got stuck in her mother's basement.

"On the beach," Alex whispered. "I think they're right below us."

"Are you serious?"

"See the shadows? Right there?"

"Where?"

Alex pointed. "Just below us. Edge of the water, over to the left."

Juli squinted in the darkness. "Wha—is that a T-shirt that just went flying through the air?"

Alex leaned forward, peering down at the beach. "Yes. And I believe it says 'Mustache rides, five cents.'"

"Ew."

"Yeah, honey, tear that bra off with your teeth! Just like that, baby—oh, careful with the dentures, that's it. You tiger! You lion! You wildebeest! Grrrr!"

"Oh, I'm gonna give it to you so good, girl. You want me to spank you like the naughty little hamster you are?"

Juli wasn't sure whether to cover her ears or her eyes. Or both. She looked up at Alex, who looked equally repulsed and fascinated.

"How do you like your eggs, baby? Over easy or hard-boiled?"

"Give 'em to me scrambled, daddy, with a little pat of butter."

"How about margarine?"

"I don't even know what that means," Juli whispered, crawling on all fours to peer through the slats of the balcony. All she could see was dark sand and the swirl of water advancing and retreating.

That was probably for the best.

"Do you think we should take notes?" Alex

whispered, scooting forward to join her. "Because a lot of this is new to me."

"I think we should be vaccinated."

There was a disturbing cacophony of smacking, giggling, and groaning, and Juli thought for a moment she might see her Denver omelet again. She tried to focus in the darkness, straining to see something, halfway afraid she might succeed.

"This is disgusting," Alex said.

"We should go inside."

"Totally."

"And lock the door."

"I'm with you."

Neither of them moved.

"Yeah, mama. You want a little hot salsa on that taco?"

"Ooh, daddy, guacamole too!"

Juli grimaced. "Do you think we should alert the hotel managers?"

"And say what? 'Someone's having really tacky sex on the beach'?"

"Well…"

"Besides, we might miss something."

Juli scooted to the left, angling her face through the bars of the balcony, trying for at least a glimpse. She felt Alex's shoulder warm against hers and reminded herself that this was gross and disturbing, not a turn-on. Not at all.

"This seems wrong," Juli whispered, feeling Alex's shoulder shake with laughter.

"You're right," he agreed. "We should have binoculars."

"I'm thinking we might need a bucket of ice water in case things get out of hand down there."

He looked at her. "You actually think it could be *more* out of hand?"

"I think these two have unplumbed depths of depravity."

"It sounds like they're doing their best to plumb them."

Alex moved closer and she felt his breath warm on her neck. She tried not to find it erotic. Truly, this was the least erotic thing she could imagine.

Wasn't it?

"Who's my little bunny? Who's my little grasshopper?"

"Right here, baby! Hop! Hop!"

"This is better than pay-per-view," Alex whispered.

"This is so not a turn-on," Juli whispered back, pretty sure that was true.

"Not even a little?"

She ignored him. "It's like a train wreck. You want to look away, but you can't."

"Ahoy, matey! Firing me cannon through your port-hole in one-two-three…"

"Bwaaack! Polly wants a cracker!"

"Shiver me timbers, baby!"

There was a disturbing amount of screaming, moaning, and the slap of water on the sand. Then a few moments of silence, followed by some soulful murmuring Juli was glad not to be able to hear.

She looked at Alex. Alex looked back at her.

"I don't know what to say," Alex said finally, sitting back on his heels and looking nonplussed.

"How can you add to that?"

He nodded sagely. "We probably shouldn't try."

"Best to just enjoy the memory."

"Think there'll be an encore?"

"I think I need a shower."

Alex nodded again. "No kidding."

Juli smiled at him and touched a hand to his knee. "Care to join me?"

—∿∿—

Alex couldn't believe it when Juli smiled up at him, mischief and moonlight sparkling in those blue eyes, and said those two simple words:

"Let's go."

"Go where?"

"Let's take a shower," she whispered. "Together, I mean."

Alex swallowed. He'd been restraining himself all evening, trying not to touch her, resisting the urge to say *to hell with it* and have his way with her.

Why was that again?

He couldn't remember, but he knew one thing for sure. He'd had more fun with her than he had with anyone in a long, long time. They'd laughed. They'd groped. They'd shared cheesecake. They'd eavesdropped on awkward sex together. Was a shower such a big deal at this point?

It's not just a shower. You know that.

Alex cleared his throat. "Shower," he repeated, just to be sure he wasn't misunderstanding. "Together."

"I'm from the Pacific Northwest," she informed him, her smile widening. "We believe wholeheartedly in conserving our natural resources. Water being one."

Alex nodded, trying to figure out whether she was serious about the shower, about the environment, or about anything.

But then she grabbed his hand and stood up, hoisting him with her.

"It's the least we can do to save the planet," she was saying, towing him forward as she moved back into their hotel room. "A moral obligation."

"Sure," he agreed, letting her pull him into the room and down the narrow hallway. "It's not easy being green, but someone has to do it."

"I'm so glad you agree."

Once they were in the bathroom, Juli let go of his hand and smiled at him—a salacious, crazy grin that made him want to boost her up on the counter and tear her panties off with his teeth.

Then she reached down and stripped off her top in one fluid motion, her arms making an erotic X beneath the pale blue cotton. Alex stared, then kicked himself for staring, then decided it was probably okay to stare under the circumstances.

"Holy Mother of God," was all he could manage.

She smiled. "Not quite. Though I understand you're quite fond of the left one."

"No bra, huh?"

"How else was I supposed to use the air conditioning to my advantage?"

Alex shook his head, remembering how much he'd enjoyed that. "Do you ever play fair?"

"Nope. Are you complaining?"

"No."

"Your turn," she said, reaching out to grab the front of his shirt.

He stood mutely for the first few seconds as she slid the buttons through the holes, her fingers clever and quick. Alex sucked in a breath as her nails made contact with his bare chest.

"Nice," she said, raking him gently.

"Urg," he said.

Classy, Alex thought, and he reached for the tie at the front of her capris. His fingers were shakier than he'd expected, fumbling a little with her zipper, and he lost his place as Juli pushed his shirt off his shoulders, palming his biceps on the way down.

"Maybe you should consider a career as an underwear model," she murmured, reaching for his belt.

"I hear the pensions are good," he replied as he slid the fabric down over her hips.

He kissed her then, savoring the softness of her lips, the lingering taste of passion fruit, the way she pressed herself against him. He cupped her bare ass, certain he was going to pass out from the pleasure of it all.

"It's the pirate-patch thong," he murmured appreciatively, circling his palms over her. He pressed his lips to the hollow of her throat, kissing his way to the curve of her neck, the wings of her collarbones. He stroked her, kneaded her flesh, fumbling to slide her panties down over her hips.

Then his fingers found the slick spot between her legs. Juli gasped and pressed against him. Alex kissed her harder, trying to pinpoint which thing he was doing to elicit the positive response.

"More," she whimpered.

Good feedback, he thought and kissed her again, circling a finger into her. He pushed against her, pinning her against the cold tile wall.

She yelped a little at that and broke the kiss long enough to smile up at him.

"We should turn the water on," she said. "That's sort of the point of a shower, isn't it?"

"Right now, I'm not sure."

Juli grinned and turned around. Alex admired the view as she bent down to twist the taps, fiddling with the temperature. She straightened up, standing on tiptoe to adjust the showerhead. Then she stepped into the steam, letting the water sluice over her as she closed her eyes, and slicked her hair out of her eyes. Alex watched, mesmerized, taking in the sight of her wet curls, her body perfect and lush and slippery.

He'd never seen anything so beautiful in his life.

She opened her eyes and smiled, curling a finger at him. "You coming?"

"No, but I'm guessing I will be in a few minutes."

"Only a few minutes?"

"It's been awhile."

She grinned. "That's okay. We've got all night."

He shucked his pants the rest of the way and stepped in beside her. The tile was rough underfoot and the steam was hot everywhere else. He breathed in something sweet and floral as Juli unwrapped a bar of soap and set it aside, grinning at him. Now that they were both naked, Alex was desperate to touch her again. He cupped her shoulders, slid his hands down over her arms, moved his mouth to her breasts, tasted her everywhere.

"Oh, God," Juli whimpered as his fingers found their way between her legs again. She slid one leg up, anchoring her heel against the back of his thigh, pulling him to her. He felt dizzy again, marveling at her balance. She twined her fingers in his hair, using her nails against his scalp.

"Don't stop," she breathed into his ear.

"Don't slip," he whispered back.

"It's a skid-resistant floor."

"Handy."

Alex slid his other hand over her hips, loving the slickness of her skin, the way she arched against him. He kissed the hollow of her throat, feeling the vibration of her moans against his lips. He slid his fingers into her softness, savoring her whimpers.

Her nails raked across his hips, moving between them, taking him in her hands. Alex groaned.

"That's quite a cutlass," she breathed in a terrible pirate accent. "What ye needs is a good scabbard."

Alex groaned again, this time not in ecstasy. Not completely, anyway. "That's bad, even for you. Don't make me gag you with the washcloth."

"Kinky," she giggled, still stroking him with a slick palm.

Alex curled a finger inside her.

"Oh, God," she gasped as he stroked her deeper. "Please, Alex!"

"Please what?" he murmured against her throat, genuinely not certain.

"You. Inside me. Now."

"Condom," he murmured, pulling back reluctantly.

"Right."

"Dammit," he groaned, grabbing the edge of the shower curtain, staggering a little as he moved away from her. *Not again. After all these times, not again with the condom thing—*

"Soap dish," she said, grasping him again with slippery fingers and pulling him to her. She smiled up at him with mock innocence. "I planned ahead."

Alex stared down at her, mystified. "You anticipated having sex in the shower?"

Juli shrugged and began to lick her way across his chest, sliding her teeth over his nipples, then moving back up to his throat. Alex groaned and closed his eyes.

"And in the bed, and on the balcony, and under the table, and beside the TV—I'm prepared for any spontaneity that might arise. There's even a condom in the closet."

"You are a rare woman, Juli Flynn," Alex murmured, reaching for her again.

Juli grinned and reached for the soap dish. Her fingers closed around a red foil packet he hadn't noticed before. She drew her hand back, her fingers already tearing at the wrapper.

Alex caught her wrist. "Wait."

She froze. "You're kidding me. Alex, if this is about—"

"Shut up," he said and kissed her to make sure it happened. He kept kissing her for a long time—minutes, hours, he wasn't sure. He could have done it for days. He felt himself getting light-headed again from all the steam and heat and naked flesh pressed against him. He drew back and looked down at her upturned face, damp and breathless.

"I'm not saying stop," he breathed. "I'm saying slow."

"Yellow light, not red light?"

"'That's not another game, is it?"

"No," she whispered and moved her lips to his throat. "No games."

He moved his palms over her body, trying to memorize that perfect curve between her hip and her waist. Already intimately acquainted with her breasts, he moved his hands up and lingered there anyway. He savored the slippery feel of her, the sharp intake of breath as he stroked her nipples to hard peaks.

Juli slid her hand between their bodies again, stroking him with fingers slick and hot and so very eager. He closed his eyes and concentrated on making this last, on savoring every second of it. Her mouth was still moving over his throat, driving him crazy with lust and a fervent desire to press her back against the shower wall and slide inside her.

"*Slow*," he reminded himself.

"Hmm?"

"Talking to myself."

She laughed, her breath tickling his wet skin as she kissed her way across his shoulder. "You do that a lot."

"And here you thought you were the abnormal one."

He kissed her again, sipped at the water that trickled over her shoulders. The pulse of the shower hit him in the face and his eyes blurred, but he couldn't tell if it was from water or plain old desire.

Juli squirmed against him, her wet skin sliding against his as she moved her mouth over his chest, nipping lightly before trailing down, then back up again. The showerhead pulsed behind her, filling the room with thick steam and the flowery scent of bar soap he'd just knocked to the floor.

He wanted to touch every inch of her at once but settled for the square inch between her thighs, warm and slippery and—

"Oh, God," she whimpered. "Please."

He smiled, his fingers still moving inside her. "I love how polite you are when you want something."

"I love how you think lust and good manners are the same thing."

He continued to tease, his fingers making gentle, slick circles. He took his time, not wanting to rush her. Not wanting to rush himself. He slid another finger into her and felt her clench around him. Her breath quickened, her eyes closed, her head tilted back as she gave a sharp little cry—

"*Oh!*"

There was no pillow this time to muffle her screams. Alex was glad. She shrieked with pleasure once, twice, three times, her cries echoing off the shower walls as he stroked inside her over and over until he felt her go limp in his arms.

She was still for a moment. Then she opened her eyes and grinned up at him. "Wow."

"Exactly."

She raised a hand and fanned at the cloud of steam hovering between them. "Very wet."

"No kidding."

She laughed, and he bent to kiss her, thinking he could never get enough of this. She kissed him back, softer this time, her fingers gliding wetly through his hair. He stroked his palms down her arms, feeling her shiver despite the heat pulsing from the showerhead. They kissed like that for a long time, lips and bellies pressed together in the steamy space. Alex felt the urgency start to build again, felt her nails rake the nape of his neck. He broke the kiss and took a small step back as Juli fumbled for the soap dish.

She grinned up at him as she tore open the condom wrapper and reached for him. She used both hands, easing the condom over him as Alex gritted his teeth and hoped to God he didn't embarrass himself.

Her eyes were teasing as she smiled up at him again. "Just in case. No rush."

He looked at her, the wet curls plastered around her cheeks, her breasts full and round and wet. He'd never wanted her more.

"Right," he said and cupped her ass with both hands.

She gave a small squeak of surprise as he boosted her up. She was lighter than he expected—practically weightless in his arms. Alex said a silent thank you to whoever installed the slip-proof shower floors as Juli wrapped her legs around his waist, her thighs slick and strong. Her arms twined around his neck and she kissed him then, hard and wet. A perfect fit. He looked down at where their bodies were almost joined.

"Last chance for something to go wrong here," she breathed. "Fire alarm, maybe?"

"Could be nuclear war," Alex murmured. "Doesn't matter."

Then he slid inside her.

Juli cried out and Alex hesitated a moment, part of him still expecting the ceiling to cave in or a band of trumpet-playing monkeys to come crashing through the door.

But the only sounds were Juli's soft gasps of pleasure and the spatter of water on the shower walls. The flowery soap had dissolved to a green lump at his feet, but Alex didn't care. He didn't care about anything but the way it felt to have Juli wrapped around him like this.

He pushed her back against the shower wall, bracing himself as Juli began to move against him—slowly at first, then with new urgency. It seemed like every inch of her surrounded every inch of him, their bodies tangled in a slick arrangement of legs and hips and arms and fingers. He thrust his hips and slid deeper, hoping he wasn't hurting her.

"Oh, God," she cried. "When you move like that I lose my mind."

"Good," he murmured and drove into her again.

He could feel her breasts pressed hard against his chest, watched her eyes widen as he pushed deeper into her, her back glued to the slick tile wall. His forehead bumped the showerhead and he saw stars for a second but kept moving inside her anyway. He didn't care if he bled to death. He didn't care if the maid found his wet, wilted carcass on the floor in the morning. He only cared about this moment right now with Juli moving against him, her whole body twining around his.

"Don't stop! Please, don't—"

She gasped and gave another cry of pleasure. He felt her legs tighten around him—felt *everything* tighten around him. He thought he could hold on, maybe keep going for another hour.

But he was already past the point of no return. He groaned and gave in to the pulse of pleasure that seized him like an electric shock. Juli's movements became more fluid, somehow slower and faster all at the same time. Alex felt everything inside him explode as he drove into her again and again and again until he was certain he'd die from pleasure.

They remained like that for a few more pulse-beats, Juli's thighs locked around his hips and the warm water sluicing over them. At last, Juli gave a little gasp and let go of him. Her arms and legs made a slick smacking sound as she peeled her flesh from his. She stepped back, her cheeks flushed and wet.

"Well, Pirate Alex," she said, grinning up at him. "You sure know how to show a girl a good time."

"The pleasure's all mine, Pirate Juli," he said and bent to kiss her.

Chapter 18

THE NEXT MORNING, JULI WOKE TO FIND ALEX GONE. She patted the bed beside her, flipping back the covers just to make sure. No Alex. No breakfast, either. She wasn't sure which was more annoying.

She laid there for a few more minutes, replaying her favorite scenes from their night together. There was a lot of slick, hot flesh. A lot of nibbling and kissing and moaning. She could say with absolute certainty now that Alex's bedroom performance rated far better than a four. On a scale of one to ten, he was probably closer to a thirty-six. His hands alone deserved some sort of medal. And the things he could do with his mouth—

Juli smiled, lost in pleasant thoughts. There were a whole lot of pleasant thoughts.

Well, okay, Cody's kidnapping wasn't so pleasant. Having a pistol pointed at her by a man she'd known since childhood wasn't so pleasant. But really, most of the rest had been good.

Juli opened her eyes and sighed, accepting the fact that bacon would not be appearing on her pillow. She flung her legs over the side of the bed and sat up, tugging the sheet off to wrap around her torso like a toga.

Somehow, the effect wasn't as sexy as she'd hoped. She took two steps and tripped, yanking the toga down over her breasts and causing her to stub her toe on the wall.

"Dammit!" she yelped, dropping the sheet entirely. She grabbed her foot, hopping on one leg as she peered at the injured toe.

"That's a good look," Alex said from the balcony, folding his arms over his chest as he watched her through the open glass doors. "Hopping on one foot naked—it's exactly how I pictured you when we first met."

Juli dropped her foot and fumbled for the sheet. Modesty wasn't her strong suit, but with the patio door wide open, she thought it best not to treat passersby to a show like she and Alex had witnessed the night before.

"Did you sleep well?" she asked, retrieving the sheet and her dignity from the floor.

Alex glanced at his watch. "Yes, the sixty-seven minutes we weren't ravaging each other were quite restful."

"You can sleep later, sailor boy. We've got an hour until Malcolm's coming back for us."

Alex stepped through the door of the balcony and into the plush coolness of the room. "You mean coming back for the rest of his books. I think we're an afterthought."

Juli tugged at the sheet, noticing the way Alex seemed fixated on the spot where it kept slipping down her left breast. She felt the heat rise up through her body, and she wanted him all over again.

"Should we try calling Phyllis and Jake?" she asked. It seemed like a safer thing to ask than *will you bend me over the dresser again*?

"Already did," Alex said, and Juli was confused until she remembered which question she'd actually asked aloud. "I called the hotel room when you were in the bathroom earlier. No answer."

"That's odd."

He shrugged. "It's early. They're probably having breakfast."

"I'm sure Cody's serving up eggs Benedict as we speak."

They both fell silent for a moment, staring at each other. Outside, the ocean crashed against the seawall. Alex didn't move. Juli looked away first, feigning a sudden interest in straightening a gold-framed painting on the wall.

Alex cleared his throat. "Look, Juli—about last night—"

"Oh, good," Juli said, looking away from the picture and back at Alex. She sat down on the edge of the bed and smiled. "I was hoping we'd have a chance to talk about our wedding now. I was thinking if we sent out our save-the-date cards in June, we could buy some time before we send out the actual invitations at the end of the summer. So then we'll have a fall wedding?"

Alex just stared. He opened his mouth to speak, then closed it again. Juli rolled her eyes.

"Relax, sailor boy. I'm kidding. Anytime a man starts a conversation with 'about last night,' it's a pretty good bet he's not going to suggest getting matching tattoos. It's okay—really."

He shook his head. "Juli—no. That's not it."

"No?" She quirked an eyebrow at him, hoping she looked more nonchalant than she felt. Her pulse was beating fast in her throat, but she tried to keep her expression serene and detached. She'd been here before, hadn't she? On the outside, looking in. She could do this again.

"Look, I'm crazy about you," Alex insisted, taking a few steps closer. "It's just—things are complicated right now. My career is in shambles, my pension's gone, and I have no idea where my life is headed. I think—well, now isn't really the best time to start something serious but—"

"And you still don't trust me."

He blinked. "What?"

"That's the main thing, isn't it? You've got doubts about who I am, what I'm after, what I might do to damage your poor little pirate heart."

The last part came out snarkier than she intended, but she let the words hang there anyway. She waited for him to argue, but he said nothing.

She took a shaky breath. "Who was she?"

"What do you mean?"

"The woman who saddled you with such a whopping pile of trust issues."

Alex looked away. He lifted his hand, and for a moment, Juli thought he might rest it on her shoulder. Then he dropped it to his side. "Fiancée," he said. "*Ex-fiancée*."

"I see."

He turned and looked at her, and his eyes were so sad, her heart nearly broke in two. She wanted to stand up and say something comforting, but she couldn't find any words at all. What the hell could she say? *Now that we've exchanged bodily fluids, you really ought to love and trust me forever.*

Not the way life worked. Not her life, anyway.

She stood up and clutched the sheet tighter around her. "I'm going to take a shower."

Alex reached out and caught her by the arm. "Wait."

"Alex, it's okay, really. You don't have to—"

"I want to try."

His voice was so soft she wasn't sure she heard him right. "What?"

"I want to try to get over it. That's what I've been thinking this morning while you were asleep. It's what I was trying to say before we got all tangled up talking about weddings and fiancées and, and—"

"Wait. You're saying you want to—what, *date*?"

He flinched a little at the word but nodded. "Yes. Look, I know I've been paranoid and you don't deserve that."

"I guess I haven't helped. I wasn't exactly forthcoming with the IQ thing or the details about Uncle Frank."

Alex sighed, his hand still warm and solid on her arm. "Let's just agree we both had secrets."

"Okay." Juli bit her lip.

"Look, I'm crazy about you. Totally, completely, ridiculously crazy about you. And last night was amazing."

She managed a small smile. "It was."

He returned the smile, his eyes never leaving hers. "So maybe we move forward from here?"

She waited, not sure what he was getting at. "Together?"

"Yes. Slowly. I mean—if you want to?"

"Okay," she said, her heart fluttering with some combination of joy and trepidation. "Right. Together."

"I'd like that."

"Me too." She smiled again. "I'm going to take a shower now, okay?"

"Together?"

She laughed. "No. Not together. Not if we're going to get out of here in less than an hour."

She stood on tiptoe and gave him a light kiss on the

cheek. He started to reach for her again, but she dodged his hand, laughing as she started to lose her grip on the sheet. She moved toward the bathroom, feeling Alex's eyes on her back.

It was a good feeling.

—————

As soon as Alex heard the shower come on, he leaned forward against the wall and whacked his head a couple times against the doorframe.

Well that was almost a disaster, he told himself. *The most beautiful, passionate, pleasantly insane woman you've ever met has mind-blowing sex with you all night long, and in the morning, you act like a mistrustful jerk and nearly blow everything.*

Idiot.

Alex whacked his head once more for good measure.

From the other side of the wall, he heard Juli's muffled voice over the rush of the shower.

"Did you need something?" she shouted.

"A lobotomy," Alex muttered, trying not to remember what had happened the last time that shower had been running.

"What?" she yelled again.

"Biscuits and gravy," Alex shouted back. "I'm going to run down and grab breakfast, okay?"

"Bring me some too! And a side of fruit, okay?"

"Sure," Alex called.

He loved her. He was pretty sure of it. Even better, he trusted her. Or he was starting to, anyway. That's more than he'd been able to do with any woman he'd dated in twenty years. It felt pretty damn good.

He moved away from the wall and began hunting for his wallet. He spotted it on the dresser next to Uncle Frank and made a grab for it. He turned and started to tuck it in his back pocket.

Clang!

His elbow hit something hard and metal and he knew without looking it was the urn. He whipped around in time to see it go toppling off the dresser.

"No!"

Over the rush of the shower, he heard her voice. "What?"

The urn fell in slow motion and Alex made a grab for it, his mind whirling with visions of ash and bone fragments. His fingers closed over thin air, and Alex shut his eyes as the urn hit the floor.

Crash.

He opened his eyes slowly. He blinked.

Gold coins. Krugerrand, to be precise, and they were covering the carpet.

"Alex?" Juli called again from the other side of the bathroom door.

He stared at the floor in disbelief. The top of the urn was still sealed, but the bottom had broken open, revealing a hidden compartment. He stared at the coins, dumbstruck. There were at least twenty of them, one-ounce pieces from the look of it. Maybe thirty thousand dollars in gold right there at his feet.

He looked toward the closed bathroom door, heard the splash of the shower on the other side of it. He looked back at the coins.

Jesus. What the hell was Juli playing at here?

"Everything okay?" she called from behind the door.

He blinked at the coins. He swallowed.

"It's nothing," he yelled. "Take your time."

Then he bent to put everything back the way he'd found it.

———∿∿∿———

Alex couldn't stop his mind from reeling. What the hell was she doing with thirty grand in gold coins? Krugerrand, the same sort of coins Tom Portelli had been running as part of his diamond smuggling operation. Was that really a coincidence? Knowing his crooked ex-boss was Juli's close family friend, could he really believe that?

He wanted to talk to her, but he didn't have a clue what to say. *I dropped your dead uncle and couldn't help noticing you're transporting a rather large sum of gold.*

As it turned out, there was no time for chitchat. Malcolm showed up early as Juli was still drying her hair, and he hustled them both down to the pier before they had a chance to eat.

"We're in a bit of a hurry," Malcolm said as he heaved a giant box of books into one of the cigarette boats. "There was a problem back on Barbados, and I need to return as quickly as possible."

"Problem?" Alex asked, wondering what else could possibly go wrong.

"Yes, apparently the U.S. Government has an interest in the ship that came to be in our possession recently—something about a criminal investigation—which is rather unfortunate, you see, since we obtained this ship for use in our important future business transactions."

Alex felt a nerve start to twitch beside his left eye. "So where is the cargo ship now?"

Malcolm shook his head sadly. "It was still there when we left but positively crawling with federal agents. They'll probably have taken it by the time we return. Such a shame, too. We had already selected a new color to paint it—really, the loveliest shade of blue—so this is quite frustrating."

Frustrating. Alex sat down hard on a box of books, trying not to lose his cool. Perhaps sensing just how close Alex was to leaping off the end of the pier, Juli touched Malcolm's sleeve.

"So, Malcolm—the cargo that was on the ship when you, um, *obtained* it—where is that now?"

Malcolm heaved another box of books into the cigarette boat and dusted his hands off. "Gone."

"Gone?" Alex croaked.

"Gone," Malcolm repeated. "All of it. Everything from every cargo hold."

"But—"

"Really, the government is welcome to it. Certainly we had no use for that sort of cargo. The boat, on the other hand—"

Alex put his head in his hands. *Jesus.* He'd been holding out hope that maybe, somehow, they'd missed something. They'd been in such a rush after Cody got kidnapped that they hadn't really searched. He'd been hoping they'd get back on that boat and find some secret nook where the diamonds were hidden. Or maybe he and Jake had just imagined what they'd seen in the cargo hold—

"So, Malcolm," Juli said, her voice much calmer than the ones screaming in Alex's brain. "Are you going to be penalized for, well, for stealing the cargo boat?"

Malcolm looked up at her, surprised. "Why, certainly not. We have an agreement with the governments of several nations—the United States included—permitting us to seize any ship we like. Naturally, we must also seize the ones they ask us to, but clearly we have proper authorization."

Juli and Alex stared at him. Seemingly unconcerned, Malcolm began shifting book boxes around in the boat.

Juli was first to speak. "The U.S. Government?"

"Well of course, my dear," he said, not looking up from his books. "Occasionally, they have a need to remove certain vessels or cargo from the high seas, and certainly we're equipped to do that. And of course, we're allowed to seize other boats as needed for our own personal use."

"But why—"

"They don't usually tell us *why*, my dear," he said, speaking as though it was the most natural thing in the world. "We're just pleased to have such a wide variety of vessels at our disposal. It's a lovely arrangement, really."

"You're government sanctioned pirates," Alex said flatly.

Malcolm laughed and hefted another box. "You didn't think we'd do this without proper health benefits and government pension plans, did you?"

Alex shook his head, wondering if he should just get it over with and drown himself in the bay.

"I chose the wrong damn career," he muttered and stood up to retrieve more stolen books from the shed.

Chapter 19

THE RIDE TO BARBADOS WAS BUMPY, AND TWICE JULI
had to turn and hurl over the edge of the boat.

Hardly the romantic morning afterglow she'd
hoped for.

The roar of the boat's motor and the crashing of the
ocean made conversation impossible, which was just as
well. She could tell Alex had slipped back into a dark
mood. Whether it was the loss of the cargo ship or something else entirely was anyone's guess.

Alex squeezed her hand. "You okay?"

She nodded and took a swig from the water bottle
he offered her. "I thought I was through being seasick,"
she yelled over the roar of the engine. "That I had my
sea legs now."

"Chop like this can make even the saltiest sailor
heave," he reassured her. "See? Even Phillip looks a
little green."

"That's because Malcolm just hit him in the stomach
for suggesting he didn't need that last box of first-edition
botanical illustration books."

Alex squeezed her knee and looked back at the ocean,
his mind clearly a million miles away.

She wasn't sure how much time passed before land
came into view and Malcolm and his brothers began
chattering back and forth in complicated boating jar-
gon. Juli stared out at the spot where the cargo boat had

been docked just a day ago. Now it was only a grayish swirl of water, an empty hole where Alex's pension might've been.

"You okay, Juli?" Alex called.

"Fine, fine. Just a little queasy still."

"Go sit down on that bench over there if you want. I'll be up in just a second and then we can head back to the hotel."

Juli nodded, not seeing any reason to argue. She wandered over to a concrete slab flecked with bird poop and plunked herself down. She waited, enjoying the view, sipping her water, wondering what the hell she was going to do with her life when this was all over.

She didn't really plan to be a pirate. It was fun pretending while it lasted, but ultimately, it was make-believe.

Dr. Gordon was right. She needed to grow up, find herself, get a real job, and focus on using her intellect for something besides high-seas thievery.

Law school, maybe?

"All done?" she asked, standing up as Alex approached, looking sweaty and disheveled.

Just like last night, she mused, then pushed the thought out of her mind as she accepted the hand he offered her and allowed him to hoist her to her feet.

"They can get the rest from here," he said. "Apparently they've got some top-secret pirate hideout somewhere nearby."

"So that's that," she said, trying not to notice Alex was still holding on to her hand.

He nodded. His eyes didn't leave hers. "That's that."

"I'd better say good-bye to Malcolm then." Juli withdrew her hand and walked back to the edge of the dock where Malcolm was barking orders at Phillip and Percy.

"Be careful with that!" he shouted at Percy. "Do you have any idea how valuable a limited edition *Madame Bovary* is?"

Juli touched his arm. "Hey, Malcolm, we're heading back to our hotel now. I'm not sure if we'll see you again, but if we don't, have a nice life."

"You too, my dear, you too," he said, grasping her hands and kissing her quickly on each cheek. "You know, your young friend Cody was quite a help to us last night and this morning. He reorganized the whole kitchen on our ship. And his dry scallops with black sesame pesto and lemon palm sugar glaze—" Malcolm kissed his fingertips. "Superb."

"I'll have to get the recipe from him," Juli said, knowing she'd do no such thing. Maybe that was it. Maybe she should learn to cook.

"My dear, it's been a consummate pleasure enjoying your company." He kissed her hands one more time, and Juli responded by giving him a chaste peck on the cheek.

"You too, Malcolm."

Percy and Phillip dropped the box they were carrying and stood up to flank Malcolm, waiting for their kisses. Juli hesitated, then rose up on tiptoe, kissing Percy first, then Phillip. Both men turned bright pink and looked down at their feet, braced for a blow from Malcolm. He looked at them both, then shook his head and picked up a box.

Juli smiled and rocked back on her heels. "Okay, then," she said. "Thanks for everything."

Malcolm nodded at her, then at Alex. "You two take care of each other."

Alex touched Juli's elbow. "Of course."

Malcolm turned and began barking orders at his brothers. Alex looked at Juli, then nodded toward the walkway.

"Shall we?"

"After you."

They strolled together along the street, headed for the same sunny yellow hotel they'd picked out just a day earlier. Had it really only been that long? It seemed like a lifetime ago. Back when they still had some hope there'd been a point to this whole mission. Juli looked at Alex and sighed.

"You okay?" he asked.

"I'm fine. I think I just need to eat something."

"I'm sure Cody has something marinating or curing or broiling."

She tried to muster her usual enthusiasm for food but found herself faking a smile instead. Something was off, but she wasn't sure exactly what.

They walked the rest of the way in silence.

When they finally reached the suite, Alex stuck his key in the lock and pushed the door open.

From across the room, Cody came galloping toward them like a spaniel with a thyroid problem.

"Hey, guys! How's it going? Did you have fun in St. Lucia? Did Malcolm tell you about the boat?"

"Hey, Cookie," Alex said as he slapped Cody on the shoulder and maneuvered around him, making his way toward the kitchenette. Juli watched the rigid set of his shoulders for a moment before turning and standing on tiptoe to kiss Cody on the cheek.

"Hey, Cookie," she said, following Alex into the kitchen. "It's been a long night. How are things here?"

Cody beamed at them. "Great. Did Malcolm tell you he offered me a job?"

Alex stuck his head in the fridge and began rummaging around. "A job?"

Cody reached up into one of the cupboards and took down three glasses, handing one to Juli. "I made fresh-squeezed mango lemonade this morning. The pitcher's there on the top shelf in the fridge."

Alex came out with the pitcher and filled each of the glasses to the brim. Juli noticed he wasn't meeting anyone's eye.

"Fresh mint garnish?" Cody asked.

"Um, thanks."

Juli smiled. "Thank you." She waited while Cody anchored the leaves on the edge of each glass before sticking a small paper umbrella in a maraschino cherry and dropping it in the lemonade.

Juli smiled. "We missed you, Cookie!"

"I missed you guys too!"

"So about this job," Alex said. "What sort of job is it?"

"Oh, Malcolm needs a cook on his pirate ship. It sounds like a pretty good deal, even if Malcolm does make me learn *The Canterbury Tales* in Old English. And the pay is really good. And he likes my lavender-injected lamb shank with goat cheese and figs."

Juli beamed at him. "Who wouldn't?"

She looked at Alex, trying to gauge his reaction to Cody's news. He took a sip of his lemonade and nodded, then gave Cody another pat on the shoulder.

"That's great. Congratulations, Cookie. You'll make a fine cook on a pirate vessel. You've already had plenty of practice."

Cody beamed as he turned to put the lemonade pitcher back in the fridge. "Thanks, Alex. I owe it all to you. I mean, without this experience, I don't know what I'd do. But now, I've really been able to find myself."

"You did that yourself, Cookie," Alex said. "You're a talented guy—it's about time you got to use those talents."

"Thanks, Alex. And I'm sure you'll find something new too. I mean, it's not like you're *that* old."

Juli winced and watched as Alex drank the rest of the lemonade in one big gulp. When he set the glass down, he leaned against the counter and looked at Cody.

"So you know the cargo ship is gone, right?" Alex said slowly. "That even if there were diamonds on board, they're long gone now?"

Cody nodded, looking grim. "Yeah. I know. Jake was pretty bummed about it too. And Phyllis was crying. I didn't even know she could cry; did you?"

"Well, there was that time she missed the audition for *American Gladiators*."

"No, she didn't even cry then. Just punched the mail-room guy."

Juli looked around, realizing neither Jake nor Phyllis had come out to greet them yet. "Cookie, where are the others?"

Cody nodded toward the closed bedroom door and gave a sheepish shrug. "I guess while we were gone, they got to know each other pretty well."

Juli raised an eyebrow at the door. "Are you sure?"

Cody's cheeks flushed pink again. "Well, Jake came out looking kind of sweaty last night and offered me twenty dollars to go buy him some condoms across the street." He frowned, looking thoughtful. "I guess he could have been making water balloons. You think that was it?"

Alex appeared to be trying hard not to laugh. "No, I don't think he was making water balloons."

Cody sipped his lemonade. "That's what I thought."

"So this is good," Juli said, lifting her lemonade in a toast. "Cookie has a new job, Jake and Phyllis are bumping uglies, and Tom Portelli is headed to jail. It's a happy ending. Well, mostly."

Cody frowned. "Tom Portelli is going to jail? What happened?"

Juli drained the rest of her glass and set it on the counter. "I'll let Alex bring you up to speed on Tom Portelli. I'm going to use the restroom."

She maneuvered around Alex, ignoring the jolt of lust that surged when his arm brushed hers. She moved down the narrow hallway, trying hard to tune out any noises coming from the master bedroom.

She had almost reached the door of the bathroom when a pale arm snaked out the bedroom door and grabbed her by the sleeve. Stumbling back, Juli felt herself being dragged into the room. She yelped, but resistance was futile.

As the door slammed shut behind her, Juli found herself face to face with a flushed, disheveled-looking Phyllis.

"Oh," Juli said, blinking against the yellowish light glowing from the bandana-covered lamp in the corner. "Got used to the bustier, huh? You can go ahead and keep that. Where's Jake?"

Phyllis darted a glance toward the bedroom door, looking nervous. "Jake's in the bathroom. Quick, I need your help. I've got a big, big problem."

Phyllis reached behind her and pulled something out from under the pillow.

Juli gasped and staggered back, trying to get away.

Chapter 20

IT WAS WITHOUT A DOUBT THE LARGEST VIBRATOR JULI had ever seen in her life.

And the way Phyllis was wielding it in front of her like a sword was, frankly, the most frightening thing Juli could imagine.

"That is a very *big* problem," Juli agreed, stepping back a little to avoid being hit with it. "Purple, too."

Phyllis looked down at the vibrator, studying it with equal parts fear and fascination. Its flesh was translucent and almost seemed to glow in the dim bedroom light.

"Well yes, but see, I'm not totally sure what to do with it." Phyllis looked back up with desperation in her eyes. "And I want Jake to think I'm worldly and experienced, but I just don't know how to use something so... so..."

"Terrifying?" Juli supplied.

"Right. In a good way, though. But see, I'm not even sure where the batteries go, or how to turn it on, or really, what I'm supposed to do with—"

"Um, Phyllis?"

"Yes?"

"Where did you get that?"

Phyllis bit her lip. "Well, see, after you guys left yesterday evening, Jake and I spent a lot of time talking. And we had a romantic dinner alone at a little seafood place around the corner with all these candles and some really great wine. And then afterward, we went for a stroll down by the harbor, and we looked at the stars, and we held hands, and he even kissed me right there in public. And everything was really very nice. Just like I imagined."

"I see," Juli said, not seeing at all how this translated to Phyllis holding the world's most disturbing vibrator.

"And while we were down there looking at the boats, we ran into one of Malcolm's brothers. I forget which one. Blythe or Winchester or Pierson or something like that."

"Okay."

"And they were trying to off-load some of the cargo from the boat, you know? They didn't have any use for it, I guess. He said they just wanted the boat, so he asked us if we wanted any of the stuff from the cargo hold."

"Stuff?"

"Well, yes. See, there were supposed to be diamonds on the boat, right? But when Jake and Alex looked, the whole cargo hold was full of these."

She toed a glossy pink box lying on the floor at the foot of the bed. Juli looked down, turning her head to admire the pictures and read the bright orange calligraphy printed on the top.

"*Diamond Delight Premier Pleasures*," she read. She looked up at Phyllis, suddenly comprehending. "You guys hijacked a cargo ship full of sex toys?"

"Shh!" Phyllis hissed, glancing at the door. "We didn't actually hijack it, remember? I mean we tried to, but—"

"So Malcolm hijacked a ship full of sex toys? Are you guys all crazy?"

"We must have gotten some bad information, okay? I mean, we thought we were going after real diamonds, but obviously there was some sort of misunderstanding or something."

"Uh-huh," Juli said, thinking that a misunderstanding was when you showed up at the wrong time for a lunch date, or accidentally patted your boss on the butt at a company meeting.

Clearly this was beyond a misunderstanding. Juli stared at the giant phallus, mesmerized. She could see right through its clear purple flesh, and couldn't help but admire the size of the battery pack in one end. She blinked at it, wanting to look away, not quite knowing how. Phyllis was still talking, waving the vibrator around, and Juli tore her eyes off it to focus on what Phyllis was saying.

"So anyway," Phyllis said, "Jake told him sure, if they were just getting rid of stuff, we could probably put something to good use. And he was getting all smiley and winking at me, so I didn't want to look like a ninny, you know? I wanted to seem womanly and experienced."

"Of course."

"So we all went down to the cargo hold and he told me to pick out whatever I wanted—*anything*. And I looked at a couple of different things and thought this one looked kind of neat, with the special vibrating love beads inside that swirl around when you turn it on. I saw that on TV once, I think. Only I thought it was supposed to look like a rabbit, and this doesn't look like a rabbit. I mean, it doesn't have any fur, obviously, and the ears are all wrong. But anyway, the pirates just gave it to me."

"The pirates gave you a sex toy?" Juli stared at the gargantuan vibrator again, trying not to notice the disturbing little ears or the odd veiny-looking surface. "A vibrator the size of a small automobile."

Phyllis blushed and looked down. "It was so pretty. And I'd never had one before. The pirates were just going to throw them out anyway, and Jake seemed so excited. Only now I can't figure out how to use it, and Jake's going to realize I'm not exotic and adventurous and—"

Juli was still trying not to stare, which was hard with Phyllis waving it around, her gestures more pronounced the more frantic she became.

Suddenly, something caught Juli's eye.

Something very, very sparkly.

"Um, Phyllis—could you stop waving the vibrator around for a second?"

"You want it?" Phyllis asked, thrusting it toward her.

Juli stepped back. "Um, thank you, no. But could you just hold it still?"

Phyllis held the vibrator upright like a torch. With her hair spiky around the crown of her head, she looked uncannily like the Statue of Liberty.

Juli squinted at the vibrator.

"Okay, not to sound like a pervert or anything," Juli said slowly, reaching out for the vibrator against her better judgment. "But I've got something a little bit like this at home. And I've gotta say, there's something really wrong here."

—∿∿—

Alex nearly fell off his chair when Juli and Phyllis came tearing out of the bedroom looking positively rabid.

Phyllis was wearing the black bustier and the look of a woman who'd been willingly ravaged by a clumsy lover. Juli was wild-eyed, waving a massive purple phallus at him and shouting something unintelligible.

Both women were talking at once, a cacophony of words and gestures and flying hair and sights he had hoped never to see in his lifetime.

There was nothing safe to look at. Alex turned to Cody. "Is there any more lemonade? With vodka, maybe?"

"Alex, look at this," Juli demanded, thrusting the giant purple penis at him.

"Really, I'd rather not—"

"Alex, seriously, you need to see what I just found."

"Juli, really—"

"Oh for crying out loud!" Juli whirled around, zeroing in on Cody. "Cookie, give me a goddamn knife."

Cody looked alarmed. He glanced over her shoulder at Alex, his eyes pleading. Alex was too stunned to say a word.

Obediently, Cody reached into a drawer and pulled out a sparkling butcher knife. He handed it to her, then stepped far, far out of reach.

Juli snatched the knife and yanked a cutting board off the rack beside the fridge. She laid the giant purple phallus on the surface and drew the knife back. Alex jumped out of his chair.

"Juli, really, if you're upset about last night or this morning—I'm sorry, really, I am, but you've made your point and I swear to you—*oh my God!*"

"Dear Lord in heaven!" Jake cried, emerging from the bathroom just in time to see Juli slice the enormous purple penis right down the middle.

There was a loud crash, and everyone turned to see Cody hit the floor. Phyllis shrieked. Alex peered down at him.

He was out cold.

"Look," Juli said, ignoring all of them as she pried apart the rubbery edges to reveal the inner workings of the vibrator. Alex winced, but Juli pressed on. Reaching inside, she scooped something out. She held out her hand and unfolded her fingers.

"Diamonds," Alex gasped, stepping forward. "What the—"

"Stop holding your crotch for a minute and take these," she said, thrusting her palm at him. "Damn right they're diamonds. Big ones."

"No shit," Jake breathed, stepping over Cody to come closer. "I mean the vibrator was big, but these are massive."

They each plucked one from Juli's fingers. Even Phyllis, who cast a quick, forlorn look at her ruined sex toy, reached for a particularly large gem.

Everyone stared at the diamonds. Alex held his, turning it over in his palm, testing the weight of it, too dumbfounded to speak. At last, he looked up at Juli.

"I missed a few things when you rattled off your list of professions a few days ago," he said, swallowing to make his voice sound less shaky, "but didn't you mention something about working as a gemologist?"

Juli nodded, looking down at the rest of the stones in her hand. She turned her palm over on the cutting board and spilled the stones out one by one. They lay there then, glittering brightly beneath the glare of the florescent kitchen lights. Alex stared, trying to keep his focus on the diamonds instead of how beautiful she was.

Juli plucked up a single stone and brought it up close to her eye. She tilted it into the light, studying it.

"Obviously I don't have a loupe or a microscope with me at the moment. But this has a high refractive index—that means it sharply bends the light that passes through it, see?"

All of them nodded. On the floor, Cody gave a soft snore.

"And look—when I set it down on this newspaper, you can't read anything through it. If it were glass or cubic zirconia or something, you'd at least see black smudges through the stone. But here—nothing. And look," she held it up again, "how the light sort of reflects gray through it?"

"I thought it was supposed to be a rainbow," Jake said, holding up the one in his own hand, turning it over in the light.

"No," Juli said, shaking her head. "Only in a fake or a real low quality diamond. Which these, obviously, are not."

"How did you know to cut open the—" Alex glanced at the dissected purple phallus and shook his head. "Never mind. These came from the cargo hold in the boat? From that stash Jake and I saw there?"

Jake nodded, looking proudly at Phyllis for a moment before turning back to Alex. "We got it last night. From the pirates. They must not have known there were diamonds inside."

Alex pressed his lips together, staring down at the pool of gems splashed across the counter. "So how many diamonds do we have here?" he asked, sweeping his hand over the cutting board. "How much do we think this is worth?"

Phyllis set her diamond down on the cutting board. "Well that's the funny thing." She smiled at Jake, and

Alex saw something in her eye he'd never seen before. Something wild and lustful and—dear God—almost beautiful. Phyllis and Jake smiled at each other and Alex felt something twist in his chest. He fought the urge to reach out for Juli's hand.

Phyllis turned back to Alex. "When I picked this out last night, the pirates were all laughing and Jake was being—well, being a guy—and I thought these vibrators were so pretty. I mean, they come in four different colors, so how do you pick? And everyone was making dirty jokes and I really wanted to be the sort of woman who'd know how to use a vibrator like this—who'd be really enthusiastic and wild and—"

"Phyllis," Alex said, glancing at Juli to see if she had any idea what was going on. Juli just shrugged. "What the hell are you getting at?"

Phyllis swallowed. "We got three cases of them. Thirty-six vibrators to a case. All they had on board. Every single one. I thought I ought to stock up."

Jake grabbed Phyllis by the arm, pulling her to his chest in an embrace that looked almost painful. He hugged her tightly, rocking back and forth and hooting with joy. Phyllis giggled—the first giggle Alex had ever heard escape her lips.

"That's my girl," Jake said. "My naughty, naughty girl."

Alex turned to Juli, his heart hammering in his chest. "Can I see you alone for a minute?"

She looked at him, clearly perplexed. "Now?"

"Now."

He caught her by the arm, not waiting for an answer as he steered her down the hall toward the back bedroom.

"You're not planning to do something obscene to me with the giant purple vibrator, are you?" she asked. "Not that I'd mind under normal circumstances, but I hardly think now is the time for—"

He shut the door hard and Juli stopped talking. Her eyes were wide as Alex leaned back against the door and studied her, weighing his words carefully.

"You saw the diamonds and Phyllis didn't."

She stared at him for a few beats. "Yes," she said, the word tinged with caution.

"You didn't have to say anything. None of us would have known. You could have just taken them and run."

She frowned. "Why on earth would I do that?"

Alex sighed. "I know about the Krugerrand in Uncle Frank's urn," he said. "I don't care, Juli. I don't care how they got there or why you're smuggling them or what your connection is to Tom Portelli. I trust you, okay? I trust you and I love you and I've been going insane these last few hours thinking there's even the tiniest chance I might never touch you again. I don't care if you're a cop or a criminal, I don't care if you're the smartest woman on the planet or the dumbest. I want to be with you no matter what."

"Alex," she said slowly, her eyes brimming with tears. "Alex."

"Yes?"

She shook her head. "What the fuck are you talking about?"

"I love you, Juli. I know we haven't—"

"Not that, you dumbass," she interrupted. "I love you too. What Krugerrand in Uncle Frank's urn?"

Alex looked at her. "The false bottom. The twenty

Krugerrand. I thought—" He stopped talking, silenced by the dumbstruck look on her face. "You honestly didn't know?"

Juli opened her mouth, then closed it, then opened it again. "He picked that urn himself. He must have thought I'd figure it out. The Feds seized his estate before he died, but I guess this was his way of leaving me something." She shook her head, her baffled gaze fixed on a spot on the carpet. Then she looked up at him.

"You honestly thought I was smuggling Krugerrand and hiding that from you?"

Alex swallowed hard. "I didn't know what to think, Juli. You had so many surprises, so many secrets. But I realized that it doesn't matter. Not to me, anyway, not now. I love you if I'm poor and you're rich, or you're rich and I'm poor, or—"

"Shut up, Alex."

He shut up.

"Neither of us is poor now. You have diamonds, I have Krugerrand—"

"No, *we* have diamonds. You were as much a part of this mission as the rest of us."

"Alex, I don't think—"

"I don't care about the money, Juli. And I don't care about the secrets. I only care about you."

She blinked at him, her eyes brimming with tears. "I care about you too." She looked down at her hand, which still held the ruined remains of the giant purple phallus. "Though if we're being honest here, I do kind of care about this."

He smiled and reached for her. She came willingly,

and he wrapped her in his arms and held her there against his chest. "Me too," he murmured into her hair. "Me too."

Chapter 21

Three weeks later

"YOU THINK THIS IS PRETTY CLOSE TO THE SPOT?" Alex asked.

Juli squinted through the lenses of her cheap sunglasses, momentarily distracted by the sight of Alex without his shirt on. She slid her glasses down the bridge of her nose, admiring the flex of his biceps as he let some tension out of the sails, slowing the boat. A wave crashed behind him, making him look like a poster boy for sailing gear.

They'd returned the hefty powerboat to the charter rental company in St. John, swapping it out for Alex's forty-five-foot Cabo Rico. Alex had told her all about the original plan—about sailing his boat down from Key West, about their quest for a seamless, peaceful heist, and their plans for a quick trip home.

Obviously, the plan hadn't quite worked. Juli, for one, was glad.

She watched as Alex trimmed the jib, his forearms flexing as he pulled one end of the rope. She smiled, noticing the faint scratch marks she'd left on his bare shoulder the night before.

"Hello?" Alex called, glancing over his shoulder, still waiting for a response. "You with me here?"

"Just admiring the view."

She tore her eyes away from Alex to survey the sea around them. Unlike the deep black-blue of the Atlantic, the water here ranged from a bright turquoise to a pale aqua where the coral reefs rose up to enjoy the sun. She was glad Alex knew what he was doing out here. And she was damn glad she got to watch him do it. She'd even gotten to help, learning about tacking and schooning and goosewinging and not even giggling anymore when he told her to come abreast.

Of course, coxswain and dinghy and ditty bag were still pretty funny.

"It's nice here," Juli said at last. "I think this seems right."

It was certainly beautiful. The sort of place Uncle Frank would have enjoyed if the weather had been this nice.

And if he'd been sober and not dead.

Juli reached for her knapsack and rummaged inside for Uncle Frank's urn. Pulling it out carefully, she rested it in her lap and looked around.

"It's a lot lighter without the Krugerrand," she said.

"I can't believe you lugged that thing around for so long and never noticed the coins."

"I was a little distracted. Besides, how would I know how much cremated remains are supposed to weigh?"

"Good point."

Juli looked down at the urn. "What do you think, Uncle Frank? You like this spot?"

Alex cleared his throat behind her. "He's not actually answering, is he?"

Juli rolled her eyes. "Of course not. He waits 'til I'm in bed before we have conversations."

"Considering I've been in bed with you every night for the last few weeks, that's disturbing."

Juli grinned. "Oh, we talk about you, mostly. Like your performance in bed, and whether you left the cap off the toothpaste and whether that little freckle on your left shoulder blade looks more like an ant or a mini chocolate chip."

"What does Frank say?"

"Chocolate chip."

Alex smiled, and Juli felt something tingly radiating all the way from her belly to her fingertips. She wondered how long that feeling would stick around. If she'd someday look at Alex over the top of her bifocals as he passed her a tube of Preparation H and she'd have a heart attack from the sheer pleasure of seeing him smile.

She hoped so.

The last couple weeks had been a bit hectic for all of them. Though Alex and the rest of the crew had already planned for how to deal with the diamonds once they had them, Juli's connections to the gem industry didn't hurt. Neither did her ability to speak Flemish on their hasty trip to Antwerp.

When the Kranston executives had called Alex's cell phone in the wake of Tom Portelli's arrest, Juli had held her breath. She'd feared the worst—an ugly legal battle, screaming accusations, a prison sentence for Alex.

Instead, they'd asked him to run the company.

Alex had been polite but firm. *Thanks, but no thanks*. There had been much mumbling about a change in priorities, a new lease on life, the fact that money didn't matter as much as he'd thought it did. Juli had tried hard not to eavesdrop, but it was tough with her ear pressed against the door.

And she'd tried not to be too hopeful when he'd said he was in no hurry to return home to Key West. Now they were back on the water, preparing for this final detail of their journey.

"So how do you want to do this?" Alex asked.

Juli looked out at the horizon, considering her options. The sun was starting to settle lower in the sky, giving everything a faintly pink glow. Frank definitely would have approved.

"I think if we just toss the ashes into the wind, they'll scatter like they're supposed to."

"You want me to head any direction in particular?"

Juli shook her head, scooting closer to the starboard side of the boat. She glanced up at the sails, trying to gauge the direction of the wind.

"Okay," she said, nodding at Alex. "Here we go."

Alex reached out and flipped the switch on his iPod. Loverboy's "Turn Me Loose" came blaring out of the speakers, just like Uncle Frank had asked.

"What about the vodka tonics?" she asked.

Alex held up a small thermos. "Got 'em right here. Ready whenever you are."

"Okay then." Juli took a deep breath. "Here we go."

She flipped the little switch on the bottom of the urn, opening the lid. The wind caught her hair and tossed it around, plastering a curl against the side of her cheek. Juli closed her eyes.

"Rest well, Uncle Frank," she said.

And then, with a little flourish, she turned the urn

upside down and sent the ashes fluttering gracefully into the breeze.

At least, that's what she tried for.

Behind her, Alex sputtered and sneezed. Juli coughed, wiping Uncle Frank from her eyes.

"Wow," she said, glancing down at her hands and arms to see Uncle Frank lodged in every little crevice and wrinkle. "Cremated remains sure can fly."

Juli turned to look at Alex, trying not to giggle.

This was a somber occasion.

"What's the proper protocol here?" Alex asked, shaking the front of his shorts to release Uncle Frank into the breeze. Pale ash clung to his lashes, making him look like a shirtless chimney sweep. "It seems rude to just spit it out."

Juli dusted a thick batch of Uncle Frank out of her hair and shook her head. "No, go ahead. Spitting out cremated remains is the sort of thing he'd appreciate."

She stood up to grab the controls for a moment as Alex spit respectfully over the side of the boat, taking heed of the direction of the wind. He twisted the cap off the thermos and took a swig of the vodka tonic, swishing it around in his mouth before spitting it over the side. He shook his hair out before dumping the rest of the vodka into the ocean for Frank to enjoy.

Then he recapped the thermos and set it next to Juli. Surrendering the controls, Juli sat back down with her feet dangling over the side of the boat.

"For future reference," Alex said, "you may want to learn a bit more about gauging the direction of the wind. If you're going to be spending a lot of time on a sailboat, that is."

Juli grinned. "Thanks for the pointer." She gave her shirt one last shake before tucking the urn back in her knapsack. "I'm sure our new pirate-themed boat charter business will have a lot of clients looking to dispose of cremated remains."

"Actually, there are two signed up already for September. Phyllis's website got several hundred hits just in the first week."

"No kidding? Might have something to do with the shirtless photo of Cody on the home page."

Alex shrugged. "Jake said they'll bring Cody with them when they all come out for our maiden voyage. As long as it doesn't conflict with one of Malcolm's pirate missions."

"Or with Jake and Phyllis's honeymoon," Juli added. "Or with the grand opening of their new sex toy shop in Barbados."

"Nice to see everyone is enjoying their retirement."

Juli smiled, looking up at him appreciatively. "Really, Alex, thanks for doing this. For bringing me all the way out here, I mean. It was really important to Uncle Frank and to the rest of my family that I get to do this just the way he asked."

"So you're grateful?" he asked.

"Oh, yes."

He smiled, stuffing one hand in his pocket as he steered the boat with the other. "How grateful?"

Juli grinned wider and leaned forward, making sure to give him a nice glimpse down the front of her shirt. She said a silent prayer her cleavage wasn't dusted with cremated remains.

"Oh, very grateful," she said. "Supremely grateful.

Back rub grateful at the very least. Maybe even blow-job grateful."

Alex raised an eyebrow at her, considering. "How about marriage grateful?"

Juli felt her heart jump into her throat. Her fingers went numb and her ears began to ring.

"Wha—what?"

Alex pulled his hand out of his pocket, clutching something in his fist. Holding his hand out to her, he opened his fingers. Sitting in the middle of his palm was the most stunning diamond ring she'd ever seen.

Juli felt her throat close up. She couldn't say a word, not even a squeak.

"I'd get down on one knee," Alex said, "but that would make it hard to keep the boat steady. So I'll just ask nicely. Will you marry me, Juli? Please?"

Juli stared at the ring. Her heart was pounding in her ears, her mouth had gone dry, and she felt like she might just throw up. In a good way.

"Look," he said, his hand steady, even though his voice trembled a little. "I know I told you a few weeks ago that I didn't want a relationship when I was broke and unemployed with my life and my career in flux, but I've realized something."

Juli swallowed. "You realized you're set for life now that you cashed in several million dollars worth of diamonds?"

"That too," Alex said, drawing a breath. "But more than that. It wouldn't matter if I didn't have a job or a pension or any money in the bank at all. As long as I have you—and that I love you and I trust you—that's what matters."

Juli felt her eyes stinging, and she was pretty sure it wasn't just the cremated remains on her lashes. Slowly, she reached out and touched the ring. She picked it up, holding it between her thumb and forefinger and lifting it up to the light.

She smiled. "Is this one of the vibrator diamonds?"

"Of course," Alex said, grinning. "Only the best for you."

Juli looked up at him as she slid the ring onto her finger. A perfect fit. "I wouldn't have it any other way."

"Can I take that as a yes?"

Juli stood up and twined her fingers in his hair and kissed him then, admiring the glint of the diamond on her left hand as the sun sank lower on the horizon.

"Yes," she said. "Arrr."

"Arrr," Alex said back, steering the boat into the sunset.

Acknowledgments

Whoever said writing is a solitary profession deserves to be pinned down and tickled until he pees.

My sincere gratitude goes out to the dozens of people who helped me along the way. Infinite thanks to Linda Brundage, Linda Grimes, and Cynthia Reese for being the best critique partners I could hope for, and to my staggeringly talented beta readers, Larie Borden, Bridget McGinn, and Minta Powelson. Without you ladies, my characters might all be badly dressed, bitchy people sitting around drinking wine while their eyes change color every couple pages. Thanks also to Dan Streck for the missing puzzle piece that inspired Juli's "issue."

Big hugs and kisses to my writer pals from The Debutante Ball, Rose City RWA, and Mid-Willamette Valley RWA as well as my Twitter friends and amazing blog readers at *Don't Pet Me, I'm Writing*. You've provided more support than even the best bra I've owned.

Thank you to the crew of *The Prima* in the Whitsunday Islands of Australia, and to the dozens of fascinating characters I encountered traveling around Barbados, Jamaica, and Fiji. Most of you will never know you inspired little pieces of this story or taught me something that helped with its creation.

Huge thanks to my editor, the fabulous Deb Werksman, publicity goddess Danielle Jackson, and the rest of the wonderful staff at Sourcebooks, Inc. I'm thrilled to be part of the team!

I can't express enough appreciation for my amazing agent, Michelle "never say die" Wolfson. Thanks for always believing in me, and for never meeting a dead horse that couldn't be beaten back to life.

Thanks most of all to my parents, Dixie and David Fenske, and my brother, Aaron "Russ" Fenske for your unwavering love, support, and encouragement. I couldn't have done this without you guys.

And thank you to Steve. For everything.

About the Author

A third-generation Oregonian who can peel and eat a banana with her toes, Tawna Fenske has traveled a career path that's led from journalist to English teacher in Venezuela to marketing geek.

She's the author of the popular daily blog "Don't Pet Me, I'm Writing" and a member of Romance Writers of America. She holds a degree in English literature and lives in Central Oregon with a menagerie of ill-behaved (albeit, well-loved) pets.

Though Tawna shares her heroine's violent allergy to seasickness medication, she has never stowed away on a pirate ship. *Making Waves* is her debut novel.

Romeo, Romeo

～ BY ROBIN KAYE ～

**Rosalie Ronaldi doesn't have a domestic
bone in her body...**

All she cares about is her career, so she survives on take-out and
dirty martinis, keeps her shoes under the dining room table, her
bras on the shower curtain rod, and her clothes on the couch.

**Nick Romeo is every woman's fantasy—
tall, dark, handsome, rich, really good in bed,
AND he loves to cook and clean...**

He says he wants an independent woman, but when he meets
Rosalie, all he wants to do is take care of her. Before long,
he's cleaned up her apartment, stocked her refrigerator, and
adopted her dog.

So what's the problem? Just a little matter of mistaken identity,
corporate theft, a hidden past in juvenile detention, and one
big nosy Italian family too close for comfort...

ROSALIE RONALDI MADE A SUCCESSFUL ESCAPE FROM the insane asylum. Okay, so it wasn't a real insane asylum; it was her parents's Bay Ridge home. But most days, it could pass for the Sicilian version of Bellevue. She pulled on her coat as the storm door snicked closed behind her, took a deep breath of cold early January air, and ran for the solace of her car.

Sitting through a typical Italian Sunday dinner at Chez Ronaldi was always a lesson in self-control. Today it had become a lesson in avoidance—marriage avoidance.

For the life of her, Rosalie couldn't figure out why her mother would push a daughter she supposedly loved down the aisle. It wasn't as if the institution had brought Maria Ronaldi any happiness. Just the opposite.

Whenever Rosalie made decisions, she measured the odds and studied the statistical evidence—something at which she'd always excelled. With the divorce rate at 53 percent, if you added the number of unhappy marriages that wouldn't end in divorce because of religious beliefs or sheer stubbornness, which she estimated was running at about 46 percent, only 1 percent of all marriages could be considered happy. A person would have to be crazy to take a calculated risk with a 99 percent failure rate.

Rosalie was many things, but crazy wasn't one of

them. As a child, she'd made the decision never to marry, and nothing in her experience since had done anything but cement her resolve. Of course, if she said that, she'd be breaking the eleventh commandment: thou shalt marry a nice Catholic boy (preferably Italian) and have babies—or go straight to hell.

Rosalie climbed into her VW Beetle and headed toward her Park Slope apartment. Turning onto the Prospect Expressway, she heard a funny thumping noise. Never a good sign. She pulled over to find her tire was as flat as matzo, and after a marathon Italian dinner, the waistband of her pants was so tight that if she took a deep breath, she'd pop a button. God only knew what would happen when she bent down to change the tire.

Rosalie opened the trunk, expecting to see her spare tire. It was supposed to be right there, but all she saw was a big hole.

Great! Just what she needed. She stared into the trunk, turned to kick the flat tire, and called her brother the nicest name she could think of that fit him. Asshole.

"*Stronzo!*" She should have known better than to give him a hundred and sixty bucks to replace her spare tire. She'd told him to buy a full-sized spare, and he hadn't even gotten her one of those donuts. "He's *proprio un stronzo della prima categoria.*"

She had no problem calling Rich the world's biggest asshole in Italian. After all, God excused cursing if done in a second language. He gave bonus points for cursing in a third. Rosalie had a feeling she'd be brushing up on her Spanish.

Dominick Romeo stood in the state-of-the-art garage of
his flagship dealership, the largest car dealership in all
of New York. He'd built it from nothing but brains and
hard work. He owned a chain of dealerships that covered
most of the East Coast, but he'd be damned if he could
figure out what was wrong with his Viper.

Nick checked the clock next to his private hydraulic
lift and decided to call it a night. He was the only one
unlucky enough to be there at five o'clock on a Sunday
evening. Anyone with the sense God gave a flea was at
home digesting a traditional Italian supper, but not him.
His car had chosen today to act up. He slammed the hood
and cringed as the noise echoed through his aching head.
Wiping grime from his hands, Nick contemplated one of
the world's great mysteries: why man had ever combined
computers and the internal combustion engine.

The weekend had started badly and gone downhill
from there. On Friday, the offer he'd made to acquire the
one car dealership he'd coveted since he was a boy had
been rejected. Then on Saturday night, instead of being
considerate about his loss, his girlfriend Tonya started
making noises about marriage, leaving him no choice
but to break things off. That led to tears on her part,
more than half a bottle of Jack on his, and a screaming
hangover Sunday morning.

The very morning he was awakened at six o'clock
by his mother's phone call reminding him it was his
turn to take Nana to church. Experiencing Mass with
Nana while hungover made him wonder whether Jesus
really died for our sins—or because dying was less
painful than listening to Nana sing. That morning, Nick
had been tempted to give the cross a try himself. His

broken-down Viper was the icing on the cake. He'd heard trouble came in threes. He must have gotten a double dose, because he was up to five at last count, which meant he had one more to look forward to.

Nick put a socket wrench away and switched off the lights. At least he knew he'd find a cold beer and a warm bed at home. But unless he wanted to drive a wrecker, he'd have to search the key box and move the cars blocking the entrance of the dealership to take a demo.

Nothing brought out the neighbors faster than parking a wrecker in front of his Park Slope brownstone. The dirty looks didn't bother him—at least not enough to spend half an hour searching for keys and moving cars. Hell, he'd lived in the same house since his birth thirty-one years earlier, back when Park Slope had almost as bad a rep as Bedford Stuy. If he wanted to park a garbage truck in front of his house, it was no one's business but his.

Nick wore his coveralls so he wouldn't get his clothes dirty sitting on the greasy bench seat of the wrecker and took off for home. He was almost there when he came across a disabled vehicle on the shoulder. A woman was kicking the shit out of a flat tire, paying no attention to the cars and trucks careening by at high speeds.

He flipped on the emergency lights and pulled off in front of the lunatic's car. At least, he hoped it was her car. If it wasn't, the owner was going to be pissed, since the woman had missed the tire and kicked the back fender. He backed up, figuring he might as well get through the remaining bad thing sooner rather than later.

The deranged woman looked like a good candidate for bad thing number six.

Nick hopped out of the wrecker and walked toward the crazy lady. Over the sound of the traffic, he swore he could hear her cursing in Italian and maybe Spanish.

"Hey lady, if you're done beating on that side of the car, you might want to start on the other side. You're liable to end up as road pizza if you stay where you are." He waited for a response, but she only looked at him as if he were an alien being. He tried again, slowly this time. Maybe she was crazy. "Lady, if you'd pop the trunk, I'll change the tire. Then you can go home and deal with the cause of your anger in person."

"What are you, *stunad*? Don't you think if he were anywhere in the tristate area, I'd have hunted him down like the dog he is and beaten him within an inch of his life?"

Nick raised an eyebrow, content to watch the meltdown from a safe distance.

"And if he'd bought the spare with the money I gave him, I would have already changed my own tire. You'd think I'd have learned my lesson when I was five and realized Richie had been robbing me blind, trading my dimes for nickels. He said nickels were worth more because they were bigger, and I believed him. I should have killed my brother years ago. Instead, I'm standing here in twenty-degree weather talking to you."

At that moment, it must have occurred to her that she was yelling at a Good Samaritan. She took a deep breath, tucked her hands in her pockets, and gentled her tone. "Not that I don't appreciate you stopping."

"Sure." Nick had a hard time hiding his grin. He'd always had a weakness for feisty women. He wouldn't want to piss her off, but damn, she was cute. A real lunatic, but cute as hell. "Look, lady, why don't you get out of the cold and wait in the wrecker? Just don't touch anything. I'll put your car on the flatbed and take you home. You can pick it up tomorrow at Romeo's."

She backed up. "You want me to get in the truck with you?"

Dominick narrowed his Sicilian blue eyes, wondering if he'd get credit for number six if he left her standing on the expressway. It wasn't as if he hadn't tried to help.

"You want me to tow your car to the garage or not?"

"Of course I do, but I'm not in the habit of taking rides from strange men."

He removed the cables he needed to hook up the car. "Good luck finding a cab at this hour. If you need to, you're welcome to use my cell phone. It's on the seat in the truck. I'll be another ten minutes if you change your mind." Nick heard her say someone should die in a pool of blood, but with the noise of the traffic rushing by, it was hard to tell who she was talking about. He hoped it wasn't him.

Rosalie wondered if the points she'd racked up cursing in Spanish were enough to convince God to send help, since, when she'd called, she hadn't found one garage open in all of Brooklyn when she'd called. It was nice to know her three years of high school Spanish hadn't been a complete waste, but then again, when something seemed too good to be true, it most often was. Wreckers didn't drive around looking for broken-down cars, did they?

If God had sent this guy, she must have scored major points. Okay, she knew she was staring, but how could she not? He looked like a large, dark Jude Law. The Italian in him only added to his good looks, not to mention the way he filled out those mechanic's coveralls. It should be illegal to be that dirty and still look so hot.

Under normal circumstances, she wouldn't have thought twice about having a mechanic drive her home, but something about him didn't add up. He wore coveralls with his name embroidered on them, and his hands were grimy, but his haircut was something you'd see on the pages of *GQ*, not *Mechanics Weekly*. He was wearing dress shoes that looked handmade, not oil-covered work boots. Then there was his accent—or lack of one. He had the Brooklyn speech pattern, said the right words, but the accent was missing. He sounded like a guy from Connecticut trying to sound like he was from Brooklyn. That made him either a rich man with amnesia working as a mechanic—or a mass murderer. The likelihood of either was slim, though a mass murderer was a better bet.

Rosalie dug though her pocketbook looking for the cell phone she'd thrown in after her last attempt to find an open garage. She dialed her boyfriend Joey, her parents, her best friend Gina, and even her cousin Frankie. No one was home, and it was beginning to snow. She called a cab. The best they could do was a forty-five minute wait. She'd sooner take her chances with a possible Ted Bundy than stand on the side of the road for the next hour. Besides, her favorite suede boots were fading fast, and she loved those boots. Damn.

She looked up to find Nick, if that was even his real name, walking toward her.

"Did you reach anyone?"

Rosalie shook her head.

"If you don't want me to take you home, at least let

me drop you off at a restaurant or bar where you can wait for a cab."

"Why don't you have an accent?" Okay, so he thought she was crazy. At least, he was looking at her that way.

"A heavy Brooklyn accent isn't good for business, so I changed mine. Now, are you coming or not?"

His reason was plausible. Even she tried to drop the accent when working. It was strange for a mechanic, but if he were a mass murderer, he could have already thrown her into the truck. What the hell, she'd take a chance and save her boots. "Home, James."

"The name's Nick," he said, pointing to the name embroidered on his chest.

"So, is Nick short for Dominick Romeo? It would make my day to be rescued by the most eligible bachelor in New York . . . well, now that Donald Trump's married again."

Her joke fell flat. Nick's scowl made her wonder if she'd do better on the expressway, but he was already helping her into the truck.

Nick closed the door and rounded the front. He jumped in and picked up the conversation, not bothering to hide his distaste.

"So, are you looking to get lucky and land a rich man?"

"Who? Dominick Romeo?" Right, like that was going to happen. She strapped herself in, trying to ignore the grease-covered seat belt and the cleft in Nick's chin. Both made her squirm in her seat, for very different reasons. "Bite your tongue. The last thing I need is a husband, rich or otherwise. I have a hard enough time cleaning up after my dog. But if you ever tell another living soul I said that, I'll have to kill you."

He laughed, and his scowl disappeared. "Your secret's safe with me. So, they're comparing Romeo to Trump now?"

"Yeah. I've heard he's Brooklyn's version of The Donald, minus the comb-over. He might not be as wealthy, but I hear he's younger and much better looking."

Nick smiled, and she felt as if she'd been hit with a tire iron. He should register his smile as a lethal weapon and be careful where he aimed it. That smile would make any normal woman throw her arms up and scream, "Take me."

It was a good thing Rosalie wasn't normal. Hell, she wasn't even single. She was in a relationship—one of convenience, but still, it was enough. Correction, it had been enough to keep her parents off her back about marrying, until today. Today her mother had informed her that it was the two-year anniversary of her first date with Joey—a date that obviously had made more of an impression on her mother than it had on Rosalie.

Joey seemed content to let things go on the way they were. She fed him several times a week; they had occasional, albeit boring, missionary-position sex; and they both had a significant other to take to family functions. It also helped that his mother no longer questioned his sexuality. For a while there, he'd said, Mrs. Manetti would ask if he'd like to bring a boyfriend or girlfriend to dinner. She'd said that a boyfriend wouldn't upset her, although she'd looked relieved the first time Rosalie joined them for a meal. Somehow, Rosalie doubted Nick had ever had his sexuality questioned.

Nick took another look at the woman next to him. Crazy Lady was giving him the "alien arrival" stare again. Too bad the only single woman he'd ever met who wasn't looking to marry a rich man was a nut job. Though, to be fair, it could be temporary insanity. He had to admit, he'd go a little crazy if someone left him without a spare.

After getting a good look at her, Nick decided sanity was way overrated. Miss Loco was every guy's wet dream. She reminded him of the Sophia Loren pinup his Great Uncle Giovanni had hanging in the back room of his barbershop. Nick liked his women curvy and built. None of those bony women who looked more like a boy than a girl for him. Tonya was always trying to lose weight, and it drove him nuts. Her ass was so small, there was almost nothing to hold. Psycho had an ass like you read about. Damn, he should ask her out for her ass alone. Plus, a guy had to admire a woman who could curse in several languages. And she was beautiful, even without makeup. He'd never seen Tonya without makeup, not even after sweaty sex, but he'd bet she wouldn't look so good. *La Donna Pazza* wasn't drop-dead gorgeous like Tonya, but he'd lay odds she didn't get Botox injections and collagen implants—and didn't have breasts you were afraid to squeeze for fear they'd pop. Hers looked like one hundred percent natural 36Ds.

He had a real problem with her car, though. The sunflower yellow VW Beetle couldn't have been girlier if she'd painted it pink. It had a freaking bud vase built into the dashboard. If he did decide to date her, he'd have to get her a new car. He couldn't date a woman who drove a car he'd be embarrassed to be seen in.

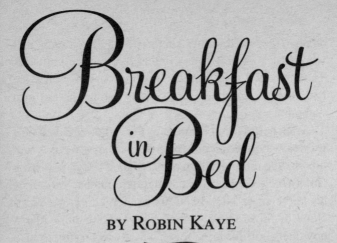

Breakfast in Bed

BY ROBIN KAYE

HE'D BE MR. PERFECT, IF HE WASN'T A PERFECT MESS...

Rich Ronaldi is *almost* the complete package—smart, sexy, great job—but his girlfriend dumps him for being such a slob, and Rich swears he'll learn to cook and clean to win her back. Becca Larson is more than willing to help him master the domestic arts, but she'll be damned if she'll do it so he can start cooking in another woman's kitchen—or bedroom...

PRAISE FOR ROBIN KAYE:

"Robin Kaye has proved herself a master of romantic comedy." —*Armchair Interviews*

"Ms. Kaye has style—it's easy, it's fun, and it has every-thing that you need to get caught up in a wonderful romance." —*Erotic Horizon*

"A fresh and fun voice in romantic comedy." —*All About Romance*

978-1-4022-1895-8 • $7.99 U.S. / £4.99 UK

Too Hot to Handle

BY ROBIN KAYE

HE SURE WOULD LOVE TO HAVE A WOMAN TO TAKE CARE OF...

To Dr. Mike Flynn, there's nothing like housework to help a guy relax, while artist Annabelle Ronaldi doesn't have a domestic bone in her body.

When they meet at her sister's wedding, Mike is sure this is the woman he wants to take care of forever. While Mike sets to work wooing Annabelle, she becomes determined to sniff out the truth of the convoluted family secret that's threatening to turn both their lives upside down.

PRAISE FOR *TOO HOT TO HANDLE*:

"Entertaining, funny, and steaming hot." —*Book Loons*

"A sensational story that sizzles with sex appeal."
   —*The Long and Short of It*

"Witty and enchanting." —*Love Romance Passion*

"From the brilliant first chapter until the heartwarming finale, I was hooked!" —*Crave More Romance*

978-1-4022-1766-1 • $6.99 U.S. / £3.99 UK

Line of
SCRIMMAGE

BY MARIE FORCE

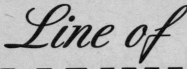

SHE'S GIVEN UP ON HIM AND MOVED ON...

Susannah finally has peace, calm, a sedate life, and a no-surprises man. Marriage to football superstar Ryan Sanderson was a whirlwind, but Susanna got sick of playing second fiddle to his team. With their divorce just a few weeks away, she's already planning her wedding with her new fiancé.

HE'S FINALLY FIGURED OUT WHAT'S REALLY IMPORTANT TO HIM. IF ONLY IT'S NO TOO

Ryan has just ten days to convince his soon-to-be-ex-wife to give him a second chance. His career is at its pinnacle, but in the year of their separation, Ryan's come to realize it doesn't mean anything without Susannah...

978-1-4022-1424-0 • $6.99 U.S. / £3.99 UK

Love at FIRST FLIGHT

BY MARIE FORCE

What if the guy
in the airplane seat next to you turned out
to be the love of your life?

JULIANA, HAPPY IN HER CAREER AS A HAIR STYLIST, IS ON HER way to Florida to visit her boyfriend. When he tells her he's wondering what it might be like to make love to other women she is devastated. Even though he tries to take it back, she doesn't want him to be wondering all his life. So they agree to take a break, and heartbroken, she goes back to Baltimore.

Michael is going to his fiancee's parents' home for an engagement party he doesn't want. A state's prosecutor, he's about to try the biggest case of his career, and he's having doubts about the relationship. When Paige pulls a manipulative stunt at the party, he becomes so enraged that he breaks off the engagement.

Juliana and Michael sat together on the plane ride from Baltimore to Florida, and discover they're on the same flight coming back. With the weekend a disaster for each of them, they bond in a "two-person pity party" on the plane ride home. Their friendship begins to blossom and love, too, but life is full of complications, and when Michael's trial turns dangerous, the two must confront what they value most in life...

978-1-4022-2006-7 • $6.99 U.S. / £3.99 UK

HEALING LUKE

BY BETH CORNELISON

She can't escape her past...

Occupational therapist Abby Stanford is on vacation alone, her self-confidence shattered by her fiancé's betrayal. Romance is the last thing on Abby's mind—until she meets the brooding and enigmatic Luke...

He won't face his future...

Scarred by a horrific accident, former heartthrob Luke Morgan is certain his best days are behind him. Abby knows how to help him recover, but for Luke his powerful attraction to her only serves as a harsh reminder of the man he used to be. Abby is Luke's first glimmer of hope since the accident, but can she heal his heart before Luke breaks hers?

"Beth Cornelison writes intriguing, emotionally charged stories that will keep you turning the pages straight through to the end. Fabulous entertainment!" —Susan Wiggs

"Healing Luke is a breath of fresh air for romance fans... a stirring novel and a five star read!"
—Crave More Romance

978-1-4022-2434-8 • $6.99 U.S. / £3.99 UK